The Series in the Chaos Legacy

IMMORTALITY AND CHAOS

Wreckers Gate: Book One
Landsend Plateau: Book Two
Guardians Watch: Book Three
Hunger's Reach: Book Four
Oblivion's Grasp: Book Five

CHAOS AND RETRIBUTION

Stone Bound: Book One
Sky Touched: Book Two
Sea Born: Book Three
Chaos Trapped: Book Four
Shadow Hunted: Book Five
Power Forged: Book Six

THE DRAGON QUEEN OF CHAOS

The Knights of Dragonwatch: Book One
Knight of Visions: Book Two
Gladiator Knight: Book Three
Knight Commander: Book Four
Knights Rift: Book Five
Dragon Knight: Book Six

THE ACTION-ADVENTURE SERIES
Lone Wolf Howls

THE ACTION THRILLER
WATCHING THE END OF THE WORLD

WRECKERS GATE

Book One of

Immortality and Chaos

by

Eric T Knight

Copyright © 2018 by Eric T Knight

Version 2.3 1/2018

ISBN-13: 978-1984301772
ISBN-10: 1984301772

Author's Note:
To aid in pronunciation, important names and terms in this story are spelled phonetically in the glossary at the end of the story.

Table of Contents

For Claudia
My love
With whom all is possible

PART ONE:
WULF ROME

CHAPTER 1

A scream came from the depths of the canyon.

General Wulf Rome held up a hand and the forty mounted soldiers strung out on the ridge behind him came to a halt. He stared down into the narrow canyon and swore softly.

"So they got Myles after all," he said bleakly. Myles was their scout. Rome turned to look at the man riding behind him. Tall and lean, with a narrow, hatchet face and a perpetually sour look, Quyloc (KWY-lock) was his oldest friend. They'd grown up in the slums of Qarath together and they'd joined the army together, more than fifteen years ago. "Now they're using him as bait to draw the rest of us into their ambush."

Quyloc didn't meet his gaze. He wasn't much for direct eye contact. "It's what I would do."

Which was true. Quyloc was ruthless. When it came to a fight, all that mattered was winning, whatever it took.

The canyon was a sharp gash cut deep into the sandstone, sheer cliffs making it inaccessible for most of its length. But below them the cliffs had collapsed, providing a way in, though a treacherous one that was little more than a long scree slope of loose stones. A turn in the canyon made it impossible to see the wounded man.

Behind them the other soldiers sat their mounts uneasily, their heads turning, eyes moving, watching. Towering sandstone buttes and mesas in every direction. They were three days deep in Crodin territory. Every man there knew the axe was going to fall. It was just a matter of when.

There was another scream from the depths of the canyon, fading slowly.

"What do you think, Quyloc?" Rome asked.

Quyloc shrugged. "We go back."

"I can't do that," Rome said. "You know what the Crodin do to their prisoners."

"Then why did you ask?"

"I've fought beside the man, Quyloc. I led him in here. I can't just leave him to die. You know that."

"So do they," Quyloc replied. He gave Rome a sidelong glance, then quickly turned his face away.

"We're going in." Rome turned in the saddle and spoke to the men he led. "Look sharp." Some faces registered fear, but on most there was only resignation mixed with bleak approval. Each man there knew if he was in Myles' place, he'd want Rome to make the same decision. Not only that, he'd count on it. Rome took care of his men.

Rome drew the battle axe that hung on his saddle and started down into the canyon, his horse picking its way carefully through the loose rock. He entered the canyon knowing that the orders he followed, the orders that sent him deep into enemy territory with an insufficient force, were not about running down one troublesome band of Crodin raiders. No, those orders were all about making sure one man died.

And that man was Wulf Rome.

It all started about a year earlier, when General Rome was summoned to a meeting with King Rix, his chief advisors, and a handful of the most powerful nobles of Qarath. Rome hated those meetings. They were one of the worst parts about his rank. Full of overdressed, preening bootlickers. None of them had a lick of real military experience. All of them came from wealth and privilege, their ranks purchased rather than earned.

Rome had risen to the rank of general two years earlier, when Qarath was embroiled in yet another of the seemingly endless wars against Thrikyl, her neighbor to the south. Thrikyl was winning that war. They broke the gates of Qarath and they were pouring into the city in a flood when Rome rallied the broken Qarathian army and drove the invaders out. The city witnessed the act and her citizens raised Rome to the status of legend overnight. King Rix had no choice but to promote Rome to general, though he clearly hated doing so.

When Rome got the summons from the king he was on the practice field drilling his men. He handed his practice axe to the sergeant and went straight away, not bothering to change clothes or clean up. The order came and he answered it. It was who he was.

2

The contempt in the nobles' eyes when he entered the opulent room in the palace was palpable. They resented the rise of this commoner into their ranks. Eyes rolled and noses wrinkled as they held perfumed kerchiefs to their faces. Rome had a thick beard and wild, bushy black hair that seemed to sprout everywhere. He'd been sweating and he stank. He knew that and he didn't care. Offending their delicate sensibilities was one small way for him to jab them back. It wasn't much, and it didn't make up for the hundred petty humiliations they visited on him whenever they could, but it was something.

There was no chair for him, of course, so he stood against the wall, his arms crossed over his chest, as Rix began to speak.

"We are going to war with Thrikyl," Rix said without preamble.

The nobles smiled. They congratulated the king and each other. There was talk of reclaiming Qarath's honor, talk of glory to be earned.

Every bit of it sickened Rome. Not a man there would actually face another man across a blade. They would command from the rear as they always did, looking like brightly colored birds in their useless, cumbersome, ornate armor and weapons, watching as real soldiers and conscripts died.

As a soldier, Rome understood that soldiers died. But he hated when they died for no reason. Suddenly, he had had enough.

"What is it this time, Rix?" he growled, pushing away from the wall and advancing on them. He did not miss the way they shied away from him. Though he carried no weapon, his armor spoke of heavy use and calculated violence.

"Did his ambassador fail to bow low enough in the court? Or are you just bored with your wives?"

The room went deathly still while King Rix's color slowly turned from white to purple. "*What did you just say to me?*" he said in a strangled voice.

"You heard me," Rome said harshly. He was surprised to feel a twinge of regret. He should have listened to Quyloc. There was going to be a heavy price to pay for this. But it was too late now. He was committed and he might as well go through with it. "You sit here and talk of war and glory. You know as well as I do that the walls of Thrikyl will not fall, but a lot of men will. Men with families to feed. If you want a war so bad, why don't you go fight?"

"I should have you arrested right now," Rix managed to spit out. "Publicly executed at dawn."

"You could try," Rome replied, once again calm. He didn't lose his

3

temper easily, but once he did, he got it back quickly. He looked at the guards who were edging closer as he spoke. They hesitated visibly and turned questioning looks to the king.

Shaking with suppressed emotion, Rix raised one hand, the order on his lips. But the order didn't come and slowly he regained control of himself. Every man in the room knew what would happen if he tried to have Rome publicly executed. There would be riots in the streets. The army itself might turn on him.

"This is not done," Rix said at last.

"No," Rome agreed.

Shortly after that General Rome was put in command of a dusty little outpost on the Crodin border. He knew the king was getting him out of the way until he figured out how to eliminate his rebellious general. And so he wasn't surprised when the orders came in a few days ago. He was to lead his meager force of men in pursuit of Trakar Kurnash and his band of raiders. They were to kill Kurnash and send his head back to the king in Qarath. No matter what it took. Failure was not an option.

"So that's it, then." Quyloc set the orders down on Rome's desk. "Rix is finally getting rid of you." He said nothing else and he kept his face expressionless, but nevertheless Rome saw something—or thought he did—and he set his jaw stubbornly.

"Go ahead and say it. You know you want to."

"Say what?" Quyloc took out the long dagger he always wore on his belt and picked at his fingernails.

"Say I told you so."

Quyloc's gaze flicked to Rome, then away. Rome stood with his fists bunched and a belligerent glint in his eye. "Just say it. We'll both feel better."

Quyloc gave the faintest shrug. "Okay. I told you so."

With the words some of the steam went out of Rome and he sat down at his desk and put his head in his hands. "You were right. I should have listened to you. You told me to keep my mouth shut, but I didn't. And now men, *my men*, are going to die on this suicide mission."

Quyloc put his knife away.

"I just couldn't help myself. You know how I get."

"Yes, Rome. I know how you get."

"It wasn't *right*!" Rome exploded, slapping the desk top with one thick hand. Rome was a big man, only a little bit shorter than Quyloc, but broad through the chest and thickly muscled, and the table jumped when he hit it. "It's still not right."

Quyloc clasped his hands behind his back.

"They sit there in their fancy chairs wearing their gold and silk and they talk about war and killing like it's this noble, glorious game."

Quyloc sat down in the room's other chair. He'd heard this rant many times. It would take a while.

"It's so easy for them," Rome continued. "It's not their blood being spilled, is it?" He glowered at Quyloc.

"No. It's not."

"Was I just supposed to do nothing?"

"It's what most people do."

"Well I'm not made like that."

Quyloc shrugged.

"I just couldn't sit there and say nothing, Quyloc. Surely you can see that."

Quyloc sighed. "Did it make any difference, Rome? Did anything change?" The latest war with Thrikyl was even then being waged to the east.

Rome slumped in his chair.

Rome and his men were halfway down the side of the steep canyon when the first arrows struck their line. The first volley targeted the horses and better than half went down, crushing men beneath them, knocking down others. Chaos reigned. Those men who got free of their horses found themselves fighting uphill against a surefooted enemy who was unencumbered by armor. Another volley of arrows and more men went down. Then the Crodin charged, stabbing with their spears.

Rome's horse went down in the second volley, an arrow sticking out of its neck right behind the jaw. Two warriors came at Rome with eager cries as he fell. Eagerness turned to surprise as Rome rolled and came to his feet faster than they expected. The axe hissed and the first Crodin fell back, his chest spouting blood. Rome shifted to strike the other one but a rock slid under his foot and he slipped. As he went down he threw up the axe, just blocking the nomad's spear thrust.

The nomad's next thrust glanced off Rome's chest plate, buying him a moment that was all he needed. He swung the axe and took the man just below the knee. Bone crunched and the man went down with a scream. Rome got up, slipped on the loose stone again, almost lost his balance, recovered, ducked a spear thrust and brought the axe around in a deadly sweep. The axe bit deep into flesh and bone.

He caught a glimpse of Quyloc to his right. Unlike the rest of the Qarathian soldiers, Quyloc wore no armor and on his feet were leather moccasins instead of heavy boots. His movements were swift and sure on the steep hillside. A Crodin stabbed at him with his spear but Quyloc slid easily to the side, letting the thrust go by. Quick as a striking snake, his right hand snapped out, grabbing the spear. He jerked the man forward and killed him with the short sword in his other hand.

A Crodin howled and leapt down onto Rome. Rome twisted just enough to make the spear thrust skip off his armor, then simply bear-hugged the smaller man and let his momentum carry them both down the hill. He swiveled as they fell so that the Crodin was on the bottom and was rewarded with the sound of cracking ribs. He smashed a gauntleted fist into the man's throat, crushing his windpipe, and got back to his feet.

This was a fight they couldn't win. Only a handful of the Qarathian soldiers were still on their feet. They were outnumbered and fighting uphill against a foe with maneuverability and footing on his side.

"Fall back!" Rome roared, his voice easily cutting through the din. "Down the hill!"

A spear thrust came from the side, too fast for him to dodge even if he did have somewhere to set his feet. So he just let go and fell backwards.

He tumbled and slid halfway down the hill before he slammed up against a boulder hard enough that he thought the sudden hot burst of pain in his chest might be a broken rib. Other than Quyloc, the rest did no better. Only nine Qarathians survived to make it to the canyon floor.

"Why aren't they coming after us?" Fouts asked. He was an older man who walked with a limp. There was blood on his face and he'd lost his helmet. The surviving soldiers were standing in the bottom of the canyon. Only one horse was still alive. The Crodin were still up on the hillside, amongst the bodies of men and horses.

"They don't have to," Quyloc replied. "Look."

They could see down the canyon now. Lying in the bottom a short way further on was the body of Myles, blood running from the gaping wound in his throat. A Crodin warrior was scaling a cliff out of the canyon, a bow strung over one shoulder, his knife in his teeth.

But that wasn't what made the soldiers stand and stare, a sick feeling growing inside each one. It was what lay further on, where the canyon ended.

Endless, towering ranks of bleached red and orange sand dunes. The Gur al Krin.

"Oh, god," Darin muttered. He was a thin, nervous youth with a meager beard. "We're going to die here."

"Not yet we're not," Rome said, clapping him on the shoulder. "Take a look up the canyon. See if there's a way out that way." He already knew there wasn't. The Crodin had planned their trap too well. But it would give Darin something to do and they needed to know all their options.

Darin took off up the canyon, looking anxiously up at the Crodin as he went. It was a long shot for a bow, but not an impossible one. However, the nomads were just standing there, watching.

Rome walked over to Quyloc, who was still looking down the canyon. "It looks like they're just going to wait us out."

Quyloc made no reply. He was staring intently at the dunes.

"Quyloc."

Quyloc shook himself and turned to Rome. "What did you say?"

"It looks like we can either wait down here and die of thirst—" Most of their water was still tied to their dead horses. "—or we can charge uphill at an enemy we won't even get close to."

Quyloc looked up the steep hillside at the Crodin. They still hadn't moved. Then he looked back at the dunes. "Or we go out into the Krin," he said softly.

Rome looked out at the dunes. It seemed he could feel their heat from here. "How long do you think we'll last out there?"

"Not long," Quyloc replied. "But all we have to do is get out of sight. Then we can circle back, come out where they don't expect."

"But won't they just follow us? Kill us out there?"

Something cold and contemptuous crossed Quyloc's face. "Not a chance."

"How can you be so sure?"

"Pirnu." Pirnu was a ragged old Crodin who lived at the Qarathian outpost Rome commanded, earning his keep by occasionally tracking for the Qarathians. Quyloc had spent a lot of time talking to him. "The Crodin fear the Gur al Krin. It is where their god, Gomen nai, lives, and he hates them. They won't go there."

"You're sure of that?"

But Quyloc had already turned away and was once again staring out into the dunes as if entranced. It almost seemed to Rome as if he was

7

listening to something. Rome had to grab his shoulder to get his attention. "I asked you if you're sure."

Quyloc scowled and there was an edge to his voice when he replied. "Of course I'm sure. I wouldn't have said it if I wasn't." He shoved Rome's hand off his shoulder. "It's not like we have a lot of choices."

Rome had to agree with him there. He stared out at the dunes, wondering at the irrational fear that welled up inside him at the thought of going in there. Maybe the Crodin god did live in there. "It would be better if we waited for dark. We don't have much water."

"If they let us wait," Quyloc replied.

The Crodin were nocking arrows and beginning to move down the hillside. Rome looked around. There was no cover here in the bottom of the canyon and they didn't have a bow among them, another item still tied on the dead horses. The Crodin could just pick them off at their leisure.

"All right," he said, coming to a decision. He turned to the surviving soldiers. "We're going into the Krin." He started unbuckling his chest plate.

"Lose the armor," Quyloc told them. "It's not going to help you where we're going, but it might just get you killed faster."

"Uh, sir, what about the firestorms?" asked Linul, a stout man who was sweating badly. His eyes were wide and there was a tremor in his voice. "Pirnu says *sklath* live in the desert. They spin the sand into tornadoes and then the tornadoes burn."

"That's just something he says to scare you," Rome replied. "Right, Quyloc?"

Quyloc shrugged. "Who knows better than the Crodin what goes on in the Gur al Krin?" Only the Crodin lived near the mighty desert. The only thing in the Gur al Krin was the dead city of Kaetria, long since buried by the sands.

Rome stepped in close to Quyloc and lowered his voice. "That's not helping," he growled.

Quyloc shrugged again. "If they're scared, let them stay here and die. I'm going into the desert."

Their armor shed, the Qarathians started for the dunes. That was when a strange thing happened. The Crodin fell to their knees and began wailing, their hands held up to the sky.

"Why are they doing that?" Fouts asked.

"They think we're going to die," Quyloc said, ignoring a warning look from Rome. "Maybe they're praying for us."

As hot as they'd been before, it was nothing compared to the heat they encountered when they took their first steps out onto the sand. It was early afternoon and the dunes were a forge, though it was winter time. Heat radiated at them from all sides and the sand was so hot they could feel it through their boots.

Right away a high dune blocked their way and they started up it, but each step filled their boots with sand and for every two steps up, they slid back one. Quyloc alone seemed unaffected, practically skimming along the surface of the sand. He reached the top of the dune before the others were halfway up and he stood there, looking into the distance.

When he started to walk down the far side Rome called out to him to wait, and though he did, Rome could sense his impatience. It was like the man *wanted* to go into the desert. It made no sense to Rome, but then much of what Quyloc did made no sense to him.

Quyloc had never been like the other soldiers in the army. When the others took their pay and headed out to drink and whore, Quyloc stayed behind, reading one of the books that he always seemed to be able to acquire. The simple fact that he could read at all was basically unheard of amongst the mass of illiterate soldiers. That he chose to waste his money and time reading made him incomprehensible to them. When he wasn't reading, he was pumping strangers for information, plying them with ale, gathering old stories and lost legends.

Rome had asked him about it more than once. What was he looking for? Quyloc always replied the same. "You already have everything, Rome," he'd say. "There's no way for you to understand."

When Rome got to the top of the dune, he walked over to Quyloc. "I'm thinking we walk along the top of this dune for a while, maybe drop off the far side a bit so they can't see us. Then, we find some place to sit down and wait for it to get dark." He waited, but Quyloc didn't respond. He was staring into the heart of the desert, seemingly lost in thought. "Are you listening to me?" he asked finally.

"Can you hear it?" Quyloc asked. "I hear something out there." He frowned. "It's a voice…I think."

"Hear what?" Rome listened. He could hear the men laboring up the dune behind them, but that was it. "I don't hear anything."

Quyloc's mouth quirked with an odd smile. "Maybe it's meant for me."

"Maybe what's meant for you? What's wrong with you?"

9

Quyloc gave him a scathing look, but said nothing. Rome walked back to see how the others were doing. Fouts' wound was still bleeding. The man was practically crawling up the dune. Rome didn't know how much longer he'd make it. He went back down and helped him make it the rest of the way to the top. Once they were all on top of the dune, Rome saw that Quyloc was gone. Muttering a curse, Rome went to look for him. Quyloc had already made it down the far side of the dune and was starting into a gap between two other dunes that led deeper into the Gur al Krin. Yelling had no effect. Either Quyloc couldn't hear him, or he was choosing not to.

"What now, sir?" asked Linul. He was pale and breathing hard.

For a moment Rome wanted to just let Quyloc go. But he knew he couldn't. The two men had been through too much together. Rome couldn't just leave him out here in the desert to die.

He looked back the way they'd come. The Crodin warriors were arrayed along the top of the canyon, staring out at them. If he and the others just walked along the top of the dune, the Crodin would simply mirror them. They might be able to slip by them once it got dark, but that still left them deep in Crodin territory and outnumbered. The smart thing to do was go deep enough into the dunes so that they were out of sight, then cut one way or the other and circle back around.

"We're going after him," Rome said. "We have to get deep enough into the Krin that the Crodin can't see us."

The men didn't like it, but they could see the Crodin as well as he could, so they fell in behind him with only a minimum of grumbling. By the time they got to the bottom of the dune, a wind had begun to blow. Sand swirled from the tops of the dunes.

"That wind doesn't help at all," Darin said. "I swear it's hotter than the sand."

It was true. The wind felt like it was searing bare skin, and the dust it raised reduced visibility.

"Pick it up," Rome said. "I want to catch up to Quyloc before he gets out of sight." Quyloc was just visible in the distance.

As fast as they walked though, they never seemed to gain on Quyloc. Yelling did no good. Time passed and the heat became even more murderous. Rome squinted through the blowing sand, which was growing harder to see through as the wind increased. Quyloc might have been a mirage, his form shimmering and insubstantial in the waves of heat that rose off the sand.

For a time, he didn't know how long, Rome seemed to lose track of himself. His body felt distant, his thoughts trapped within themselves. Someone seemed to be talking to him, but he couldn't tell what the voice said, only that he wanted very badly to hear it better. He forgot about the Crodin. He forgot about King Rix and the vow he had made to himself to bring his men out of the desert and make the king pay. There was only the blistering heat, the wind, and placing one foot after the other, always in pursuit of the ghostlike figure of Quyloc in the distance.

The first thunderous boom echoing across the dunes was like a slap in the face, bringing Rome out of his thoughts. He spun, stunned by what he saw.

CHAPTER 2

Coming up fast behind the soldiers was a towering pillar of fire. Moments later whirling tornados of dust sprang up on either side. As Rome watched in disbelief, first one, then the other, exploded into flame with crackling booms.

Pirnu was telling the truth.

Rome turned back around. Quyloc was in the distance, waving his arms wildly. Rome squinted and then saw the rock pile on the horizon beyond Quyloc. Something about the stones looked unnatural, but there was no time for that now. Rome turned back to his men. One of them, Fouts it looked like, straggled far in the rear. Rome saw in a glance that he wasn't going to make it. Realization and action happened in the same instant and Rome began running towards him.

As he passed soldiers, he yelled at them to run, follow Quyloc, there was shelter up ahead. The blowing sand grew thicker as he went. Visibility was dropping fast. The sand stung his skin and made his eyes burn. The burning pillars grew closer, the heat coming off them increasing.

Rome was choking by the time he found Fouts. The man had fallen to the ground and wasn't moving. Rome grabbed him and dragged him to his feet.

"Move, soldier!" he screamed. "That's an order!"

He slung one of Fouts' arms around his neck and began dragging him. The heat and blowing sand grew worse. Each breath was torture, the sand driving deep into his lungs. He could hear the tornados of fire all around him, roaring like beasts deprived of their prey. The day was a vicious red color. Blisters rose on his neck and face. Fouts was a dead weight hanging around his neck.

Somehow, Rome carried on. Every muscle cried out to stop. Self-preservation demanded that he drop Fouts and run ahead. Stubbornly, he continued on, though the sand became too thick to see through and he was stumbling blind.

Suddenly, out of the reddish gloom, a figure loomed. It was Quyloc. "This way!" he yelled. "We can make it!"

The pillars of fire pressed close on all sides. Rome's uniform was smoldering, his exposed skin raw and blistered. Each breath felt like it would be his last. But he fought through it. Quyloc was there. Quyloc would lead them to safety.

Huge stones loomed out of the gloom. They stumbled toward them, into their protective embrace.

Suddenly the heat and roaring subsided. Blessed calm flowed over Rome. The air was still filled with sand, but it was manageable and the pillars of fire couldn't get to them here. Rome set Fouts down and collapsed to the ground, coughing.

Outside, the firestorm raged, but they were safe for now.

"Did everyone make it?" Rome asked when he had regained his breath.

Voices spoke up, then Darin said, "I don't think Linul made it. He was right behind me but I didn't see him come in."

"I don't think Levin made it either," another said.

"How are you doing, Fouts?" Rome asked. There was no answer. He felt for a pulse and found none. He swore silently. That meant they were six now. More deaths to lay at Rix's feet.

A few hours later the firestorms gave up and dissipated. When it had been quiet for a while, Rome said, "I'm going outside to take a look around. Quyloc, come with me."

It was night time. The sky was a black bowl glittering with thousands of stars. The dunes stretched silently in every direction. "What happened, Quyloc?"

Quyloc didn't answer for a while. Finally, he said, "I don't know. There was a voice. It seemed to be calling me, offering me something. Something I want more than anything." His voice was bleak and empty. "I...lost myself in it. Then the firestorms started."

You've killed us all, Rome wanted to say. But when he looked into his memories he realized he had followed the voice too. It seemed like lunacy now. "I heard it too," he admitted. "Remember that entertainer we saw in that tavern? The one who hypnotized that man and made him meow like a cat? I felt like that man."

"Can you hear it now?" Quyloc asked. "The voice?"

Rome listened, then shrugged. "I don't know. It seems like I can, but when I try, it slips away. I don't know what to believe."

"How are we going to get out of here?"

"We let the men rest a couple more hours, then we start back. If we're lucky, we make it out while it's still dark."

"And the Crodin?"

"If they see us, we fight. We'll lose, but we're getting out of this desert one way or the other."

Quyloc nodded, the motion barely visible in the starlight. The two men were turning back to their shelter when Quyloc grabbed Rome's arm suddenly.

"What's that?" he hissed.

A moment later Rome felt it too. A vibration underneath the sand. A feeling of something huge and powerful coming fast.

"We have to get them out of there!" Quyloc yelled.

But it was too late.

The vibration turned into a crunching, grating sound. The ground buckled under their feet, knocking both men down.

Something huge burst up out of the ground underneath the piled stones. Stones flew up and out.

Rome got to his feet. There was a crater where their shelter had been.

Then something rose out of it.

It was three times the height of a man. Its body was covered in a black shell and its two arms ended in pincers. From one hung the body of a soldier, twitching feebly. Its armored head swiveled and a row of dimly glowing eyes fixed on them.

"HE WAITS!" the thing thundered. It tossed the body aside and then climbed back down into the crater and disappeared.

"What was that?" Rome yelled.

Quyloc didn't answer. He went to the body the thing had flung down. It was Darin. He was dead. Together they searched the debris, looking for the others. Two lay crushed under huge stones. They couldn't find the last one. While Rome was searching he noticed something strange: the stones had been cut. They were the ancient remains of some kind of structure. He looked around, wondering if there were more, buried in the sand. He walked to the edge of the crater and looked down into it.

Quyloc joined him. They stood there for a while in silence. Then

Quyloc began making his way down into it. After a moment, Rome followed.

The voice was back. And it was calling them.

Neither man saw the three creatures which watched them from the top of a nearby dune. Once Rome and Quyloc had disappeared into the crater, the three creatures made their way down off the dune and followed.

Rome and Quyloc wandered in darkness deep into the earth beneath the Gur al Krin. The darkness was absolute, but neither man stumbled in the rocky, uneven tunnel, guided as they were by the voice. Immersed as each was in listening to it, they did not speak to each other, were barely aware of each other's presence. They walked for hours or days. Neither would ever know for sure. Time disappeared. Hunger and thirst became distant and unreal.

The tunnel led steadily downward at a steep angle. As they walked, they became aware that they were approaching something poisonous, something antithetical to life. It was as though they approached a place where life itself was unwelcome. As the feeling grew stronger, they shivered and looked around in the darkness, wondering what it was.

But still they did not slow. The voice gripped them, drawing them on with its promise. What that promise was neither man knew, but it spoke to their deepest desires, their most earnest hopes and hidden fears.

A cold, white glow appeared in the tunnel ahead. It bathed their faces as they drew closer, casting sharp shadows. The tunnel opened up onto a vast cavern. On the far side of the cavern was a glowing, white wall. It was seamless and extended out of sight in either direction.

The wall was clearly not stone. It looked almost like it was made of ice, but as they drew nearer they saw that it wasn't that either. There was a hint of deep purple rippling under its surface. A low, discordant buzz came from it. There was a feel of vast, unnatural energies barely contained within it. They knew instinctively that to touch it would mean death.

The voice called again and both men's heads turned. They followed the wall, careful to avoid coming too close to it. As they walked they began to jockey for position, subconsciously aware that only one could receive the promise of the voice.

They walked for several minutes. The wall curved slightly. Something different appeared.

Set into the wall was a roughly oval section of gray granite, easily ten feet tall and half that wide. They stopped before it. The voice was coming from the other side of it.

Further on, the monster that had killed the other soldiers waited, crouched down, watching. It was well away from the white wall, as if it feared its touch as well. Its shell was dull black and scarred by countless years. Part of one of its pincers was broken away. The row of eyes watched them unblinking. The two men ignored it.

"Where is it?" Rome demanded. His voice was rusty. Dust coated his beard and his face and there was dried blood on his shirt.

"It's here," Quyloc replied, his eyes moving over the granite. "But I can't find it."

"You promised," Rome said loudly. "We came." The white glow from the wall was blinding, seeming almost to throb.

There was a concussion from the other side of the granite, as if it was struck by something heavy. A small cracking sound followed, loud in the stillness, and then a single flake of stone fell away.

There was something there now. They peered at it. Something black. A clawed hand or foot, which it was they couldn't tell.

Rome stepped closer, started to reach for it—

"No!" Quyloc cried, shaking himself as if awaking from a dream. "Rome, don't—"

But Rome had already taken hold of it. He frowned, then slowly pulled it free of the wall.

The black-shelled monster stood. Something glittered in its eyes. A faint crack ran through the center of the granite.

But neither man noticed.

They were staring at the thing in Rome's hand. It was a black axe, but it was clearly no normal axe. It was made of translucent black stone. Carved into the sides of the head were closed eyes. Cut into the lower edge of the blade was the suggestion of a mouth. The haft was the body of a strange creature, stretched out, claws emerging from the end.

The black-shelled monster touched the wall. There was a flash of light, a silent explosion of power, and both men were flung to the ground, where they lay motionless. The black-shelled creature's arm was blown off. It staggered, black ichor pouring from the stump, then slumped to the ground.

CHAPTER 3

Three creatures emerged from the tunnel and made their way across the silent cavern.

The first was tall and skeletally lean, its skin white and smooth and hairless. It had no eyes. Its face was completely featureless except for two slits where a nose should be and a short, vertical slash underneath, approximating a mouth.

The next looked like a gaunt, emaciated man, its bones clearly visible under its skin. It was bald. Its eyes were empty holes, its mouth gaping and toothless. There were weeping sores over much of its body.

The last looked like it was formed of blocks of red granite. Its fists were the size of small boulders. A deep gash ran diagonally across its face, through one eye and across its mouth. From the depths of the gash came a flickering red glow.

They stood over the unconscious forms of Rome and Quyloc, staring at the crack in the stone.

The binding is broken. You are free of the Gur al Krin now, came the voice from beyond the wall. *Go now. Prepare for our return. Leave these two on the sand. See that they do not remember what happened here.*

The white-skinned one held out its hands, palms outward. In the center of its forehead a single, red-rimmed eye suddenly opened. "Kasai hears and obeys," it said.

The mouth of the emaciated creature stretched unnaturally wide and a high, piercing voice came from it. "Gulagh hears and obeys."

The rock-like creature slammed its massive fists to the floor with a thunderous boom. "Tharn hears and obeys," it grated.

Gulagh placed one hand on each of the unconscious men's

foreheads and an eerie, moaning sound came from it. When it was done, it stood and started for the tunnel. Tharn picked the men up and followed. Kasai gathered up the black axe, wincing as it touched the weapon, and followed the other two. None glanced back at the dead form of the black-shelled creature.

CHAPTER 4

How long they'd been crossing the Gur al Krin Rome could no longer say. All he knew for sure was that he was close to dying. The dune he and Quyloc were climbing seemed to have no end, and he wasn't even trying to stand anymore. Crawling was good enough. It was all he had left. Momentum and sheer stubbornness had kept him going this far, but even that was fading. His tongue had swollen to fill his mouth completely. He thought he could feel the tip of it protruding from between his blistered lips. The world tilted and blackness crowded the edges of his vision hungrily. Quyloc was a vague form somewhere ahead of him.

When he finally made it to the top of the dune it took a moment for the fact to register. He raised his head, expecting only to see more sand dunes ahead. Instead, he saw something unbelievable. Quyloc croaked something. Rome closed his eyes, rubbed them, then opened them, afraid to believe what his eyes told him. They'd shown him many things in the last few hours, all of them lies.

Far below, at the foot of the dune, the sand trickled away to nothing. A narrow canyon ran off at an angle, crowded with rock spires and jagged boulders. A few stunted trees sprouted from the bottom of the canyon amid tufts of iron-gray grass. And right there, in the canyon, behind a crude earthen dam, was a muddy pool of water hardly big enough for a dozen men to crowd around. Paradise. The water swelled and exploded in his vision and Rome knew, at last, that this was no lie. Eager noises came from him as he started crawling head first down the dune.

Quyloc grabbed his arm and croaked again. Rome tried to push him off, but Quyloc was insistent. "Crodin," it sounded like he said. He held out a shaking finger.

Rome followed the finger with his eyes and nearly wept at what he saw. Huddled in the shade of a cliff wall were a handful of hide tents, painted with garish symbols in orange and red and yellow. A dog padded listlessly through the camp and flopped down in a patch of shade. No Crodin were visible, but that did not mean they were not there. It was midafternoon, the height of the daily furnace. Only idiots and dying men moved at this time.

"I'll kill them," Rome said, or tried to. The sounds coming from him didn't sound much like words. He felt for his battle axe but the only weapon that met his fingers was the strange black axe he'd found…somewhere. Every other weapon was gone. He didn't have so much as a dagger. The black axe couldn't be very useful. It felt like it was made of glass. Likely it would shatter if he so much as dropped it. He wished he hadn't lost his other axe.

"Nightfall," Quyloc croaked.

Quyloc was insane. The sun wouldn't go down for hours. He'd never live that long. He didn't care what the Crodin did to him. He was going down there now. But when he tried to crawl forward once again he couldn't move his legs. He turned his head, saw Quyloc lying across his legs.

"Circle around. Find shade."

Rome fought him anyway. He didn't want shade; he wanted water. But he couldn't seem to reach back to where he could get a hold of Quyloc and after a moment he had to stop. The sun made all movement so difficult. He sagged down onto the hot sand. "Okay."

Quyloc rolled off him and then helped him pull himself back up to the crest of the dune and down the other side, out of sight, where they began the laborious process of circling around, finding a place where they could hide from the sun without being seen. A process made so much worse by the knowledge that water, life, salvation, lay so close at hand.

Sunset found them southeast of the Crodin camp, huddled under the overhang of a chipped boulder. Rome had his eyes squeezed tightly shut, trying not to look, not to think. He wasn't having much luck. He was sure he could smell the water. The Crodin were up and moving about their camp now, talking sometimes. They were camped too close to the water. If he was to start for it, just stand up for two good steps, one of them would see him. They were always vigilant, these people.

He could see the way their eyes always moved, scanning the rocks and canyons that were their home. They lived among too many enemies, including their own people, to ever be fully secure. Two seconds after they spotted him he'd be sporting a coat of arrows.

How long since he had last had water? How many years had he spent in this blasted desert? Was there no end to the heat, the thirst? The days were a blur of sun and sand and boiling heat, broken only by the nights, blessedly cool at first, biting cold before morning so that at first the sun was a welcome sight, but not for long. If ever he was lucky enough to come upon water again, like a river or a lake, he would never leave it. He shook his head, trying to stop his thoughts from wandering. The sand blew through his mind, clouding and obscuring everything.

He shifted and felt the black axe under his hand. It was cool. Even after a long day in the sun it was cool. His fingertips were sore. The first day, when they stopped for a rest, he tested the edge on the weapon, and it bit deep. He yelled and dropped it, and when he looked up he did not expect the look he saw in Quyloc's eyes. Sudden, pure hatred. But when he blinked the look was gone and he thought he might have imagined it. What sense would that make? What reason could Quyloc have to hate him? It was just the sun, up to more tricks.

At last night fell and they began to creep forward, one agonizing foot at a time. Lucky that the wind was blowing towards them. All it had to do was shift, and the Crodin dogs—mangy, yellow-eyed beasts with slat ribs—would be on them in a heartbeat. If that happened, Rome wasn't sure if he would fight or run—straight towards the water. One way or another he'd drink first, before he died.

The pond was close now. The dirt was damp under his fingers. The air felt different. Firelight flickered on the rocks around them, blotched now and then by huge, twisted shadows as men and women passed close to the fire. Their voices were gnats buzzing around his head. He cared for nothing but the water.

Then his hands sank into the thick, slick mud and Rome thought he would cry out. It was all he could do to put only his face into the precious liquid, to sip and not gulp. Slowly. Slowly. Too much and he would be sick, worse off than before. The water smelled of decay and the thing floating by his hand looked like a dead bird, the feathers coming loose as it rotted, but it was better than the finest wine he'd ever drunk.

They had filled their water skins and were starting to back away when Quyloc stopped and turned his head to the side.

"Do you hear what they're saying?" he whispered.

"Who cares? Let's get out of here." Rome understood a little Crodin, acquired over the years by necessity.

"They're upset about something. Wait a minute. Let me listen."

Rome stifled a groan. That was Quyloc. Probably he wanted to write this down in one of his unending journals. "This isn't the time," he growled. The water was flowing through his veins now, like a flood over parched terrain. He could feel his strength, his very life, returning. He took another drink.

"They're afraid of something. Something's happening."

Then Rome did listen. It took a bit. His Crodin wasn't as good as Quyloc's. But they definitely did sound afraid. Something about their god, Gomen nai, walking the sands again, stepping forth from his dark fortress at Har Adrim to devour their souls. At least that's what it sounded like. "I hope he kills all of them. Now let's get out of here."

It was hours later when they crested a long ridge that led generally northwards. The Crodin camp was a lost flicker in the darkness behind them. The pale moon frosted the bare rocks jutting up around them. Quyloc started to follow along the top of the ridge when Rome stopped him.

"Not that way."

"What are you talking about? We have to get out of Crodin territory as fast as we can. In the morning they'll find our tracks and they will follow us."

"Thrikyl is this way."

Quyloc just stared at him. The moonlight left his face in shadow. A breeze flapped his torn clothes on his lean frame. He might have been a scarecrow.

"I owe Rix a debt."

"Rix isn't in Thrikyl."

"No, he isn't. But his army is."

"They'll arrest us."

"They'll try." Rome pulled the black axe from his belt. The moonlight winked off its surface. "But I have a feeling there's other things might happen."

"You don't know what that thing is." It was the first time Quyloc had referred to the axe since Rome found it. He hadn't looked at it, hadn't asked to see it. Nothing. As if it wasn't there. Which was really strange, for Quyloc, who was curious about everything.

"You're right. I don't." Something was starting to come to life inside Rome, a whisper of a future that might be. "But I will find out."

Quyloc's face twisted suddenly and his hands came up clenched. "It's not *yours*," he snarled.

"It is now."

Quyloc stood there for a moment longer, his mouth opening with words he would not let out, then he whirled and stalked away, down the ridge, down the way Rome wanted to go.

Rome stared after him, wondering what Quyloc was angry about. He looked down at the axe. Why couldn't he remember finding it? He remembered the pillars of fire and taking shelter in the rocks with his men, but nothing after that. Did he find the axe in there? And what happened to the rest of his men?

The sentry rubbed his eyes twice before challenging them. He was dozing at his post when two apparitions appeared out of the late afternoon haze. The picket line was loose out here; the Qarathian army had no reason to expect any trouble from the west and the sentries were mostly a formality. The sentry started to draw his sword, paused, put it back and said, "General Rome? Is that you?"

"More or less," Rome said, returning the man's salute. He figured he probably looked pretty bad. Dirty, bedraggled, footsore. Without money they'd had no way to buy horses at the one small town they passed. Besides, when a person is starving, food was a lot more important. They'd traded Quyloc's dagger for enough food and water to get here. "We could use some water if you have it."

The sentry handed over a water skin. While Rome drank, the soldier looked over his shoulder at Quyloc, then back to Rome. "I thought you were posted to the Crodin border. What are you doing here?" Though there was no one nearby, he kept his voice low. Word travels fast in an army and every Qarathian soldier knew that King Rix had sent Wulf Rome to the border as punishment.

"I came to fix some things," Rome said grimly.

Just then the sentry noticed the black axe hanging at his belt and his eyes widened. "What's that?"

"Believe me, if I knew, I'd tell you. But I don't."

They gave the sentry back his water skin and continued on. The land was hillier here than it was around Qarath. Sharp, steep hills, some of them big enough to be small mountains, all with tufts of pine trees clustered on the tops. Like Qarath, the city of Thrikyl sat with its back against the ocean, completely enclosed by high walls. Those walls had never fallen to a siege.

"I hope you know what you're doing," Quyloc said, when they had left the sentry behind.

"Not really," Rome replied. "I'm hoping it will come to me." Over the past days he'd wondered many times what he would do when he reached this point, and he still didn't have any real idea. All he knew for sure was that he couldn't go back to Qarath. Rix would have him executed for failing to follow his orders. The thought of fleeing to one of the other kingdoms never occurred to him. He was Qarathian. He could be nothing else. And besides, Rix had to answer for the men who'd died because of his orders.

Near the center of the camp were the bright tents and pavilions of the nobles, flags fluttering from their peaks, but out here there were no tents, just dead cook fires, piles of bedding, broken weapons, refuse. It looked as though yet another desultory attempt on the walls had been repulsed. A few men were still retreating beyond bowshot range, dragging wounded with them. There was an air of sullen resentment that changed to surprise as the men looked up and saw the Black Wolf among them. A number called out to him, and he nodded back but did not speak.

They made their way to the command tent. The guards posted outside crossed their halberds at the two men's approach, but when they saw the look on Rome's face they settled them back to the ground, though one turned to announce his presence to those inside.

Tairus was the first man Rome saw when he stepped into the tent, his stumpy form bent over the map table, his mail covered in dust, a battered helm on the ground beside him. Tairus turned, his eyes taking in their tattered appearance. "You look like you should be dead."

"Almost," Rome said, glancing at the other two men in the tent. Fortunately, neither was one of those fool nobles, with an ornamental sword and feather-brained notions of winning glory through the shedding of other men's blood. Both wore mail like Tairus, with short swords and dirks strapped to their sides. He didn't know either of them well.

Tairus followed his look. "Tarn, get these men some food and wine. Pol, roust up some new clothes. Hurry." The two men left and he turned back to Rome. "Tell me what happened."

"Rix sent us on a suicide mission," Rome said flatly. "The Crodin ambushed us and we had to go into the Krin."

Tairus gave a low whistle. "You went into the Gur al Krin? No wonder you don't look so good." His eyes fell on the black axe. "Is that where you got that?"

Rome nodded.

Tairus scratched at the stubble on his cheek and looked toward the front of the tent. They wouldn't be undisturbed much longer. Word of Rome's return must be spreading like wildfire. "Why'd you come here?"

"I'm going to make Rix pay. For that I need an army."

Tairus shook his head. He'd known Rome long enough to know that Rome didn't say what he didn't believe. "I can see where an army would help," he conceded. "But if you're thinking of getting the men to rebel and follow you...well, they're none too happy, but I don't see them turning against their king."

"What are you doing here?" a new voice demanded.

In the entrance stood a man wearing a satin tunic striped with black and gold. A sword hung at his side, the hilt and scabbard crusted with gems. His mustache and hair were long and neatly oiled. He stepped the rest of the way into the tent. "So, it is true," he said, curling his lip. "The great Black Wolf himself is here. Pray, have you come to deliver us? Maybe you have heard how poorly the siege goes and have come to take Thrikyl by yourself?"

Something struck home when he said that. It was as if Rome found the thing he had been looking for all along. He smiled broadly. "Truth is, Lord Field Commander Ilus," he said, "that's exactly what I'm going to do."

Rome started to leave the tent, but Ilus scowled and stepped in front of him, drawing his sword as he did so. "I didn't give you permission to leave." Ilus was half a head taller than Rome and just as broad, but his girth was fat, not muscle.

Rome looked at him steadily, ignoring the blade in his face. "If you get out of my way now, I won't kill you." The words were said simply, without threat or swagger. It was a statement of fact. Ilus' eyes bulged and his face began to turn red.

"*What* did you say?"

"He said if you get out of his way he won't kill you," Quyloc said.

Ilus' face went purple and he drew back his sword to strike.

Rome stepped in and punched him in the stomach. Ilus folded in half and went down without a sound.

"You'll pay for this," he moaned from where he lay on the ground.

"I'll see you dragged back to Qarath in chains."

Rome walked past the fallen man without giving him another look, but when he heard the gasp of pain he knew that Quyloc hadn't been so kind. A sharp kick, probably. Ilus had once dressed down Quyloc in front of all the men and then had him lashed, all because Quyloc did not stand when he went by. Quyloc didn't easily forget a slight.

Rome held the axe loosely in one hand as he made his way through the camp. The men were gathering as news of his presence spread. They crowded around his path, many fresh off the battle field, armored and carrying weapons. Some were wounded, with bloodstained bandages wrapped around heads and limbs, hobbling out of the medical tents to see what the noise was about. There were scattered cheers as he made his way through them, Quyloc and Tairus close behind, and a number fell in behind him.

When it became clear that he was headed for the walls of Thrikyl the cheers began to die off and bewilderment and concern began to show. Did he mean them to mount a new attack on the impregnable city? Especially now, when they were already bloodied from the day and the sun was slipping close to the horizon? Many of them drew back, whispering among themselves. The Black Wolf wore no armor, his clothes were rags and he carried a strange-looking axe. Had he gone mad?

At the edge of bowshot Rome turned to Quyloc. "Wait here."

"What are you doing?" Quyloc hissed, trying to keep his voice low enough that the soldiers couldn't hear. "Are you crazy?"

"Probably," Rome admitted. "If I am, there's no sense in you or anyone else getting killed too."

"I have to agree with Quyloc," Tairus put in. "I don't see how getting yourself killed is going to do anyone any good." He looked back at the massed soldiers, every eye watching intently. "They respect you. Hell, they *love* you. Talk to them. Maybe they will follow you."

"And if they do, what then?" Rome asked. "We march on Qarath and besiege it, kill our own people in a bloody civil war?" He shook his head. "No. I have to do this. If it doesn't work, Rix will get what he wants and no one else dies. If it does..." *What made him think this would work? What did the days in the Gur al Krin do to his brain?* he wondered.

Except that the axe seemed to be humming slightly in his hands, and he had an inexplicable feeling he knew what it was capable of.

Alone he started across the empty battlefield, looking at the high stone walls before him. They were massive, a good hundred feet tall. It was said that the walls of Thrikyl had been built by the gods and while that might not have been true, what was true was there were no visible seams in the stone. It might have been raised whole from the very bedrock. Those walls had never fallen.

Rome thought he heard a voice urging him on, perhaps one of the men waiting behind him. Perhaps only his own imagination. He shifted the axe to hold it in both hands. Too light for a proper weapon, but beautifully balanced.

He was halfway to the walls when he heard the hurrying footsteps behind him and knew it was Quyloc. Always Quyloc backed him up, ever since they were boys. Now Rome felt his smile break out. This was the way it should be. With Quyloc behind him there was nothing he couldn't do. His brawn and Quyloc's brains. "Just like when we took down Dirty Henry," he said, but didn't think Quyloc heard. It didn't matter. What mattered was that all this ended right here. Now.

Two armies held their breath as the two figures made their way across the battlefield. Later, men from both sides would wonder aloud why the defenders never fired on them. They could have killed Rome, stopped everything that came after right there. But others swore it wouldn't have mattered even if they had.

"Rome had the hands of the gods shielding him that day," they said. "They would have turned aside any arrow, any ballista bolt."

Whatever might have happened, the fact is that none raised a hand against Wulf Rome and Quyloc as they marched on that wall. It was as if a glamour held them all spellbound, made them all mute witnesses to a drama far larger than mere mortals. The fact is that *something* was in the air that afternoon.

Rome stopped at the foot of the wall and raised his eyes to look at the men on the top, thinking to warn them, give them a chance to get out of the way. Fighting was his business, but he never killed if he didn't have to. But as he opened his mouth, Quyloc hissed, *"Now!* Strike *now!"*

Rome swung.

The axe whistled through the air and bit deep into the wall. The wall groaned. A crack as wide as Rome's fist appeared, arcing upwards jaggedly. Men yelled from on top of the wall, and arrows flew but they went wide because the wall was shuddering like a wounded beast.

Rome struck again and again. The crack became a rent. A hollow boom came from inside the stone as fissures spiderwebbed all across the face of the wall. The axe was wild and alive in his hands. He was swinging wildly when Quyloc grabbed him and pulled him backwards.

"We have to get back! It's coming down!"

A whole section of the wall collapsed with a groan. Stones crashed to the ground, throwing clouds of dust into the air.

Then a roar went up from behind them and thousands of Qarathian soldiers surged forward.

Rome left half the army in charge of the captured city and marched back to Qarath. The gates were wide open, the populace turned out en masse and universally jubilant. The hated Thrikylians had been defeated, the Black Wolf had returned triumphant and change was in the air. Things were about to get better.

King Rix's royal guard manned the defensive wall around the palace and their captain was defiant, if more than a little pale. Those soldiers whose job it had been to hold the walls of Qarath against Rome "to the last man" were all with Rome. Not a single one had so much as drawn his sword, except to wave it jubilantly during the victory march through the city.

"Turn back!" the captain yelled from on top of the wall. "We will resist." Rome hesitated, not wanting a fight. But a moment later there was a strangled cry and the body of the captain flopped lifelessly to the ground at Rome's feet. Rome looked down on him somewhat sadly. The man had, at least, been loyal—as he himself had once been—if to someone who did not deserve it. Others of the guard opened the gates and Rome entered the castle. Only Quyloc came with him. He knew he didn't need more.

Rix himself met them at the top of the steps leading to the main doors of the palace. Rome stopped and looked up at him. The old man had gone downhill badly since he'd seen him last. His skin was an unhealthy gray pallor, his eyes sunken, his hair nearly gone. He stood as tall as he could for a moment, then removed the crown from his head and threw it to bounce on the stone between them.

"There it is," he said as fiercely as he could. "What you've wanted all along. May it weigh as heavy on your head as it did mine. It's a miserable, ugly place at the top." Rumor said he'd poisoned his father and had his two brothers strangled in their sleep to gain the crown. He tried to glare and then broke down abruptly.

He flung himself at Rome's feet, gabbling with tears and piteous cries for his life. He swore to run away into exile, become a slave, anything to keep his life. And, despite himself, Rome was moved. This thing before him had been a man once. He was pitiful and disgusting, something to scorn, but as he looked down on him he found he could not hate the man. He started to turn away, to call for someone to take Rix away until he could decide what to do with him, when Quyloc acted.

In one smooth step he was beside Rix. With his left hand he took a handful of thin hair and yanked his head up and back. A knife appeared in his right and he slit the fat throat ear to ear, so deep the head nearly came loose in his hand.

"He would have been a rallying point for the nobility," was all he said, before ordering the body hauled away and thrown on the city trash heap.

CHAPTER 5
(Six months later)

"It was all a waste of time, Quyloc," Wulf Rome growled, throwing his leather riding gloves on the table. "The rebels were gone by the time I got there. No threats or bribes were enough to get anyone to talk. We never found out who was behind it." Scowling, Rome leaned on his knuckles on the table, the muscles in his thick arms knotted.

In contrast to Rome, Quyloc was the picture of calm. He sat in a chair on the other side of the table, his elbows on the armrests, hands steepled before him, face expressionless. His white-blond hair was thin and cut short. He wore a fresh green cloak and a green cotton tunic tucked into soft breeches. His sharp-featured face was scrubbed clean, his fingernails precisely trimmed. His voice, when he spoke, was careful and measured, nothing wasted, taut and clean. "You believe it was one or more of the nobility who stirred them up."

"Of course it was. Who else would it be? Every time I turn around those coyotes are nipping at my hamstrings. I'm sick of it!" The slight breeze through the open window behind Rome did little to dissipate the odors of sweat and horse and leather that emanated from him. The two men were in a small room high up in Bane's Tower. The window afforded a clear view of palace and grounds down below. Beyond that lay the city of Qarath itself, spread around the high point that the palace and tower stood on.

Quyloc pulled his dagger out and spun it in one hand. "So execute the lot of them. If you don't know which nobles are behind the troubles, kill them all."

Rome slumped into a chair, the steam gone from him suddenly. Quyloc wondered if he had ridden here nonstop from Thrikyl. His face was lined with dirt and sweat, his eyes bloodshot. His thick black hair and beard were matted. There was a black smudge high on one cheek, just over the old scar that ran from his cheekbone back to his ear. Quyloc could see him turning these words over in his mind and knew his old companion was thinking that conquering Thrikyl was turning out to be easier than ruling it. The former ruling class of Thrikyl had raised intrigue and political ferment to an art form, and they never stopped finding ways to agitate.

By contrast, Qarath's nobility was quiet these days, almost docile. Even the most belligerent had to see how rabidly the masses were united behind their new king. He was the Black Wolf, the man who singlehandedly defeated Thrikyl and ended the war. On top of that Rome had made himself even more popular by throwing open the gates of the prison—where so many had been wrongly imprisoned for so long—and the royal granaries—giving away food to every one of the poor who showed up with his hands out. Within a few days of taking power he slashed the oppressive taxes that had done so much to grind the people down and turned over much of the nobility's lands to the peasants who worked them. That was right about the time he booted the nobles out of the palace and down into the streets where they had to face the same laws and the same justice as the common folk.

It was a vast understatement to say that Rome was popular in Qarath.

Just thinking about it all still made Quyloc's head hurt. He'd missed out on a great deal of sleep in those first heady months, dealing with the ramifications of Rome's hasty acts. Nor was it over yet. The royal treasury would be some time recovering from the loss of all the grain supplies, not to mention the pay raises he'd given all the soldiers.

The countryside was chaos, the populace fighting over who got what land. At least they'd finally stopped trying to burn every manor house they could get their hands on. Again and again Quyloc had tried to impress on Rome the importance of consulting with him before making any major decisions, but he hadn't had much luck. The big man got an idea in his head and he ran with it without stopping to think. That his decisions were almost all wildly popular among a populace too long downtrodden didn't go far in ameliorating the problems afterwards.

"I don't like it," Rome said at last. "My rule is based on law. I won't execute anyone without proof."

"Then your problems will continue," Quyloc said. "And every day that this drags on will embolden others to join the unrest. Give it enough time and eventually you *will* have full-scale, open rebellion."

But Rome continued as if he hadn't heard him. "It's the sort of thing Rix would have done. It's not right. I won't be like him." As he spoke, Rome drew the black axe that was strapped to his back and laid it on the table between them.

The axe.

The weapon that started it all.

As always, the weapon drew Quyloc's eye. The haft was carved to look like the body of some unusual creature, with its legs folded in close to its body. On either side of the head was carved a closed eye. The lower part of the cutting edge was split slightly, as if to convey a partially opened mouth.

Whoever had done the carving had been very skilled. The work was meticulous in its detail. There were even tiny scales—or feathers, it was hard to tell—carved into the body.

It wasn't made of steel. If Quyloc had to guess, he would have said it was made of obsidian, the black volcanic glass that traders from the far south sometimes brought to Qarath. It had the same milky, almost translucent look to it.

But he didn't think it was obsidian. No weapon made of obsidian could have done what he'd seen that axe do in Thrikyl. No weapon ever *made* could do what he'd seen that axe do.

Quyloc frowned. He wished he could remember where they found the axe. He remembered fleeing into the Gur al Krin and he remembered the firestorms that forced them to find shelter in that tumble of huge stones. And he remembered crawling out of the Krin, half dead from thirst, Rome carrying the axe.

But in between there was nothing.

Where did they get the axe? What happened to the other soldiers?

It bothered him, not being able to remember. He had a feeling something important had happened during that lost stretch of time, something they *should* remember. One time, a couple months ago when he and Rome were sitting in this very room late at night, he'd asked Rome about it.

"Do you remember how we got it?" he asked him.

"Of course I remember." The axe lay on the table before Rome like a slice of night and he was stroking it with his fingertips. "It was…in a cave or something. Buried in the dirt I think."

"You don't remember either."

"Not exactly," Rome said irritably. He didn't like to talk about the axe, and for the most part Quyloc never brought it up because he didn't like to talk about it either. He was afraid if he talked about it his envy and his bitterness would show.

It should have been mine, was the irrational thought that always came to him when he looked at the thing. *It was promised to me.*

"But what difference does it make?" Rome continued. "It's here, it got me this kingdom. Beyond that, who cares?"

To which Quyloc had had no answer, no more than he had now. What difference *did* it make, after all? What mattered was that it did what it did. The rest was details. Except that Quyloc was not a man who could accept things at face value and let them be, like Rome could. Life had taught him all too clearly that no hand was completely open, that nothing was given without a price.

Coming out of his reverie, Quyloc said, "The farmers are complaining again. They don't like your order to open the royal granaries and distribute the grain to the poor. They say the bottom's dropped out of the market now, and it's driving them all to ruin."

Rome gave him what was almost a sheepish grin. "Is that true?" When Quyloc nodded he went on, "I never thought of that. I just hate to see people hungry while good food goes sitting. You'll look into it, won't you, Quyloc? Find a way to keep giving those people that grain and still take care of the farmers' problems?"

Quyloc couldn't suppress one irritated sigh. He'd come from the same dirty alleys Rome did. He didn't like to see people starve either. But this was what Rome always did. He saw a problem, a knot, and instead of stopping to figure out how to untie it, he simply slashed it and went on his way. Then he turned to Quyloc to pick up the pieces. But all Quyloc said was, "Of course I will."

Rome gave him a relieved look and cracked his knuckles. "Thanks, old friend. You know how I hate all that administrative grackle. Who'd've thought being a king could be so dull?" He gave a short, barking laugh. "Well, if that's all, I think I'll head down to the barracks and find Lucent. He bet me a pot of ale his nag could beat mine in a race and he lost. I'm going to collect."

His look grew pained when Quyloc picked up a heavy sheaf of official-looking parchments from the table and dropped them with a meaningful thud. "Did I mention how tired I am? We rode almost straight through." He'd come into the city with only a handful of men. The rest of the soldiers he'd left Thrikyl with were probably a day behind. It was hard to keep up with Rome once he got moving.

Quyloc's answer was forestalled by a new presence in the room, as a voice neither man had ever heard before said, "Unfortunately, you men have far bigger problems to deal with than farmers and uprisings."

CHAPTER 6

Rome spun away from the table and into a battle stance, the axe suddenly in his hand, a frozen black shadow. Quyloc was out of his chair, his dagger ready.

"How did you get in here?" Rome barked.

A man stepped forth from the shadows in the corner of the room. *There was no way he could have been there all along*, Rome thought. *No way one of us wouldn't have seen him in full daylight like this.* It was almost as if he stepped right out of the wall.

"How I got in here does not concern you." The stranger walked toward them. He carried a staff made of some black wood, but he did not lean on it. He had white hair and was wearing a simple white shirt and brown breeches. Though his hair was white, he did not move like an old man. In fact, it was hard to tell how old he was. His face was curiously unlined but deeply weathered at the same time—Rome's impression was of a stone statue left exposed to the wind and the rain for centuries.

"That's far enough," Rome said. He couldn't see any weapons other than the staff, but he knew how effective a staff could be in the right hands.

The stranger paused.

"You didn't answer my question. How did you get in here?"

The stranger brushed the question away with an irritable gesture.

"Why are you here?" Quyloc asked. Rome glanced at him. His head was cocked slightly, and he had a curious look on his face, as if he were puzzled by something.

"There. That is the question you should be asking," the stranger said. He started forward again.

"I told you to stop. I won't warn you again." Rome raised the axe. It felt light and cold and strangely eager in his hands. He had not used it since Thrikyl. In truth, though he would never have admitted it, he was almost afraid to use it. He was afraid of what it might do, of whether he could actually control it. He wished he had his old war axe with him, but somehow he had forgotten and left it attached to his saddle.

The stranger turned hard gray eyes on Rome. "Your childish posturing is beginning to anger me. You pose no threat to me."

"We'll see about that," Rome said grimly. Despite the stranger's words, Rome caught the look he flashed at the axe. It was a look of wariness, as if he had seen the axe before.

As the stranger came closer, Rome and Quyloc moved aside. He passed between them and walked to the window. He looked out the window for a few seconds while Rome and Quyloc exchanged looks. Then he began speaking.

"When the world was young, it was populated only by beings you call gods. Immortal, ageless, they dwelt in the Great Spheres of Stone and Sea and Sky, endlessly shaping. But the world was a cold, lifeless place, the Spheres motionless but for their wills. All that was changed when one of their number, she who came to be known as Xochitl (so-SHEEL), reached into the three Spheres and took pieces from each of them to create something different.

"Life.

"Life was something new. Its denizens grew of their own accord, flowered, prospered, and died. They were endless variety and creativity. In time, Xochitl molded her greatest creations: man and woman.

"Among the immortal beings was one second only to Xochitl in power. This was Melekath, and he was trusted by Xochitl. But he was jealous of the love humans had for their creator and wished for the same for himself. When he tried and failed to create his own race, he instead created what he called the Gift. When he offered the Gift to humankind, most were smart enough to reject it. But some were not and those were corrupted. So were born the Children of Melekath, perverted humans with great powers and greater hungers. They built a city named Durag'otal and from there they began to build an army to topple Xochitl and kill those humans who had stayed loyal to her.

"Xochitl and seven of the other greatest immortals led an army against Durag'otal. The destruction was horrific, but at last they prevailed. Melekath and his spawn were sealed in a prison of stone and sunk deep in the earth, never to threaten the world again."

At his words, Rome felt something inside him lurch and he had a strange feeling of unreality. For a moment he did not see the room around him; he was lost in a deep cavern and there was a cold, white glow that blinded him. He put up his hand to shield his eyes and the moment passed. He blinked and looked at Quyloc. His friend had a dazed look on his face. Their eyes met and Rome had the strongest feeling that he was on the verge of remembering something vitally important, but it was like ashes thrown into the ocean, gone before he could collect it.

Rome shook himself. "Thanks for the history lesson, but I don't see how this has anything to do with us."

"On the contrary, it has everything to do with you." The stranger turned and looked at Quyloc, as if expecting a response from him. But Quyloc said nothing.

"The prison had a flaw." The stranger's eyes flicked to the axe in Rome's hands.

Rome shrugged. "So?"

"Melekath has cracked the prison. Soon he will be free. That is why I am here. To prepare you."

"Really?" Rome asked skeptically. "You expect us to believe that?"

"I expect nothing of you. Quyloc, however, is another matter." The stranger was again staring at Quyloc, as if looking for something. "You know something is happening, don't you? You're not like him. You're not like any of them. You *feel* things. You *feel* this."

Rome looked at Quyloc and was surprised by what he saw. Quyloc looked thoughtful, not skeptical like he'd expected.

"You have heard the stories," the stranger continued, still talking to Quyloc. "There is an eyeless, white-skinned creature that burns people with a touch. Another that looks like a diseased man who spreads plague and pestilence wherever he goes. And a third, like a pile of stones walking, that can knock down the strongest walls with its fists. Those are the Guardians, Melekath's lieutenants."

Quyloc nodded. "I've heard."

"Those are just rumors," Rome interjected. "Things like that don't exist."

"What do you think?" the stranger asked Quyloc, leaning toward him slightly, awaiting his answer. Rome found himself awaiting Quyloc's answer also, as if a great deal depended on what his old friend said next.

"Something is happening," Quyloc said at last.

The stranger nodded. "How do you know this?"

Quyloc's look turned inward for a moment. "I just do. It's…a feeling."

The stranger nodded again. "I was right to come here then."

"Does someone want to tell me what is going on?" Rome demanded. "What are you two talking about?"

"I don't know," Quyloc admitted.

"The end of the world," the stranger said.

"What?" Rome stared at the man. "Are you crazy? The end of the world?"

The stranger said nothing, only continued to stare intently at Quyloc.

"I don't think he is crazy," Quyloc said.

Rome turned on him. "You too? Did everyone fall over the edge this morning and forget to tell me?"

"I've felt…something," Quyloc said to the stranger. "I thought it was just me. It's getting stronger. What is it?"

"It is Melekath, reaching into the world once again," the stranger replied.

"That's enough," Rome sputtered. But the other two ignored him.

"The Tender holy book claims Melekath's prison is impregnable," Quyloc said.

"Impressive," the stranger replied. "You know your history. I was not sure I would find any who still knew it."

"But you're saying that the prison isn't impregnable."

"There was a flaw. It took thousands of years for Melekath to exploit it, but finally he has."

"No," Rome said firmly. "No, no, no. I'm not swallowing this at all. What's wrong with you, Quyloc? You don't honestly believe this man, do you?" A strange feeling passed over him as he said the last part and he found himself wondering if the stranger was really a man, or if he was something else. There was something undeniably different about him.

"I'm not sure yet," Quyloc replied, still staring at the stranger.

"It is only reasonable to be skeptical," the stranger said. "It is not every day a stranger appears in your midst and turns your entire world upside down." His eyes hardened. "Make no mistake, though. Your belief, or lack thereof, changes the facts not one wit."

"Right," Rome said. "And those facts are what? That some old god no one remembers is escaping his prison and coming to kill us all? Funny, but there are at least a dozen children's stories that say pretty much the same thing. It's ridiculous."

"Children's tales come from somewhere."

"Except when they don't. They're just stories, that's all. Made up by parents to frighten their children into being good."

"I'm not so sure about that," Quyloc said. "Variations of this same story appear in every region I know of. The details change, but the same thread is always there."

"But those are just legends."

"And what about what you did with that axe at Thrikyl?" Quyloc countered. "In a thousand years won't that just be a legend?"

"That's different. It really happened." Though privately Rome had to admit to himself that there were times when he wondered if it really did happen the way he remembered it. It seemed so implausible.

"So did this," the stranger said. "You feel the truth of it, don't you, Quyloc? Be honest with yourself. You aren't like him." A faint gesture toward Rome. "You aren't like any of them. You are sensitive to the flow of hidden energies. You know what I am saying is true."

Quyloc sat in silence for long moments, seemingly fixed by the stranger's gaze. Finally, unwillingly it seemed, he nodded.

"Well, I don't feel anything," Rome said, trying to shake off the coldness that was seeping into his gut. "It's just rumors and legends. The wilder they are the more people believe them." The other two both ignored him.

"How do you know all this?" Quyloc demanded suddenly, his voice almost angry.

"Because I was there."

The words hung in the silence and then Rome laughed. Or tried to. This couldn't be real. *What was it he couldn't remember?* "Now you've gone too far," he said. "You almost had me believing you but that last part…" He tried to laugh again.

"You're *him*, aren't you? Lowellin." Quyloc's eyes had gone wide.

The stranger nodded. "I am the Protector. I am the one who will do anything, sacrifice anything, to defeat Melekath."

"And you're thousands of years old." Rome tried to sound sarcastic, but he didn't quite succeed.

"Xochitl herself set me to this task, to watch over her creation."

Quyloc's gaze had turned inward once again.

"I saw the flaw from the beginning." Lowellin's face had grown very hard and his free hand was curled into a fist. "We were so close. The prison was nearly complete and Melekath would have been gone forever, but she—" He bit the words off. "She let weakness interfere with her resolve. I saw it happen. I knew this day would come."

"But why have you come to us? What can we do?" Quyloc asked. "Why can't the gods who built the prison fix it?"

Lowellin scowled and something dangerous flashed in his eyes.

"The gods are gone. They have left mankind to its doom."

CHAPTER 7

"The gods are *gone*?" Quyloc asked. It was hard to imagine. He was not a devout man by any means—in his experience the gods cared little for the affairs of their followers—but it was still hard to accept the idea that they were gone.

"Ran away. Hid. We are on our own."

"*All* of them are gone?" Rome asked. "Even Bereth? And Gorim?"

"All of them," Lowellin replied without looking at him.

"But why?" Rome asked. Something in the tone of his voice caught Quyloc's attention. There was a note there he hadn't heard before.

"They're afraid," Lowellin sneered. "They were afraid then —afraid to do what needed to be done—and they are afraid now. They know Melekath will not hesitate to do to them as they should have done to him."

"But without the gods' help…" Rome seemed to be having trouble getting the words out. "What chance do we have?"

"Not much," Lowellin said grimly.

"That's not very reassuring."

"I'm not interested in reassuring you. I'm here to see if you have the courage to fight back. If you do, and if you do exactly as I say, there is a chance—however faint—that we can stop Melekath. There are weapons, but they are dangerous. In the right hands they give us a chance. In the wrong hands…" He stared at Quyloc for a few seconds before continuing, challenging him. "They will turn on us."

Quyloc felt something respond in his heart, something he longed for that he dared not dream of. "What weapons are you talking about?"

"Some will be for the Tenders."

"The Tenders?" Quyloc responded, instantly irritated. "What good are they? Their power was broken long ago. Without Xochitl they are nothing." The Tenders worshipped Xochitl, but she had abandoned them long ago.

"We will see about that."

"And the other weapons?" Quyloc heard the sound of his own need in his voice and hated it, but he could not stop it.

"*One* other."

"What is it? What is this weapon you speak of?" Quyloc asked before Rome could speak. He could not help but think of the black axe as he spoke. He would not miss his chance again.

"Only the right person can wield it. Only the right person even has a chance of obtaining it."

Quyloc swallowed, his mouth oddly dry. He felt a tremor in his hands and made an effort to still them. "I want to know more."

"Even if what you say is true," Rome said. "We had nothing to do with the prison. How do we know Melekath won't just go after the ones who put him there? Maybe he will leave us alone if we stay out of this."

Lowellin's eyes blazed as he turned on Rome. "You have no idea what you are saying. You don't know what we're dealing with."

"That's what you say. But we have only your words and nothing else."

Lowellin's lip curled. "Wise words, my king," he said mockingly. "But hear me now. A human army stood with Xochitl and the other gods when they besieged Durag'otal. Melekath and his abominations have had three thousand years to contemplate the injustice done to them.

"*Three. Thousand. Years.*

"It is a long time to hate, don't you think?" He waited, and finally Rome nodded.

"After all that time, do you think they will be *reasonable?*"

Rome looked at Quyloc, but Quyloc had nothing for him. Finally, he shook his head. "Perhaps not. But that still doesn't mean we should trust you."

Lowellin stiffened. "Then I have wasted my time coming here. I will look elsewhere for those who will fight."

He started for the door, but Quyloc held up one hand. His opportunity, what he had waited so long for, was getting away. "Wait." To Rome he said, "Don't dismiss him so quickly. You don't know what's going on here."

Rome gave him a surprised look.

"I want to know more about this weapon," Quyloc said.

Lowellin looked from Quyloc to Rome and back. "If you doubt, even a little, you will fail. I cannot take that risk." He made again as if to leave.

"Let us talk about this together before you decide," Quyloc said quickly. "It's a lot to accept all at once."

Lowellin hesitated.

"Just one day. That's all I'm asking."

Lowellin considered this. "I have not yet spoken with the Tenders here." He nodded. "Okay. You have one day. I will return and we will speak of this again."

He brushed past them and headed for the door. Partway across the room he stopped and turned.

"It is only a matter of time before the Guardians begin building an army to help their master. We will need one as well, to fight them." This time he was looking at Rome, who suddenly looked interested.

"Your little army won't be enough by itself. For this war you must conquer the rest of them. Forge Atria's rabble of worthless kingdoms into one force."

"You're talking about rebuilding the Kaetrian Empire," Rome said.

"No. I'm talking about building a new empire, led by a man whose soldiers would follow him to the gates of Durag'otal itself. Is that man you, Wulf Rome?" He did not wait for an answer but moved through the door and was gone.

"Did he just say empire? Do you think we could really do it?" Rome set the black axe down on the table and turned to Quyloc. He felt lit up with possibilities. *Empire*. He liked the sound of that. He definitely liked the sound of that.

Then he realized Quyloc hadn't responded. He was standing there with that distant look he often got when he was lost inside his own thoughts. Rome frowned. That couldn't be good for a man.

"Did you hear me, Quyloc? Are you listening?"

Quyloc shook himself and looked at Rome blankly.

"I said, do you think we could do it?"

"Do what?"

"Build an empire. Do you think it's possible?" Rome felt suddenly charged. He wanted to start right now.

"*That's* what you took away from what just happened?" Quyloc looked incredulous. "A man appears out of nowhere, says some ancient god is about to come crashing down on us, but that he has some dangerous weapons that might help if we just do what he says. Oh, and he claims to be thousands of years old. But all you hear is the word empire?"

"It doesn't sound so good when you put it like that."

"No. It doesn't."

"But you don't really believe any of that stuff he said, do you?"

Shaking his head, Quyloc sheathed his dagger. "You were here, right here in this room, right? You saw him appear out of nowhere."

"Not actually. He might have—"

"He *appeared out of nowhere*. But that's only part of it. Surely you noticed that he was no ordinary man, that there's something unusual about him. And what about that staff of his? There's something really bizarre about that thing." He rubbed his temple. "It was starting to give me a headache."

"You're overreacting. I admit that Lowellin is a little unusual, but that doesn't mean he's thousands of years old or that any of that stuff he said is really going to happen."

"And what if it is? What if you do nothing and it all comes true?"

Rome sat down. It felt like all the miles he'd traveled suddenly caught up with him at once. A few hours of sleep would be good right now. "You really believe him, don't you?"

"I do."

"Why? How do you know what he's saying is true?"

"The same way I knew the old lady with the puppets had put poison in the wine," Quyloc snapped. Years before, when Rome and Quyloc were still privates in the army, they went out one night when they got off duty. While walking down a small street in the meaner part of the city they came across an old woman putting on a puppet show on the street corner. The old woman was very skilled, and they stopped to watch her show. At the end she sold cups of watered wine for a copper, but just before Rome drank his Quyloc had a feeling and knocked the cup out of his hand. The man next to him wasn't so lucky and died right there in front of them.

Rome had learned to trust Quyloc's feelings. They weren't always accurate, but they were often enough.

"Okay. We'll go along with this for now. But I don't trust him, not at all. We need to keep a close eye on him. He's playing his own game here and using us."

"I agree with you on that." Quyloc turned and started for the door.

"Where are you going?"

"I don't know."

Quyloc stepped out onto the landing. Lowellin was nowhere to be seen. He started to walk down the stairs, then hesitated. He closed his eyes and concentrated.

After a moment he could hear something coming from up above, maybe on the roof. It wasn't something he heard with his ears, though. It was deeper than that, more than a sound, almost a feeling.

It had to be Lowellin. He wasn't sure how he knew it was, only that he *was* sure, and he'd learned to trust his instincts on this.

It was only two flights of stairs to the top. The trap door to the roof was open. He climbed the iron rungs set into the stone wall.

The view from on top of Bane's Tower was impressive. To the west and south, beyond the palace grounds, lay the city of Qarath. Beyond the city wall lay miles of open, rolling countryside, covered with fields and a few copses of hardwoods here and there. A handful of manor houses were visible out there, summer homes for the nobility. Two of them had been burned down.

Close by to the north lay the Eagle Mountains; the palace grounds sat on the very fringes of its foothills. The Cron River tumbled down out of the mountains, passing through the city.

To the east was the sea. The tower stood on the edge of high cliffs, the waves crashing against their base.

Lowellin was standing at the parapet, looking out to sea. He did not turn or acknowledge Quyloc as he approached.

"Somewhere out there, deep beneath the surface, hides Golgath."

The name sounded familiar to Quyloc, but it took him a moment to place it. Then it came to him. Golgath was one of the Eight, the gods who besieged Durag'otal and created the prison.

"Golgath hides because he fears Melekath, and he hopes to escape his wrath. But he is wrong." Lowellin sounded angry. "Hiding only means that he will be vulnerable when the time of reckoning comes. He deserves whatever Melekath does to him. Those too stupid to prepare for a coming threat always deserve what they get."

Quyloc did not miss the point of what Lowellin was saying. Hiding from the threat of Melekath would only leave them helpless when the time came. He wondered if Lowellin had approached Golgath and been turned away. Had he approached all of the Eight?

"We talked about what you said. We would like to know more."

"So it seems you have more sense than they do."

"Rome is still skeptical, but he will come around."

"And what about you? Do you believe what I say?"

"Of course." Privately, Quyloc still had his doubts. Trust came slowly for him.

"No, you don't," Lowellin said, surprising him. "But you want what I have to offer, and so you are willing to pretend. For now."

"What makes you say that?"

"Because I am no blind fool. I saw how you responded when I spoke of the weapon."

Quyloc had no response for that.

"Why do you want the weapon so badly?"

Quyloc hesitated, considering what he should say. "It is merely prudence. If what you say is true, then we will need all the help we can get."

"Save your lies for the fools who surround you."

Quyloc glanced at him. Lowellin still wasn't looking at him. He sensed Lowellin's anger growing. This was not someone with much patience.

"What do you want me to say?" Quyloc asked.

"The truth. Is it power, is that what you want? Would you make yourself king in place of that oaf?"

This question required no thought. "No. Absolutely not. I have no desire to be king." That much was completely true. The thought of being responsible for the whole kingdom horrified him. He often regretted agreeing to be Rome's adviser and would have quit the post already were it not for the fact that it gave him the resources to continue his search.

"Then why do you want it so badly?"

They were back to the beginning. Quyloc had never told a soul of the strength of his need, how badly he needed answers. It was why he spent his time and his money on old books, on questioning anyone he found who might have clues.

"How long have you known you were different?" Lowellin asked, surprising Quyloc by suddenly turning to look at him.

"I don't know what you're talking about."

"Then there is no reason to continue this conversation. I made a mistake when I approached you. I will have to find another."

Quyloc's stomach fell when he heard the words. He'd searched for so long and found so few real answers. This might be the only chance he ever got.

But it meant taking a risk. It meant revealing more than he ever had before. Quyloc had learned long ago that no one could really be completely trusted. Share too much with anyone and sooner or later they would turn it against you. Survival meant keeping secrets.

"Last chance."

"Okay, I'll tell you." Quyloc realized sweat had broken out on his brow. He took a deep breath. "I've known, guessed, since I was a child." He hesitated. This felt wrong. But he had to know. "It wasn't a single incident. I was always better at stealing than the other orphans. I just had a sense about when the merchant's attention was distracted, when the best moment to snatch something came. At one point I realized the other children didn't have that sense."

"It got stronger as you grew older."

Lowellin was staring at him so hard it hurt. Quyloc couldn't hold his gaze. "It did," he admitted, looking away.

"And now you are growing desperate. You've searched everywhere, but no one, no person, no book, has the answers you're looking for." He paused. "Or they won't share what they know. That's why you hate the Tenders, isn't it?"

Quyloc feared Lowellin would see the tremor in his hands. He felt the urge to flee.

"Tell me the truth," Lowellin demanded.

"Okay. Yes, I hate them. They claim their knowledge is forbidden to men." There was more to the story, but the shame cut too deep and he wasn't letting Lowellin know about it.

"And always it's been that way, hasn't it?" Lowellin asked, his voice softening somewhat. "Those willing to share know nothing worth sharing. Those with true knowledge won't share what they have, leaving you always on the outside."

It was true. No matter where he looked, he found only dead ends. And meanwhile the itch inside him, that sense of unseen energies, of unseen potential surrounding him, only grew stronger. Many times he'd despaired of ever finding answers.

"I have the answers you seek," Lowellin said. "I can tell you all that you long to know. I can pull back the shroud and show you what truly lies behind the world you see."

Quyloc didn't dare look at him, knowing his eyes would betray how deep his need was.

"You can still turn back."

"Why would I want to do that?" Quyloc said.

"You have no idea what it is you are about to get into. The weapon I speak of is found in another world, a shadow world underneath and beside our own. Once you go there, once you see it, it will in return see you."

"So? I am not afraid."

"Then you are an idiot. Because in this shadow world there are no second chances. Every denizen of that world, the world *itself*, will try to trap you."

"I've faced death before."

"Oh, but it's not that easy. The shadow world doesn't want you dead. It wants you *alive*."

CHAPTER 8

Rome was sitting at the table in the tower room when the door opened and Tairus came in. Tairus was a short, stout, dark-skinned man with a bald head and a long mustache. He and Rome went back a long way, to when they were both in the same squad as green privates. One of the first things Rome had done as king was make Tairus his First General, in charge of Qarath's army, second only to Rome himself.

Tairus walked to the table and flopped into a chair, breathing heavily.

"Took you long enough," Rome observed.

Still trying to master his breathing, Tairus said, "You've got no one to blame but yourself, Rome. Gorim's beard, what is it about you and this damned room?" He coughed, hauled himself out of the chair and went to the window to spit. He sat back down. "You got a whole palace full of rooms down there, you know, in case you forgot. Ever think about using any of them?"

"Not if I don't have to. I really kind of hate that place. Everywhere I turn there's someone bowing and scraping, and there's always someone who wants something."

Tairus searched for a gap in his leather armor and scratched his chest. "It's called being king."

"I know," Rome said. "I just never thought it would be so…so..."

"Inconvenient?"

"Yeah. That."

"Shoulda thought of that before you cut Rix's throat."

"That wasn't me. It was Quyloc."

"Whatever. You're getting no sympathy from me." His breathing was finally returning to normal. "Couldn't we at least meet lower down next time? Why do you have to choose the eighth floor, when there are seven perfectly good floors beneath this one? None of those would work?"

Rome gestured at the window, which was about four feet square. "See that? It's a real window. I can see the whole city from here. The lower floors just have arrow slits. Can't see a thing."

"If you say so." Tairus was clearly unconvinced. Rome was idly stroking the black axe, which was lying on the table still. "I wish you'd put that thing away. I don't like to look at it."

"I took it with me to Thrikyl. I thought the people there might need a reminder of how I took their city."

"I keep waiting for the eyes to open one day."

"That'd be something to see."

Tairus shook his head vehemently. "No. No, it wouldn't. It'd be damned horrifying, that's what it'd be. Thing comes to life and starts running around killing people." He shuddered.

"You sound like a child," Rome replied. "It's made of stone or something. It's not going to come to life and start killing people."

"You don't know that."

"Yes, I do."

"I was there at Thrikyl, remember? Who knows what that thing's capable of?"

"I know one thing it's good for. It got me a kingdom. Got you a good promotion too, if I remember right."

"Don't mean I have to like it," Tairus groused, a sour look on his face.

"Forget about the axe." Rome slid it to the side. "That's not why I called you up here." He hesitated. "You're not going to like this."

"Like what?"

"What I'm about to tell you." Tairus was a solid, feet-on-the-ground kind of person. He had no use for anything unnatural or supernatural. Except for Musicians, of course, but then, everyone liked the Musicians.

"Well, get it over with then. The day's not getting any younger and neither am I."

"Something pretty strange happened a little while ago."

Tairus groaned. "You're right. I hate this already."

"Quyloc and I were in here talking and this man appeared out of nowhere."

Tairus looked around the room. "What? You mean he was hiding somewhere?" There wasn't much in the room besides the table and chairs.

"No. I mean he appeared out of nowhere."

"You probably just didn't see him."

"Really?"

"You get distracted."

Rome waved it off. "That's not the strange part."

"You sure? I think it sounds strange enough."

"Stop interrupting me! I've got something to say here." Grumbling, Tairus went quiet. Rome proceeded to tell him what Lowellin had said about the prison breaking open. When he finished, Tairus was shaking his head emphatically.

"No, no, no. I'm not swallowing one bite of that. It's just crazy talk from some madman who was probably hiding in the corner. That kind of stuff doesn't happen."

"You can't be sure of that."

"You know what I like about the gods, Rome? They stay off in their corner and leave us alone in ours. It's a perfect system. We build them temples and they leave us be. There's no point in upsetting that. It's worked fine for a long time."

"But what if he's right?"

"He can't be. It's impossible."

"You weren't here. You didn't see him. There's something really unusual about him. Quyloc believes him."

"That's Quyloc's fault. He's always sticking his nose into things best left alone."

"I hope you're right, Tairus. I really do. But I think we need to listen to him, just in case."

"Why not just clap him in chains next time he shows up? Wouldn't that be better?"

"Somehow I don't think it would be that easy."

Tairus sighed. "I got a bad feeling about this, Rome."

"He did say one thing that you'll want to hear. He says we're going to need a bigger army to fight Melekath. He wants me to conquer the neighboring kingdoms and found a new empire."

"Why would I think that's a good thing?"

"Come on. Aren't you a little bored these days? Wouldn't you like a challenge?"

"What I'd like is to retire from the army and go back to farming. Get old and fat and have lots of kids. That's what I should be doing. I should've never joined the army."

Rome chuckled. It was a familiar refrain from Tairus. Whenever he was tired or having a bad day he always said the same thing. Rome knew Tairus would hate farming. He was a soldier, through and through.

Rome stood up. "That was a long ride and I'm parched. Let's head down to the palace and get something to drink."

Tairus looked at him in disbelief "I just walked up here and now you want to leave? I wish you'd make up your mind."

"Stop complaining. I'll buy you an ale."

"You're the king. You're buying a lot more than one ale."

They were on the bottom floor of the tower, heading for the front door, when it opened and a man entered. He was wearing tight black breeches and a short black jacket over an immaculate, ruffled white shirt. His shoes were black and shiny. His hair and mustache were trimmed neatly and held firmly in place with a thick layer of oil. When Rome saw him he groaned audibly. Then he turned on Tairus.

"Did you tell him? About the tower?"

Tairus gave him an innocent look and shook his head. "I haven't said a word."

"What are you doing here, Opus?" Rome asked the man. "Gods, you're not going to start cleaning this place, are you?"

Opus had whisked a cloth out of the inside of his jacket and was running it over a trunk that stood up against the wall. "It's filthy in here," Opus said, grimacing at the dust that streaked the cloth.

"It's not so bad," Rome said. "A little dirt never hurt anyone."

"While I doubt the truth of that statement, Sire, I will not argue it with you at this point," Opus replied. "I must protest your behavior though. You are the king of a powerful kingdom. You should not be skulking about in a storehouse."

"I am not skulking," Rome snapped. It didn't help that the smile on Tairus' face was getting bigger by the second.

"You slink out here when you think no one is watching. If someone does see you, you threaten him into silence. If that is not skulking, what, pray tell, is?"

Rome glowered at him but Opus did not cringe or back down, steadily returning his look. "Okay, maybe it is skulking," Rome said at last. "But this isn't a storehouse. It's a tower, the last line of defense if invaders should overrun the city."

"Unless these invaders are very small, I do not believe our downfall to be imminent. At any rate, this tower's sole purpose has been as storage for many years now."

"Well, I'm using it for important meetings now," Rome said, rubbing his temple. Opus had a knack for giving him a headache.

"Very well," Opus said with a slight bow. "I will have staff in here tomorrow to begin cleaning." Seeing Rome's scowl, he added, "At least the room you have been using."

"I already cleaned it."

"I'm sure you have," Opus said, tucking the cloth away. "Now, will you tell me which floor it is on, or do I have to go through them all?"

"That won't be necessary," Rome said hastily. "It's on the eighth floor." There was an old cot on the fourth floor and he liked to sleep there. It wouldn't do to have Opus find that. He'd want to fill it with furniture, maybe put curtains on the arrow slits.

Shaking his head, Opus turned to leave. He had just put his hand on the door when he turned back. "Oh, Sire, one more thing."

"What?"

"It has come to my attention that you have not been sleeping in the royal quarters."

Rome sighed.

"May I presume that you have taken one of the rooms out here?"

Rome nodded wearily. It looked like Tairus was going to start laughing.

"May I also presume that were I to remind you that, in this, you are not upholding the decorum of your office, it would be to no avail?"

That made Rome's head spin. He didn't even know what decorum meant. "What?"

"Sleeping in a store room is not becoming of a king," Opus said. "But reminding you of that will not change anything, will it?"

"No. It won't."

Now it was Opus who sighed. "Very well," Opus said. "However, please be aware that I will send a servant to clean that room as well."

As Opus exited the tower Rome said, "Make sure the servant comes during the day when I'm out. When I'm in the tower I'm not to be disturbed for any reason. Am I clear on this?"

Opus bowed slightly. "Very clear, Sire."

The door closed behind him.

"You sure have a knack for managing the servants, Rome," Tairus said with a laugh.

"Shut up," Rome growled.

"Seriously, why do you put up with that? Why don't you just toss him out?"

Rome snorted. "If only I could."

"Meaning?"

"Little bastard runs the whole palace. He takes care of everything. Without him the place would probably fall apart." Rome also had to admit that the little man was very good at what he did and he grudgingly respected him for that. Opus ran the palace and directed its small army of servants with all the precision of a military commander. Rome had spent enough years in the army commanding people that he valued subordinates who knew their jobs and did them well.

Which meant putting up with Opus.

"It doesn't mean I have to like him, though," Rome added, causing Tairus to laugh some more.

They left the tower and Tairus slapped his forehead and said with a groan, "I'll have to take that ale later. I forgot I was supposed to meet with the quartermaster this morning." He left and Rome was alone once again.

A broad walkway connected the tower and the palace, leading to a set of double doors, but Rome left the walkway on a smaller path that led through an elaborate garden complete with fountains, flowers and hidden benches. A smaller path led off that to a narrow door that was a servants' entrance. Rome preferred the servants' entrance to the main doors. It was easier to get in and out without being noticed.

He walked down a dark corridor, passing a room where servants were folding clothing and gossiping. He went around a corner and was almost run over by a lanky, teenaged boy in a hurry. The young man turned white when he saw who it was.

"Sire," he gasped, trying to bow and kneel at the same time and accomplishing neither. "I'm sorry...I didn't see you and..."

"Hold on there," Rome said, putting his hand on the servant's shoulder and standing him up. He was shaking. Rome frowned. "Easy, boy, I'm not going to hit you. Stop acting like a rabbit." He gave him a little shake. "Look at me when I'm talking to you." He was trying not to get irritated, but it was difficult. All the servants were like this. They acted as if he was going to eat them. It was all those years under King Rix and the nobility that had made them spooky.

"What's your name? I like to know who I'm talking to."

The servant shot him a round-eyed look. "My what?"

"Your name. You do have one, don't you?"

"R-Ronen, my Lord."

"Good, Ronen. Now here's what I want you to do. Go fetch Perganon, you know, the librarian with the yellow whiskers? Tell him to meet me in the... What's that room called, the one with all the soft red chairs?"

"The Velvet Chamber?"

"Yeah, that's it. Tell him to meet me there and to bring the history with him." The servant started to scurry away but Rome stopped him. "Then fetch me a bottle of that peppered liquor the Karthijinians make and a loaf of bread, hunk of cheese, whatever you can get your hands on. I'm starving. And one more thing," he said, stopping the boy again. "What's a strapping boy your age doing here?"

"Here? I was on an errand for–"

"No, I don't mean that. I mean here. In the palace. You look like a strong kid with a little bit of sense in your head. Why would you want to be hidden away in this stuffy old place?"

Ronen considered this. "I don't know. It's what I've always done. My parents sent me here as a boy to work in the kitchens."

"Hmm." Rome scratched his beard. "Well, Ronen, I don't know what the rules were before, but that doesn't make you a slave. If you ever wanted to do something else, like join the army, just go out into the yard and ask for Lucent. Tell him I sent you. He'll find a place for you." The idea pleased Rome. If Qarath was going to be an empire, her army would need lots more young men just like this. "It's a little more exciting than drudging around in here. Nothing like a uniform to turn the girls' heads." He slapped the boy on the shoulder and sent him on his way. He'd have to talk to Lucent about actively recruiting more soldiers.

Perganon was a wizened little man with sparse yellow whiskers turning to white and gnarled, misshapen hands. He showed up promptly with the heavy volume of history and a pair of spidery spectacles that he used for reading. Rome didn't know anyone else with spectacles but then, he didn't know anyone else who could read either, aside from Quyloc. Maybe it was reading that made your eyes go bad.

Rome was leaning back in a chair with his feet on the table when Perganon arrived. He'd already had a glass of the peppery liquor and was working on some food. A silver tray loaded with cheeses and different kinds of breads and sausages sat on the table. It had showed up a few minutes before carried by a small squad of liveried servants, all bowing and scraping, the leader of them apologizing for the poor fare and promising that a proper meal would be arriving shortly, along with wine and so on. Rome told him to forget it, that this was all he wanted and to go away and leave him alone. He added the last when it became clear that one or two of them seemed bent on staying and probably spooning food into his mouth. No wonder the old king was so fat. The man obviously didn't do a single thing for himself. Rome couldn't seem to convince the servants that he was a grown man and didn't need everything done for him. It was another reason he avoided the palace as much as possible.

Perganon stood hesitantly by the door until Rome waved him in. "Come in. Have a seat. How're the old bones today?"

"Not too stiff, my Lord." The old man laid his hands across the top of the book and rubbed his puffy joints gently. "Shall I pick up where I left off, Lord?"

The writer of the book, Tilus, had just finished describing a huge battle fought against the Sertithians and the tactics used in it. Rome had learned a lot from that. From the whole book really. Tilus wasn't afraid to describe defeats as well as victories, carefully going over the lessons to be learned from each.

Perganon was describing the disposition of forces for another battle when Rome stopped him. "Hold on. What was the title of that Kaetrian general?"

Perganon's eyes followed back down to the tip of his finger. "'Macht', Lord."

"And a macht is…?"

"The supreme military leader of all the armies. In times of war the macht was in many areas answerable to no one, not even the emperor."

"That's it!" Rome exclaimed, snapping his fingers. Perganon's eyes widened behind his glasses, but he said nothing. "That's the title I've been looking for."

After a long pause, Perganon hesitantly said, "Lord?"

"Macht. It's perfect. I'm not a king, never have felt like one, at least not the way people think of a king. Macht Wulf Rome. That's what I am. That's what I'm going to be called from now on."

Perganon sat there for a long moment, clearly unsure how to proceed, while Rome rolled the new title around on his tongue. Finally, he simply resumed reading.

But Rome wasn't listening. He kept thinking about what Lowellin had said about an empire. Was it really possible? Some of the closer kingdoms, like Yerthin and Opulat, had weak leaders and would be easy to take. The biggest problem was Karthije. They were more powerful than Qarath, but if he waited to take them on until he'd built up his forces with soldiers from the conquered kingdoms he should be able to beat them.

The more he thought about it, the more he became convinced that it was possible, and the more excited he became.

Empire.

Was that not the dream of every ruler? Rome drifted off into his plans. The army would need more training. Tactics were only useful insofar as the troops were disciplined enough to carry them out in the heat of battle. Time and again the Kaetrian armies had won battles against larger forces in hostile terrain simply by virtue of being highly disciplined. They did not break and run, continuing to hold their ranks and execute their orders even when the losses mounted.

Rome realized suddenly that Perganon was still reading. The old man's voice was hoarse and cracking. How long had he been going on while Rome was lost in his own plans? "You can stop now," he said, leaping to his feet. The old man broke off gratefully. "Sorry about that. I got a bit lost there for a while. Here, wet your throat." He filled a glass with the liquor and held it out to Perganon.

Perganon shook his head, looking somewhat alarmed behind his glasses. "No thank you, Lord—er, Macht."

"I insist. You've earned it. And leave off with the titles, okay? You don't have to use one every time you speak to me. Not in here."

Perganon took a sip, then another, larger one. "Good tiare is hard to find," he murmured appreciatively.

"Yeah, one of the benefits of being king," Rome said, pouring him some more. "I mean macht." He sat down and gnawed some cheese while the old man drank some more. The ideas and plans were still whirling around in his head. "Better have something to eat with that," he said, shoving the tray over to Perganon. "It goes right to your head otherwise."

Perganon's cheeks seemed brighter, and he didn't try to refuse this time. After a bit, Rome said, "You are a learned man. You must have read hundreds of books." Such a thing didn't really seem possible to Rome. *Hundreds* of books? He was just complimenting the man. But Perganon nodded and lowered his glass. "So tell me what you think. Is it possible to make Qarath into an empire?"

Perganon blinked, clearly surprised. He licked his lips. "Well, I'm sure that under your fine leadership–"

"Knock off the lip talk," Rome growled. "I asked you what you think, and I want to know what you think. I'm not going to have you executed for saying you think it's a fool's plan. But I will get mad if you only tell me what you think I want to hear." He topped off Perganon's glass. "So tell me what you *think*."

Perganon drank and stared into the depths of his glass for several breaths. Abruptly he took off his glasses and looked Rome in the eye.

"Yes. I do. The lands around the city are fertile. With better management they could be made to produce more food with fewer farmers working them. No country has true wealth without the agricultural base to sustain it. And the nearby mountains hold rich deposits of iron ore for weapons.

"You are a good leader. The people love you. With the right coaxing I believe they would follow you anywhere. Certainly your soldiers will, but you will need the citizenry united for this." He said this last matter-of-factly, not as flattery, but a straightforward representation of the facts.

"You also have Thrikyl's wealth to tap into—their gold and silver will go a long way towards paying soldiers. Finally, there's the fact that, with the very big exception of Karthije, your closest neighbors are weak. If you can keep Karthije out of it until you get stronger, you should get a good start on your empire."

Rome was stunned. He'd thought of this man as nothing more than a doddering old shut-in, obsessed with his books, slipping toward senility. He realized suddenly that that guise was a mask the old man wore, probably as a way of staying unnoticed. And he wondered how many others he misjudged every day, as they presented him with the faces they thought he wanted to see.

"Would you like to hear more?"

Rome could only nod and take a drink off the bottle.

"Karthije is key. Their army is bigger and better in the field than yours." Rome winced. It was true. The one time he'd led men against the Karthijinians had shown him that. They had a lot of mounted cavalry and their infantry fought in tight blocks bristling with spear points and shields that were nearly impossible to crack.

"How do you know so much? That can't all be in those books of yours."

For the first time, Perganon smiled. A real smile. It made him look decades younger. It was the smile of a man finally recognized for his achievements. "No, it's not," he said, draining his glass and holding it out for more. He appeared to weigh Rome for a minute, clearly wondering how much to give away, and then decided to give it all. Maybe it was the liquor. Maybe, like any other man, he simply needed to talk to someone about what he'd done.

"I have assistants who help me. Men—and a few women—who live other places. They keep their eyes and ears open and send me letters when they can. None of it is secret. They are not spies. They are ordinary citizens. Most I met when I was a much younger man. I traveled a great deal back then, though it was not easy. The roads between cities were no safer then than they are today. In some cases the correspondence has been taken over by children or even grandchildren as their parents have died or gotten too old to continue writing. In return I send each a small annual stipend."

"You crafty old bull," Rome said with genuine respect. "Where do you get the money? I've seen the library. It didn't receive first priority from Rix's treasury."

"Shall I just say that I saw an opportunity years ago and the king graciously signed an open-ended letter of annual funds? It is not a sizeable amount, I assure you. But I administer it judiciously."

"Remind me not to get drunk around you," Rome said with a laugh. "Also remind me to double whatever you're getting. I want to know more. Lots more. But I want to keep it secret, just between you and me. Carry on like you have been but get whatever you can from your assistants." His mood sobered. "You really think we can build an empire here?"

"With a lot of luck, you can. Never forget that, Macht. Luck plays an important part. If the wrong day goes against you, you could lose it all."

"The gods know I understand that." Rome touched the scar across his cheek. "If the man who gave me this hadn't slipped as he was swinging, I wouldn't be here to talk with you. And there have been more than a few other times."

"May I go now, Macht Rome? I am an old man and I fear the liquor is going to my legs as well." Rome nodded. Perganon paused at the door. "I almost forgot the most important aspect." To Rome's unspoken question he replied, "Roads."

"Roads?"

"Not just roads. Good roads. Roads that don't turn to quagmires in the rain and then harden into impassable ruts. To have a real empire you have to have good roads, paved with stone if you can. When the empire gets large there's no way you can keep enough troops to adequately garrison every corner of it. But with good roads you don't need to. Good roads allow an army to travel quickly from one place to another, greatly extending its range. And they're good for trade too. You'll need a lot of money to get this beast moving and keep it moving. That money comes from taxes. People can't pay taxes if they don't have money. The first thing you need to do with any new city you take is to drop the import taxes on both ends. Clean out the road bandits and provide good roads and trade will follow. Trade is your lifeblood. Don't forget that. The Kaetrians understood the need for good roads. They paved everything with stone and some stretches of their old roads still exist, still better than anything built since then. Take that page from their book if you take nothing else."

He left and Rome sat wondering at the luck of finding such a gem right under his very nose. If Qarath was going to grow into an empire, he was going to need a lot more such luck.

CHAPTER 9

"**If** it isn't the FirstMother of the Tenders, come to grace my simple establishment with her grand presence," the shopkeeper said. "What will it be today?"

"Maybe today I'll finally turn you into hoptoad," Melanine replied. Out of habit she looked over her shoulder, making sure no one had heard what Ronse said. Qarath was a reasonably safe place for Tenders, but it was still best to be careful, especially these days with the strange rumors going around. Frightened people liked nothing so much as a scapegoat and she didn't feel like being one.

"Last week it was a mole," Ronse teased. "You should make up your mind."

"So long as it's something that can't speak," Melanine replied. "You talk too much, even for a shopkeeper."

Ronse laughed. "It's a curse all the men in my family have. That's what my wife used to say."

Melanine grunted, but didn't reply. Ronse's smile faded. "That bad, is it?" He set down the rag he'd been dusting with and came around the counter. "There's always rumors." He took a chair from the corner of the room and set it out for her.

Melanine sat down gratefully and leaned her cane against her leg. It seemed her back hurt more every day. Getting old wasn't much fun. "You're right, but this time it's different. These are more than just rumors."

The rest of Ronse's good humor disappeared. "What are you saying?"

Once again Melanine looked around the shop. Candles filled every available inch of shelf and counter space. A few of them were colored or molded into fanciful shapes, but most were the dull golden brown of simple tallow. Ronse's shop didn't see much beyond the poorer folks of Qarath. As before, there was no one there to hear her, but a lifetime of caution was too ingrained to ignore now.

"I can hear it in the Song. Something bad is happening. Something really bad." She spoke frankly. She and Ronse had known each other for almost thirty years. He wasn't a follower of Xochitl, but he was an old friend and she could trust him. She'd healed his son of the spotted sickness all those years ago and Ronse wasn't the sort to forget.

Ronse pulled up a chair opposite her and sat down. "What do you think it is?"

For a moment Melanine felt too weary to answer. Why did this have to happen now? She was old. She'd be lucky to make it another two winters. All she wanted was to finish her life in peace. "It frightens me even to say it," she whispered hoarsely. She took a deep breath. "I think the prison is breaking. Melekath is returning to the world."

Ronse said nothing for a long moment, a confused look on his face. "Who's Melekath?" he said at last.

"He is the one who betrayed Xochitl. She warred on him and imprisoned him and his followers in the earth."

"Oh," he said. "*That* Melekath." Clearly he still did not know who she was talking about. But that wasn't a surprise. Few knew who Melekath was anymore. Much had been forgotten. "That's bad, isn't it?" he asked.

Melanine nodded.

After a bit he said, "Just know you can come here, any time of the day or night. I'll help you however I can."

Melanine leaned forward and patted him on the knee. For a moment the doom which had been haunting her the past few weeks lifted somewhat. Ronse meant what he said, even if it cost him his life. His wife was dead for three years now and his son lived on the other side of the city with his own family.

Both turned as the door to the shop opened. A man with white hair entered, carrying a black staff. His clothing was ordinary, as were his features, but there was something unusual about him, something that didn't quite fit.

The second his eyes fixed on Melanine the sense of doom came rushing back.

Melanine struggled to her feet as he approached, for some reason reluctant to face him sitting down. She leaned heavily on her cane and stared into his gray eyes. She knew before he spoke that this was no ordinary man.

"FirstMother," the stranger said. It was not a question.

Melanine nodded fractionally.

"I need to speak to you and your order."

"Not something you can just tell me then, I take it?"

His eyes bored into her. She had the curious sensation that he was digging through the depths of her life, judging her in a way she'd never been judged before. Then he seemed to pull back and she knew without a doubt that she had been found wanting.

"Is something wrong, Melanine?" Ronse asked. He'd stood too, and was twisting his cleaning rag in his hands. The look in his eyes said he wanted to run, but his loyalty to his old friend was too strong.

"Yes, there is," she replied, turning to him. "But there is nothing you can do about it." She clasped his arm briefly. "Thank you. For everything."

Without saying another word, she followed the stranger out of the shop.

Melanine led the stranger out into the sunlight. They passed through the trades quarter and down a side street into a meaner area. The streets were narrower here, the buildings jammed together, with filth piled along the edges. She made no attempt to speak to him as they walked and he remained silent. Who was he? she wondered. Why did he want to speak to the Tenders? She realized that she was in no hurry to find out. There was plenty of bad news in the world and she'd learned there was no need to rush toward it. It would come in its own bad time.

The street twisted and went down a short decline. A woman dumped a bucket of some brown liquid out of an upstairs window, narrowly missing the two of them. The FirstMother frowned, but the stranger didn't seem to notice.

The street dead-ended at a rough dwelling, two stories tall, with heavy shutters over the windows and a stout door. Melanine FirstMother banged on the door with her cane. "Open up, Lenda!" she yelled.

There was the sound of footsteps, a bar being lifted, and at last the door opened.

"Here we are," she said, leading the way inside. "Thank you, Lenda." Lenda was a skinny woman with short brown hair and a lazy eye. She was staring at the stranger as if he had two heads.

"FirstMother, I…a *man*," she said breathlessly. "You brought a *man* here. Why?"

Melanine shrugged. "He asked to come speak with us. Stop staring, girl. It's rude." She gave her a gentle push. "Go tell the others to meet in the common room. And bring some tea." She watched Lenda scurry away. "She has a good heart, that one does. Just a little simple is all. She was living on the street when I found her. I couldn't just leave her there now, could I?"

The stranger said nothing, but Melanine hadn't really been talking to him anyway. Lately she talked to herself more and more. Another of the byproducts of getting old.

They walked down a short hallway that led to a fairly large room with a rough, scarred table in the middle. A lamp with a smoky chimney provided the only light, and not enough to reach the corners of the room. The floor was rough stone flags and there was a smell of old grease in the air. Lurking in the gloom at the other end of the room was a statue. Two women sat at the table, their heads together, speaking in murmurs. When the FirstMother and the stranger entered they sat back and looked up guiltily.

"FirstMother, we didn't expect…" one started to say, rising. She had a long face and two of her lower teeth were missing. She broke off as she saw the stranger and her eyes widened. She shot a look at the other Tender with her—a stout woman with thick, muscular forearms and streaks of gray in her brown hair—but the other woman wasn't looking at her. Her attention was fixed on their visitor.

"He wants to talk to us, Velma," the FirstMother said. Stiffly she moved to the table and sat down. When did a simple walk become so hard?

They waited in silence then, the four of them, while the lamp flickered uneasily and mice scurried in the rafters overhead. The statue seemed to lean towards them. From somewhere down a hall a door creaked open and then slammed shut. There were scurrying footsteps. Voices and more doors and then they began to emerge, one after another, like rabbits coming out of their burrows, looking on the man in their midst with curiosity and fear. Finally, Lenda came into the room and said breathlessly, "I told them all."

"Good," Melanine said. "The tea, Lenda. Don't forget the tea." Lenda threw up her hands and hurried out again. To the stranger she said, "We are all yours. Speak."

He stood at the edge of the light, the statue seeming to loom behind him, not speaking, only looking at them. Once again Melanine had the feeling he was measuring them. His gaze roamed over them one by one and each one shrank slightly in her chair as he found her wanting and moved on. Last was the stout woman with the gray streaks in her hair. She met his gaze as he stared at her for what seemed like a long time. "I am Lowellin," he said finally, speaking to her. "Lowellin who was named Protector by Xochitl."

Most of the Tenders only stared at him stupidly, aware that this name should mean something to them, but not knowing what it was. Their knowledge of who they were, their roots and history, had gone dim and gray in this battered age. The light of the Order of the Tenders of Xochitl was slowly but surely going out.

"So you say," the stout woman replied. She might have been an attractive woman, in a strong, masculine sort of way, but years of hardship and disappointment had drawn the lines too deep on her face and her eyes held too much suspicion. Suspicion that surfaced now. "But we have only your word on this, don't we? Why are you here, now?"

Lowellin's eyes glittered faintly in the lamplight. He looked taller than Melanine remembered. He seemed almost to glow. "You know why I am here, Nalene. You have heard the dissonance in the flow of LifeSong. In your heart you know what it means."

Nalene's eyes widened. "No," she whispered.

"What is he talking about?" Lenda asked, coming into the room with a kettle and several cups on a tray. "What's 'dissonance'?"

The other women exchanged worried looks but Melanine knew at least half did not know what the stranger was talking about. They were Tenders in name only, unable to hear more than the faintest whispers of LifeSong.

"The Book of Xochitl says the prison cannot be broken," Nalene said, still staring at the stranger. The Book of Xochitl was the Tender holy book, written in the days shortly after Melekath and his spawn were defeated.

"In this, the Book is wrong," he replied.

"Can someone please tell me what is going on?" Lenda asked irritably. "I'm confused." She was still standing in the doorway holding the tray.

"Our visitor claims the prison is failing," Melanine said. "He says Melekath will soon be free."

Frightened babbling erupted around the table. Lenda gave a little cry and dropped the tray with a crash of broken pottery. Only Melanine and Nalene stayed quiet, watching the stranger. Finally, Melanine took her cane and banged on the table several times until they settled down.

"That's better," she said. "You sound like a flock of chickens, disturbed during the night." She looked at the stranger again. "Go on."

"I have come to find those who are ready to fight."

"Fight?" Velma said. "What can we do?" There were nervous nods in agreement.

"Are you not the Tenders of Xochitl?" Lowellin challenged them in a booming voice. "Did not an army of Tenders march with Xochitl when She laid siege to Durag'otal? Did your order not help defeat Melekath before?"

"We call ourselves Tenders," Nalene said bitterly. The perpetual frown on her face settled in deeper. Melanine had never liked Nalene. She was too cold, too angry. She ran roughshod over any who stood in her way. But she had grit; she had to give her that. She didn't back down to anyone and she didn't back down now. "But it's only a name now that the Mother has withdrawn Her favor. If you really are Lowellin, you know that."

"I do know that. But what has been lost could be reclaimed."

"Is Xochitl coming back? To help us?" Lenda asked suddenly.

"No," Lowellin replied.

Lenda's face fell. "So that means She still doesn't forgive us, doesn't it?"

Dead silence greeted her words, and every eye went to Lowellin, hoping against hope that he would gainsay her. The Mother had been silent for so long now.

"Not yet," Lowellin said. "But this is your chance. I offer you the return of power, though not the same power you once knew. Use it wisely this time and Xochitl will look favorably on the Tenders once again."

"These are Xochitl's words?" Melanine asked. "She told you to tell us this?"

"Do you question my right to speak for Her?" Lowellin demanded, looking at Melanine for the first time. "Do you know nothing of your own holy book?" The Book of Xochitl spoke of Lowellin as the mediator between the Tenders and their god. According to it, Xochitl spoke through him and he interceded on their behalf with Her.

"It has been a long time since you appeared to us. You did not once appear during all the dark years. How are we supposed to know if what was true then is still true now?"

Before Lowellin could reply, Nalene spoke up again. "You said our power will be different this time. How?"

Why are you so hungry for power? Melanine wanted to ask. *Have you forgotten what happened before?* The Tenders of Xochitl had been very powerful during the days of the Kaetrian Empire, but they had misused that power, let it seduce them so that they forgot the task set for them by Xochitl—to tend to all living things. It was generally believed by the Tenders that the reason Xochitl did not answer their prayers, why their power was gone, was because She was punishing them for what they had done.

"There are weapons out there, powerful enough even to kill a god. But they will not come without a price," Lowellin said. "There will be pain. They may turn on you. Not everyone will be strong enough to wield one."

Nalene raised her chin. "I am not afraid. I will do whatever it takes, whatever the Mother requires of me." She swept the rest of them with a look that dared them to follow her. Most did not meet her eyes. They had been beaten down for too long.

Lowellin nodded. "It is this we must have if we are to win this war," he said. "More like you." He stood. "Think on what I have said. Think on who you are and what you will do to protect Life as you have sworn to." He paused and swept them all with his gaze one more time.

"Think on what you will do to redeem yourselves in the eyes of Xochitl."

When he was gone they sat around the table in silence. Melanine sat at one end of the table and Nalene at the other. It was still subtle, but Melanine noticed that most of the women had slightly altered their positions so that they were oriented toward Nalene. Melanine was too old to fight, she didn't even know if she should fight, but she had already lost.

"I do not trust him," Melanine said, knowing it was hopeless, but determined to say her piece anyway.

"You doubt he is Lowellin?" Nalene threw the words down the table at her, daring her.

"No," Melanine admitted. "I think he is. But I still don't trust him."

"He was named Protector by Xochitl Herself," said Velma. With her tongue she poked at the gaps where her lower teeth were missing. She was sitting at Nalene's right hand. She followed Nalene in everything.

"Xochitl has been gone a very long time."

"Meaning?" Nalene asked.

Melanine turned her palms up. "Things change. Who knows the will of the Mother anymore?"

"If anyone does, it must be the Protector," Lenda said stoutly and then hesitated, looking at the others, wondering if she had spoken wrongly. Relief flooded her when others nodded in agreement.

"It says in the Book that the Mother trusted Lowellin over all others," Velma added. She checked with Nalene to see if she approved, but Nalene was staring hard at Melanine.

"It also says that in the beginning it was Melekath who was closest to Xochitl. You know how that turned out." According to the Book, Melekath became jealous after Xochitl created humankind. It was because of his jealousy that he created the curse known as the Gift, which he used to subvert those who came to be known as his Children.

That stopped them. More than one face creased in a frown as a Tender considered this new idea. But Melanine knew it would not last. The hatred and scorn their order had suffered for centuries had a very bitter flavor and what Lowellin offered was too sweet to be rejected.

"I think you are afraid," Nalene said, spitting the words out as if they tasted bad. "You are old and afraid." She looked at the others. "Lowellin said it would be painful. He said it would be hard. But look around you." She gestured at the drab, dimly lit room. "When have our lives ever been anything but hard?" She fixed a hard gaze on Melanine once again.

"Now our chance has finally come. We can once again be something! I cannot speak for you, but as for me nothing can be more painful than what I live with every day.

"I will follow where the Protector leads. I will do everything he commands." Then she began to recite the vows, the words the Tenders were supposed to begin every day with:

"I vow to pay any price, to make any sacrifice in fulfillment of my duties to Xochitl and all She has created.

"My life for the land, and all its creatures.

"This is the will of the Mother, which I will never again forget."

By the time she reached the end, the rest had joined in with her and Melanine knew she had lost them. There were other things she could still say, but what was the point? What made her think she was right anyway? She said nothing as Nalene stood and left the room. She sat there alone as they silently filed out after her.

CHAPTER 10

Quyloc had trouble concentrating all day. After Lowellin's frankly frightening comment about the shadow world wanting him alive, he'd refused to reveal any more information.

"I'll find you tonight. I'll tell you more then."

"Where do you want to meet?"

"Where would you like to meet? Where do you feel safest?" Lowellin asked him with an odd look.

Quyloc's first thought was of his chamber underneath the tower, but he didn't want Lowellin to know about it. Only Rome knew about it and he wanted to keep it that way.

"How about your secret chamber?" Lowellin asked.

Quyloc started to ask him how he knew about it, then changed his mind. Clearly Lowellin had been watching him for some time. It was the only way to explain how he knew so much about Quyloc. Quyloc didn't like it, but there was nothing he could do about it.

After it got dark, Quyloc headed for the tower. Before he entered he looked around, making sure no one was watching. Once inside, he lit the lantern that stood on a shelf.

On the bottom floor of the tower was a room, about half full of crates and barrels. Quyloc slid some aside, revealing a trap door, cunningly concealed in the floor. Quyloc would never have found it on his own. He'd seen it on an old set of plans stored in the library. Those plans were no longer in the library.

He pulled up the trap door, revealing iron rungs set into the side of a shaft that led straight down. He made his way down the rungs, pausing to close the trap door behind him.

When the rungs ended he was in a rough-hewn passageway that led to stairs. The stairs were rough and uneven. He went down several flights and found himself in another passageway, this one even rougher than the first. The floor was uneven and stones had fallen from the walls and ceiling, making walking difficult.

At one point the passageway sloped down steeply. Where it leveled out there was a wide crack cutting across the width of the passage, like something that might have opened up during an earthquake. It was too far to jump so Quyloc had brought two planks down and laid them across it. Warm, sulfur-tainted air flowed up from the depths of the crack. The one time Quyloc had turned off the lantern and looked down there, he thought he saw a faint, reddish glow.

Further on, the passageway forked. The left fork led steeply down, the stairs finally ending in a natural cave at the base of the cliffs. At high tide the cave was completely filled with water, but at low tide it was possible to walk out onto a narrow strip of beach at the base of the cliffs.

The right fork led to a small room. The room had one small window that opened onto the cliff face, about halfway down the cliffs. Quyloc had no idea what the room was for. When he found it, it was empty except for a badly rotted chair and a rusted sword. The passageway down to the base of the cliffs made sense as an emergency escape route, but that didn't explain the room. Nevertheless, it appealed to Quyloc. Here he could store his most secret books and know they would not be disturbed.

He had brought a rough cot down into the room, along with a simple desk and a chair. Along one wall he'd set up some bookshelves and they were filled with the books he'd collected over the years. They were old histories and every bit of arcane lore he'd been able to get his hands on. He'd read every one more than once.

Setting the lantern on the desk, he pulled out a heavy volume with a battered leather cover. It was a copy of the Book of Xochitl. Very rare. Very hard to obtain since most of them were destroyed after the fall of the Empire, when the angry mobs vented their pent-up hatred on the Tenders, burning temples and havens, killing the Tenders. After the Tenders refused to help him, he'd begun searching for a copy of this book, thinking it would hold the secrets he sought. It didn't, but he had still learned a great deal from it.

Quyloc reread everything he could find in the book about Melekath, the creation of the prison, and Lowellin. It corroborated everything Lowellin had said, except for one important point: there was no mention of a flaw in the prison. The prison was supposed to hold Melekath forever.

Suddenly Quyloc realized he was not alone. He stood and turned. Lowellin was there, holding his black staff.

"Are you ready to start?"

Quyloc nodded.

"We will go first to the edge of the shadow world, which is more properly known as the *Pente Akka*. I will begin teaching you there."

Before Quyloc could react, Lowellin reached out with the staff and jabbed him in the chest with it. Quyloc fell backwards.

When he regained his balance and looked around, his heart stopped.

He was no longer in the secret chamber. He was standing on yellow sand in darkness. The sky was black tinged with purple. Lowellin was standing a short distance away, looking at him, his hands resting on the top of his staff. There was something about the staff. It looked different. He had the sudden, irrational thought that it was watching him.

The first thing you need to learn is not to let yourself become distracted or careless. The place will try and trap you. Your only chance of surviving in the Pente Akka *is to be focused at all times.*

Quyloc heard Lowellin's words clearly, but in his mind, not in his ears.

You will need this. Lowellin used the end of the staff to flip something over to Quyloc. Quyloc looked down. On the sand at his feet lay a knife.

Pick it up.

Quyloc did so. It looked to be made of bone.

Do not lose it. Without it, you will be unable to leave the Pente Akka.

What do I do with it?

You use it to cut an opening in the Veil.

What is the Veil?

Look behind you.

Quyloc turned around. What looked like a very fine, gauzy web stretched out of sight in both directions and disappeared into the sky overhead.

Beyond that is the Pente Akka.

This was moving too fast for Quyloc. He had expected Lowellin to lead up to this, maybe explain some things to him first. He could see vague shapes beyond the Veil and they frightened him. He needed some more time to prepare. *We're not going in right now, are we?*

I'm not going in at all. Only you are.

Feeling truly alarmed, Quyloc backed up. *I'm not ready for this.*

You never will be. Not really.

I need to know more first.

In order to leave the Pente Akka, *you will have to summon the Veil yourself. Once you pass through it, I will not be able to help you.*

His fear grew. *I don't know how to do that. I don't think that I can do that.*

Then you will be trapped there. And I will look for another to take your place. There are no second chances in that place.

Almost, almost Quyloc threw down the knife then and there. He was insane to be doing this. It couldn't be real. It had to be a dream. None of this made any sense.

It is all too real, Lowellin said. *What you call real has many facets. You have viewed it only from one angle.*

I can't—

Then you are of no use to me. Go back to your little world and I will find another with the courage to wield this power.

Wait! Quyloc held his hands up. *I just...I need to know more before I go there.*

Look at the Veil. Look at it very closely.

Quyloc did.

What color is it?

It's white. Grayish white.

You're not paying attention. Look again. What color is it?

Quyloc tried to stare at it, but he was having trouble. He kept thinking of what waited for him on the other side. He pushed the fear away, concentrated only on the Veil. Then he saw it.

There is purple in it, very faint.

How does the weave run?

What?

How does the weave run? Is there a pattern? Is it random?

I don't know.

Then you will not be able to summon it and you will be trapped in there. Only if you can picture it exactly in your mind will you be able to summon it.

Quyloc stared at it some more. There *was* a pattern. It was intricate. *Okay,* he said. *I see it.*

Close your eyes. Can you still see it?

Yes.

When you want to leave, picture the Veil in your mind. Picture it perfectly and it will be there. Get one detail wrong and you are lost.

I can do that.

Then there is no more time to lose. Do not stay too long. Look around, then return. If you see the hunter, leave immediately.

Quyloc started to ask him what a hunter was when Lowellin shoved him in the back with the staff.

Quyloc fell forward, into the Veil.

It was a strange landscape Quyloc found himself in. There was no sun in the sky. The sky was a dull bronze color, the light emanating from it diffuse. He was standing on a vast, grassy plain. The grass was waist-high and was topped with heavy seed pods. Waves and ripples moved across the grass, though he could feel no wind. That bothered him and for some time he stood staring at it, trying to see if the movement was caused by some creature. But he could see no pattern and after a while he gave up.

When he turned around he saw a rocky knoll in the distance. Since it was the only feature anywhere in sight, he tucked the odd bone knife in his belt and started towards it.

How long it took him to get there he could not have said. There was no way to judge the passage of time. The light never changed. It was hard to tell if he was actually moving. He might have simply been walking in place.

However, at some point when he looked up at the knoll he realized he was standing almost at the foot of it. It was about thirty or forty feet tall and made up of jumbled whitish boulders. Some kind of shrub sprouted from the gaps between the stones and near the top two stones leaned against each other in such a way as to create something of a cave between them.

Something hopped out of the depths of the cave, stopping right at the mouth. A moment later another one hopped into sight. They appeared to be some kind of bird, though their feathers were silvery and their necks were very long. They had very narrow, hooked beaks. As Quyloc began to back away, they fixed bright eyes on him. They began opening and closing their beaks, making loud clacking noises.

Then they jumped into the air and flew straight at him.

Quyloc's first thought was to flee, but there was nowhere to go and he wouldn't be able to outrun them. Next he remembered the Veil but they were closing fast on him and he couldn't remember any details about the thing, much less picture it closely enough to summon it.

They dove at him and at the last moment he remembered the knife. Yanking it free, he stabbed at the first bird, then ducked as the other tried to rake him with its claws.

They wheeled in the sky and dove at him again. This time he was able to wound the first bird, sending it veering away with a shrill cry, but in doing so he left himself vulnerable to the second one. There was a sharp pain on his arm as it slashed him with its beak.

The birds then flew away and disappeared into the distance.

Quyloc looked at his arm. Blood dripped from a shallow wound on the back of his forearm. Though the wound was not serious, it alarmed him. It was time to leave. But the adrenaline was coursing through his veins, his heart was pounding wildly, and he couldn't remember anything about the Veil except that it was gray-white. He needed to calm himself. He needed to focus.

He took deep breaths, trying to get himself under control. But it didn't seem to help. His thoughts were in utter turmoil. He couldn't stop looking at the wound. Blood was dripping from it, way too much for such a small wound. Then he realized that his blood didn't look right. It looked almost black.

When he looked at the ground he got a new fright.

There was no stain where his blood fell, no puddle. It looked as though the ground was absorbing his blood completely.

The spot where his blood was falling began to move.

A hole opened and something like ants, but with too many legs, boiled out.

Quyloc jumped back.

There was a howl in the distance, joined quickly by two more. He spun, eyes straining to locate this new threat. Far off in the distance the grass was rippling wildly, and the disturbance was getting closer.

Shrill cries from the sky made him look up. The birds were coming back. Only there were hundreds of them now.

It was his blood. His blood was attracting these things.

Panic threatened, but Quyloc fought to get control of himself. If he gave into his fear now, he had no chance.

It wants you alive.

Lowellin's words echoed in his mind. He was running out of time. The birds were almost on him. More of the bizarre insects were coming out of the ground with every second. The Veil was his only chance.

Though every instinct was screaming at him to run, Quyloc forced himself to stand still. *Focus!* he told himself. *Focus!* He closed his eyes to block out everything else, trying to picture the Veil.

All at once it was there, but it was hazy and when he opened his eyes it was nowhere to be seen.

The birds were blotting out the sky. The grass all around him tossed as if in a storm. The insects were swarming up his legs.

He closed his eyes, trying desperately to block it all out, knowing it was already too late.

All at once the Veil was there in his mind in shining perfection, the whole darkly beautiful pattern.

Quyloc opened his eyes. There was the Veil. Birds were diving at him. The insects were a solid mass running up his neck, onto his face. Something toothy and covered in yellow fur leapt at him from the side.

He slashed at the Veil and dove through the rent.

He opened his eyes and he was lying on the floor in his room under the tower. The lantern flickered dimly.

Gasping, his heart still pounding hard, Quyloc climbed to his feet and stumbled to the narrow window. He stood there, breathing hard of the fresh sea air. When he had calmed somewhat he realized he was still gripping the bone knife tightly in one hand. He laid it on the desk and looked for the cut on his arm.

There was no wound.

Looking closer, he saw a faint purple line where it had been.

He touched it. The skin felt numb, like touching an old scar. For a moment it seemed he could hear howling in the distance.

Quyloc sank into the chair. *What just happened?*

CHAPTER 11

The Haven was quiet the next morning when FirstMother Melanine awakened. Through the window she could see that the sun was not yet up. She breathed in the currents of LifeSong and listened to the slow rumble of the inhabitants of the city, just beginning to stir. This was her favorite time to rise, when the day was pure, full of endless potential. So much could be accomplished before the masses fully awakened and began to move about. With most of Qarath's people sleeping, the flow of LifeSong was like a stream not yet muddied by people stomping around in it, churning up the mud and debris.

But not today. Today she lay there, knowing what she needed to do, prepared for it, but still having trouble finding the strength to take the final steps.

She had not tried to convince any of her sisters to believe as she did about Lowellin. What could she offer them anyway? She could only have said that it was what she believed. But what was belief? Perhaps her beliefs had been wrong her entire life. And what difference did it make what she believed anyway? Her belief or disbelief did not change the pillars of reality one bit.

Tired and angry suddenly, she pushed herself up off the bed. Maybe she was wrong. Maybe Lowellin was their savior. But she would not be a part of what was to come. She would walk away; let the consequences fall on the heads of the others.

She opened a chest at the foot of her bed and took out the white robe that lay on top. Age and long use had made the garment more gray than white. Robes were the official attire of her order; the white color signified that she was of the Arc of Humans, those Tenders tasked with tending to humankind. She looked at the robe for a minute, then put it on. Normally the robe was only worn when the women in her Haven were performing a ritual or celebrating a holy day and they never wore them outside, not wanting to endure the harassment that would occur if they were recognized for what they were.

She started to turn away from the chest, then stopped. She knelt back beside it once again and dug through the clothes until she came upon a heavy object wrapped in oiled canvas. It had the weight and the heft of gold, though she had not taken it to a jeweler to find out for sure. It might be lead, but she doubted it. It came from a time when the Tenders did not need to make their adornments out of base metals.

Before she unwrapped it she shot a look over her shoulder at the window, but it was small and high up in the wall. Nearly impossible for someone to be peeking in, though she could not be too sure. Not with something this dangerous. Slowly she peeled the cloth back, holding her breath. As big as one of her hands with the fingers splayed, it was a many-pointed star enclosed in a circle. It was a Reminder, the holy symbol of the Tenders, and it was about the most dangerous thing she could own.

She had found it several years ago, up in the ruins of Old Qarath. What compelled her to go up there she did not know. Certainly she was too old to go climbing up the side of a mountain just to wander around in some old tumbledown buildings. But she had felt confined that day, tired of being enclosed by the squat gray buildings of Qarath. She needed to get out, and somehow she found herself walking up the old road to the abandoned city, and finally to the foot of the great ruined temple of the Tenders itself. And the Reminder was there, on the steps leading up to the main entrance, glittering in the sunlight, waiting for her.

Once, during the days of the Empire, Reminders had been everywhere. At the height of the Tenders' power Reminders adorned the flags fluttering atop every imperial building, even the Emperor's palace itself, flying at an equal height with the Emperor's golden lion. Reminders were carved into every public building, into every helm and shield of the Tenders' private armies. The wealthy and powerful wore them in golden brooches or necklaces, the poor in simple wood or even cloth. The starburst inside the circle, symbol of the Mother's many-faceted presence inside the Circle of Life. Wearing one was meant to bring good fortune, a blessing from Xochitl. More importantly, wearing one might keep a body from getting hauled in to face the Tenders whose job it was to root out unbelievers and blasphemers wherever they might be hiding.

This symbol that Melanine held in her hand was still illegal in Qarath. Its appearance in public would get its wearer dragged in to face the magistrate immediately, if a citizen did not deal with the offender first. She turned it over in her hands. This was an ornate one, probably worn by a Tender of high rank. The symbols of the different Arcs—Human, Animal, Bird and Plant—were carved on the outer ring.

She should have disposed of it. She should never have picked it up. Beyond the fact that it was dangerous, it stood for everything she did not believe in, the arrogance and blind power of the order at its depths. It repelled her, and it drew her. Ghosts held onto it, whispered past her when she touched it. They pressed their cold lips to her now, and with another guilty look over her shoulder, she settled the heavy chain around her neck.

The metal was cold. All at once she seemed to see herself at the head of a bristling army of steel and leather, herself more powerful than all of them combined. She stood on a pedestal and looked down over cities…

Abruptly she yanked it off with trembling hands and threw it back into the chest. Xochitl's curse lay upon the thing. She might be an old fool, but she would not bring that upon herself as well.

Melanine stood quickly, and swayed as a wave of dizziness swept over her. When it had passed she went out into the common room. It was empty, though at this time of the morning the other Tenders should have been gathering to say the prayers and to renew their sacred oaths. But they did not gather for morning prayers anymore, had not for years. Only on holy days did they gather, and not always then. All the old rituals were slipping away. Now she stood there and wondered how she could have been so blind. Why had she not insisted they continue, insisted that every sister attend every day?

Before the statue of the Mother at one end of the room she knelt and looked up at the eyes that stared into nothing, the hands that reached up to emptiness. Dust lay thick on the Mother's shoulders; a cobweb stretched from one hand to the side of her head. She had not been much of a FirstMother, Melanine knew. History would not remember her. Her own sisters would quickly forget her.

She bent her head and tried to pray one last time. There were voices behind her and she turned. Nalene and Velma entered the room, murmuring to each other. With the help of her cane Melanine stood. When they saw her they stopped by the long dining table, their eyes wary. What would she say now? What would she do? She was still FirstMother and that still meant something. If she officially forbade the Tenders to have anything to do with Lowellin, it could be difficult.

"I'll save you the trouble," she said, walking towards them, wondering why her voice sounded so high and shaky. "I quit."

They recoiled. Velma said, "What?"

"I renounce my vows. I won't be part of this."

Velma was blinking rapidly, trying to absorb the sudden news, but Melanine saw the calculation in Nalene's eyes and knew what it meant.

"You are wondering who I will name as the next FirstMother, aren't you?"

"No, FirstMother," Velma protested, but Nalene said nothing. The calculation in her eyes grew hooded, but it did not disappear completely.

Melanine stopped across the dining table from them and stared at Nalene. "What would you do if I named someone else besides you? What if I named Velma here instead?"

"I would follow your will, of course," Nalene replied, but Melanine had seen the flash of anger that preceded her words and knew the lie within them.

"Please don't!" Velma blurted out, her eyes wide. "I don't want to be FirstMother. I'd be terrible at it." At least she was sincere. Velma did not possess the guile or the ambition to lie about such a thing.

"I won't do that, Nalene. I will name you my successor. Just as you have always wanted."

Nalene nodded.

"But not because I believe you are best suited to it. No, I believe either Mulin or Perast would be a better FirstMother."

Nalene's jaw tightened.

"I name you my successor because I believe you would wrest the title away anyway, and I would save my sisters the strife."

"In the war that is coming, the FirstMother will need to be strong. There are none here stronger than I."

"Do not confuse strength and ruthlessness," Melanine snapped, suddenly furious and wanting nothing more than for this to be over. "Now that you are FirstMother you should have this as well."

She pulled something out of the pocket of her robe and threw it on the table.

All three women stared down at the table in surprise.

"It's a *Reminder*," Velma said in awe.

Melanine fell back a step, suddenly confused. *I put that thing back in the chest. I'm sure of it.*

Nalene reached for it. She stroked it once, reverently, then picked it up.

"It's a sign," Velma sighed. "A sign from Xochitl."

"Where did you get it?" Nalene asked. Her eyes were fixed on it hungrily.

"I...I found it." It was hard to get the words out. The walls were pressing in on her and she couldn't breathe. Down the hallway she heard the front door creak as it opened and she turned, knowing instantly who it was.

"I will not be part of this," she gasped, and headed for the back door.

Nalene didn't even see her go. She stood staring at the Reminder, transfixed. First Lowellin, and now this. It was her vision, coming true at last. It had to be. Footsteps were coming down the hall. Without looking up she ordered Velma, "Don't just stand there. Escort the Protector in." Velma scurried away.

Lowellin entered the room, Velma bobbing around him, murmuring apologies. He strode to the table. "I have come for your decision."

Nalene nodded. "We are ready." To Velma she said, "Go get the others. Tell them to hurry."

When they were alone, Lowellin looked at the Reminder and said, "I have not seen one of those in a long time."

"They are forbidden," Nalene said.

"Times change," he replied. "What was feared becomes a symbol of security. Those who were ridiculed become protectors."

"This has gone on too long," she said, her voice bitter. "I will not put up with it anymore." She clenched the Reminder in her fist, then looked up and met his eyes. "You don't know what we have been through. You don't know how they treat us."

"I know more than you realize. I knew when I walked in here yesterday that you would be the one to lead the Tenders back to greatness."

His words went through her and suddenly it was hard for Nalene to look at him. She wanted so desperately what he offered, but she didn't want him to see the need in her eyes. "We deserve to walk the streets openly. To speak the truth about Xochitl without fear. To leave this—" she gestured around her at the dark room with its cracked floor, sagging ceiling, worm-eaten furniture, "—this hovel behind, for good."

He only stared at her. She could feel his eyes and she did not know what color they were. His strength filled the room like the throbbing of a forge. At length he said, "It will not be easy." She made a gesture of dismissal. "It will require sacrifices, some of them painful."

"So?" she said, angry now. Her anger made it okay to look at him. Her anger was her strength. "What do those things mean to me? My whole life has been a sacrifice."

"Not like this," he warned.

"At least this sacrifice will be *for* something."

He nodded, as if hearing what he had expected to hear. "History will remember you as a great FirstMother."

"I have earned it," she told him, and settled the Reminder around her neck. It felt cool and strong against her skin. It felt right.

When the others entered the room their gazes traveled from Lowellin to Nalene, sitting at the head of the table wearing the Reminder, and they shrank. Tension and fear and hope radiated from them. Most proved unable to meet the gaze of either Nalene or Lowellin and simply took their seats quietly.

Nalene looked down on them and saw a huddled group of broken women, afraid of their own shadows, clinging onto shreds of the past while they waited for death to release them from their own inadequacy. They didn't have a complete backbone among them. They did not look like the core of an army that could stand against Melekath. They did not look as if they could have stood before a band of vegetable peddlers.

Suddenly they disgusted her. She wanted to shout at them, tell them to stand up straight and be proud, shove the Reminder in their faces and show them a symbol of all they had to be proud of. They had been heirs to the world once before. They would be again. Couldn't they see that?

Lowellin moved from the table to stand before the statue of Xochitl and Nalene followed and stood beside him.

"This is a new day," he said. He stood with his back to them, his hands resting lightly on his staff, looking into the statue's carven face. "Never will there be one like this again. The next age is arriving, and it will be born in fire. It will be born in pain. But if you are strong, if you stay true to your faith, you will survive. You will emerge victorious and the shame and humiliation of centuries will be forgotten."

The women quivered and a sigh swept the room.

"It will not be easy. It will be more difficult than you ever imagined."

Lowellin turned around and fixed them with a burning gaze. When he spoke his voice had taken on a new intensity. "This is a war. A war with all Life at stake. If we lose, Melekath will break the Circle and everything will die. *Everything*. Never forget that. When what I ask you to do seems too hard, too frightening, remember what is at stake."

He stared at them while his words sank in, measuring, judging.

"I have been preparing for this war for a very long time, since the prison was made, in fact. Remember this and do not doubt me, no matter what I ask of you. We do not have time to waste. I do not want Tenders who will question and doubt and fall short. If you are not completely committed to this, if you are unsure or hesitant, stay where you are. You must trust what I say implicitly and completely if we are to have any chance of defeating Melekath." He seemed to have grown larger as he talked, as if taking the hood off his inner fire, and he blazed across the room, sweeping darkness and fear before him.

"It is time to choose. Those of you who are ready will now come forward and kneel before me."

The gathered Tenders exchanged fearful looks. They were unprepared for this, Nalene saw. They had spent too many years hiding. Lowellin's light was too strong. She, on the other hand, was ready. The scorn and humiliation she had suffered had prepared her exactly for this. Nalene wanted to shout with joy. It was time.

But she knew she had to act quickly and decisively or the moment would be lost. They would falter and Lowellin would turn his back on them as the Mother had done.

Nalene knelt before him and bowed her head. He placed one hand on her head. "Repeat after me: In defense of the land and all Life, I will not hesitate. I will never surrender, never yield. My own life is nothing. There is no sacrifice too great."

Nalene started at the words, so similar to the Tender oath, but she did not hesitate to say them. In truth, she did not need to speak them aloud. With her whole being she surged toward his light, ravenous for it after so long in the dark. He placed his hands on her head and she felt his light wash through her, filling her with a sense of purpose, of sureness.

Velma was next. She nearly flung herself at his feet. "I will follow you anywhere, Protector."

When she stood up after intoning the words she looked fierce, determined. She took her place beside Nalene and glared at the other Tenders, daring them.

Perast was next, her thin face composed as she knelt before the white-haired man. Like Velma, Perast looked changed when she stood up, and crossed her arms over her chest as she took her place beside Velma.

Any lingering indecision was gone then, as the Tenders jostled each other to make their obeisance before the Protector. Eagerly, fearfully, like chickens racing to get inside the coop before darkness comes and leaves them outside with the wolves, they came forward and the room was charged with new life as they took their oaths. All of them except a young, round-faced Tender named Minel and simple Lenda.

"I am with FirstMother Melanine on this," Minel said softly, putting the slightest emphasis on the title. "I will be no part of this."

Lenda looked from Minel to the women at the front of the room, indecision on her face. She and Minel shared a room. Minel had taken her under her wing from her first day in the Haven.

"I cannot help you in this decision," Minel said to her gently. "You must listen to your own heart."

Lenda stood poised there a moment longer, her soft features twisting. But she could not stand before the weight of such a majority and with a small cry she darted for the others and knelt as well.

Then Minel stood alone, her hands clasped before her, her eyes turned to the floor.

"Go," Nalene said roughly. She wanted this woman out, fast, before she poisoned others with her weakness. Every moment she stayed was like a finger of guilt pointing straight at Nalene.

"I will need only a few minutes to collect my things." Minel started for the hall leading back to their quarters.

"And this is our first lesson," Lowellin said, his voice calm. "Not all will fight. But we will make the land safe for all of them. Our blood will make their meekness possible."

Minel did not reply, but she lowered her head further as she walked out, as if his words were lashes.

Then they all stood there, none sure what they had just done, what they would do now. "This is your new FirstMother," Lowellin said, resting his hand on Nalene's shoulder. "Obey her."

Then he walked for the door, motioning to Nalene to join him. To her he said, "I will return in a few days, and I will show you the weapons that even Melekath fears."

CHAPTER 12

Quyloc was exhausted after his narrow escape from the *Pente Akka*. He laid down on the cot and fell into a fitful sleep for a couple of hours. When he awoke the sun was up and shining in through the narrow window. He felt groggy and disoriented. It was difficult to stand up.

Did that really happen? he wondered, rubbing his eyes. Was it just a dream?

But there on the desk was the bone knife. He walked over to the window and looked at his arm where the bird had wounded him. The purple mark was still there, almost like a bruise. It ached, though the feeling was distant. He touched the mark. The skin felt cold.

Suddenly he couldn't bear the thought of being down there in that little room, alone, the stone pressing down on him from all sides.

Leaving the bone knife on the desk, he hurried up the passageway and the stairs, then out of the tower and into the sunlight. By the time he got outside, he was breathing hard and feeling dizzy. He stopped and put his hands on his knees. Everything looked strange. The sunlight was too bright. The world around him looked fake, two-dimensional. He blinked to clear his vision. It didn't really help.

He needed to find Lowellin. He needed answers.

Weaving slightly, he walked toward the palace. Much of the area between the palace and the tower was covered by gardens and footpaths. He chose a path that took him around the north side of the palace. This area had once been lawns, places of leisure for the wealthy and powerful. Now much of it was taken up by soldiers training. Hasty barracks had been erected along the inside of the defensive wall that surrounded the palace grounds.

Quyloc saw Rome talking with Tairus and walked over to him. Rome spotted him before he got there and gave him a concerned look.

"Are you feeling okay? You look terrible."

"I'm fine. I just didn't sleep very well."

"It looks worse than that," Tairus observed.

Quyloc gave him a sour look. He and Tairus had never gotten along all that well. Which wasn't all that surprising; Quyloc didn't get along with anyone very well.

"Have you seen Lowellin? I want to talk to him."

"Not today," Rome replied. "Why?"

"I just do," Quyloc snapped.

"Easy there," Rome said, holding his hands up. "Only asking."

Quyloc rubbed his temples. He was developing a terrible headache. "I need to ask him some questions."

"Isn't he supposed to meet with us today?"

"That's what he said. But he didn't say when, and I need to talk to him now."

"He said something about talking to the Tenders."

Quyloc had forgotten about that. He started to walk away.

"What's that on your arm?" Tairus asked.

Quyloc clapped his hand over it. "Nothing. Only a bruise."

"Not like any bruise I ever saw."

Quyloc walked away, thinking. Lowellin might be at the Tenders right then. He could go down into the city and find out. He knew where their Haven was.

But it was too soon for that. He wouldn't go there until he had to.

He went into the palace, ignoring the servants that bowed as he walked by. He went to his office. His aide, a middle-aged man with a strangely high-pitched voice, was sitting at his desk outside the door.

"Get me Frink. Fast," Quyloc told him. Frink was part of the small information network Quyloc had set up since becoming Rome's adviser. All told Quyloc had a dozen people, men and women from various walks of the city, that he paid to keep an eye on certain people, keep him apprised of the word on the street, that sort of thing. Part of Frink's duties included watching the Tenders. He would know if Lowellin had been there.

"Don't bother me," he told his aide. He went into his office and sat down at his desk. There was a large pile of parchments waiting his attention. He took the top one off the pile and looked at it, but the words swam before his eyes, and he couldn't keep his thoughts steady. He kept thinking about what had happened in the *Pente Akka*, how close he'd come to getting himself killed.

No, not killed.

It wants you alive.

What had he agreed to? Was it really worth it?

Was it too late to back out?

The door opened and his aide looked in. Quyloc glared at him. "I told you not to bother me, Robson. I told you to find Frink."

The man quailed. "I sent a boy for him right away."

"Then what are you doing in here?"

"It's Lord Atalafes, sir. You had a meeting with him?"

Atalafes was the leader of a delegation of nobles that was always pestering Quyloc, always lodging formal complaints largely related to their hatred of having to treat the common folk like actual people instead of livestock. Quyloc couldn't stand him. He wished the man would give him a reason to have him arrested. He would enjoy that.

"Tell him I'm busy."

Robson's eyes grew very large. When he spoke next his voice was so high-pitched it was nearly piercing. "He *insists*, sir. He says he won't be denied."

Very calmly, Quyloc said, "Tell him if he comes through that door today, for any reason, I'll put my spear through him. Use those exact words."

"But, sir—"

Quyloc simply stared at him coldly. Robson squeaked and backed hurriedly out of the room.

A door in one side of his office led to his private quarters, three rooms and a balcony with a clear view of the sea. Quyloc went through the door and locked it behind him. He didn't want to be disturbed and there was a good chance that others would show up and intimidate Robson into bothering him. He should replace Robson. Frink would know enough to knock.

He went out onto the balcony. It had a small table and two chairs on it. This corner of the palace was closest to the sea, which was the main reason he'd found it empty and unused when Rome took power. From the balcony he could look down over the edge of the tall cliffs— easily four hundred feet high—that lined the back border of the palace. He could almost see the waves breaking on the base of the cliffs when the tide was in. To the left he could see Bane's Tower. To the right, down the slope a bit, was the castle wall, and beyond that the city.

People were afraid of the sea. It was an old fear, going back to the ancient wars between the gods of the land and the gods of the sea, when humankind was still young.

According to the legends, the sea gods resented Life from the moment Xochitl—who was one of the gods of land—created it, and threatened many times to destroy it. Despite their threats, they tolerated Life until Xochitl created humans. In time, they made war on the gods of the land—the gods of the sky stayed neutral—and tried to exterminate the humans.

During the war, the gods of the sea created droves of new sea creatures, monstrous things whose sole purpose was to kill. Most were confined to the sea, but some were capable of coming onto land and they did a great deal of damage during the war.

Traveling across the sea became impossible, every boat crushed and its crew destroyed within hours of putting out on the water. Even living near the sea became untenable and all coastal cities were abandoned.

With the end of the war, the sea gods withdrew, but first they warned that any who went into their domain would be ruthlessly killed.

In the millennia since, humans had gradually reclaimed the coasts of Atria. But they still did not go out on the sea. As for the people who lived beyond the sea, it was not known if any of them were still alive, or if they had all perished during the war.

Personally, Quyloc didn't fear the sea. What happened, happened millennia ago—long before Melekath's prison was created—if it actually happened at all. Nothing had attacked from the sea within memory. There were no records of such an event in the official histories of the Kaetrian Empire that he'd seen.

Further cementing his belief that the sea was no longer hostile was the Sounders. The Sounders were a cult who worshipped the sea. They were thought to be extinct, wiped out by the Tenders during the days of the Empire.

But Quyloc had found one a few years ago. The man was pitiful, the last of his order that he knew of, but he swore to Quyloc that the sea gods—he called them *shlikti*—no longer sought to kill the humans they encountered. He claimed to even have a small watercraft which he swore—this was too much to be believed, but still—he had gone out onto the sea in many times and communed with the creatures he called forth there. Quyloc didn't believe much of what the man said, but clearly he did not fear the sea.

All of which led Quyloc to believe that one day ships would put forth on the sea and those lands beyond would be recovered.

Not very many people believed as he did. Most still feared the sea.

That was why Quyloc had chosen these rooms. He liked that most people were uncomfortable from the moment they saw the balcony. Some wouldn't even go near it.

Those men Quyloc found especially irritating, like Lord Atalafes, he liked to invite to sit with him out on the balcony. On a windy day, a man could feel the sea spray on his face.

It made dealing with them much easier.

There was nothing to do now but wait for Frink to report. Quyloc went back into his rooms and lay down on his bed. There was very little furniture in the suite; two of the rooms were completely empty. Quyloc cared not at all for more than the bare minimum. Luxury held no appeal for him.

It seemed he had barely closed his eyes when he had a sudden sense of wrongness and he opened them again.

He was no longer in his quarters.

He scrambled to his feet. He was on the sand, looming sand dunes nearby, the sky a weird, purple-black. His arm was hurting, and he looked down to see that the wound on his forearm had begun to bleed once again.

But it was far too much blood.

He looked down. The blood was pooling at his feet. It looked black in the strange light. The pool became a stream that ran across the sand and toward the Veil, a short distance away.

The blood touched the Veil, and a jolt ran through Quyloc. He took a step back.

The blood solidified, changed.

Right at the Veil it became a link in a fine chain. More links appeared in rapid succession, running across the sand and up to Quyloc's arm.

Disbelieving, Quyloc grabbed the chain and tried to pull it free, but it wouldn't come loose. It seemed to grow right out of his arm.

Slowly the chain began to slide across the sand, links disappearing into the Veil. Quyloc pulled harder on it, trying to free himself.

The chain grew taught. Quyloc was dragged forward one step, then another.

Fear turned to panic, and he fought wildly. But he couldn't properly get hold of the chain with his free hand. It kept slipping through his fingers. He dug his heels in, but the sand offered no purchase. He was dragged closer to the Veil.

Then, a new horror.

A shadowy figure became dimly visible on the other side, pulling on the chain.

Quyloc threw everything he had into the fight, but it did no good. He was dragged closer and closer.

The Veil was less than an arm's length away when he heard a loud series of concussions behind him.

He opened his eyes and found himself back in his quarters.

His heart beating wildly, he sat up and looked at his arm. The wound looked angry, but there was no chain.

There was no chain.

A series of loud knocks from the door leading to his office and a voice calling to him.

"Lord Quyloc, sir! Is everything all right?"

Shakily, Quyloc stood up. There was blood on his bed. He pulled a cover over it and went and unlocked the door.

Frink was on the other side, Robson hovering anxiously in the background. Frink had a dagger in his hand. "You were yelling, sir. Is someone in there?"

Quyloc fought to compose himself. "It was only a bad dream is all."

Frink's eyes roamed around the room, but he said nothing. Robson bowed and scurried back to his desk.

Quyloc pushed past him and closed the door to his quarters. He went to his desk and sat down. His heart was starting to slow down, but his hands were still shaking badly. He put them in his lap, out of sight.

"Have you seen a man with white hair going into the Tender Haven today?"

Frink nodded. He sheathed the dagger and came to stand before the desk. There were unspoken questions in his eyes, but he wisely kept them to himself.

"Aye, and yesterday afternoon as well. I was coming to report to you when the boy found me." Frink was a solidly built man with curly black hair and piercing eyes that missed little. He was dressed like a common laborer in simple clothes, the kind of man one saw everywhere. The kind of man it was easy to overlook in a city.

Quyloc sat forward when Frink spoke, then relaxed back, trying not to look too eager. "Do you know where he is now?"

Frink shook his head, and Quyloc's heart fell. "Figuring you'd want to know about something as unusual as a man going into the Tenders' home, I followed him when he left. Both times. But each time I lost him. Each time he got into the shadows, and then he just wasn't there anymore. Damned peculiar." Frink frowned. He took pride in his skill at following people. He'd worked as a spy for one of the nobles before Quyloc hired him, and he knew what he was doing.

"Was it the same place both times? Maybe he went through a hidden door you just didn't see." Quyloc knew that wasn't the case, but he had to ask.

"No. Different places. Nowhere he could really go. Like I said, just disappeared."

Quyloc sagged back, deflated. "Go back and keep a close eye on the Tenders. It's your only duty now. Learn anything you can." He stopped Frink as he was leaving. "Pass the word onto the rest of my informants. Their highest priority, their *only* priority, is finding Lowellin. If anyone finds him, they're to tell him I need to speak with him at once."

After Frink left, Quyloc sat there in his office staring at the wound in his arm, his thoughts black.

One time. He'd only gone into the *Pente Akka* one time and already the place had trapped him. Worse, it had reached into his world and tried to drag him back.

It was too late to turn back. If he didn't find a way to break the chain that bound him to the place, he was going to be dragged in there.

It wants you alive.

He had to find Lowellin.

He thought again about going to see the Tenders himself, then rejected the idea. He wasn't that desperate yet. Frink would pass the message on to Lowellin if he saw him.

He took another parchment off the stack. It was a report on the stores of seed corn for the coming season. As he read it, he felt his eyes growing heavier and heavier. His head drooped. Angrily, he shook himself awake and forced himself to keep reading the report.

Suddenly he realized that his head was on the desk and he was falling asleep.

Alarmed, he jumped up. He took the report and several other parchments and went into his quarters, then out onto the balcony. Spring wasn't really here yet and the air blowing off the sea was chilly. It would keep him awake.

He sat down and started reading again. Almost immediately his chin dropped to his chest. He slumped forward, the papers slipping from his fingers.

"Sir! Sir!"

Quyloc jolted upright. For a moment he didn't know where he was. For a moment all he saw was purple darkness and yellow sand.

Robson was running around on the balcony, chasing papers that were blowing free in the wind. "They're getting away!" he yelped, grabbing two of them but missing a third, which was lifted up over the edge of the balcony and blown out to sea.

Quyloc leapt to his feet, stunned that it had happened again. He was tired, but he shouldn't be this tired. Was the *Pente Akka* trying to make him fall asleep so it could take him?

"I'm sorry, sir," Robson said, his voice quavering. "I know you said you didn't want to be disturbed but I went into your office and I saw the door open and when I looked in…" He held up the papers he'd retrieved.

"It's okay," Quyloc told him. "You did the right thing. Put the papers on my desk on your way out."

"Begging pardon, sir, but you look like you could really use some sleep and this isn't such a good place. A body could pick up a fever in this cold wind."

"There's worse things than fevers." Quyloc decided right then that he couldn't wait any longer. He had to go see the Tenders, however humiliating it was. He couldn't stay here any longer.

Quyloc stood before the rough wooden door, his hand poised to knock. The planks in the door had weathered badly and large gaps showed between them at the bottom. The rest of the building was in no better shape. The crude plaster was peeling off the walls in sizable chunks. Tiles had come loose in several places on the roof and the shutters sagged on rusted hinges.

Unbidden, his mind turned to Arnele, the old Tender he'd known years ago. He was around fifteen or sixteen when he saw her the first time—as an orphan he had no way of knowing for sure—and he and Rome had recently joined the army. He didn't know she was a Tender at first. She was just an old woman begging outside the barracks, her hands and feet swollen with the winter gout. The other soldiers ignored her or mocked her as they went by, but Quyloc knew right away there was something different about her.

His short time in the army had already underscored just how different he was from the others. Oh, he'd tried to be like them, spending his money on drink and women, all the foolish displays of empty masculinity that went with that age, but it never felt right to him. That world held no interest for him. He was different. It was useless to deny it.

It wasn't just the intuitions he had about people and what they were going to do either. He also had vivid dreams. The dreams were the worst. Many of them were terrible and poisonous, Qarath reduced to a smoking ruin, the river clogged with the dead. At times they drove him from sleep with a scream. The other soldiers teased him when he did that, so that he went to sleep each night fearing that he would humiliate himself once again.

He also sometimes heard something that no one else heard. It was like a soft, gentle melody playing far in the background. It was beautiful, alluring, carrying with it a sense of peace beyond anything the world had to offer. He could find no source for it, no matter where he looked. It drew him, offering something that he had never known in his short, turbulent life on the streets of Qarath. The need for it grew with each passing year, encompassing his life.

When he saw Arnele that first time he sensed she held answers he sought. So he slowed down until the other soldiers had gone into the barracks, and then he crouched beside her.

"Coin?" she said, her filmy eyes moving to him. He realized then that she was blind. The hand she stretched out to him shook badly.

"Who are you?" he whispered. "*What* are you?"

A hint of smile touched her wrinkled cheeks, and she thrust out her hand again. "Coin."

Quyloc opened his coin purse and put a copper on her palm. She shook her head and said again, "Coin." He put another copper in her hand. She closed her fist on it and tucked it away safely.

"It's LifeSong you hear, boy," she said in her cracked voice. Most of her teeth had rotted away and the shift she wore was little more than rags.

"What are you talking about? How do you know what I hear?"

"How do I know? Why did you stop to talk to me? Surely you didn't stop for my womanly charms." She ran gnarled fingers through her white hair.

Quyloc looked around, making sure no one was watching. "What is LifeSong?"

"It's the melody in the background."

His heart leapt into his throat. Was he really going to finally know the source he'd chased for so long? "Tell me more."

She shook her head. "Help me to the wine seller first." She held out one grimy hand.

Looking around again, Quyloc helped her to her feet, picked up her walking stick and handed it to her. The walk to the wine seller's shop was agony, one slow step at a time. Several times he tried to get her to talk, but each time she rebuffed him with a shake of her head.

She clasped the flask of wine to her bony old chest like a lover and sank to the cobblestoned street with a sigh. It was on that day that Quyloc first discovered the magic that was alcohol. He'd never liked the stuff himself and could never understand why the others he knew sought it so eagerly. It dulled his mind and slowed his reactions, both deadly to survival. But as he watched Arnele suck at the flask, wine dribbling down her cheeks, he suddenly understood how alcohol could help him get what he wanted.

When half the wine was gone, she finally started talking.

"I'm a Tender, boy, or at least I was. Lost it to the drink but it wasn't worth anything anyway."

That surprised him. There weren't many Tenders left. Quyloc had never met one that he knew of. "What is LifeSong?" he asked.

"It's the energy that flows through all living things. It's the reason you're alive."

"It sounds almost like music."

"That is does." She took another drink of the wine. "I'll need more. My mouth doesn't work too good when I'm thirsty."

When he'd brought her more she continued. "You're not hearing it with your ears. You're hearing it in here." She tapped him on the chest with one bony finger. "Most people are closed to it."

Quyloc listened raptly, drinking up every word as greedily as she drank up the wine.

After that he sought her out on a daily basis, whenever his duties gave him the free time. The other soldiers inevitably saw him, of course, and mocked him unmercifully until Rome stepped in and told them to shut up or answer to him. Which they did. Even back then it was obvious to all that Rome was born to command.

Unfortunately, Rome couldn't command them to like Quyloc and he could see in their faces how they felt about him. He understood then that his chance to be one of them was gone forever, but he didn't care. Arnele held the secrets that he desired more than life itself. That was more important than the approval of others.

Then came the day when she told him no. It was when he asked her to teach him the method the Tenders used to go *beyond* and *see* the flows of LifeSong which, according to her, were like threads of light connected to every living thing.

"That knowledge is forbidden," she said, and drank deeply from the flask he had just bought her.

"Why?"

She lowered the flask and fixed her sightless eyes on him. "You are a man. No man may know this. Xochitl has forbidden it."

Something akin to panic arose within Quyloc at her words. "I don't understand."

She shrugged. "Gods are like that."

"But you left the order. You told me so. Surely Xochitl's restriction does not apply to you."

She shook her head stubbornly and drank more wine. Nothing he said, no amount of wine he poured down her, could get her to change her mind. He went away desperate and furious. That something from so long ago, some ancient myth, should keep him from what he so badly needed, seemed the worst injustice of all.

The following days yielded no better results and his anger at the old woman grew. Finally, he followed her to see where she slept, thinking she might have a copy of the holy book she had spoken of and he could steal it. He followed her to a crumbling hovel in the Warrens, down by the Pits.

But there was nothing there. Nothing but a pile of rags she slept on and a scattering of empty wine flasks. Enraged and desperate, he threatened her. But she spat at him and cursed him so that he finally snapped.

When the madness lifted, she was lying motionless on the ground. Guilt and shame rose up in a cloud and engulfed him. Desperate to hide what he had done, he set fire to her hovel and fled into the night.

Quyloc banged on the door. Several minutes passed, then he heard a bar being lifted and the door opened a crack. A skinny woman with a lazy eye peered out. "What do you want?"

"Let me speak to the FirstMother," Quyloc said.

"About what?"

"I need to find Lowellin."

That seemed to frighten the woman. She slammed the door, and the bar dropped into place before Quyloc could react. He banged on the door again.

"I am the advisor to the king," he said. "I will speak to the FirstMother or I will return with the city watch and we will break this door down." It was a threat he did not want to carry through. He didn't want anyone to see him here. But he would do it if he had to.

There was the sound of running feet on the other side of the door and more minutes passed before footsteps returned. The bar lifted and the door opened. The skinny woman stood there, shifting from one foot to the other nervously. "The FirstMother will see you," she mumbled, not meeting his eye.

He followed her into the gloom. The place smelled of decay. There were cracks in the walls and spider webs in the corners. She led him to a room lit only by a guttering lamp, with a long table in the middle and a statue of what he assumed was Xochitl against the wall.

"Wait here," she said, and scurried away before he could say anything.

The time dragged by, and the FirstMother did not appear. Quyloc drummed his fingers on the table. He paced the room and inspected the statue. By the time the FirstMother appeared he was angry.

She was a stout woman with graying hair and thick forearms that spoke of strength. She was wearing a heavy gold Reminder and a robe that was more gray than white. She took a seat at the end of the table and stared at him without speaking.

Quyloc knew immediately that she had kept him waiting deliberately. This was a bitter woman who faced him, misused by the years and determined to pass that bitterness on to others when she could.

"I do not like being kept waiting," Quyloc said. "Do you not know who I am?"

"I am well aware of who you are, Advisor," she replied calmly, a touch of a smirk on her features. "I was busy and could not receive you sooner."

Quyloc swallowed the retort that came to his lips. Fighting with this woman would yield him nothing. "I need to find Lowellin."

She gave him a calculating look. "How do you know of him?"

"He came to the palace first, *FirstMother*." He said her title mockingly, emphasizing how little it meant. "You are not the only ones he has been recruiting."

Her jaw tightened. "Why do you wish to speak with him?"

"That is no business of yours."

"I have not seen him."

"That's a lie. I know he has been here twice."

"Since you know so much, you do not need me. You may go." She started to stand.

"If I go before you answer my question, you and all your women will be in prison before the sun sets."

"So this is the new king's vaunted justice," she sneered. "You can run about the city threatening a house full of women at your whim and there is nothing we can do about it."

Quyloc took a deep breath. This was getting him nowhere. "I need his help."

"But you are the king's *advisor*," she said mockingly. "What help could you possibly need?"

Quyloc gritted his teeth. He held out his forearm and showed her the purplish mark. "I need his help with this."

"With a bruise? Would not warm milk be more useful?"

Quyloc wanted to scream at her. "It is no ordinary wound. I received it in…another place. There is something going on and only Lowellin can help me."

She frowned. "Another place?"

"Not in this world."

Now she looked angry. "You're not making any sense. Are you drunk?"

He ignored the jab. "Just answer the question." He swallowed. "Please."

She smiled as if she had won a victory. He knew she would not forget it. "Since you have finally asked properly, I will help you."

He waited, and when she said nothing more he said, "And?"

She shook her head. "I do not know where he is. He left here this morning, and I have not seen him since."

Quyloc fought the urge to rip the dagger from his belt and bury it in her chest. "Did he say anything about where he might be going?" he grated.

"I would not dare to question the Protector and if you are wise, you will not either."

Quyloc stood up so quickly his chair tipped over. "You have made an enemy of me this day, FirstMother. I promise you, you will regret it."

"Somehow I don't think so, Advisor. Something tells me that the world is changing. Those who were oppressed are once again returning to power."

CHAPTER 13

It was night time and Rome was in his room in the tower that he usually slept in, about to blow out the lantern and go to sleep. There wasn't much in the room besides a cot, a table, a couple chairs and the heavy chest he kept the black axe locked in. He had spent all day going over the army's tallies, the number of soldiers in uniform, weapons, supplies, horses. He had called the royal treasurer to him and even looked into the financial end of it. Then he had simply ridden through the city, looking at his people, judging their mood, seeing how many able-bodied men and older boys there were, candidates for the army. And, after all he had learned, he still had no idea if it was possible to build an empire with Qarath as its center, but he couldn't stop thinking about it.

In the back of his mind there rested always Lowellin's warning about Melekath, but in the light of day it seemed frankly ridiculous. Some ancient god breaking free of his prison, bent on taking revenge on the world? Things like that were for children's tales, not the real world.

A couple times he wondered what was going on with Quyloc. He'd looked pretty bad when Rome saw him that morning, and there was something weird about the mark on his arm. Did it have something to do with Lowellin and the weapon he talked about?

The door swung open and Lowellin walked in.

Rome jumped up off his bed. "How did you get in here? Are my guards completely useless?"

"I'm here to talk about your axe." Lowellin sat down on the chair and laid the staff across his knees.

Rome went to the table and poured himself a drink from the bottle of rum that stood there. Then he sat down, looked at Lowellin and scratched his bare chest. He was wearing only a thin pair of cotton undershorts. "Why?"

"I want to know if it is what I think it is."

Rome made no move toward the chest. The key to it hung on a chain around his thick neck. "What do you think it is?"

Lowellin planted the staff before him and gave Rome a hard look. "What I think is that you are not taking this seriously. This is still a game to you."

Rome took a drink of the rum, stared into the depths of his cup and put it down. He met Lowellin's gaze. "Why should I?" Leaning against the wall next to him was his battle axe, but he found himself wishing he had the black axe there rather than locked in the chest. This man, or whatever he was, made him more uneasy than he liked to admit.

"Understand this," Lowellin said, pointing the staff at him. Rome didn't like that thing either. There was something weird about it. "Melekath is real. He is going to escape. And when he does there will be war. Not the wars you are used to. A war for the future of everything. *Everything.*"

Rome scowled. "It feels a lot like you're threatening me."

"I *am* threatening you." Rome tensed, prepared to jump aside if Lowellin swung the staff at him. "But *I* am not the threat. Melekath is. Whether you believe me or not, this war will happen. It is not a matter of if, but when. When it does, you and your entire race have only one chance to survive.

"*Me.*" He lowered the staff to the floor.

Rome relaxed fractionally. "So you say. But I'm still not convinced that Melekath's fight isn't with you and the rest of the gods and you're just trying to drag us into it. I'm still thinking that if we stay out of it, he will leave us alone."

Lowellin stared at him for a long minute and Rome held his gaze, though it was not easy. There was something about his eyes, a sense that they hid something unnatural.

"Surely you can admit that it will not hurt to tell me where you got the axe," Lowellin said finally.

Rome took another drink of rum before he replied. "It was in the Gur al Krin desert."

Lowellin's thin lips pursed. "That's a start, but I'd already guessed that much. I need more. *Where* in the Krin did you get it?"

Rome frowned. As always when he thought back to that time he encountered a fog that clouded his memory. He remembered the Crodin ambush and fleeing into the desert with the survivors. He remembered pillars of fire and seeking shelter in a pile of stones. But after that there was nothing. "We took shelter in the stones. I found it there, I think." He shrugged. "That has to be it. Nothing else makes sense."

"But you do not remember actually finding it."

"No."

"Has it never seemed strange to you, that you cannot remember what was the singular event in your life?"

Rome laughed. It came out a little shaky. "Lowellin, *everything* about that axe is strange. I just try not to think about it too much."

"After all, with it you defeated Thrikyl and took the crown. What else matters?"

Rome finished his rum. "That's the way I look at it."

"You are a fool," Lowellin said. "As is your entire race. You blind yourselves to the sun and call it wisdom. I will never understand what she saw in you."

He stood and walked to the door.

"Wait," Rome said. Lowellin turned back. "Quyloc's looking for you."

"I know."

"Are you going to go see him?"

Lowellin shrugged. "Tomorrow, maybe."

"What about now?"

"He's busy now. You could say it's a matter of life and death."

"What does that mean?"

"Why don't you ask him?" Lowellin opened the door. "We will speak of your axe again." Then he left.

"I can't wait," Rome said. What did Lowellin mean about Quyloc being busy with a matter of life and death? What had Quyloc gotten himself into?

He considered going to look for Quyloc right then, but discarded the idea. Quyloc was probably in that little chamber carved out of the stone underneath the tower. Rome hated it down there, all damp and closed in. It was hard to breathe down there, window or no. He couldn't imagine why Quyloc liked it so much. But then, he couldn't imagine the why of most of the things Quyloc did. He'd known the man most of his life and Quyloc was still a mystery to him.

Rome pulled the chain over his head and unlocked the chest. Taking out the black axe, he went to the table, sat down and poured himself more rum. He pulled the lamp closer and looked at the axe. It looked almost like glass. Quyloc said it most resembled a black volcanic rock called obsidian. The axe was cold to the touch. It always was.

He traced the outline of the closed eye carved into the head of the axe. The carving was very cunningly done. The eye was so lifelike, as if it might open at any moment.

The carvings on the haft were just as well done. It really looked remarkably like the body of some unknown creature, the forelimbs folded back against the body, the hind legs extended. The haft ended in very realistic-looking sharp claws.

Where did he get it?

CHAPTER 14

Quyloc hit the end of the day a defeated man. When the sun went down and he still hadn't found Lowellin he knew he was out of options. He'd spent the whole day moving, afraid to even sit down because he knew he'd fall asleep and be dragged into the *Pente Akka*.

What now? he wondered. How far through the night could he make it before sleep claimed him? He stood at the back of the palace grounds, looking over the low wall on top of the high cliffs, looking out over the sea as darkness fell.

When it was completely dark he turned away. At first he headed for the palace, then he changed his mind and turned toward the tower. Maybe Lowellin would show up in his secret chamber as he had the night before. It wasn't much of a hope, but it was something.

Back down in his secret chamber his eyes fell on the bone knife, still lying on his desk where he'd left it, and an idea came to him. He went back above ground and walked to his palace quarters, where he retrieved his spear and a long dagger. Then he went back to the secret chamber. He tucked the bone knife in his belt. With the spear in one hand and the dagger in the other, he lay down on the bed.

If the *Pente Akka* was going to take him, at least he was going to go down fighting.

He fell asleep almost immediately and when he opened his eyes he was on the sand under the purple-black sky. The chain connected to his arm was already sliding across the sand.

But the spear and the dagger were gone. He was empty-handed.

The chain tightened and he was jerked forward a step. A shadowy figure, easily half again as tall as he was could be seen on the other side of the Veil.

Desperately, Quyloc yanked the bone knife from his belt. It was pitifully small and would probably shatter immediately, but it was all he had. He tensed to run at the Veil, hoping to land a blow with the help of the element of surprise.

A hand fell on his shoulder.

Quyloc tried to turn, but was jerked forward another step closer to the Veil.

Use the bone knife. Cut the chain.

Quyloc acted without thinking, slashing at the chain with the bone knife.

It didn't work.

Quyloc was jerked off balance and fell to his knees.

You weakened it. Keep trying.

Quyloc began hacking at the chain wildly, the Veil getting ever closer. The shadowy figure was clearer now, a black thing of hard, bladed edges. Red eyes were fixed on him.

Just as his arm touched the Veil, Quyloc hacked one more time and this time the chain split.

He fell backward, then rolled away from the Veil and stood up.

That was close. The voice sounded amused.

Quyloc turned. It wasn't Lowellin who stood there. The figure was shorter than Lowellin and wearing a long, hooded cloak. No face was visible. The hands were lost within the wide sleeves.

Who are you? Quyloc asked the figure.

The figure shook its head. *In time. It's too risky right now. I don't want Lowellin to know I'm here.*

Quyloc put the bone knife in his belt. *What happened to my weapons?*

Things of the physical world don't come with you here. You're not strong enough yet.

Quyloc looked down at himself. *But...I'm here.*

Are you really? The figure reached out with a pale, slim hand and the hand passed through Quyloc.

How'd you do that?

That is not really your body. It is more the idea you have of your body. A thought, really. It's what the Tenders call the spirit-body. You can't take your physical body into the shadow world. You'd die instantly. Nothing living can go in there and survive.

Quyloc was silent as he struggled to make sense of it all. He'd read about the spirit-body in the Book of Xochitl. But there was still something that didn't make sense. *If I am only here in my spirit-body, then how come I had that purple mark on my arm when I got back to my world?*

The mind is a very powerful tool. You believed your arm had been injured and so you manifested the wound where you believed it should be.

But how come I bled when I was attacked?

That wasn't blood.

Then what was it?

It was your life-essence, what the Tenders call Selfsong.

Quyloc thought about that. He supposed that made sense. He drew out the bone knife. *Why is this here?*

You already know, don't you?

He turned to look at the Veil. *It comes from in there, doesn't it?*

A Tender brought it back from there long ago. It has been lost for millennia. Somehow, Lowellin found it.

A Tender brought it back? Quyloc thought about this. Suddenly something occurred to him, and he turned back to the cloaked figure. *That's why Lowellin needs me, isn't it? He wants me to bring back a weapon from that place that he either can't get himself, or doesn't want to take the risk to get.*

The cloaked figure nodded. *You are a sharp one, somewhat less dull than the rest of your species at least.*

If he needs me to retrieve a weapon for him, then why did he leave me to die?

Why don't you ask him that?

I would, but I can't find him.

I have a feeling he will find you soon.

Who is he really?

He is who he says he is, the one the Tenders call the Protector.

Is Melekath really escaping?

Yes, he is. The figure sounded troubled by this.

Can I trust Lowellin?

Something that sounded like laughter came from the figure, but it wasn't human laughter. *Can you trust me? Can you trust yourself?*

Tell me more about this weapon I'm looking for. Where do I find it?

Later. I have to go. Lowellin may come to check on you. Remember, do not tell him about me.

Wait! How do I get back home?

But it was too late. The cloaked figure turned, took two impossibly long steps, and disappeared. Quyloc was left alone on the sand. He turned back to look at the Veil. He could still see the shadowy figure. It seemed to be watching him. He shivered.

How was he going to get home?

He stood there for a while, thinking, then he got an idea. He could summon the Veil by picturing it in his mind. Could he do the same with home?

He closed his eyes and pictured his secret chamber, drawing every detail in his mind. A minute later he opened his eyes.

He was back home.

CHAPTER 15

"I see you figured out how to cut the chain."

Quyloc opened his eyes and sat up. Lowellin was standing over him. Morning sunlight was coming through the narrow window. He quickly got to his feet and put some distance between himself and Lowellin.

"No help from you."

"Exactly. No help from me." Lowellin's voice was light, almost cheerful.

"Where were you? I was looking for you all day."

"I know."

"And still you avoided me?"

"I did."

"Why?"

"Consider it a test. I was waiting to see if you had the intelligence to figure out a solution to your problem." He pointed at the bone knife. "I had already given you the only tool you needed."

"And if I didn't figure it out? If I was dragged into that place by that…that *thing* on the other side of the Veil?"

"Then right at this moment you would be in a great deal of agony. And I would know you were not the one I have been looking for and I would have to start my search anew. So I think this way works out better for both of us, don't you?" Lowellin went to the chair and sat down. "Don't look so angry. You survived, didn't you? Very few would have made it this far."

Quyloc was so angry it was hard to get the words out. "You *used* me!"

Lowellin nodded. "Of course I did. What did you think, that I chose you because I wanted to be friends? If it helps, think of me as your general and you as my loyal soldier. The general does not explain the reason for the orders he gives the soldier, or worry about the soldier's life. He merely uses that soldier to perform a function. As I have—and will—use you."

"That's heartless."

"From your point of view it probably is. But that's because there's no room in your tiny brain for the big view of events. You can't see very far because you have lived only a few short years. I have lived for millennia beyond your ability to count. I see *very* far." His face hardened and his voice grew serious. "What angers me is that you and that idiot king still don't truly believe me. You still don't want to believe that the future of all life is at stake here. *All life.* Against this, your little life is completely unimportant. I would throw away you and ten thousand like you without a second's hesitation if it gave me the slightest advantage against Melekath. Do you understand?"

After a long moment, Quyloc nodded. His anger was not lessened though.

"Then stop your mewling. You survived. Be glad about it and move on. I have much to do and I'm not going to sit around here all day and hold your hand while you cry."

Quyloc clenched his fists, but said nothing.

"Good. Then we can resume. Now that you have shown that you might survive for a little while, I expect you to go back into the *Pente Akka* again tonight, and every night."

His words chilled Quyloc. *Every night.* He never wanted to go in there again. Swallowing, he said, "Where do I go? What am I looking for?" He couldn't resist one angry comment. "Or are you just going to make me go in there blind as part of some new test to see if I survive?"

"Really, Quyloc. Petulance is not becoming to you at all." Lowellin sounded almost cheerful once again. "But I am willing to overlook it. For now. You are looking for a large river. Once you find that, I will give you your next orders."

"That's it? That's all you're going to tell me. Look for a *river*? Can't you give me any more clues than that?" Quyloc made no effort to keep the bitterness out of his voice.

Lowellin pointed the staff at him and scowled. "You're doing it again. I don't have nearly as much patience as you think I do."

"I need to know more." This time Quyloc tried to keep his voice more neutral and he succeeded, to a point.

"The river will be found in a broad valley, filled with dense vegetation. Depending where you hit it, you may see a volcano beside it. Have you seen anything like that so far?"

"Where I went was a broad, grassy plain. There was no sign of any features at all, other than a low hill."

"Try passing through the Veil at different points. Each place you enter through will put you in a different spot in the *Pente Akka*. You may want to avoid the plain for now. I expect you have drawn the attention of the hunter there, what with spilling your blood everywhere. That really was a foolish move."

"I didn't do it on purpose," Quyloc snapped. "The birds surprised me."

"Yes, well, if you are that easily surprised, you probably won't survive much longer." Lowellin stood up to go.

"You're leaving already? Isn't there anything else you can tell me?"

"Look for the river. Try to not do anything too stupid. I think that's enough for now."

"Why didn't you tell me that I don't go there in my body?"

Lowellin gave him a sharp, surprised look. "How did you figure that out?"

"Maybe I'm not as stupid as you think I am."

"I doubt that. However, I am somewhat surprised, I must admit. What else did you figure out?"

Quyloc almost admitted to knowing more, but he stopped himself. Lowellin was looking at him suspiciously and he remembered the cloaked figure's warning. "That's it."

"How did you figure it out?" Lowellin was watching him very closely.

Quyloc had to think quickly. He held out his forearm. "My wound. In there it is a cut. Here it is just a mark. And I have read of what the Tenders call a spirit-body. The two facts fit together."

Lowellin seemed to be gauging whether or not to believe him. Quyloc held his breath. Then he nodded. "It is true. The Veil serves as some sort of barrier to living things. The spirit-body is the only way to travel there."

"I tried to take weapons with me last night, but neither of them made it. Only the knife did. Did the knife come from the *Pente Akka*?"

"It did," Lowellin admitted.

"Am I looking for something like it?"

"You are. But that is enough for now. I need to leave."

"One last thing. How do I get back to the Veil from here?"

"You made it back here from the Veil, didn't you? It's all the same." Lowellin walked to the door and left.

CHAPTER 16

"Can we meet in the palace this time?" Tairus asked. "Maybe a room with comfortable chairs? And no stairs?"

Rome laughed and clapped him on the back. "When did you get so old?"

"Since you became king and put me in charge of your army maybe," Tairus grumbled. "If I'd known how many details and how many meetings go into being general, I would have arrested you when you showed up outside Thrikyl and turned you over to Rix myself."

"Macht. I'm not the king, I'm the macht." Rome had gone through with his plan to change his title and he'd sent criers through the city proclaiming it to the people.

"Sure, *Macht*," Tairus said. "But I've been on my feet all day running *your* army—did you know I had to meet with the chief quartermaster three times today? I can't stand the man. You'd think every sword and bent horseshoe belonged to him—and I'm tired. I want to sit down and have a servant bring me something to drink."

"Okay, the palace it is," Rome agreed. They were in front of the palace, in the grand, circular carriage way. Under Rix the carriage way had frequently had opulent carriages coming and going, ferrying the nobility to and from meetings with the king. Now the carriages were all gone and the only wheeled vehicles coming and going were wagons and carts, carrying food, weapons, and building supplies. Now when the nobles wanted an audience with their macht they had to leave their carriages outside the gates and make it the rest of the way on foot. They hated that.

Rome and Tairus walked into the palace. Two servants converged on the two men immediately, but Rome waved them off. "I hate having

111

them bowing and scraping," he told Tairus in a low voice. "It makes me uncomfortable."

"So order them not to," Tairus responded.

"When I do that, they just look miserable. I can't win with these people."

"Which is why you hide in the tower," Tairus said.

"I don't hide in the tower," Rome said indignantly.

"Call it what you want. Seems like hiding to me."

They were in a large entrance hall. Statues stood in niches along the sides and tapestries draped the walls. Colored tiles covered the floor. Ornately-carved stairways climbed up both sides of the room to galleries on the second floor. Hallways led off in three directions. Everything was encrusted in gilt and filigree.

Tairus stopped and looked up. "I never noticed that before," he said, pointing. On the ceiling high overhead was a mural depicting a majestic king leading troops into battle. "Is that you?"

"Of course it's not me. Why would I wear gold armor? Talk about making yourself a target." Rome squinted at it. He'd never really noticed it before either. "I should have it painted over." He waved his hand at the rest of the room. "I should tear all this out. It's awful."

"Give it time. You'll get to like it."

"I don't want to like it," Rome grumbled. "Come on." He started up one of the stairways and when Tairus protested he said, "Oh, it's only one floor. There's something I need to do up here first." At the top of the stairs he strode down a hallway, waving off another servant who appeared seemingly out of nowhere.

"You know, you could have one of them bring us some ale before you run him off," Tairus said.

"Don't worry. There'll be another one. There always is." They went down the hall a short way to a set of double doors. Rome opened one door and went in, Tairus following. The room was large, with a massive four-poster bed, heavy, ornately-carved furniture, and a big mirror hanging on the wall.

Rome walked over to the bed and proceeded to mess it up, pulling the blankets back, tossing the pillows around. He looked at it critically for a moment, then lay down on the bed and rolled around on it some more. He got up. "That should do it."

Tairus gave him an incredulous look. "What are you doing?"

"Opus wouldn't stop bothering me, so I told him I'd sleep in here once or twice every week," Rome said, lowering his voice overheard.

"I'm trying to make it look like I did."

"You know that's crazy, don't you?"

"You don't know Opus like I do. Trust me, this way is easier."

Just then a servant emerged from a door near the back of the bedchamber, carrying a stack of linens. When she saw the macht she stopped. "Forgive me, Macht. I didn't—"

"It's okay," Rome told her hastily. He saw her looking quizzically at the bed. "Just do one thing for me, will you? Don't tell Opus about this. This is our little secret, right?"

After the servant had mumbled her agreement and hurried from the room, Rome turned to Tairus. "She's going to go straight to Opus and tell him."

"How do you know that?"

"I just do. Come on. Let's leave before he shows up."

They continued on down the hall until they came to another door. "Let's try this one." Rome opened it and looked inside. It seemed to be some kind of living quarters, with a bed, some heavy furniture and a door leading out to a small balcony. "No, that's no good," he said, backing out and closing the door. "It seems like half the rooms in here are bedrooms. I'm told all the important nobles kept quarters here in the palace. So they could be close to the king, I guess. Not anymore though." He gave Tairus a wicked smile. "Kicking those lickspittles out of here was one of the best things I've ever gotten to do. You should have heard them." Their outrage had been the talk of Qarath for a month and only served to make Rome even more popular with the ordinary citizens.

The next door opened on some kind of meeting room, with a large, circular table surrounded by chairs. "This will do," Rome said, leading Tairus in.

"The ale?"

"Oh, right." Rome went back to the door and leaned out into the hallway. A woman was sweeping a few doors down, her back to him. "Hey, you!" he called. She looked up, startled, tried to curtsy and dropped her broom with a clatter. "Get us some ale. Bread and cheese too." She stared at him openmouthed, then hurried away.

Rome came back into the room shaking his head. He sat down with a grunt and put his feet up on the table. "Tell me what you found out," he said to Tairus.

Tairus proceeded to fill him in on the efforts to recruit new soldiers. He followed that with some details on what they had on hand in weapons and armor and how fast the smiths could turn out more. Then he went into horses, feed, training. Rome had asked for an overview of the army and how fast Tairus thought it could be built up.

While he was talking servants brought in ale, bread and cheese. One tried to stay and serve them but Rome chased him off. "I'm not helpless. I can pour my own ale," he said.

Tairus finished by saying, "We can put thirty thousand soldiers in the field tomorrow and maybe another ten thousand within a month, though they won't be much good until they get more training. That's not counting the five thousand garrisoned at Thrikyl. I don't want to cut those numbers down more than that, not until we're sure there isn't going to be another uprising."

"Nobody but Karthije can put more than half that number up against us," Rome said. "If we can take a couple of the smaller kingdoms before they react, we can add some of their soldiers to our own and then we should be able to beat them."

"So you say," Tairus said sourly.

"You still don't think much of my empire, do you?"

"No. I don't. I think it's a fool's dream. I told you that before and I still believe it." Tairus took a long drink from his ale and wiped foam from his mustache.

"But what if the threat from Melekath is real?"

Tairus belched and drank more ale. "Have you seen this Lowellin since the first time?"

"I did. He popped up in the tower a couple nights ago, when I was getting ready for bed."

Tairus grunted. "Sounds like he likes popping up in the tower. You sure there aren't some secret doors in that place?"

"I'm sure."

"What did he want?"

"He was asking questions about the black axe, where I got it and such."

"What did you tell him?"

Rome shrugged. "Not much. There isn't much to tell. I found it in the desert."

"How did he like that?"

"He didn't. He accused me of not taking him seriously."

"I don't trust this man. I don't trust him at all. He's playing his own game and using us as pieces. We need to get rid of him."

"You have any good ideas how to do that?"

"Post some guards in the tower. Arrest him the next time he shows up."

"And if he really is who he says he is?"

"Then you won't be able to arrest him, will you?"

"I don't know. There's something about him, something unnatural. Put that together with the rumors about those things roaming the countryside and the other weird stuff that's going on…"

"What other weird stuff?"

"You know, the axe."

"Okay, something is going on. I'll admit that. But it doesn't mean some crazed god is getting out of prison and coming to attack us."

"No, it doesn't. But if it does, Lowellin may be our best ally."

"Or our worst enemy."

Both men drank in silence for a few minutes. Then Tairus spoke again.

"I saw Quyloc this morning. Is he sick? He doesn't look too good."

"I don't know what's wrong with Quyloc. He won't tell me. I hope he figures it out soon, though. He's been skipping out on most of his work and eventually the city's going to fall apart without him."

"He asked me if I'd seen Lowellin."

"He asked me too. There's something going on there."

"This isn't going to end well," Tairus predicted gloomily.

"That's what you said when Rix sent me off to fight the Crodin," Rome said, draining his glass. "And look how that turned out." He held up his empty glass. It was a dainty thing, holding no more than two swallows. "Why do they bring me stuff like this?" he complained. "One or two swallows and it's empty. It's more trouble than it's worth."

"Well, I better get going," Tairus said, finishing his glass too. "I have to go talk to Lucent. Someone needs to tell him we're trying to attract new recruits to the army, not run them off."

"Best of luck with that," Rome said. They both knew how Lucent was. He'd been training new recruits seemingly forever; he'd trained both of them when they were new. He was a holy terror with only one volume and that was loud. He believed in beating down green recruits until they cracked. He believed those that didn't might be worth something someday. Those that did deserved what he gave them.

Tairus left and Rome sat there alone, forgoing the glass and drinking straight from the pitcher of ale. Then the door opened and Opus came in.

"Pardon, Sire," he began. "I came to remind you—"

He saw Rome's feet on the table and gave a strangled cry. "*What* are you doing?" He hurried over to the table. "Take them off. Take them off this minute."

The table was carved from heavy, black maple. Mother-of-pearl was inlaid in the legs, and silver filigree traced its way across the top. Rome's boots had scratched the wood rather badly. "The table of Loness!" he cried. "You've destroyed it!" He produced a cloth from inside his jacket and wiped ineffectually at the scratches.

Rome belched and set the pitcher down. "I didn't mean to, Opus. It was an accident."

"An accident. You, Sire, are the accident. You have no sense of the propriety of your position. No sense of how a king should act."

"But I'm not the king. I'm the macht."

"So you say. Titles, titles. In the end you are the king and I would perish of joy if you would actually act like one." Opus's attention shifted from the table to Rome himself. "Look at yourself." He tried to brush some of the dirt from Rome's shirt. Rome had helped hold a horse that one of the farriers was shoeing that morning and had gotten kicked soundly for his troubles. His shirt was torn and there was manure on his pants. "How will people respect you if you won't even try and act the part?"

"I'll try, Opus, really I will." The truth was that Rome did feel somewhat bad. It was a nice table. He hadn't meant to scratch it. Some of the hobnails must be coming loose in his boots.

Opus gave up and stepped back, tucking the cloth away again. He took a deep breath and composed himself. "I assume from your attire that you have forgotten your appointment with the delegation from Managil, Sire."

"Delegation?" Rome frowned and scratched his head. His scalp was itchy. Maybe he did need a bath. "Is that today?"

"Yes, it is. They are already waiting for you in the audience hall."

Rome winced. "Can't you find Quyloc and have him meet them? He's really a lot better with delegations than I am. You remember what happened with the ones from Rahn Loriten." A delegation had come from that kingdom shortly after Rome took power, to offer gifts and acknowledge him as king. Rome got drunk and ended up in a fight with the ambassador. He broke the man's nose and, though he'd apologized sincerely afterwards, relations were still strained with that kingdom.

"Believe me when I say I do remember," Opus said solemnly. "If I could locate the Advisor I would certainly have him present."

"You can't find him?"

"He can be more elusive than you, Sire."

"Can we just put them off until you find him?"

Opus straightened his collar and shook his head. "They have waited an entire day already. You must meet with them."

"Okay, I'll meet with them," Rome said grudgingly. He finished the ale in a long pull and stood up.

Opus held the door for him and as he passed through, he said, "May I suggest a bath, Sire? And some clean clothes?"

"I can do that," Rome agreed, scratching again. Were there fleas in his cot?

"I will have a servant draw the water and set out suitable attire."

"But not the crown," Rome said. "That thing hurts my head."

Opus sighed. "No crown, then." As Rome started down the hall, Opus said, "One more thing, Sire?" Rome stopped and turned around. "Are the royal quarters to your satisfaction?" Something gleamed in his eyes. "Is the bed there to your liking?"

CHAPTER 17

"Let's give him a few more minutes," Rome said. "He's probably just finishing up with something important."

The delegates from Managil exchanged troubled looks but said nothing. They were sitting in the audience hall, a vast chamber with a high ceiling, its walls covered with the filigree that Rome so loathed. The long table was inlaid with gold leaf, the windows were covered with heavy, velvet curtains and there was a massive chandelier overhead that probably took an army of servants to light.

Rome sat at the head of the table and the three delegates were seated to his left. Hoping that Quyloc would show, Rome had arrived late, but there was still no sign of his adviser. He'd been stalling them for some time and it was starting to look like he'd have no choice but to start the meeting without Quyloc.

Rome drained his wine glass and reached for the bottle, but the servant waiting behind him was faster, snatching it up before he could get a hold of it. Rome suppressed his irritation and set his wine glass down so the man could refill it. "Have some wine while we wait," he said to the delegates. They nodded and raised their glasses to their mouths but, as before, it didn't look like they were actually drinking any. Rome frowned. Did the people in Managil not drink wine? He tried to remember if he'd ever heard anything to that effect, but came up with nothing. He'd faced their soldiers in battle twice, and he knew something about how they fought, but he didn't know anything about how they lived. Maybe their god forbade drinking. He took another drink of wine. That was the problem with religion. The gods were always interfering in people's lives, telling them what they could and couldn't do.

This was getting bad. Where was Quyloc? This was his job. He was supposed to handle anything that resembled diplomacy, not Rome. He'd rather fight these three than talk diplomacy with them. Fighting was so much simpler. Not that the delegates looked like they'd put up much of a struggle. Judging from their paunches, they did their battle at the dinner table. They also looked like they were seriously upset about something.

Rome tugged at the collar of the purple wool coat he was wearing. It was far too hot in here for a coat, but under it was a god-awful frilly shirt that he would never have worn if he didn't have the coat to hide it. He could feel the sweat starting to run down the back of his neck. How much longer could he stall these guys? He was probably insulting them by doing this. Maybe he *would* have to fight them. He had to say something.

"Does it seem warm in here to you?" Rome asked, nerves making his voice a little too loud. The men flinched and the one in the middle— Rome thought he'd said his name was Analeen or something like that, though what kind of name that was for a man he couldn't imagine— agreed somberly that it was. He didn't miss the sideways looks the men shared. If Quyloc didn't show up by the time he'd finished this bottle of wine, he was canceling this meeting; he didn't care who was offended.

Just then the door opened and Quyloc entered. Quyloc looked worse than he had the last time Rome had seen him, which was yesterday. There were dark rings under his eyes and his clothes, usually so neat, were wrinkled and there was a stain on the front of his tunic. Rome got up and met him halfway.

"Are you all right?" he asked quietly. "You look bad."

Quyloc gave him an irritable look. "No. I'm not all right." Then he brushed past Rome and went to the table. The delegates stood and bowed.

Rome went back to his seat. Worried about Quyloc, he missed the first few sentences from the lead delegate, but what the man said next caught his attention and he turned to look at the man. "Say that again?"

The speaker was a heavy, florid man and his right hand trembled on the table before him. "There is something wrong in Nelton."

Rome shot Quyloc a look, but his old friend seemed lost in his own thoughts.

The man continued. "Our representative there did not report when scheduled. When the king sent messengers, they did not return. So he sent more. Only one of those returned and he was badly shaken. He said something is happening to the people there. They gather every night in the main plaza to hear a man speak, and after they do, they are changed."

"That doesn't make sense," Rome said. "How could listening to someone speak change people?"

"He could not say. He did not attend the gathering. The others with him did and afterwards they were changed."

"How were they changed?"

"They became fanatical followers of someone they called Gulagh. They babbled about the return of a god named Melekath, and they called him Father."

"Gulagh?" Quyloc asked, looking up for the first time.

The man nodded.

"What about the king?" Quyloc asked. "Where is he in all this?"

"Our messenger did not see King Uren," the man replied. "It is his belief that the king has been changed as well.

"We have been sent to seek an alliance with you," the man continued. "King Chisan is concerned by these developments. According to our messenger, Gulagh's followers are increasing in number as people flow into Nelton from the surrounding towns. Our king believes that you will see Nelton poses a threat to you as well."

Rome nodded, thinking. This cast Lowellin's assertions about Melekath in a new light. Suddenly his dire pronouncements seemed a lot more real. He asked some more questions, but the delegates did not have much to add. He dismissed them, telling them he would have something written up that they could take back to their king once he'd had a chance to consider it further.

When they were gone, he turned to Quyloc. "You recognized the name. Who is this Gulagh?"

"He is mentioned in the Book of Xochitl as one of the three Guardians," Quyloc replied.

"Guardians?"

"Melekath's generals. They were trapped when he was."

"You think it really is Gulagh?"

"I don't know," Quyloc said wearily. "But it could be. I don't think any ordinary man could do what they said he's doing."

"And the other two we've heard rumors about? You think they're Guardians too?"

"It makes sense."

"So you think Lowellin is telling the truth."

"I *know* he's telling the truth. About some things at least."

"How do you know?"

At first Rome thought Quyloc wasn't going to answer. He looked away and seemed to be struggling with something. Then, in a low voice he said, "I've been…to another world."

Rome stared at him in alarm. "What do you mean by another world? Where is it?"

"I can't answer that. I don't know where it is. I'm not sure it's anywhere. I don't go there in my body."

"Have you lost your mind? Nothing you just said makes any sense."

"I wish that was all it was," Quyloc said. "I wish it was just in my mind. But it's all too real. It already almost trapped me once, the first time I went there, and every time I go back I just barely survive."

"Why didn't you tell me about this?"

"Because I knew you wouldn't believe me."

"It's a lot to believe."

"I know. I'm still having trouble with it myself."

"Why are you going there? Is this something to do with Lowellin?"

"That's where the weapon is he was talking about. He says it can be found near a river, but I can't *find* any river. I can't find anything at all. Things attack me every time I go in there almost immediately. I don't know how much longer I'm going to survive this." Quyloc's voice was pure anguish. Not once did he look at Rome. He stared at his hands, his fingers clenching and unclenching.

"Stop going there, Quyloc. We can't trust Lowellin. Maybe he's just trying to get you killed."

"If he was just trying to kill me, I'd already be dead. Nothing holds him out. He goes wherever he wants. He's already been in my secret chamber twice."

"Then maybe he isn't trying to kill you. But he may have some other motive for sending you there. He's just using you."

"You think I don't know that?" Quyloc snarled. "Of *course* he's using me. I don't think he can go into that place himself. That's what he needs me for."

"So why do you keep going?"

Quyloc gave Rome an odd look, then looked away again. When he spoke, his voice was barely a whisper. "I *need* it."

"What did you say?"

Quyloc struggled to get a grip on himself. "We need that weapon.

Add it all up, Rome. Your axe, Lowellin, the Guardians. The prison is breaking. We can't fight a god with steel."

Rome stared at him, knowing he wasn't telling him the whole truth. Quyloc clearly needed the weapon—if there really was one—for reasons that were solely his own. But he also knew Quyloc wouldn't tell him until he was ready to.

"Is there anything I can do? You want me to go with you?"

Quyloc looked at him, and Rome was surprised to see a moment of pure gratitude there, before his old friend looked away again. "You can't come with me. This is something I have to do by myself."

"Okay. I trust you in this. If anyone knows what he's doing, it's you. But keep me informed. I want to know about any progress you make or any new problems that arise."

"I will." Quyloc stood up to go.

"What should we do about Managil?"

"Accept their offer of alliance. We're going to need all the help we can get." Then Quyloc left.

CHAPTER 18

Quyloc left the palace grounds and wandered through the streets of the city in a black cloud. The sun was going down, another night was approaching, and he didn't think he had the courage to face the *Pente Akka* again.

He'd been back twice more since cutting the chain from his arm. The first time he'd stepped through the Veil and found himself in a bleak, rocky area. No mountains or hills in any direction. Just the bronze sky and a massive tree, reaching halfway to the sky. As he started to back away from the tree, hornets the size of his fist suddenly boiled out of it and swarmed toward him. He barely managed to summon the Veil and escape before they got to him.

The second time he was in a hilly area. He climbed one of the hills to get a look around. The ground started shaking underfoot and cracks appeared, spreading out to cover the entire hill. He didn't wait to see what was coming that time, just fled quickly.

The Veil was huge. There could be thousands of places to pass through it. Who knew how long it would take to find the spot that would bring him to the river Lowellin spoke of? He needed some guidance, someone to point him to a spot.

He also needed some way to defend himself. The knife was too small. He was too small. He was like a rabbit in a world of wolves. It was only a matter of time before he was too slow.

He'd looked for the cloaked figure outside the Veil, thinking he might get answers there, but no luck so far.

As he came around a corner, lost in his thoughts, he ran into a beggar and staggered back. The beggar was a big man, wrapped in a long, dirty coat.

For a heart-stopping moment the face Quyloc looked on was one from his distant past. The same hulking figure, the same coat, the same sickening stench. In that moment he was once again a skinny, dirty street rat, trying to survive on the streets of Qarath, and before him was Dirty Henry, coming to finish off what he'd started.

Quyloc threw up his hands, an involuntary cry coming to his lips.

The beggar mumbled something and hurried on by, leaving Quyloc shaking, trying to get a hold of himself. *It's not Dirty Henry*, he told himself desperately. *Dirty Henry died long ago. We killed him. Rome and I killed him…*

Quyloc was nine the year that Dirty Henry finally caught him. Or at least, he thought he was nine. Growing up without parents, with only the other street rats for family, made it impossible to be sure of such things. But Quyloc needed more than anything to be sure of things and so he maintained that he was nine, even when the other kids teased him and said he was too small for that age.

One thing he'd been sure of for a long time was that sooner or later Dirty Henry would catch him.

Dirty Henry was a leper. He lived in the remains of a sprawling, rundown structure at the southwest corner of the city, hard by the offal pits, stinking, filthy holes in the ground where the city's butchers dumped the remains of their livelihood, those parts too diseased or useless to grind into anything. Each day a team of men shoveled dirt over the day's deposits, but it was never enough. Flies covered everything and carrion birds gathered in clouds. It was a wasteland. No one went there who didn't have to. Disease was in the air, carried on a stink so bad it made the eyes hurt just to be near it. It was the perfect place for Dirty Henry.

By day he lay against the wall just off Piper Square—hard-packed dirt that doubled as an open-air market for the city's poorest—always wearing his black greatcoat, no matter how hot it was. At night he wandered the streets looking for children. Specifically, the street children. He was smart enough to know that his time was numbered if he went after the children of the decent folk of Qarath. But the street children—the unwanted, the pests, thieves and runners—they were a different matter. They were less than vermin in the eyes of the city watch and what was the harm if a few of them disappeared anyway?

These were the children that Quyloc and Rome called family. They lived among a jumbled maze of fallen-down warehouses and abandoned homes called the Warrens. Back then, Quyloc and Rome weren't friends. They knew each other, all the street rats knew each other, but no more of each other than names, and names were something that each child earned. It was a rough life and they died often, their names quickly forgotten.

Quyloc was always smaller than the other kids. He always stayed back, out of the light, trying not to be noticed. Because he had learned that if you were noticed, sooner or later someone was going to try and hurt you. He never questioned it. It was simply the way the world was. He could either try to survive it or be swept away by it. And Quyloc was a survivor.

As long as Quyloc could remember he had lived in fear. Very vague and distant was the fear of his father, a mean drunk with a heavy hand. Back in the shadows was a mother, also a drunk, but kind in her own weak way. When she died it was only his father and then there wasn't even that, as the old man threw him out to make it or die on his own.

Fear was the reality all the street rats had in common. They all had it, but none could admit it. Fear was weakness and weakness killed. That was the one iron rule of life on the streets.

There were lots of things to be afraid of. The city watch was one. They savagely beat any street kid they caught stealing, even throwing the bigger ones into the stocks or the city jail for a time. Some of the men on the watch were sadists, plain and pure, and street rats were good for venting on.

There was also the fear of starvation. The fear of disease that came so suddenly and killed so surely. Fear of the packs of wild dogs that roamed the same hovels they lived in and wouldn't turn away from bringing down a child on his own.

And there was the fear of Dirty Henry.

Kids he caught were never seen again. He wrapped them up in his black greatcoat and hauled them off to the Pits and what he did with them no one ever knew, though they spent many nights huddled around their little fires talking about it, scaring themselves and each other with every shadow thrown by the flames.

Once Quyloc and two other boys—he couldn't remember their names now—ventured down to the Pits in the daytime and saw one of Dirty Henry's victims. It was Spit, a tough, wiry kid who talked constantly and was quick with his fists. What was left of him didn't look so tough. His own mother, had she still been alive, wouldn't have recognized him. Wouldn't have taken his body into her arms, that was for sure.

Then came the night Quyloc got caught out late. He'd gotten some legitimate work, helping a man unload manure for his gardens. As the sun dipped down he'd begged the man to let him go, but the man told him he wouldn't pay for less than a full day's work and Quyloc badly wanted that copper.

Free at last, he ran down dark alleys, empty except for snarling dogs and the occasional slumped shape of a passed-out drunk. He was small, but he was quick, and he was smart. He knew how to stay to the shadows and he knew how to squirm away from reaching hands. He could make it back to the dubious shelter of the Warrens if he was lucky.

He almost did.

It was the fireworks that betrayed him. A celebration was going on up on the hill, where the palace was and where the nobles lived. The first shell went up and he stopped to watch, enraptured as always by the colorful lights. He was almost home, only a few blocks from the Warrens. Surely he was safe, just for the moment. With one hand on the corner of the wall he turned back to watch the colored lights explode and slowly fade away. He wondered about the children up there who watched the same lights he did. He wondered if they went to bed afraid every night. If it was even possible to not be afraid. It was something he could not even imagine.

Then the hand clamped down on his wrist and he remembered his own fear. He knew instantly who it was, but no matter how he twisted or fought, it would not let go. He was pulled in to the stinking, rotting face, staring in horror at the one remaining eye of Dirty Henry.

"Looks like we caught ourselves a little fish tonight," Henry rasped. His teeth were gone; his mouth stank of corruption. "We'll eat good now."

Quyloc did the only thing he could, the thing that would bring him out of sleep for nights to come, sweating with shame and self-disgust: he pissed himself. His bladder let go and soaked his ragged trousers.

That made Henry grin bigger. "You'll be good company, I promise."

Quyloc screamed. He screamed like a girl. Like a rabbit caught by the wolf. He screamed and he struggled but it did no good.

Dirty Henry jerked him close and wrapped him up in his black greatcoat, stifling Quyloc's screams and nearly suffocating him. Down the narrow alley they went, staying out of the light, Henry giggling and Quyloc screaming.

Quyloc screamed for the other boys to come save him. He screamed for his mother to come back from the dead. He screamed even for his father, whose beatings were gentle compared to the fate that awaited him. None of them came to help him. The Pits drew closer.

He never knew what happened. Maybe Dirty Henry slipped in a patch of mud, or maybe he tripped in a hole. But suddenly he fell, losing his hold on his wriggling parcel. The greatcoat opened and spilled Quyloc onto the cobblestones. In a heartbeat he was on his feet and running, tears blinding him, not knowing or caring where he was going, as long as it was away.

He stayed outside all night that night, unable to go back to the hovel in the Warrens he shared with the other street rats, sure that they would see his shame on his face, smell it in the urine that slowly dried on his pants. He spent the night cursing his helplessness, cursing himself for his cowardice. He could have fought, done something, anything, but all he did was piss himself and scream like a baby. He hated Dirty Henry and he hated himself.

The other kids were surprised to see him the next day, sure that Dirty Henry had gotten him. But he offered no explanations and ignored all their questions. Every night after that he awakened from nightmares and every shadow he passed held the diseased man in the black greatcoat, waiting to grab him and finish what he had started. It was only a matter of time. He knew that. Dirty Henry had marked him and eventually he would come for him. There was nothing he could do. Nowhere he could run. No place to hide.

Time passed and Rome made his inevitable way to the leadership of the street rats. He was bigger than kids several years his senior, already with a shadow of a beard, a deep voice and thick arms when those his age were still clearly boys, with slim, smooth bodies and high voices. But it was not just his size and fighting skills that took him to leadership. It was his charisma. Even as a boy Quyloc recognized that in him. When he spoke, other children listened to him. Where he went, other children followed. True, Rome fought his way to the leadership of the street rats, but even the boy he defeated for that place held no grudge afterwards.

A few weeks after Rome took what was clearly his rightful spot as leader, Dirty Henry struck again. This time it was a curly, blonde-haired boy who called himself Piper, a joker, well-liked by all. The next day Rome decided it was time to do something about Dirty Henry.

"Tonight, I'm going down to the Pits," he said, holding up the knife he had fashioned recently. It was made from a blade with a bent tip that he'd found in a refuse pile and lashed to a makeshift handle. "I'm going to finish Dirty Henry for good. So he never bothers us again." He must have been twelve or thirteen at the time, his shoulders already taking on the width that would make him a powerful man. And though what he said seemed unbelievable to the other street rats he had a way of saying things—as if they were already done and all that was required was for the proper time to pass—that made them believe him. "I'm going in right before dawn, when he's sure to be asleep."

The other kids looked up at him in awe, Quyloc included. Dirty Henry was the nightmare that had ruled their nightmares forever and Rome stood before them and calmly announced that he was going to go at night—at night!—and slay the monster. Had he said he would pin the dread god Gorim's tail to his back they couldn't have been more impressed. It was at that moment that Quyloc knew all he wanted in life was to be like Rome. And felt the sudden bitter bite of the knowledge that he never would be, no matter how hard he tried. The most he could ever hope for was to be close to this boy and hope some would rub off on him. Love and envy sprang forth within him at the same time.

"Who will come with me?" Rome said it casually, not the frightened child who needs others to come with him to bolster his courage, but a man turning before he goes to see if others wish to come and share in what he does.

No one spoke. There must have been two dozen of them and Jef was probably fifteen, but none of them could meet his eye. Rome merely said, "Okay," and let it go. He didn't harangue them or lash out at them, he just said, "Okay," and went about getting ready for the thing he was going to do. Quyloc watched, ashamed because he could not stand up and go too, his heart and lungs so full of terror he could barely breathe, and felt another surge of the same confusing mix of love and envy. How could Rome do this thing that none of the rest of them could even dream of? How could they stand by and let him go alone?

True to his word, Rome left an hour or so before dawn. He looked grim and resolute in the light of their fire as he stuck the knife in his belt and bid them goodbye. They followed, of course. All of them in a tight knot. They couldn't help themselves. They were drawn after him like iron filings in the wake of a magnet.

They followed him through the maze of the Warrens until the protective walls ended and the bulk of the city wall loomed in the distance. To the east the sky was just growing light. Between the edge of the Warrens and the Pits was an open space, a stone's throw across, a no-man's land. Broken timbers stuck up from the earth like shards of bone; pieces of brick and broken wheels were mixed in with fluttering bits of rag. Rome paused there. Just beyond the open space lurked the wreckage that was Dirty Henry's home. Maybe a dozen rooms, two stories. The doors were gone or hung crookedly. One whole corner had simply fallen down and from the way the thing swayed in the wind that had sprung up, soon the rest would follow suit.

Rome set his shoulders, drew his knife and started across. But no further did the rest of them follow. Here they were still offered some measure of safety. Out there was none.

Quyloc watched him go, despising himself for not going too. Despising Rome for going and exposing him for the coward that he was. Afraid suddenly that Henry would get Rome and take away Quyloc's only chance, his only hope. Rome was nearly across the open stretch when Quyloc suddenly jerked out from the safety of the pack and lurched after him.

The ground seemed to rise up and try to stop him. He tripped over unseen things in the dark pools that resisted the coming morning. Sharp points jabbed his legs and the air was thick with the foul odor of the Pits. He fell several times and came up the last time clutching a heavy chunk of wood, full of splinters. Gripping it in both hands, he ran on.

When he reached the doorway to the place, Rome was nowhere to be seen. He stood there, framed by the darkness, unable to move his legs. His breathing was harsh and loud, too loud. He couldn't go in, couldn't go back. Even now Dirty Henry was circling around behind him, waiting to grab him from behind. Rome was already dead.

Quyloc lurched forward, moving his legs blindly. He gripped the makeshift club tightly, feeling the splinters dig into his hands. His heart had stopped. He couldn't feel his legs at all. Dirty Henry was reaching for him. He wanted to scream but there was no air in his lungs.

After an eternity he came to a doorway lit by a dim glow. He crept up and peered around the edge. Dirty Henry was in there, curled up in his greatcoat by the embers of a dying fire. Rome was there too, not sneaking like Quyloc, but striding across the room until he stood over the sleeping man.

He could have done it the easy way. He could have stabbed Dirty Henry in the back right there while he was asleep. It was what Quyloc would have done if he could have summoned the courage. But even then Rome's sense of fairness would not allow him to attack another unsuspecting.

Rome kicked him in the back and yelled at him to get up. With a groan Dirty Henry rolled away from him and sat up, mumbling incoherently. "Get up!" Rome yelled again.

Now Dirty Henry's mumbling was thick with threats of pain and violence. He pushed himself to his knees and slowly came to his feet. As he straightened, Rome dashed in and sank the knife in his belly, then darted back, still gripping the blade, even then his instincts telling him not to let go of his weapon.

Dirty Henry's hand went to the hole in his gut and his face turned up disbelievingly. He screamed and staggered forward and Rome attacked him again, a slash across the throat. Dirty Henry fell to his knees, holding his throat, and the paralysis gripping Quyloc finally broke.

Screaming his hatred and fear he burst across the room and swung the club with all his might. He hit Dirty Henry square on the side of the head and dropped him like a stone.

Quyloc stood over the fallen man. Dirty Henry didn't even move. Something in the way he lay there said his neck was broken.

Calmly, Rome looked at Quyloc and said merely, "I knew you would come, Quyloc. I knew I could count on you to watch my back." And stuck out his hand.

Numbly, Quyloc stared at him, then slowly extended his own to grip it. Rome let go and bent over Henry, rolling his head back. "He's dead, all right. He won't trouble us anymore."

And Quyloc almost told him, right then and there. Almost blurted out his shame and fear, how Henry had grabbed him and all he'd done was piss himself. But if he did he knew he'd lose Rome forever. Rome would turn away in disgust and there would be nothing left for him. So he kept his mouth shut and dropped his club and followed Rome back out into the dawn.

Rome was a hero after that. Surprisingly to Quyloc, he was too. Even more surprising was that Rome let him share in the glory, not once telling the other kids that after all, he alone had killed Dirty Henry, and all Quyloc had done was hit him with a stick when he was nearly dead anyway. From then on Quyloc stuck close to Rome, always right behind him, and for his part, Rome began to listen to him, to ask him for advice on things. Thus was a friendship born.

Almost two decades had passed since then, and Quyloc had never truly understood the confusing mix of love and envy that lay at the base of their relationship.

X   X   X

The beggar was limping away. The late afternoon shadows were growing long. Quyloc ground the heels of his hands into his temples, as if he could force the memory out of his head. It was all so long ago and yet still so vivid for him. He and Rome had never spoken of that incident, though Rome had told the story many times within Quyloc's hearing. From the way Rome told the story, Quyloc had been essential in overcoming Dirty Henry, coming in with his club at just the right time, rather than as it had truly been. He wondered if Rome even remembered how it had actually happened. He wondered if Rome could have any inkling of how much Quyloc hated that story, hated having the lie of his bravery perpetuated again and again. These days, when Rome told the story, he had to leave the room.

The truth was that his whole life to this point was built on a lie. He had lived his whole life as a coward and soon he would die one.

He turned and slowly made his way up the hill toward the palace and the secret chamber under the tower.

CHAPTER 19

Quyloc was on the sand under the purple-black sky once again, the bone knife clenched in his fist. This time the cloaked figure was there, waiting for him.

Water is what you seek, the cloaked figure told him.

Water?

In the Pente Akka, *water is power. Find water and dip the knife into it. It will imbue the knife with power and you will no longer be easy prey to every creature that dwells there. They will see that you have teeth and can bite back.*

Are you talking about the river? Quyloc asked. *Is that what I'm to put the knife into?*

No. You are far from being strong enough to do that. If you come that close to the river, it will sweep you away. You want still water, a small pool. You should be able to handle that.

That sent a chill through Quyloc. He *should* be able to handle it? What did that mean? What if he couldn't? What would happen?

I don't know where to find water in there.

I can show you a place. Follow me.

The cloaked figure led him along the edge of the Veil, then stopped. *Here. Enter here and you will find water.* The cloaked figure began to walk away.

Wait! I have more questions.

Not now. He is too close. In moments the cloaked figure was gone.

Quyloc turned to the Veil. Should he follow the cloaked figure's advice? He wasn't fool enough to believe that the cloaked figure helped him out of any altruistic motives. The figure used him just as surely as Lowellin did.

But he also didn't have a lot of options. He was at the mercy of everything in that place and sooner or later something was going to catch him.

The question he needed the answer to was why? Why was the cloaked figure helping him? It clearly didn't want Lowellin to know, so from that he could safely assume that it opposed Lowellin. Which meant that he was caught between two powerful adversaries. Which was very bad news for him. However, he might be able to find a way to play them off against each other if he was careful and very, very lucky.

It was likely that the cloaked figure didn't want the weapon Quyloc was seeking to fall into Lowellin's hands. Which meant it wanted the weapon for itself. He could also assume that, like Lowellin, the cloaked figure wasn't able to enter the *Pente Akka*.

Where did that leave him?

With too many questions and not enough answers.

Quyloc steeled himself and plunged through the Veil.

He found himself in a broad, flat area. The soil was gray and had dried in irregular, interlocking geometric patterns that had peeled up on the edges. It looked like a dried lake bed.

In the distance was a large mound of dirt, probably thirty feet high, topped by a ring of standing white stones, like jagged teeth. There were no other features visible, so Quyloc headed for it.

Quyloc climbed the mound. Partway up he heard a howling sound in the distance and turned to look. Far off was a small cloud of dust, thrown up by a pack of fast-moving, four-legged creatures. He didn't have more than a few minutes before they would be on him.

He made it the rest of the way to the top. There were gaps between the stones and squeezed through one. He worked his way forward until he could see beyond. The center of the mound was hollowed out. Down in the bottom was a small pool of water.

But it was what was waiting beside the pool that made his blood run cold.

Easily twenty feet long, it looked like a giant centipede, its body as big around as a man's torso. It was a dull red color, its legs bright yellow and hooked on the ends. The head was black with long antennae.

Quyloc's first thought was to summon the Veil and leave. There was no way he could get past that thing. He doubted the bone knife would be able to pierce its armored exoskeleton even if he could strike it squarely.

But if he left now he was no better off than before, and there was no guarantee he could find his way back to this same spot again. He was going to have to take the risk.

He needed some way to distract the thing long enough for him to get to the pool and dip the knife in. What happened after that…well, he just had to hope that the cloaked figure wasn't lying to him about water being power. If it was, then he was doomed. He looked at the knife. It seemed awfully small. Even if dipping it in the pool did what the cloaked figure said it would, it still wasn't much to bring to a fight with something that large.

He must be crazy to even be considering this.

He needed to act before he thought about it too much and lost his nerve completely.

On the ground were several fist-sized chunks of rock. He picked up two of them and moved to the very edge of his cover. In rapid succession he threw both rocks at the standing stones on the other side of the mound.

The centipede thing came instantly awake and scurried around the pool and up the other side to investigate.

As soon as it did, Quyloc took off at a dead run for the pool. He ran as quietly as he could and at first it looked like he was going to make it there before the centipede thing noticed.

But before he was halfway there his foot struck a loose stone, which rattled down the slope.

The centipede thing whirled—surprisingly fast for such a large creature—its black, expressionless eyes fixing on Quyloc, and raced toward him.

He wasn't going to make it. The thing was moving too quickly. But he also knew it was too late to run away. Before he could make it to the cover of the standing stones it would be on him.

In the instant it took for the thoughts to race through Quyloc's mind his pace never faltered. He was less than ten feet from the pool when the centipede thing intercepted him.

It rose up over him, its front half lifting off the ground. Its maw opened and curved fangs extended, glistening with venom.

It struck at him.

But Quyloc had anticipated the strike, and he threw himself inside the attack, toward the monster, tucking and rolling as he did so. The monster just missed him, the fangs clicking together inches from his head.

The underside of its body hit him, knocking him out of his roll so that when he came out of it, instead of being right at the edge of the pool where he planned, he fell into it.

Not the whole way; he got his hands under him and caught himself.

As his hands struck the water, something powerful and painful jolted through him and he cried out.

In almost the same instant he hit the water, he recovered and threw himself to the side, rolling again. A split second later the centipede thing struck the very spot where he'd been, sending up a spray of water, some of which splashed onto him, each drop like fire.

Quyloc rolled onto his knees, then back to his feet, where he froze for an instant, dumbfounded by what he saw.

His hands were burning with purple-tinged fire.

There was no time to understand. The centipede thing had recovered already and was striking at him again. Frozen by what he'd seen, Quyloc couldn't possibly move in time.

So he did the only thing he could.

He stabbed the thing in the face with the bone knife.

He struck with power and speed beyond anything he'd ever experienced. The knife tore clear through the creature's head, shearing most of its jaw away. Yellow ichor sprayed wildly in every direction.

The thing fell backwards and began thrashing wildly on the ground.

Quyloc looked at his hands. The purple-tinged fire flickered and went out. Time to leave.

He summoned the Veil and, as the first howling things broke through the ring of standing stones, calmly slashed an opening in the Veil and stepped through.

Quyloc paused for a moment on the other side of the Veil and looked back the way he'd come. Did he really just do that?

He turned away, closed his eyes and visualized his secret chamber. When he opened his eyes he was back home. The lantern was still burning. It was still dark outside.

He was exultant. He'd done it! He'd gone into the *Pente Akka* and faced down one of its dangers and he'd not just survived, but killed the thing.

All his earlier fear and exhaustion were wiped away. He felt strong, unstoppable. He wanted to shout his triumph from the tallest building.

There was no way he could sleep now. He needed to go outside, to move around. He had too much energy. It was burning through his veins.

He put the bone knife on the desk and as he did so he noticed something strange. His hands and wrists had turned white. He turned them this way and that, looking at them in the weak light. It was like all the pigment had been bleached from his skin wherever the water touched him. He frowned. He flexed his hands, but they seemed all right. There was no pain, only a thrumming that filled every inch of his body.

He shrugged it off. If this was the price he had to pay, he was willing to pay it. He left the room and walked back up the tunnels, through the tower and outside.

Once outside the tower, he stopped. It was amazing. It was as if all his senses blazed with life. He could *hear* the presence of people nearby, hundreds of them, like a faint buzzing in the corner of his mind. Right now they were all mixed up together—a veritable barrage of emotions and sensations—but he had a feeling that with practice he could learn to focus on just one at a time.

Behind all that was something else, something that filled Quyloc with excitement. It was the beautiful, gentle melody of LifeSong. How long had he longed to hear it more clearly?

He sensed someone approaching and stepped back deeper into the shadows of the tower.

It was one of the guards, making his patrol along the edge of the wall. He wasn't paying much attention—there was really no risk of anyone scaling the high cliffs and entering the palace grounds this way, but Naills, the castellan, was nothing if not meticulous in his duties—and he didn't see Quyloc at all.

The guard seemed to glow with a soft light that covered his body, though it was very faint and when Quyloc blinked he wasn't sure he saw it at all. For just a moment Quyloc saw something deeper, a shadow within that light and into his mind came the thought that the shadow was an illness growing within the man, but still so faint that he was not yet aware of it.

The guard passed by and Quyloc stepped out of the shadows. He was starting for the front gates, with the thought of walking around in the city, when the pain hit him.

He grunted involuntarily and bent over, the pain shooting throughout his body. With the pain came nausea so intense that he retched.

There was a presence beside him and Quyloc managed to look up. It was Lowellin.

"Help me," Quyloc said.

The guard came running up then, but before he could say anything, Lowellin turned on him. "This does not concern you. I will handle it. Return to your rounds."

The guard hesitated, but Quyloc managed to gasp out, "Go!" and he hurried away.

"You need to be on bedrock for me to help you. Follow me," Lowellin said, walking to the tower door. He made no offer to help Quyloc, who staggered after him.

Once in the tower, Quyloc collapsed and curled up into a ball. Shivers ran up and down his body in continuous waves. His heart was beating too fast. His skin was hot, too tight for his flesh. At any moment he felt he would split open like an overripe melon.

Lowellin crouched beside him and placed his palms on the stone floor. "Don't move." Lowellin warned him.

Another spasm of pain racked Quyloc and he clamped his teeth together, trying not to move.

The stone around Lowellin's hands began to glow red. The glowing area grew until it encompassed Quyloc. Strangely, no heat came from the glowing stone, but Quyloc felt a painful pressure beginning to build, as if a great weight pressed on him from all sides. The pressure built until he began to fear he was being crushed.

"It's too much!" he cried.

"Not yet," Lowellin replied grimly. "Not until all the poison has been leached from you."

The pressure increased and it was all Quyloc could do to keep from screaming. He thought that surely he was about to die.

Then the pressure began to recede. As it went, the burning pain inside him receded as well, as if drawn into the stone. A few minutes later the pressure and the pain were all gone, though Quyloc felt raw and sore. The glow was gone as well.

With an effort, Quyloc sat up. Lowellin had lit a lantern and he held it by Quyloc's face, examining him.

"I was not sure that would work," he said. "Living things are far too delicate for stone power. Usually they are killed by it."

"What did you do?"

"I encased the chaos power in stone and sealed it away."

"I don't understand. What is chaos power?"

"It is the power of the abyss, the place from which the *Pente Akka* springs. But that is not important now. What is important is that you nearly killed yourself." He sounded angry.

"So?" Quyloc retorted. "I thought you didn't care if I lived or died."

"I don't. But you have shown promise and if you die now precious time will be wasted finding one to replace you. And the bone knife would be lost. Such an object is extremely rare."

"I'm so glad you have my best interests at heart."

Lowellin was looking at his hands. "You touched water."

"It was an accident."

Lowellin's eyes narrowed. "You *accidentally* found water there, where it is very rare except in the river, and then you *accidentally* touched it?"

"It was a small pool in this hollowed-out mound."

"And it was not defended?"

"Not at first," Quyloc said, hoping Lowellin wouldn't hear the lie. "I went over to look at it and that's when this thing, like a giant bug, attacked me. I fought it off, but while doing so I got the water on me."

Lowellin's suspiciousness did not abate. "It sounds like you were incredibly lucky."

"I don't feel so lucky right now."

"Did someone tell you that water holds power there?"

"Who?" Quyloc asked defiantly. "Who would tell me that?"

"Maybe you read it somewhere."

Quyloc felt the trap there and he didn't take it. Best to stick with his original story. "It was an accident, like I said."

"It seems unlikely, not just to find the water, but to find it undefended, even for a moment."

"Unlikely, but not impossible. Think about it. What else could it be? Where would I get the information? I saw the water and something about it drew me. When I got closer I was attacked and accidentally got some on me. If you're worried that I'll do it again, don't be. That was enough of a lesson for me."

Lowellin still didn't look like he really believed Quyloc, but he didn't accuse him again.

"What is chaos energy?" Quyloc asked.

"You don't need to know that right now. For now, it's enough that you know the energy of that place is deadly to you. When you find the river I will tell you more." He stood up.

"Yeah, about that. It would be helpful if I actually, you know, *could* find you when I need you."

"You don't need to. I will find you. Wherever you are." The way he said the last words sounded like a threat.

CHAPTER 20

Rome feinted to the right, shifted back to his left and brought the axe around in a low, whistling sweep.

His opponent, a squat, heavyset man with a gray beard and thick jowls, brought his short sword around, redirecting the blow so that it skipped harmlessly past him. He stepped in towards Rome, moving faster than seemed possible for his age and size. The sword flashed towards Rome's chest, who barely got his shield up in time to stop it.

With a wicked smile on his face, the heavyset man hooked his foot behind Rome's and threw his shoulder into the shield.

Rome stumbled back, throwing his arms wide to catch his balance, and found himself looking at a blade held up to his chin.

His smile stretching wider, the heavyset man lowered the blade and backed up. With a mocking bow to Rome and to the watching recruits he said, "*That* is how you handle a taller, bigger opponent in battle." He spun the short sword in his hand, then tossed it to one of the recruits, who caught it awkwardly.

"Well done, Sergeant," Rome said. He'd known Lucent was going to pull that trick and he'd left himself open to it—this was a demonstration for new recruits—but it still surprised him how fast the old sergeant was after all these years.

He felt a presence then and looked up. Lowellin was standing at the edge of the practice field, both hands resting on the black staff, staring at him. Rome had a sinking feeling he wasn't going to like this. Handing the practice weapon to Lucent he patted the older man on the shoulder and walked over to Lowellin.

"What do you want?" Rome asked.

"You have learned that the Guardian Gulagh is in Nelton. I assume this means you believe what I am saying now."

Rome crossed his arms and gave Lowellin a long look. Lowellin's eyes were like chipped quartz today. Whatever he was thinking, it didn't show there. "Yeah. I think I do. Something's going on anyway."

"I can wait no longer. I have to be sure of the origin of your axe."

"I've told you everything I remember."

"It's what you don't remember that concerns me. That's what I'm here for." Lowellin took a step forward and reached toward Rome's face.

"Hold on," Rome said, backing up. "What are you doing?"

"He blocked your memories. I can release them."

"I don't want you touching me. Why are these memories you say I lost so important to you anyway?"

"If I am right, and that axe is what I think it is, then you are the one who freed Melekath."

Rome gaped at him. "You're crazy! How would I...? You think *I* released Melekath?"

"There is only one way to be sure," Lowellin said, raising his hand once again.

Rome realized that a number of the recruits were looking at them. "Let's talk about this somewhere else." He led Lowellin off to a quiet area.

"You're saying Melekath hid my own memories from me. Why would he do that?"

"So he would have more time before he was noticed. He knows I am watching."

Rome nodded. "That makes sense. But I still don't want you in my head."

"You don't care that Melekath hid your own memories from you?"

"I don't know for sure that he did that. I have only your word on it."

"So you think maybe you just *forgot*? Is that it?" Frustration was becoming evident in Lowellin's voice.

Rome shrugged. "I'm not sure what happened."

"Don't you wonder what else he might have hidden from you?"

"Yeah. And I also wonder what you're hiding from me."

Lowellin's anger was apparent now. His voice was sharp, his gaze hard. "I tire of your constant suspicion of me. We have the same enemy. We are on the same side. You can trust me."

"We may have the same enemy, but that doesn't mean I trust you. I think you are hiding things from me."

"Of course I am," Lowellin snapped. "As you hide things from me. Because we are allies does not mean we must share everything. Nor does it mean we must like each other. All that is required is a recognition of a common enemy. Are you too dense to see that?"

Rome took a deep breath and stared hard at Lowellin. His gut told him not to trust this…*thing* that wore a man's form. But he also knew that what Lowellin said was true. They had a common enemy. He needed all the allies he could get.

"Tell me what you're doing to Quyloc."

"I'm not *doing* anything to him. What he does, he has chosen of his own free will."

"You know what I'm talking about. You're sending him to some kind of other world, telling him he can find some kind of weapon there."

"And it is there."

"He says he nearly died."

"More than once. What he is attempting is extremely dangerous."

"I don't like it."

"This is war. People die in war. You are a soldier. You, of all people, should understand this. The weapon he is looking for is vital to our war against Melekath. Why would you think such a weapon could be obtained with no risk?"

Rome stared at him. He made sense, everything he said made sense. His gut told him not to trust this man, but his head said wars were not won without taking risks. All at once he decided.

"Okay."

"You will let me release the memories?"

Rome nodded.

"Do not move. Once I start this, hold very still. I am trying to bring out one specific memory without damaging others. If you move, I cannot be responsible for the result."

"You better know what you're doing," Rome replied.

Lowellin placed the fingers of one hand on Rome's forehead. Rome stiffened. It felt as if something was crawling around in his mind. He wanted very badly to strike Lowellin, but he held still.

"This will hurt," Lowellin said.

A sudden, sharp, searing pain and Rome gritted his teeth, his hands balling into fists. There was a tearing sensation and all at once he remembered. It all came flooding back, the creature that came up out of the earth, killing the rest of his men, the tunnel into the earth, the vast wall underground.

"That's it." Lowellin pulled back and Rome slumped and almost fell.

"It wasn't an axe when I pulled it out, though I remember hoping that was what it would be," Rome breathed. "It started to move, then it changed, taking on the shape of an axe." He drew a shaky hand across his brow. "What *is* that thing?"

"I don't know for sure. I haven't been able to learn that."

"Is it *alive?*"

Lowellin gave him a strange look. "I don't know that either." He started to leave, then paused. "Be careful with that thing. It may turn on you."

Rome stared after him, thinking. The axe might be alive. He'd found it underground, stuck in the wall of the prison. *He* was the one who freed Melekath? It was too much to take in.

Tairus came walking up right then. "Are you feeling okay? You don't look very good."

"It's not every day you find out you caused the end of the world."

"What? What are you talking about?"

"Later," Rome said, turning away. "I need to find Quyloc right now."

He left Tairus staring after him and went to Quyloc's office. His secretary, Robson, looked up when he came in and without a word jumped up and opened the door for him. Quyloc was standing at the window behind his desk, staring out.

Rome slumped into the chair in front of Quyloc's desk. "You won't believe what just happened," Rome said, still having trouble grappling with it.

Quyloc turned around. Rome broke off what he'd been about to say and gaped at him. Quyloc's hands had turned white. There were white speckles on his face and neck. "What happened to *you?*"

"The *Pente Akka*," Quyloc said grimly, sitting down.

"Will it go away?"

"No, Rome. I don't think so."

"Are you okay?"

Quyloc gave him a wan smile. "I think so. For now, anyway. I might not get so lucky next time."

"What in the hell have we gotten ourselves into?"

"I don't know. I really don't. What happened to you? You look terrible."

"Yeah, I guess I do." Rome rubbed his eyes and then sighed. "I think maybe I'm the one who let Melekath out."

Now it was Quyloc's turn to be incredulous. "Where did you get that idea?"

"Lowellin. He did something to me, pulled out some lost memories from our little trip into the Gur al Krin. I know now where I got the black axe." He then proceeded to tell Quyloc what he'd learned. As he did so, the memories began to return for Quyloc as well so that by the time he got to the part where they first saw the wall of the prison, Quyloc stopped him.

"How could we both forget this?"

"Lowellin says Melekath made us forget, to buy him more time."

"When you pulled that thing out of the wall, what made it turn into an axe?"

"The only thing I can think is that I was thinking about an axe, hoping that's what it was. If that makes any sense."

"Somehow it responded to your thoughts."

Rome shrugged. "Maybe. I don't see where it makes much difference now. I guess Lowellin's been telling us the truth all along."

"It looks that way."

Rome sighed. "Gorim's tail, Quyloc, I think we might be in over our heads on this one."

CHAPTER 21

Lenda came hurrying into the room, the one that had belonged to Melanine, the old FirstMother, but was now Nalene's. Melanine had not been seen since the day she abdicated her title. She'd left the Haven and never returned.

Nalene was still getting dressed and she looked up and scowled at Lenda. "Have you forgotten how to knock?" she asked acidly.

Lenda wilted. "I'm sorry, FirstMother. I was in a hurry and I forgot."

"Yes, just as you *forgot* the stew you were cooking yesterday and burned it so badly no one had any dinner. Just as you *forgot* the candle burning in your room and nearly lit your bed on fire. Is there anything you *cannot* forget?" Nalene had not slept well and besides that she was irritable because there had been no further contact with Lowellin for days. It was as if he had completely forgotten the Tenders and forgotten her. After the intense surge of optimism and hope she'd felt the day they all swore to follow him, it was a bitter letdown. Making it worse was the odd visit from Quyloc, saying he couldn't find Lowellin either.

After waiting and praying her whole life for something to finally happen, Nalene didn't think she could bear the thought that Lowellin might have gotten her hopes up, only to crush them.

"I don't know, FirstMother," Lenda said, hanging her head.

"Well?"

"Well, what?"

"Why did you barge into my room?" Nalene just managed to avoid shouting at the woman. She knew if she did that, Lenda would simply dissolve into tears and fall apart. It could take hours to find out what she came in for.

Lenda blinked, thinking.

Nalene crossed her arms and tapped her foot. "I'm waiting."

Lenda's eyes grew very wide, but still she did not speak.

"You are beginning to anger me."

"FirstMother!" she cried. "I forgot!"

"You *what*?"

"I forgot why I came in here. You scared me and now I can't remember."

"That's it, Lenda! Get out of here before I lose my temper!"

Lenda squeaked and bolted out the door. Just beyond the threshold though, she stopped dead. "FirstMother!" she exclaimed, turning around, her face lighting up. "I remember!"

"Praise the Mother," Nalene said sarcastically. "What is it? A lizard you found dead under the table? A bee that got in your hair when you were at the market?" Lenda had a tendency to get oddly excited over the strangest things.

"No, that's not it at all. It's about the Protector."

Nalene suddenly went very still, though her heart sped up. She took hold of Lenda's wrist and pulled her back into the room, none too gently. "What is it, girl? What about the Protector?"

"He was in the common room earlier, sitting at the table."

"This morning?"

Lenda nodded. "He was so still and quiet I didn't see him and when he spoke I screamed." She lowered her eyes. "Just a little."

"Forget that," Nalene fairly snarled. "What did he *say*? Is he still here?"

"No, he left." Lenda wrung her hands, unsure if she was going to be yelled at about this.

Nalene took her by the shoulders and fought the urge to shake just the tiniest bit of sense into her. "Tell me what he said."

"He said…he said for you to meet him tonight, inside the ruined temple."

"In old Qarath?"

"I guess. I don't know any other ruined temples."

"Did he say anything else?"

"No. That was all."

Nalene let her go and Lenda scurried away. She realized she was shaking and she went to her bed and sat down. This was it. It was finally happening. This was the day the Tenders would begin their climb back into the light. This was the day they would begin to prove to Xochitl that they were once again worthy of Her.

Nothing, *nothing*, could be allowed to go wrong.

By the end of the day, Nalene was a nervous wreck. She'd been on edge the entire day, jumping at sudden noises, barking at the other Tenders' smallest mistakes. Twice during the day she'd reduced Lenda to tears.

The sun was close to setting when she sat down at the dining table with the rest of the Tenders and picked up her spoon. All of them avoided looking at her. No one spoke. Nalene ate a spoonful of soup and quickly spat it back out.

"It's cold!"

All of the women stared hard at their bowls and tried to look as small as possible. Nalene glared at the lot of them.

"It's bad enough that I have to eat slop that's barely fit for an animal. Is it too much to ask that it at least be warm?"

Dead silence. No one moved. Then Velma said timidly, "We're out of coal for the cookfire. There wasn't enough to heat the soup."

"Out of coal? I told you two days ago to buy more!"

"There's no coin. The last few coppers went to buy cloth for—"

"I don't care!" Nalene yelled, standing up and throwing her bowl against the wall, where it shattered into a thousand pieces. "I can't stand it anymore! I won't live like this, huddling in this hovel like beggars. We are the chosen of the Mother and it is time the world remembers it." Breathing hard, she leaned over the table, pointing at them. "I promise you this. Things will change around here. Do you hear me?"

The women stared at her in alarm, none of them daring to respond. Lenda had turned white and was shaking.

"I want you all to understand something," she continued. "I will do anything, *anything*, to restore this order. I will not let anything stand in my way. If any of you doubt this, if you are not completely and absolutely dedicated to this task, then you need to get out of this building now!" She punctuated each word with angry stabs of her index finger.

The other Tenders sat there paralyzed. Then Lenda started nodding furiously. "I'll do it, FirstMother!" she babbled. "I'll do it. Just tell me what to do." Tears streaked her face.

Nalene's expression softened somewhat. "Good. That's one. What about the rest of you?"

Heads bobbed all around the table.

Nalene stared at them for a minute longer, gauging their

commitment. She still thought them too soft, too weak, but she felt marginally better. Maybe they weren't hopeless after all. Maybe she could forge them into something.

"Get my robe. I'm going to meet the Protector."

The Tenders all surged to their feet.

"Just one of you. Velma, you go. And get the Reminder as well."

Velma's eyes grew very large. "FirstMother, are you going to wear the Reminder in public? Is that…is that…?"

"The time for timid half-measures is past. The Mother has no use for those followers who are afraid to take risks in the war that is coming."

Velma hurried out of the room. "Sit down," Nalene told the rest irritably. They sat.

When Velma returned with the robe, Nalene let her help her on with it. Then she lowered her head to let Velma set the Reminder around her neck. She faced all the women proudly, her head held high.

"Let history remember this moment, when the Tenders first climbed out of the muck and moved back into their rightful place.

She left the room without another word.

But when she stepped outside, with sunlight still in the sky and watching eyes seemingly everywhere, she suddenly felt very exposed. Wearing the Reminder in public could get her dragged down the street and beaten. After making sure the door to the Haven was closed and no Tenders were watching, she tucked the Reminder inside her robe.

Then she set off down the street. She walked quickly and avoided eye contact with people. The old white robe she wore didn't really stand out all that much and wouldn't necessarily mark her as a Tender, but today she didn't want to take the risk. If something happened and she wasn't able to make her meeting with Lowellin, he might conclude the Tenders were not capable of handling their role in the coming war. And they might not get another chance.

Of course, she could have chosen not to wear the white robe at all, but she didn't want Lowellin to think she was frightened. He had chosen her because she was strong and she was determined to prove to him that she was.

She left the city through the smaller north gate and started up the rutted, abandoned road to old Qarath, which sat higher up on the foothills of the Eagle Mountains.

Old Qarath had been a mighty city during the days of the Kaetrian

Empire, nearly as large and as wealthy as the capital city itself. The Tender temple there was even larger than the central temple in the capital city, which was fitting since Qarath was the ancestral home of the Tenders, being the city where Xochitl lived back when she still walked amongst her children.

After the fall of the Empire—triggered by the events at Wreckers Gate and the loss of the capital city to the sands of the Gur al Krin— the temple in old Qarath stood for some time against the chaos and anarchy that swept the land.

But the Tenders holed up in the temple were few in number and as their powers continued to erode it became clear they could not hold out much longer. The mobs outside the temple walls grew larger and angrier with each passing day, the citizens of the city convinced that it was the treachery of the Tenders that had led to the fall of the Empire.

What happened next was mostly lost in the dust bin of history, but the Tenders inside the temple made one last, desperate attempt to survive. The story that Nalene had always heard was that the Tenders joined their dwindling powers together and sought to tap directly into the River, the Source of all LifeSong.

But the power they unleashed was too much for them to control. Raw, uncontrolled Song exploded outwards, killing the remaining Tenders instantly and causing an earthquake that cracked the great temple in half.

But that was not the only damage caused. Something the Tenders did tainted the raw Song and as it burst outward across the city every living thing it touched was affected. Some things merely fell ill or were rendered unconscious. But others were fundamentally changed. People and animals were mutated, driven insane.

The survivors fled the city and began a new city, further down the foothills of the Eagle Mountains.

It had been nearly a thousand years since that day and there were people who made a living scavenging in old Qarath, finding bits and pieces to sell, but most still avoided the place. There were always stories floating around about ghosts and other dark things that supposedly waited within the abandoned city.

One thing everyone agreed on: it was lunacy to go into old Qarath at night.

Which helped to explain why Nalene set out for the city while it was still light. She wanted to be inside the old temple before it got dark. She didn't really believe that old Qarath was haunted, but she also knew it was one thing to discard superstitions in the light of day, and quite another thing to do so in the darkness.

Nalene made it to the shattered gates and entered the city just as the sun was setting. Centuries of neglect had greatly diminished the once-proud city, but had not defeated it entirely. Most of the stone buildings still stood, though the colors were gone and facades had crumbled away. There was an elegance of craftsmanship still visible in the buildings and in fallen statues and weathered sculptures that was not present in modern Qarath.

The cracked dome of the temple was visible at the city's highest point, turning orange in the sunset. The main boulevard leading up to it was littered with broken stone and Nalene had to pick her way carefully. The shadows grew longer.

She heard footsteps behind her and she stopped and looked back the way she had come. The street was deserted. Telling herself it must have been her imagination, she continued on.

But before long she heard the footsteps again. This time they sounded closer. She spun, her heart speeding up. There was nothing but growing shadows.

She began to move faster. She glimpsed something between two buildings and thought she saw the flash of a face. She gave up all pretense and started running. Her footsteps echoed hollowly off the ruined buildings.

She was gasping and sweating by the time she finally reached the temple. The twin spires that had once graced the grand entrance had collapsed and lay broken in thousands of pieces and she had to climb over some of them, scraping her knee, in order to gain entrance to the vast courtyard that lay before the mighty dome itself.

Once inside the courtyard she stopped and looked back into the street. The sun had completely set and she could not see far or clearly, but she thought she saw a figure in the distance, standing in a doorway, staring at her.

She turned back around and hurried toward the cracked dome, hoping that she would be able to take shelter there.

Inside the dome she stopped again. There was no movement in the courtyard. Had whoever—or whatever—been following her given up? Or were they even now creeping closer?

Stop being ridiculous, she told herself. Even if someone was following her, it was surely nothing more than a filthy scavenger. She was the FirstMother, she was in the ancient seat of Tender power, she was about to meet the Protector, and she would run no more.

She turned her back on the outside, pulled the Reminder from under her robe, and went deeper into the temple.

She'd been here once before, during her Songquest, the ritual all Tenders went through at the end of their initiation. The purpose of the quest was for young Tenders to have the vision that would guide them through their lives, the vision that would map out their future. They endured three days of fasting and praying, then set out to wander until their vision came to them.

It was hard for Nalene to imagine how idealistic and hopeful she had been back in those days. Unlike many Tenders, who saw the quest as a waste of time, she'd undergone hers eagerly. She'd been excited to see what the Mother had in store for her and she believed that—unlike most of the other Tenders, who got nothing but sore feet—the Mother would grant her a vision.

For the first few days nothing happened, and her hope began to dim, but things changed when her steps led her up the slopes to old Qarath and the ruined temple.

She'd reached this very spot and, too weak to walk anymore, fallen to her knees and prayed as she never prayed before. Finally, she fell asleep, and that was when she had her vision. It came to her in a dream.

In her dream she found a small, hidden door in the temple that opened onto a long, steep stairway leading down. A shimmering, humanlike figure was waiting for her on the stairs. For what seemed like hours she followed it down into the darkness.

At last the shimmering figure stopped, and turned to her with glowing eyes. They were in a small cavern with a high ceiling. In the center of the cavern was a huge tree, made completely of crystal. It was beautiful. She stared at it, entranced, and understood that it was the tree of Tender history. Each branch was a piece of the Tenders' past, and on the leaves were written the names of famous Tenders.

Then the shimmering figure pointed and she saw a new branch at the bottom, just sprouting from the trunk. At the end of the branch was a single, crystal leaf and on that leaf was written her name.

When she reached for it, a great wind began to howl through the cavern. The limbs of the crystal tree thrashed wildly, limbs cracking away, leaves falling off.

It took all she had, but she fought her way through the storm and wrapped her arms around the trunk of the tree. The storm tried to tear her free, but she refused to let go. Finally, the storm subsided. That was when she woke up.

She walked back to the Tender home that morning a changed woman, scarcely aware of the poverty and ignominy the sisterhood lived in, filled with what she had experienced. She interpreted the dream to mean that the Tenders were going to face a terrible crisis, but that she would be the one to lead them through it if only she was strong enough. The vision was what drove her life from then on.

But the years passed and nothing happened. Her vision grew tattered, ever harder to take hold of. Reality proved too much for faint promises. And the reality was that the Tenders were a shattered remnant. Their power from the days of old was gone and there was no way they were ever going to reclaim it. She would die a nobody among nobodies. That was the reality she had to live with, had to harden herself to. The Mother had deceived her. It was all a lie.

Until Lowellin arrived. When he named himself and spoke of his mission everything changed, as suddenly as a lightning bolt from the sky. All at once her vision burst forth once again, as bright and fresh as the day she'd received it.

Nalene walked down the long entrance hall. Massive columns lined the hall, the arches between them leading to other rooms and areas of the temple. Something scurried up a column to her right, dislodging bits of rock as it went. Much of the hall's ceiling had collapsed in the earthquake and there were jagged chunks of stone that she had to pick her way around, but at length she made it into the great dome itself.

A massive crack bisected the dome, the last of the daylight coming in through the crack enough that she could still see fairly well. The inside of the dome was a huge amphitheater, big enough to hold thousands of people. Set high up on the inside of the dome were the symbols of all the Arcs of the Circle of Life: Human, Animal, Bird, Plant, Reptile and Insect. The last two had always seemed odd to her. There were no Tenders of those Arcs now. Many didn't believe they'd ever existed at all, especially the Insect. Why would a Tender devote her life to bugs? There was only one oblique reference to the Reptile Arc in the Tender history books, and the Book of Xochitl made no mention of either of them.

Though it was too dark to see them now, she remembered that between the symbols, in alcoves angled to look down on the gathered worshippers, were statues of the greatest Tenders: Fea, who tamed the savage tribes of Caldea and brought them to the faith; Termina, who wrote most of the Book of Xochitl shortly after the Mother left;

Veriana, who turned back the godless hordes of Sertith when they threatened the entire Empire; Hame Terinoth, who stood with the Eight at the creation of Melekath's prison. There were others, too badly broken to be recognized.

Covering the inside of the dome itself was a great mosaic. The colors had faded and much of the work had fallen out in great chunks, but the picture was still visible. It showed Xochitl, standing with a great host at her back. She was pointing at a beast-like figure, who cowered and slunk away toward a gaping hole in the earth. Crawling and groveling beside the beast-like figure were numerous warped and misshapen parodies of humans, following their master down into the hole. It was the Banishment, when Xochitl defeated Melekath and his spawn and imprisoned them.

There was no altar in the great worship hall, only a raised, circular dais in the center of the room. It was there that the FirstMother stood in the days of glory, presiding over a room filled with kneeling thousands. Throughout the city were numerous circular plazas. During worship everyone who wasn't too old or too sick to move knelt in those plazas—it was a crime to avoid worshipping the Mother—all facing towards the Temple.

Legend had it that it was there on the dais where the last FirstMother, Shireen, conducted the ritual that led to the destruction of the temple.

It certainly looked like it. A huge crack split the white stone in half. The crack zigzagged across the floor of the worship hall, up the walls and across the ceiling. The stone along the edges of the crack was blackened and melted as if in a great fire.

In her imagination, Nalene could picture what might have happened, the Tenders linked in a *joining circle*, using their combined power to summon the River. Then the power getting away from them, the sudden explosion and great gouts of white-hot fire. Did they realize during that last, fateful moment their mistake? Or did it happen too quickly?

Nalene climbed up onto the dais and walked over close enough to the crack so that she could look down into it. It might have reached to the center of the earth. Cold, dank air wafted up out of it. She shivered and started to back away—

All at once the edge gave way and she plunged into the crack, clawing at empty air.

CHAPTER 22

A hand grabbed the back of Nalene's robe, stopping her fall, but not pulling her back to safety.

"Help me!" she gasped, her heart beating wildly. "Pull me back!"

"Are you the one? Are you the FirstMother who can lead the Tenders to war?"

"I am, I am!" She dangled like a puppy from his grip. Panic threatened to overwhelm her. One foot found purchase, then lost it. The chasm yawned beneath her. Dislodged stones clattered against the sides, but she didn't hear any of them strike bottom.

"I told you to trust me. If you don't, we have no chance against Melekath."

"I do trust you! I promise!" She thought she heard a seam in the robe rip. She tried to turn, to take hold of his arm, but she couldn't.

"Then why do you struggle so? If you trust me, then why do you fear I will drop you?"

"I'm afraid. I don't want to fall and die."

"So you *do* doubt me."

"No. I…I trust you." There was a loud ripping sound, unmistakable this time. She dropped several inches as the old fabric began to give way.

"Your words say one thing, but your actions betray a different truth. I do not know that you are the one I am looking for."

With a supreme act of will, Nalene forced herself to stop struggling. She took deep breaths, trying to slow her breathing. "I'm sorry, Protector."

"Apologies are no good to me. Apologies will not defeat Melekath."

"I know that. Only strength and courage will." Her mouth was dry and it was hard to say the next words. "If I am not the one, I would rather die." As she said those words, she knew they were true. "I accept your will in this, Protector." She closed her eyes and tried to prepare herself for death.

All at once the fabric gave way completely and she fell—

A hand like stone grabbed her arm and dragged her up out of the crack and back onto solid ground.

Nalene lay there on the ground for a moment, trying to get a hold of herself, trying to get the sick feeling of falling to leave. Then she sat up and dragged herself to her feet, forcing herself to meet Lowellin's eyes.

"Thank you, Protector." There was within her a question: *Did she fall into the crack, or was she pushed?*

"Your thanks, as your apologies, are meaningless. Only one thing matters. Do you understand me?"

"I understand. I will not fail you."

He stared at her, gauging the depth of her determination. It was strange how clearly she could see him in the quickly-fading light. His face might have been cut from raw stone, the angles in it were so sharp. There was no facial hair at all, beyond the merest suggestion of eyebrows.

"It is time to claim your weapon."

"I'm ready."

Just a hint of a smile. "No, I don't think you are. You're just ignorant."

She tried to match his iron will. Her shoulders were square, gaze steady, hands still by her sides. "Nevertheless."

"It waits for you in the River."

That surprised Nalene, though she tried not to let it show. The *River*? How could her weapon be *there*? What was it? "Are you going to summon the River, then?"

"No. Ilsith will take you there."

Nalene looked around. There was someone else here?

"For this, you need the clear vision of *beyond*. Go there now."

"I...I need a few minutes." Going *beyond* had once been commonplace for the Tenders, as natural as breathing. Now, only a few were able to make it there. Nalene had only managed to go *beyond* a few times, and only with a great deal of effort. "I have to calm myself."

"I have other things to do this night." Before she could react, he reached out and tapped her on the forehead with his finger.

She blinked, and she was *beyond*. *Beyond* was not a physical place. It could more correctly be said that it was a state of heightened perception, where LifeSong could be perceived, though not with the eyes, rather with deeper senses.

Her body was not visible there, only the glowing outline of her *akirma*, the shell that contained her Selfsong, the energy that kept her alive. But it was vague, partially obscured by the mists that enshrouded *beyond*.

"Come, Ilsith, my Other."

She heard his words as if from a great distance. Lowellin himself was not visible.

Then she felt a new presence, there in the mists with her. There was something frightening about it, something alien.

Suddenly she wanted very badly to leave *beyond* and return to the familiar world.

A black, sinewy shape appeared in the mists and slid toward her. She tried to get away from it, tried to will herself back to normal perception, but she could not leave.

"Ilsith will take you to the River. Do not resist or it may injure you."

Nalene tried to call out to Lowellin, to tell him she wasn't ready. She didn't want that thing to touch her. Maybe this was all a very bad idea. But she felt trapped and from here she could not find the control over her own body.

The black, sinewy shape wrapped itself around her *akirma* and dimly Nalene felt pain, which surprised her. She had been taught it was not possible to feel pain *beyond*.

Ilsith tightened its grip, then jerked. There was a moment of disorientation and then Nalene realized she was *seeing* her own *akirma* from outside herself.

She was in her spirit-body.

Before she could fully grasp the enormity of what Ilsith had done, it raced away with her and her *akirma* faded into the distance.

They went deeper into the mists, though it would not be accurate to say that they went down. Or up. Or sideways. Only deeper.

The mists whipped past them, then faded and disappeared altogether. Nalene had never been this deep *beyond*, though she had read about it. Without the mists to obscure them, the flows of LifeSong that sustained all living things became visible, like glowing threads of golden light, branching this way and that in the velvety darkness.

The golden threads led to pinpoints of light, some white, some with a golden brown hue, some blue, most in varying shades of green. Each pinpoint of light was a living thing, kept alive by its individual flow of Song.

It was, quite simply, the most beautiful thing she had ever *seen*.

Or it would have been, had Ilsith not kept her tightly in its grip as it hurtled ever deeper *beyond*.

The tiny pinpoints faded and disappeared. The golden threads of light joined to larger, thicker flows, like the branches on a vast tree. The Life-energy contained in one of those branches was enough to sustain hundreds or even thousands of people, Nalene knew. In the days of the Empire, the more powerful Tenders were able to tap into those branches and use the power contained therein to do remarkable things.

Deeper still and the branches led back to a trunk, shining golden in the darkness, rippling as the constantly-flowing energy of Life passed through it. There was power great enough to sustain an entire city or, as happened once, destroy an entire city.

But none of it prepared Nalene for what she *saw* when they reached their destination.

The River.

It looked like a vast, golden river suspended in darkness. Its ends were lost in the distance, but the Tenders believed that it flowed in a huge, never ending circle. Mighty currents swirled within it, all the Life-energy of an entire world contained within it.

The sight was so awesome that for a moment Nalene forgot her fear, forgot all about Ilsith and even the Protector. The power radiating from it was so vast that she knew in an instant that there was no way the Tenders holding out in the temple in old Qarath had ever attempted to harness that power, regardless of how strong they were or how many of them there were. It simply could not be done, no more than the ocean could be tamed by humans. Even to go too close to it would be certain destruction.

Ilsith raced toward it.

In that distant, supernatural place where sound did not exist, Nalene screamed. Maybe her body, still back in the temple, screamed as well. She had no way to know. All she knew was that the raw power of the River was tearing her apart. Her *akirma* was being shredded like a cobweb in a hurricane, her Selfsong snuffed out like a candle.

Yet somehow, miraculously, she was not torn apart. Somehow Ilsith was strong enough to keep her intact.

Then they were right by the River, close enough to touch it. Awestruck, Nalene stared into its depths—

And that was when she saw them.

Tiny, wriggling creatures swam in the River, like pale, bleached tadpoles. They seemed utterly frail, far too weak to survive there, but somehow they did. Not just survived, but thrived, riding the currents as easily as a hawk rides a thermal high in the sky.

An appendage shot out from Ilsith, snatched one of the creatures and tore it from its home.

It pulled the thing in close and they began the journey back to the normal world.

Nalene opened her eyes to darkness and the sound of someone gasping for air. It took a moment before she realized that it was herself she heard.

She rolled onto her side, gasping turning into coughing. Her body felt distant, unresponsive, as if she had been gone from it for a very long time and it had forgotten her.

Gradually she became aware of something on her chest, just above her breast. She sat up and pulled her robe down so she could see what it was.

Moonlight was streaming in through the broken dome and it lit up something lying there, nestled against her skin. It was milky-white and smaller than her thumb, as perfect as a tear. It was the thing Ilsith had pulled from the River.

"What is it?"

"It has no name. Such a thing has never been in the world before. Call it a *sulbit*, for that is what it is for."

"And this…this is the weapon you spoke of?"

"It will be. When it has had time to grow and you have trained it properly. A creature of pure Song, for controlling the raw power of Song."

"It's beautiful."

Lowellin made no response to that, merely stared down at her, his hands clasped over the head of his staff.

"I will take care of it," she said fiercely, some forgotten, elemental mothering instinct rising within her suddenly. "I will make sure it is safe."

"It will need to be fed if it is to grow."

"What do I feed it?"

"It feeds only on Song, nothing else."

That made sense. It came from the River after all. But she still didn't understand. "I don't know how to do that. I don't understand where this Song will come from."

"It will come from you."

She looked up at him, chilled by his words. "It will feed off *me*?"

He shrugged. "For now." He started to leave and she reached for him.

"Wait. I have so many questions."

"They can wait. Care for the creature. Prepare the other Tenders to receive theirs."

He strode away and was gone.

Nalene tried to get to her feet but she felt dizzy and had to give it up. She would rest here for a while before walking home.

Just a little while.

Nalene awakened stiff and cold on the stone floor. Her eyelids fluttered open and nothing she saw made sense. Where was she? Bits of rock bit into her cheek; her neck was sore. Haze filled her mind. Gingerly she sat up.

Then it came flooding back to her. She pulled the neck of her robe down and there it was.

It was even more beautiful in the daylight. It seemed to glisten slightly. It was pale, cloudy like a pearl, smooth and perfect, curving and tapering at one end like the hint of a tail. With the tip of her finger, she stroked it gently.

When she touched it, something happened. It was like a link opened between them. She became aware of its presence in a new way, like a faint murmuring at the edge of her heart. Very dimly she sensed the world as it sensed it and knew that it was confused and frightened at the change in its environment.

"It's okay," she murmured. "I'm here. I'll take care of you. I won't let anything hurt you."

Its fear seemed to ease some then, and she smiled.

She looked around and what she saw awed her.

The world was *different.*

Colors were sharper than ever before, every sound clearer. She was aware of her body and her surroundings at a level she had never known. She could feel the tiniest breeze tickling the small hairs on her arms. She felt an ant running across the edge of her robe.

It thrilled her and for several minutes she sat there, savoring the feel of it all. Her *sulbit* had opened a whole new world to her. It was amazing, wondrous, new.

But there was too much to do to sit here. She took her hand away from the *sulbit* and at once the day faded. She felt dry and empty and listless. She had small pains everywhere from sleeping on the floor. Her mouth was dry and had a metallic taste.

Shakily, she stood up. Judging by the light, it was about an hour after sunrise. The others would be worried. They would be wondering if she would return.

She walked outside and on the steps of the temple she stopped, breathing in the morning air, looking out over the ruins of old Qarath. This morning was like no morning before it in the history of the world. She had taken the first step, gone where no Tender had ever gone before, and brought something back into this new day. It overwhelmed her, made her feel how small her entire life had been to this point. It excited her to think where this might all lead, once she learned the boundaries of her new power.

She would be the master of LifeSong and she and her sisters would use that elemental power to defeat Melekath. Xochitl would smile on them once again. The Tenders would return to their rightful place. They would be honored. People would look at them in awe as they passed. As if in a vision of the future she saw the pitfalls that awaited them, the traps of pride and wealth they had fallen into during the Empire. But she had plans for that, ideas on how to steer her order clear of those traps.

She walked through the ruined city like a woman walking on clouds. The decay and destruction around her was nothing. Once Melekath was defeated she would see to it that this symbol of glory was again restored to its luster. There were no limits to what she and her Tenders would do. She would be known as one of the greatest Tenders, spoken of for thousands of years.

She had left the city behind and was walking down the pitted road toward Qarath when she was assailed by a sudden, powerful hunger. But it was no normal hunger. Then it came to her.

This hunger wasn't hers.

She pulled down the neck of her robe and looked at her *sulbit*. Was it her imagination, or had it lost some of its luster? She needed to feed it.

The thought of being fed on frightened her. She tried to tell herself that it would be no different than what a normal mother would feel, nursing her baby, but that didn't really help.

There came the smallest pinch from where the *sulbit* was nestled against her. Hard after that came an enervating feeling, as if something vital was draining away.

The *sulbit* was consuming her Selfsong.

Her knees started to buckle and she had to sit down. The urge came to rip the creature off her breast and toss it away but she resisted it. The Protector had told her this would happen. The Protector would not have given her the *sulbit* if he didn't think she could handle it.

She bit her lip and let her new child feed off her.

CHAPTER 23

The Guardian known as Gulagh left the city of Nelton and walked out into the desert. Behind Gulagh walked a young man with loose, dirty blond hair. He was shirtless, his trousers ragged. The young man followed Gulagh with his head down, his gaze distant and unfocused. He didn't question where they went, didn't speak at all or make any sound.

They walked south for several hours as the sun dropped toward the horizon. They came to an area of badlands, where an ancient volcanic flow covered the ground for miles. The rock was like black glass, smooth and undulating except in those places where an air bubble trapped in the lava had broken open, leaving sharp edges. The young man cut his bare foot on one, but still made no sound. Afterwards he left a faint trail of blood to mark his passage.

Near dark they came to a hole in the ground. It was almost perfectly round and about three feet across. It was a new hole, created over the last six months by Gulagh, starting shortly after it escaped the Gur al Krin. It had only finished the hole the day before.

At the edge of the hole Gulagh wrapped its arms around the young man, then jumped in.

It was a long fall. As they neared the bottom, Gulagh began to slow their descent using its legs and one arm. The impact at the bottom was still enough to break one of the young man's ribs, but he survived, and that was the important thing.

Because Gulagh needed him alive for what it planned to do next.

At the bottom of the shaft Gulagh had scooped out a small cavern, big enough for a person to lay down in. Despite its depth, the small cavern wasn't dark, but was lit with an odd purple light. The light came from the floor, which was some kind of translucent stone.

With one clawed finger Gulagh scratched the young man's chest. The wound was deep and blood began to flow immediately.

It lay the young man face down on the floor. When the young man's blood contacted the translucent stone floor, something happened.

There was a bright flare of light from the other side.

The young man began to scream.

He tried to push off the floor but he couldn't break away. The glow grew brighter.

Something began to seep through the floor.

It soaked into the young man's body. He continued to scream, his limbs thrashing as he fought futilely to get free. Terrible lesions broke out all over his body. Weird bulges formed under his skin, one on his throat, the other on the side of his head.

The slender thread of Song attached to him began to change, a cancerous yellow taint spreading up its golden purity.

The taint crept up and up the flow, spreading after a while into the larger feeder line of Song that it was connected to, and from there into the even larger trunk line.

At last it reached the River and dripped into it. A stain appeared in its golden purity.

Without looking down at the young man, who was still screaming and thrashing, Gulagh climbed out of the shaft and returned to the city of Nelton. The young man was strong enough to survive for several days and during that time he would serve as a conduit passing the poison of the abyss into the River, thence to spread out to the rest of the living world.

After several days he would have to be replaced, but that was not a problem. Gulagh had plenty more to choose from in the city it now controlled.

PART TWO: NETRA

CHAPTER 24

In the beginning was Xochitl, first of all the gods to awaken. She looked on a world that was empty, silent, and She was lonely. She breathed onto the world and there was life, the plants, the animals and the birds. But still She was lonely. So She took of Her own essence and molded it into a shape like unto Herself. To this shape She gave intelligence and free will and a name: humankind. Then did the new world have meaning and She was no longer alone.

The Book of Xochitl

The woman stood barefoot in the dark majesty of the desert night with her eyes closed, her hands clasped before her. Her lips moved in a silent prayer to Xochitl, the Mother of Life, while a coyote howled in the distance and a soft breeze stirred her long, black hair. Crickets called to each other and bats squeaked overhead as the minutes passed and a sliver of moon began to rise. When it had cleared the sharp ridges on the horizon she gave up and opened her eyes.

Her prayers brought no answer, so now there was no way to go but forward. The dreams that filled her nights constantly now gave her no choice. She could no longer sleep and she could barely force herself to eat. The lack of sleep was slowly driving her mad. Maybe it already had. She had even started to hear voices.

Or at least one voice.

She had to have answers, no matter what the risks were.

Slowly she undressed, removing the brown robe of simple homespun and then the light, cotton shift underneath. Then she was naked except for a small animal skull hung on a piece of twine around her neck. She drew the necklace over her head and laid it gently on her clothes.

Behind her was a small, rounded structure, with a dying fire beside it. It was modeled after the one described in the garbled writings known as the Book of Sorrows, penned by a frantic Tender in the final hours before she took her own life. It was woven from hundreds of gaunt, black, arthritic limbs taken from greasewood bushes, the waxy-leafed shrub that grew everywhere in the Tark Valley. Over the limbs were packed handfuls of brown desert mud, layer after layer until it was solid, leaving only a narrow entrance that could be closed with a mat, thickly-woven from more limbs.

She knelt and crawled into the structure—peering out at the night for a long moment like one who believes she will never see it again—then pulled the door shut behind her. Inside it was barely large enough for her to sit upright with her legs crossed. In a scooped-out hollow in the center of the floor was a pile of stones, glowing red. She hesitated, while the clamor in her brain increased so that she winced. A pouch on the ground beside her contained a whitish powder. She took out a pinch of the powder and held it, fearful of the next step. It had not gone well for the last Tender who went before her down this path. But, like her, that woman had also been desperate. All at once she tossed the powder onto the stones.

Smoke billowed around her, hot and thick and choking. She clutched her head in her hands and rocked side to side, making small animal sounds. Pain started in her chest and spread throughout her body. An unbearable pressure built up inside her, then she was torn asunder and thrown out of the everyday world. Out into a far vaster, crueler dimension, where the soft fabrics that protect the living from harsh reality are torn away, revealing the bladed edges underneath.

When the eyes of her soul opened and she looked on the source of her dreams, she began to scream.

CHAPTER 25

Netra was sitting on a bench in the common room of Rane Haven next to Cara, her best friend. They held an old history text between them, trying to decipher the faded script in the dim light. On the other side of her sat Brelisha, the old Tender in charge of their lessons. Tallow candles sputtered in wrought-iron sconces on the walls, lighting faded murals and cracked plaster. A large, old sycamore tree stood in the center of the room, reaching with its bent arms towards the cracked skylight overhead.

Netra sat up, stretching her back and rubbing her eyes. She and Cara had been trying to decipher this text for over an hour and she was mortally sick of it. Who cared about what happened thousands of years ago anyway? Those people got to live their lives; why did she have to waste hers reading about them?

A warning hiss from Brelisha—the stern-faced woman seemed to always have an eye on Netra, just waiting for her to slip up—and Netra bent dutifully over the text once again, though not without an aggrieved sigh. Cara shifted and gave her a pat on the shoulder, as always trying to cheer Netra up, but Netra was having none of it. She was almost nineteen, an adult. Would the lessons never end?

Netra gave up trying to make sense of the text. Still pretending to read, she listened in on Karyn and Gerath's conversation. As usual, they were talking about the past.

"The temple at Qarath was big enough to hold over five thousand people in the main worship hall. And the whole floor was tiled in rose quartz, brought in from hundreds of miles away," Karyn said, shaking her head, her frowsy hair bouncing with the movement. She had pale, unfocused eyes that masked a keen intellect. "Can you imagine? When

Thelin FirstMother led services there, people fought to get in. The power of her voice was so strong that the mad were healed just by listening to her."

"True," Gerath replied. She was a stout woman who carried an air of perpetual superiority. "But, as great as Thelin undoubtedly was, I don't think she could hold a candle to Klie Gerthon, FirstMother during the reign of Justus the Third. It was said that she could hear the illness in a person's Song from a mile away and then..."

Dull, dull, dull. Every night it was the same thing with those two. They were as bad as the history book. Netra tuned them out and focused her attention on listening with her inner hearing. When they tried, about half of the Tenders at Rane Haven could hear at least a little LifeSong. The ability to do so was what traditionally marked a woman as Chosen, and thus eligible to join the Tenders. These days the Tenders counted themselves lucky simply to find women who would endure the poverty and scorn that went with being a member of their order; they couldn't afford to be too particular about whether that woman was Chosen or not.

Netra was one of the ones who could hear LifeSong. She couldn't remember a time when she hadn't been able to hear Song. In fact, as a little girl she remembered feeling surprised when she learned most other people couldn't hear it. It was a part of her life. She heard it all the time, without trying. It was a faint melody playing in the background, a familiar, reliable companion. It was not something she heard with her ears; no amount of ordinary noise could drown it out. It was more something she heard inside her mind. She thought of it as inner hearing.

Over the years she had learned to distinguish between the primary, background melody of LifeSong and the secondary melody of Selfsong that radiated off of other people and animals. It was like hearing a rushing river in the distance and picking out the sounds of smaller creeks and streams nearby.

Selfsong was unique to each individual. It carried within its rhythms a wealth of information—about a person's mood, health, and so on. Netra was still learning to interpret what she heard, but she was getting better at it all the time.

Cara's Selfsong was content, quiet. Cara was like that. Steady, calm.

Gerath's had a hint of irritation in it that was growing as she got deeper into her argument with Karyn.

Suddenly, Netra's inner hearing picked up another Selfsong approaching. She heard the fear first, so strong her heart speeded up in response. Then she heard the pain, so intense that she dropped her side of the book, her hands feeling like they were on fire.

A moment later she knew it was Jolene who approached, coming in through the back door. She rose up from her chair just as the dark-haired woman stumbled into the room, tears pouring down her face, her skin glistening with sweat. Her hands were doubled into fists, driven under her arms.

Netra hurried to her. "What is it, Jolene? What's wrong?"

Jolene didn't reply. Her thin form was shaking uncontrollably. Netra helped her to a chair near the cold fireplace and lowered her into it, where Jolene immediately curled up, eyes closed tight, moans coming from her.

For a long moment none of the other Tenders in the room moved, frozen in place by something they didn't understand, almost an animal instinct for danger. It was as if they sensed that what Jolene brought into their midst would change their world forever.

Then Siena entered the room. "Jolene!" she cried, and hurried to her. The paralysis broke and suddenly everyone else was moving too, crowding around the woman, exclamations and sounds of concern filling the air like the nervous clucking of disturbed hens.

"Hush," Siena said, and they quieted. She turned back to Jolene, and knelt beside her. "What happened? Are you all right?"

Jolene raised her tear-stained face, still keeping her eyes closed. Slowly she stretched forth her arms and opened her hands. They were a ruined mess of burned, blistered skin.

There was a collective gasp and the room broke into excited babbling again. Brelisha's voice cut sharply through the din as she ordered Karyn to bring bandages and ointment.

"What happened?" Siena asked again, an unusual urgency in her voice. Netra heard a note of fear in the older woman's Selfsong and she wondered why.

Jolene opened her eyes and looked at the Haven Mother. "I built a...I used the dream powder. I had a vision."

The hush fell again. Dream powder. After what had happened to the Tender who wrote the Book of Sorrows, dream powder was forbidden to all Tenders, the doorways it opened too dangerous to go through.

"Fool girl," Brelisha hissed. "You might have lost your mind—or worse."

"Easy, Brelisha," Siena warned. "She has suffered enough this night." Turning back to Jolene she said gently, but still with that same odd sense of urgency, "What did you see?"

But Jolene was bent over herself again, weeping silently, shaking her head. Karyn arrived with the bandages then and Siena stood. "I think we had better help her to her room, get her to bed." She stepped back and all at once Jolene leapt to her feet.

"Someone has to go to Treeside! Soon!"

"Why, Jolene?" Siena asked, and Netra could sense the effort it cost her to remain calm. Something beyond what had just happened here was bothering the Haven Mother. "What's at Treeside?"

Jolene shook her head and sagged against Siena, the tears starting anew.

"Bronwyn. Donae. Take her to her room," Brelisha ordered. The two Tenders took hold of her arms and led her away. "Go with them, Karyn. Give her something strong to help her sleep." Karyn was already halfway to the door. The remaining Tenders looked around at each other uncertainly.

"This is a perfect example of why dream powder is forbidden," Brelisha said sternly, addressing Netra and Cara. "There was a time when it was a powerful tool of our order, but that time is long past. We are no longer what we were. No longer do we have the strength to deal with the rigors of what it puts a person through."

"I knew it was a bad idea when she started reading the Book of Sorrows," Gerath put in, returning to her seat and shaking her head dramatically. Gerath followed Brelisha's lead in everything. She folded her hands across her stomach, peering at the room through the little spectacles she wore. Netra had looked through those spectacles once, when Gerath left them on the table. They distorted her vision so badly she couldn't see the other side of the room, and she suspected they did the same to Gerath, which was why she always wore them so far down on her nose. It was her belief that Gerath just wore them to make herself look smarter. "I knew it could only lead to evil, full of dangerous ideas and blasphemy it is. I don't know why we still have the book, why we haven't just taken it and burned it and be rid of it forever."

"We haven't burned it because we aren't children," Siena said suddenly. Netra still felt the fear in her, but there was something else as well, an angry edge that was growing.

Gerath spluttered and Brelisha cut in swiftly, never one to miss a chance to disagree with Siena. "You see what it's done to that poor weak-minded woman and yet you still say that?"

"Jolene is not weak-minded."

"What is she then?" Brelisha asked acidly. She had returned to her seat and picked up the darning she was working on, but now she set it aside and gripped the arms of her chair, as if about to fling herself out of it and into a fray. Her hair was white, straight and thin like she was and swept back in a tight bun. She had perpetual scowl lines around her mouth and her deep set eyes. She looked like a hawk, Netra thought, or rather a vulture, getting ready to swoop down.

"I don't know," Siena replied, her eyes drifting to the hallway Jolene and the other Tenders had disappeared down. "I've never known."

"Well, I still say it is foolishness, dangerous foolishness," Brelisha declared, as if she had said the last word on the issue. "These aren't the days of the Empire, and we Tenders need to know where our proper boundaries are." Gerath nodded vigorously in agreement.

But Siena seemed not to have heard her. She turned back to the room and for some reason her eyes went to Netra, but when she spoke, it was for everyone. "Some of us will have to go to Treeside. As soon as possible."

"What?" Brelisha cried. "You're going to encourage her madness?"

"I am going to encourage any chance given to us by the Mother, even if it seems foolish." There was a sudden iron in her voice that was surprising. Brelisha disagreed with Siena often—in fact she seemed to make a point of it—and usually Siena was restrained, almost passive, in her response.

"But the dream powder—"

"Is an old wisdom given to us by Xochitl in the early days, a way of going directly to her for answers." Siena had her arms crossed and the stare she gave Brelisha showed no signs of wavering.

"This is madness," Brelisha insisted. "That path to the Mother was closed long ago. Yuon She proved that. The Mother has withdrawn her protection and there are things lurking on that path far too dangerous for any of us. Who knows what kind of evil waits for us in Treeside?"

"Which is why I will only ask for volunteers." Again Siena's gaze went to Netra and Netra felt a thrill of excitement go through her. This was too good to be true. A chance to go on a journey? Anything for that.

"Madness," Brelisha repeated. "I won't stand for it."

"I'm not asking you to, Brelisha. This isn't your decision to make. I'm the Haven Mother here. It's my decision and it is made." Still her gaze was locked on Netra. Brelisha looked poleaxed. Her face was turning red.

"I'll go!" It was all Netra could do not to jump up and down, but she managed it. Cara looked at her in horror.

"Good," Siena said, before Brelisha could get her next angry words out. "Anyone else?"

"Gerath will go too," Brelisha grated, her jaw tight. She looked like she was strangling. Gerath's loftiness disappeared as she gave Brelisha a startled look that was not all that friendly. The portly woman complained of the distance to the privy. To get to Treeside would be a full day's walk, and some of it uphill. Brelisha ignored her. "At least I know Gerath will be clearheaded about it—whatever it's supposed to be."

"It is decided then. You two will leave the day after tomorrow." Siena left the room.

Brelisha stayed where she was for perhaps a minute longer after Siena left the room, stabbing at the piece of fabric in her hands, her lips a thin white line. Then she slipped and stuck one of the needles into her thumb. She threw her needlework down on the table beside her— muttering something under her breath that Netra was reasonably certain wasn't a prayer—and marched over to the door Siena had gone through.

Netra had returned to her seat on the bench by Cara and she sat there as long as she could, but finally she couldn't help herself. She had to know what was going on. She stood up and stretched casually. Gerath gave her a sour look, and Netra, assuming her most innocent expression, mouthed the word, "privy," and started out of the room. Cara caught her eye as she left and she gave the blonde girl a look that was meant to say: Whatever I learn, I'll tell you.

Once she got outside, she didn't head for the small wooden building set off by itself behind the Haven, but stood for a moment in the darkness, letting her eyes adjust. Then she made her way along the edge of the Haven, a sprawling stone and timber structure built in a time when there were three times as many Tenders as there were now, and servants besides. The granite blocks were rough under her fingertips, the night breeze cool on her skin. Out here, deep in the Mother's embrace, she felt alive in a way she never did indoors, like she was part of the night. She felt each twig through the thin soles of her sandals, caught the faint musky odor of a coyote, heard the swoosh of a nighthawk and the tiny squeak of its prey.

She eased her way around a squat cholla cactus and ducked into the deep shadows of a mesquite tree, only a few feet from the outside wall of Siena's quarters. To her dismay she saw that the shutters over Siena's window were closed. That was surprising. With summer coming on, they should be open to let in the cool air. She eased up to the window and pressed her ear to the shutters, but all she could hear were low murmurs. She couldn't tell what they were saying at all. She started to go back inside the Haven, then changed her mind. Why waste such a beautiful night?

She lowered herself to the ground and sat cross-legged. Then she reached inside her robe and withdrew her *sonkrill*. *Sonkrills* were talismans intended to help Tenders connect with Song. Their use came about in the chaotic years after the fall of the Empire, as the remnants of the Tenders of Xochitl faced the awful truth of how they had abused their power and sought new ways to recover it, ways they hoped would be smiled upon by the Mother. Only a handful of Havens sought *sonkrills*, and generally they were of the Arc of Animals.

She held the *sonkrill* up and looked at it closely, hoping, as she always did, to see the glow she had only seen once before. The talisman remained dark and she sighed softly. Gripping it in both hands, she closed her eyes, focusing on drawing each breath deep into her lungs, then slowly releasing it. In and out she breathed, slipping further inside herself with each breath. Closing off the noise and clamor of the outside world and her own thoughts. Stilling her mind until it was a placid pool. As she had been taught, she visualized each inhalation as a slow tide of LifeSong that flowed first into her lungs and then through every fiber of her body. With each exhalation she felt LifeSong withdraw from the far reaches of her body, narrowing to a single point in the center of her chest, then flowing up and out through her mouth.

When her concentration was strong enough, she took hold of the incoming LifeSong, then let go of herself. As she exhaled and LifeSong withdrew, it pulled her out of herself.

There was a lurch, and she was *beyond*.

The desert night faded, overlaid with a new world. In this new world a thick mist swirled around her, though she knew it was not really mist, just as she knew she was not seeing it with her eyes.

Going *beyond* was the primary goal of every Tender's early training, for it was there that a Tender could *see* LifeSong, which was a vital step toward controlling it. It was their ability to manipulate LifeSong which for centuries had made the Tenders so powerful.

These days, only a few Tenders actually managed to make it *beyond*, but once they did they were helpless. The stronger ones could part the mists and *see* LifeSong, but they could not take hold of it or bend it to their will.

Netra had only managed to go *beyond* for the first time a few days ago. So what if there were no powers to be gained by coming here? There was a peace here, a sense of oneness with the Mother and all of her creation that surpassed everything else. Other than Cara, she hadn't told any of the other Tenders about it yet. Right now she just wanted to keep it for herself.

Netra concentrated on the mists, focusing the power of her will to try and part them. After a few minutes, her efforts were rewarded as the mists thinned, revealing threads of light that glowed with a gentle golden color. One was connected to her *akirma*. There were smaller threads of light as well, connecting to the plants and various creatures around her.

Looking around, Netra *saw* two other threads of light similar in size to hers nearby. Those flows probably connected to Siena and Brelisha. She followed the flows until she could *see* two glowing figures ahead. Siena and Brelisha's *akirmas* glowed with a warm, white light, though hints of other colors surfaced here and there, indicating strong emotions or sensations. The white light was Selfsong, that Life-energy held within a living thing's *akirma*.

In the center of each woman's *akirma* was a brighter glow. That was her Heartglow. Selfsong could bleed away and yet life remain, but once Heartglow left the *akirma* there was only death.

Something caught Netra's attention and she looked down. Drifting near her was an unusual flow. Not only was its normal golden glow tinged with a cancerous yellow color, but it was not connected to anything. It seemed to be drifting aimlessly.

Then it snapped forward and struck her. Netra felt a sudden burning pain and she jerked back and fell out of *beyond*.

She scrambled to her feet, her heart pounding. What was that odd yellow flow? Where had it come from?

Suddenly she felt very exposed and alone out there in the darkness and she hurried to the back door of the Haven and went inside.

CHAPTER 26

"I can't believe Jolene was foolish enough to use the dream powder. Surely you don't believe she had an actual vision?" Brelisha folded her arms over her narrow chest, daring Siena to gainsay her. "Why are you going to let Netra go? She's so young. Bronwyn would be better qualified to make a judgment on whatever she finds there—if there's anything to find." Her tone clearly indicated what she thought of that possibility.

"Netra is—"

"She's undisciplined, is what she is," Brelisha snapped. "You've let her run wild for too long."

"She has to feel her wings to know how far they will stretch," Siena said with a sigh. It was an old argument between them.

"That's what Qualin said about Netra's mother—and you know what happened to her."

The mistakes of the past hung between them then and Siena looked away as the old pain bit anew. She and Shakre had been the best of friends and what happened to her still hurt. As she had so many times before, Siena wondered if she had been wise to keep her old friend's secret all these years. More than once she had decided to go to Netra and tell her the truth, but she'd never been able to quite do it. The last thing Shakre asked of her was her oath never to tell her daughter what happened to her mother, and no matter how she tried she couldn't seem to break it.

"Has Netra gotten any closer to entering the mists yet?" Siena asked, hoping to change the subject.

"No. At least, not that I know of. I wouldn't be surprised if she could do it but she was hiding it from me."

175

"Give her time. She'll get there when she's ready."

"It would help if she would apply herself more and not spend so much time running around in the hills like some kind of wild animal. I've tried and tried to break her of it, but it doesn't do any good. You're the only one she'll listen to at all. No amount of discipline seems to get through to her. And now you go and reward her by letting her go to Treeside. You've wrecked what little progress I've made with one stroke."

"I'm sorry, Brelisha. For that I truly am."

"So you'll change your mind about letting her go?"

"No." Brelisha's face tightened at Siena's words. "I don't know how to explain it, I really don't. But I just have this feeling that Netra needs to go."

"If you ask me I'd say the feeling is guilt. You still feel guilty about what happened to her mother. That's why you've been so easy on her all these years."

Perhaps Brelisha was right, Siena thought. If she had chosen differently, if she had gone to the Haven Mother with what she knew, maybe she could have averted what happened.

Siena sighed again and sat down at her desk. Brelisha tired her so. Why did it have to be this way between them? Why must they argue so all the time?

But she knew the answer to that, knew it all too well. The anger, the arguments, all grew out of one decision nearly fifteen years ago. One decision among many made by Ivorie, Haven Mother before Siena. The last one she made in that role. The day came when Ivorie announced her retirement, knowing that her death was coming soon. And all the Tenders at Rane Haven knew who she would choose to succeed her. After all, Brelisha had always been her favorite, the Tender most like her in temperament. Ivorie had never hidden her love for her.

But then she lay here on her bed in this very room, the Tenders all gathered around, and handed the Haven's one battered copy of the Book of Xochitl to Siena. Siena would never forget Brelisha's look when Ivorie did that, the way her face seemed to close in on itself like a fist, clenching on the hurt that sprang up there like a dark flower. After that she didn't speak to a soul until after Ivorie's death and when she finally did, it was to argue one of the first decisions Siena made as Haven Mother.

Looking at her now, Siena could see that hurt still festering there and she wanted to just give it to her right then. Simply abdicate, say, *It was a mistake. It should have been you. I don't want to be Haven Mother.* Because the truth was that she didn't. She'd never wanted the responsibility. She would have been perfectly happy to remain a follower.

But even as she thought this Siena knew she couldn't do it. Ivorie was a woman who had always seemed to know just what she was doing, as if the Mother were always there, whispering in her ear. Even after fifteen years Siena couldn't shake the feeling that if Ivorie chose her as Haven Mother, she must have had her reasons. She must have been right. Neither Siena's nor Brelisha's feelings changed that at all. She gathered herself before meeting Brelisha's gaze once again.

"You've heard it too, haven't you?"

Brelisha was girded for battle and that surprised her. But she recovered quickly, as she always did. "Heard what?"

"The dissonance in LifeSong."

Brelisha's arms fell to her sides and she stood there for a moment, blinking at Siena. Then she sat down abruptly in the chair that faced Siena's desk. The candlelight cast her eyes in deep shadows as she studied her hands. Siena thought she saw them shaking slightly.

"Then it really is there." Brelisha took a deep breath and her next words were very soft, almost inaudible. "It's so faint I wasn't sure I heard it." In a whisper she added, "I thought maybe the dissonance was in me."

Siena knew, right then, that Brelisha's hurt went clear to her center. And why not? All these years, wondering if Ivorie passed her over because there was something wrong with her inside. Always that fear deep down, eating at her every day. No one she could share it with. Nothing she could do about it. Siena felt a surge of compassion for the other woman and wished she had shared her fears with Brelisha days ago, when she first heard the dissonance. But she'd thought that maybe she was imagining it, and she hadn't wanted to face Brelisha's acid tongue, hadn't wanted to fight to convince her of something that might have no substance at all.

"It's getting worse, isn't it?" Brelisha said.

"I think so." And then the big question. "What do you think is causing it?"

Brelisha's gaze went to a tattered tapestry on the wall. It was a very old depiction of the Banishment. The colors were badly faded, but one could still see the towering figure of Xochitl, clothed in white light, pointing a commanding finger at the dark shape of Melekath, as he slunk towards a gaping hole in the ground. "I keep telling myself it can't be that," Brelisha said. "I've never believed the Book of Sorrows is anything more than the babblings of a madwoman. I've never let the girls read it." The Book of Sorrows contained the apocalyptic revelations of the Tender, Yuon She. In the dark days following the fall of the Empire, Yuon She used the dream powder ceremony to seek a vision of the Mother, and what she saw drove her over the edge into madness and despair, for the vision showed her that Melekath's prison was not unbreakable, as the Book of Xochitl claimed. The Banishment was not permanent. Someday Melekath would free himself and he would return to take his revenge on those who sided with Xochitl against him. Shortly after her vision, Yuon killed herself. The pages that came to be known as the Book of Sorrows were found clutched in her dead hand. "But now I don't know what to believe."

"I don't either," Siena admitted. "But something in my heart tells me..." She broke off, unwilling to say the terrible words.

They sat there in silence for long minutes, neither woman able to look at the other. Finally, Brelisha said, "If Jolene really did have a vision, then Treeside could hold some answers."

"I don't know what else to do," Siena said. "I have read the Book, I have prayed, and I just don't know what to do. I don't have anything else to try."

"And if that's really what it is?" Brelisha said, gesturing at the tapestry.

"Then the Mother help us, because nothing else will."

When Brelisha was gone, Siena looked at the tapestry on the wall once again. She'd never liked the thing. It made her uneasy. If it was up to her she'd have thrown it on the trash heap years ago. But it had hung in this Haven, in this very room, since the time of the Empire. It would be here after she was gone. Some traditions were stronger than mere people.

She opened a drawer in her desk and removed a wooden box. Inside was a rib bone from a spikehorn, highly polished so that it shone in the lamplight. Her *sonkrill*. The ribs protect the heart, Ivorie had told when she returned with it after her Songquest. She had never completely understood what the Haven Mother meant by that, as she did not understand so many other things that enigmatic woman said or did.

She picked it up gently. There was a time when she carried it with her constantly. She remembered sitting in her room late at night, just holding it. There were nights when she was sure that it was aware of her, that it knew her touch and responded to it. Her faith was a living thing inside her back then, a vital core she could not imagine losing.

When did she stop carrying her *sonkrill*? When did she lose her faith?

She sighed, put the talisman back into its box, and the box back into the drawer.

Netra shut the door behind her and took a deep breath, relieved to be back inside the Haven. Her arm throbbed slightly and her heart was pounding. What happened out there? What was that strange yellow flow? She wanted to see if it had left a mark on her, but this room was unlit, as was most of the Haven. Money was scarce, too scarce to spend burning candles in a room no one was using. The sound of her name being called interrupted her thoughts and she started down the hall towards the common room, rubbing at the sore spot as she went.

Gerath gave Netra her most disapproving look when she entered the room, one that she seemed to have copied from Brelisha. Netra had often wondered if she practiced that look in front of the mirror.

"That took you long enough."

"I was—"

Gerath waved off the rest of her words, clearly not interested in another excuse. "Go help Owina. She's in the garment room." Her eyes narrowed. "What's wrong with your arm?"

Netra dropped her hand quickly. Whatever happened, she sure didn't want to talk about it with Gerath. "Nothing. Bumped into something, I guess." She tried a self-deprecating smile. "You know how clumsy I can be."

Gerath just frowned at her and Netra realized that she must blame her for this unexpected trip to Treeside. *I'm not the one who's making you go,* Netra wanted to say. *I don't even want you to go. I'd rather go alone.* But she didn't. She'd just get into more trouble and that was something she couldn't afford right now. Not with a chance to finally do something so close. So she mumbled something conciliatory and left the room.

Her walk down the echoing hallways to the garment room wasn't exactly hurried. Helping Owina in the garment room could only mean one thing: another ceremony. Which one was it this time? The Feast of Dead People She'd Never Heard Of? Good Mother, did they ever do anything else around here? There were so many holy days and rituals and ceremonies Netra couldn't count them all. They just blended together in one big blur, each one duller than the one before it.

The garment room stood at the end of a hallway in a back wing of the Haven. The doorway stood open, candlelight spilling from it. She stopped at the edge of the light and held her forearm up. In the dim light she could just see a faint purplish blotch on her left forearm. Was the flow that touched her tainted somehow? Was that even possible? She shivered, reliving the moment, and hurried into the room, not wanting to be alone.

The room was small, made smaller by the boards nailed over the broken-out windows. In the center of the room was a lone table, a pair of stubby candles burning fitfully on it. Lying on the table were a number of fanciful garments. Owina was sitting on a bench, a needle and thread in one hand, squinting at a white garment streaked with every color of the rainbow. The garment's hem was tattered and one of the sleeves had begun to part ways with the rest of it. All the ceremonial outfits at Rane Haven were in similar shape. It had been a long time since there'd been money to replace any of them.

In stark contrast to the moth-eaten garments was Owina herself. Even on a rough-hewn bench in a barren room, Owina managed to look, if not elegant, at least prim and neat. Her hair was tied neatly back and secured with a pair of plain wooden combs. Her brown robe fit well; somehow she managed to make what looked like a loosely-tied sack on everyone else look like a tailored gown on her. Her back was straight, the movements of her slender fingers graceful as she turned the ceremonial garment this way and that. Netra had always thought she looked like she belonged in a big house somewhere, married to a rich trader or even a nobleman. More than once she and Cara had speculated on what could have possibly led a woman like Owina to join the lowly Tenders. Of course, they never asked her outright. Tenders left their past lives behind when they joined the order. It was considered very improper to ask another Tender about her past.

Netra didn't have a past. At least not before the Haven. Where the other women had either been discovered through Testing as young girls or had come here on their own when they were older, Netra had been born here. All she knew about her parents was what she'd been told: they were traders passing through, her mother died in childbirth and her father left her here to be raised as a Tender.

"There you are. I was beginning to wonder what had become of you," Owina said, without looking up.

"You're not the only one."

Owina raised her head, a consoling smile on her lips. "I know you don't want to do this, Netra. I know you'd rather be outside looking at the stars or something. But I need your help or I'll never finish tonight."

"It just seems like such a waste of time," Netra said, taking a seat on the bench and poking at the garments stacked on the table.

"Ceremony often does to the young," Owina said gently. "It's not until you get older that you see the importance of such things."

"How can these empty motions ever be important?"

"That's all you think they are? Empty motions?" The prim woman shook her head almost sorrowfully. "It's all in how you look at them, I suppose. But what seems empty to you is comforting to some of us."

"I don't see how."

Owina set the garment she'd been working on down and turned toward Netra. "Sometimes the storms of life grow too strong and threaten to sweep us away." She touched her hair and looked down, the perfect picture of the demure lady. "When that happens, ceremony and ritual give us something solid, something comforting, to cling to."

Netra started to reply, then thought of the yellow flow in the mists again and closed her mouth. "Oh," she said softly. "I never thought of it that way."

And, oddly enough, she found it to be true—in a way. During the next hour as she sat there in the silence broken only by a word of direction here and there by Owina, or the rustling of clothes as they finished with one costume and moved to another, Netra did find herself calmed. Slowly the encounter in the mists faded back, pushed away by the humdrum of the routine, and when at last they were finished and she pushed back from the table to leave, she found that it didn't quite seem as frightening as it had before.

"There," Owina said, patting her hand and smiling kindly, "it doesn't seem as bad as all that now, does it?"

"Thank you," Netra said, looking at the small woman, her face so smooth even though she had to be in her fifties. For a moment she was tempted to tell her what had happened. She needed to tell someone. But then Owina took up the needle she'd set down on the table, put it in its case and stood, gathering up the costumes—"Go on, I'll take care of it from here."—and the moment was gone.

Netra made her way back through the dark, echoing halls towards the room she shared with Cara. Her friend was sitting at the room's only desk, copying from a tattered, leather-bound book onto an old slate. Cara looked up and smiled at her, but then she saw the look on Netra's face and her smile slowly faded.

"What happened? Something happened out there, didn't it?"

Netra sat on her bed heavily, feeling suddenly very tired. "I don't know." Her hand went to the purplish mark again.

"Did you do something to your arm?" Cara got up from the desk and came over to the bed. "Let me see." She took hold of Netra's arm. "What is this? It looks strange. Did you burn yourself or something?"

"Not exactly," Netra admitted. She leaned back against the wall and told her friend what happened. Cara was the only one who knew she could go *beyond*, so she wasn't surprised by that part of the story, but her expression grew awed when Netra told her how she went deeper, past the mists, to the point where she could *see* the *akirmas* of Brelisha and Siena.

"I didn't know you could do that, Netra."

Netra shrugged. "Neither did I. Not until tonight anyway." She took a deep breath. "But that's not all of it." She touched the mark on her arm again. Was it her imagination, or did the skin feel kind of cold to the touch? "I *saw* something else in the mists. It was a flow of Song, but not a normal one. It was yellow, not golden like they're supposed to be. It…touched me."

Cara's eyes went very round and she seemed to stop breathing. Abruptly she jumped up. "You have to tell Siena right away."

"No."

"What do you mean, 'no'? Netra, something attacked you *beyond*! That's not even supposed to be able to happen."

"I never said it attacked me."

"Well, it did something to you. Look at your arm!"

"It doesn't hurt anymore." It really didn't, Netra was sure of it. Any lingering ache had to be in her imagination. "If I go to Siena with this now, I'll be up half the night, explaining. Surely it can wait until tomorrow."

Cara just stared at her, her mouth working slowly. "Are you crazy? That thing could have…it could have poisoned you."

"It didn't poison me," Netra scoffed, though the thought made her a little nervous now that she considered it.

"But you don't know!" Cara's face was anguished. "Oh, Netra, I couldn't bear it if something happened to you. I just couldn't." Tears were gathering in the corners of her eyes.

"Come on, Cara, sit down," Netra said, taking her arm and pulling her down to sit beside her on the bed. Now she was feeling a little embarrassed. If there was one thing she found difficult to manage with her friend, it was Cara's propensity to burst into tears over every little thing. "You're getting too worked up. I feel fine, I really do."

"Then what can it hurt to tell Siena? Can't you at least have Karyn look at it?" Karyn was the Haven's best healer.

"It really can't," Netra admitted. "But I still want to wait until tomorrow."

"But why?" Cara fairly wailed.

"I just…I want some time to think it over first."

Cara hung her head and then she did cry, silently. A little awkwardly, Netra put her arms around her friend. Things like this always made her feel so out of place, as if she never quite learned how to deal with them. Cara was so gentle and delicate, so pretty, so…feminine. Next to her Netra felt almost crude, taller than all the other Tenders except Bronwyn, her hands and feet big and ugly, not small and pretty like Cara's.

"It will be okay," Netra said, and repeated it a few more times as if that would make it true.

In time Cara's sobs subsided and she looked up at Netra, her face streaked with tears. "Are you sure you feel okay?" she asked.

"I'm sure," Netra said, and tried a smile she hoped was reassuring. "Trust me, Cara. You know I always land on my feet."

"Except for that time you fell out of that tree and broke your arm."

"Except for that," Netra admitted.

"You'll tell Siena in the morning? You promise?"

"Of course I will, only…let me tell her in my own time, when it's right for me, okay?" However she broke this, she knew it was going to cause problems. Brelisha would be furious that she hadn't told her she could go *beyond*. She'd grill her for hours and then come up with a thousand more boring exercises for Netra to practice. Why did everything have to come with so much regimen and discipline? Why couldn't she be allowed to just enjoy the Mother's gift and leave it at that? A new worry occurred to her then: what if Siena changed her mind about letting her go with Gerath to Treeside? She couldn't bear that.

Later, after Cara had gone to bed, Netra stood before their dresser, and took the tie from her braid. She ran her fingers through her hair and then began to brush it. It was so thick and coarse that if she didn't brush it every night it turned into a hopeless nest of knots and tangles. When she was done, she removed her brown robe and hung it on a hook on the wall, feeling, as always, relief at being rid of it. It was so cumbersome, so bulky. Wearing it was like wearing a horse blanket. Trousers made so much more sense, were so much more practical for crawling around in the desert.

Fortunately for her she did own a pair of trousers and an old cotton shirt that laced up the front. She went into Tornith alone one time, without permission, and traded some crystals she'd found for the clothes. She kept the clothes hidden in a cloth sack tied to a tree behind the Haven and she changed into them secretly whenever she went for her longer walks. She wasn't concerned about any of the other Tenders seeing her. They hardly ever walked more than a stone's throw from the Haven.

She pulled on her nightshift and sat down on the edge of her bed, looking again at the purplish blotch on her left forearm. Despite what she'd said to Cara, it did frighten her. Something far outside the realm of the ordinary had happened to her tonight. She shivered, wondering what would have happened if she hadn't been able to get away from that sickly yellow flow. As always when she was upset, her hand went automatically to her *sonkrill*, hanging around her neck. Hers was not dead and empty like the others, she told herself. It was aware, just like the *sonkrill* of old; she was sure of it.

Netra touched a scar on her right forearm and thought of her Songquest, undertaken more than a year ago. She had been young for a Quest, and at first Brelisha refused to even consider it. But she took her case to Siena and the Haven Mother overruled Brelisha, saying that it was not up to them to decide who was old enough to receive the Mother's blessing. After the prescribed cleansing and purifying rituals, Netra set out on her own.

Her Seeking—that period of time when a Questing Tender wanders the land, guided by the Mother, waiting for the Mother to reveal Herself—lasted for nearly twenty days, far longer than most. During that time she fasted, drinking only water, and praying ceaselessly. To this day she couldn't say where, exactly, she went. Most of that time was a fog. Certain features, a rock, a cactus, a cliff, were very clear in her memory, but she could not say where she saw them.

At one point she stumbled into a cave. It was dark, but for some reason she could see quite well. Mist blanketed the floor and the weariness and hunger which were her constant companions were gone. She felt weightless, almost insubstantial, but extremely lucid and aware. Knowing that this was where she was meant to be, she sat down to wait for her spirit guide.

Sometime later her spirit guide appeared, in the form of a huge rock lion with glowing eyes. It stalked towards her, the mists swirling with its passing. She was frozen by the sight of it, utterly overwhelmed by its presence. She could still remember clearly every detail of its appearance, the green-gold hue of its almond-shaped eyes, the silver coat, every hair tipped with white, like a layer of frost.

When it turned and walked away she followed. They went deep into the cave, walking for what seemed like hours. Finally, the lion stopped and Netra looked around her. There were no bones on the floor, as she had been taught to expect. Then she looked closer. Lying on the bare stone floor was a single rock lion claw. She picked it up and held it in both hands, mesmerized by the pure, simple beauty of it. Dimly she was aware of the spirit guide circling her.

The spirit guide moved faster and faster, until it was a blur. Suddenly it stopped and roared. The sound echoed around the cavern.

As the echoes died out a whistling, howling noise started in the upper reaches of the cavern. A beam of fierce blue light stabbed down out of the darkness and struck the claw.

A different sound, like the roar of a waterfall, joined the first, and a beam of deep emerald light lanced down and struck the claw as well.

After that came a deep rumbling, like the movement of stones deep beneath the earth, and a blazing red light struck the claw.

Netra stared in awe as her hands were surrounded in a nimbus of light. From the corner of her eye she saw the spirit guide leap forward and slash at her. Pain streaked down her arm and she cried out, her eyes going to the line of blood welling on her forearm. Then, from the wound came a thin beam of white light—her Selfsong—mingling with the other three lights. Their combined light was so bright it was hard to look at, but at the same time she could not look away. The colors blended together, coalescing into a globe of brilliant golden light that surrounded her.

In time the lights faded away and Netra looked up to see that her spirit guide was gone and she was alone. She realized then that she was seated on the ground near the entrance to the cave. Did she simply imagine it? But there in her hands was the claw and when she held it up she saw a faint amber light glowing in its depths. She held herself very still, listening very closely with her heart, and it seemed she could hear the smallest whisper coming from it.

Over and over as she made her way slowly back to the Haven she stared at that light, but before she was home it had faded away completely. There were many exclamations over the claw, for rock lions were very rare and one had not appeared to a Tender as a spirit guide in a very long time.

But in the Selfsongs of the other Tenders Netra heard disbelief and knew several of them did not believe it was a *sonkrill* at all, that she had simply stumbled across it and told the others she was led to it by a spirit guide, to save herself the shame of returning empty handed. She could not blame them for feeling that way, knowing that some of them had done that very thing.

She never told any of the others what she had seen, or about the rock lion clawing her, not even Cara. She explained the scratch away as an accident on the return trip, caused by her own weakness from lack of food. She knew they wouldn't believe her if she told them the truth, but that wasn't why she kept it secret. She kept it secret because she was convinced that the Mother had marked her, because she was special, because she was destined to do great things in Xochitl's name. She had a feeling that if she shared it with others, the magic of it would slip away through her fingers.

Since then she often woke up in the middle of the night and held her *sonkrill* before her, looking for that glint of amber. It was never there, but that did not mean she had imagined it. It was simply waiting for the right time.

She traced the scar with her finger reverently. With this scar, the Mother had marked her as her own.

A chilling thought came to her then:

Had some other god marked her tonight as well?

Jolene was waiting when Siena went outside later that night to get a breath of fresh air before going to bed. She stood alone by the stone bench underneath the willow tree, her perpetually tousled black hair and dark robe making her a shadow in the moonlight. The bandages on her hands were very white.

"I need to talk to you, Haven Mother."

"I know," Siena said wearily, not surprised to see her. *I should have stayed in my room*, she thought. *I'm not ready for this.* Abruptly she asked, "How did you burn your hands?"

"I couldn't find my way back. I couldn't break free of the dream," she said softly. "I grabbed hold of the hot stones." Jolene raised her head. "Do you believe what the dream powder showed me was true?" Jolene asked hesitantly.

She had been at Rane Haven for ten years and still Siena didn't think any of them really knew her. She was a solitary figure, driven by voices and visions none of the rest of them could hear or see. Siena suspected the others were harsh on her sometimes because she made them nervous. And there was something unsettling about her. It was as if she wasn't quite all there, as if part of her were off somewhere else, beyond a curve in the world that the rest of them would never know.

Siena made herself move closer and laid her hand on Jolene's arm. "I want to say that you haven't told me enough to believe or disbelieve." She hesitated for a moment and drew a deep breath. The slope she stood on was turning into a cliff. "But somewhere in my gut is a feeling that you did see truth and that what you saw is further proof of what I fear is happening."

Jolene lowered her head, and her hair hung down about her face like a shroud. Her voice when it emerged was distant, lost. "I saw the abyss. I...I—" and here she choked on the words, "saw down into it."

She trailed off and Siena's grip on Jolene's arm tightened in alarm. Jolene saw down into the *abyss*? The abyss was the netherworld. It was what Xochitl and the Eight reached into to create the prison. The Book of Xochitl said the abyss was the complete antithesis of the normal world, utterly hostile to it. She wanted to squeeze so hard that Jolene would scream, run away, anything but continue. More than anything, she didn't want to hear what the woman would say next.

"Haven Mother, I...the abyss is leaking into our world."

Now Siena needed her grip on the woman's arm to keep herself upright. The night spun around her. Bad enough the thought that the prison was breaking, that Melekath was returning to the world, but *this*? Could this be the reason for the dissonance she'd been hearing in LifeSong recently?

"You must be mistaken." The words were feeble. They did nothing to deny the fear that gripped Siena.

Jolene hung her head and said nothing. There was nothing left to say.

CHAPTER 27

Netra woke up the next morning with Cara shaking her. "Okay, okay, I'm awake," she mumbled. "Is it morning already?"

Even in the dim light, Cara's face looked pale. "I said your name twice and you didn't even move. I was afraid that…"

"I'm fine, I'm fine," Netra said, giving her a reassuring smile. "Just a little tired."

"How's your arm? Does it hurt?"

Netra looked at her forearm. The purplish blotch was hardly visible. The events of the night before had faded as well, so that they seemed hardly real. "It feels fine."

"Are you sure? When are you going to tell Siena?"

"One thing at a time," Netra said, swinging her legs over the edge of the bed and pushing her hair back out of her face. She stood up and stretched. "Let me wake up first."

"But you will tell her today, won't you?" Cara hovered next to her, looking like a mother waiting to catch a sick child if she should start to totter.

"Of course I'll tell her. Just let me do it in my own time, okay?"

Cara's soft eyes looked into hers for a long moment and then she nodded. "I just don't know how you can be so careless about this. First Jolene uses the dream powder and burns her hands, then something attacks you *beyond*. What's happening?"

"I don't know," Netra said. "I don't think anyone does. But I think it's going to be all right. Have a little faith, my sister." She gave Cara a hug, wondering the same thing herself. What was happening? Is this it, Xochitl? she wondered. Is this what you have been preparing me for? She found, to her surprise, that she didn't feel scared. In fact, she almost felt excited. Anything had to be better than the mind-numbing boredom that ruled her life. And what could be better than a chance for the Tenders to redeem themselves in the eyes of their god?

"We better get going or we'll be late for morning vows," Netra said, releasing her friend. Cara nodded and brightened a little. She liked morning vows as much as Netra did.

Outside it was still the gray light of predawn, but the sun was nearing the horizon. Already the slopes of the Firkath Mountains above the Haven were painted golden with the first rays. The chapel was a fairly large stone building set off from the Haven itself, encircled by tall willow trees. Though it had clearly once been an impressive building, with a spire, high, arched windows and elaborate stone work, it was gradually falling apart, surrendering to the ravages of time. Some of the stained glass windows were broken and had been boarded up. There was a hole in the roof and one corner, where the ground underneath was too soft, had sagged.

The inside looked no better than the outside. Lighter patches on the worn wooden floor showed where pews had once stood—long since sold for the expensive wood in them. Gone too were the ornamentation and artwork. All that remained was a statue of the Mother standing behind the altar, and one of her arms was broken off. The other Tenders were already gathered inside, some already kneeling, most standing about, yawning and rubbing sleep-filled eyes. Netra knew that most of them didn't want to be here. During the winter several of them had gotten together to ask Siena formally to either change the morning vows to once a week, or move them to later in the morning. Siena curtly told them no and, to her credit, for once Brelisha backed her up.

Siena knelt just before the altar, her head bowed in prayer. Next to her was Jolene, who was nearly face down on the floor, her bandaged hands stretched out before her in supplication.

As the first rays of the sun poured through the chapel windows Siena raised her arms and said, "Mother, hear our vows."

The women went to their knees and together they spoke again their vows:

"I vow never to kill, never to take a life.

"I vow never to stand by while life is lost without doing all I can to prevent it.

"I vow to nurture and protect all life, for every living thing is part of Xochitl's creation and it is all sacred to her.

"I vow to pay any price, to make any sacrifice in fulfillment of my duties to Xochitl and all she has created.

"My life for the land, and all its creatures.

"This is the will of the Mother, which I will never again forget."

Always they were the same words. Every day, always reminding themselves, hoping against hope to recover what had been lost for nearly a thousand years. The vows were born in the dark years following the fall of the Kaetrian Empire. They came about as the remaining Tenders of Xochitl faced the horrifying reality of what they had become, how far they had strayed from the Mother's path.

The morning vows finished, Siena led them in some hymns. Netra and Cara loved these hymns and poured their hearts into them. Netra always clasped her *sonkrill* to herself during them, feeling her connection to it, reliving the wonder of its creation. Sadly, Netra was aware of how different this was for most of her sisters. There was no intensity, no depth, to the words they sang. They only mouthed the words. Their hearts were elsewhere, remembering some slight from the day before, wondering what was for breakfast, if the garden would have to be watered again today.

Every day it was like this. Netra felt keenly their distance, the way disillusionment and despair grew like weeds in their hearts, and every day she feared that as the years passed she would become like them. That for her too, the words would lose all meaning, her *sonkrill* would become only an empty relic, *beyond* just a mist-shrouded, unfriendly place, filled with currents she could not touch.

Netra remembered a night when Karyn said outright that Xochitl had abandoned them for good, that they would never be forgiven. Hoping otherwise was pointless, she said, and no one argued with her.

Is that how I will become some day? Netra wondered. Will I give up on the future and spend my time in the past?

Netra finished clearing away the dishes from breakfast and stood for a moment outside the back door to the kitchen, looking at the morning. It was time for her daily lessons but she didn't want to go inside yet and be cooped up for another beautiful day. The sky was clear and blue. Though the season was young, the heat of summer was already beginning to make itself felt. The birds, which had been so noisy only a half hour before were quieting down, settling in the shade. Off at the edge of the large garden she saw a coyote pause on its way to hole up for the day.

She envied the animal, free to roam at will, without lessons to attend or chores to do. At that moment she wanted nothing more than to follow its tracks as it faded back into the desert. To spend the morning watching the stink beetles trundling through the dirt, or the speedy striped-tail lizards as they raced from the shelter of one bush to another. It was tempting, but she consoled herself with the knowledge that tomorrow she would be going to Treeside at this time, and it would be stupid to do anything to risk that. Already Brelisha would be wondering where she was, sharpening her tongue for her arrival.

With a sigh, Netra let the door close and headed for the old library, which adjoined Brelisha's bedroom. The Haven was lacking in many things, but books were not one of them. They completely lined two walls of the room. The room, as always, was dim, since Brelisha kept the shutters closed to avoid the chance of any sunlight falling on the books and aging them. All of the books were extremely old and brittle and she and Cara had been enjoined many times never to touch any of them without permission. If there was one rule Netra actually followed, it was that one. There was little in them that interested her half as much as any given hillside or dry wash. She wouldn't even come in this room at all, if she didn't have to. Cara, on the other hand, could often be found in here when she wasn't busy at her chores, a book open on the table before her, studying some forgotten bit of information or lore.

Cara was already seated at the round table when Netra entered. Brelisha was standing at one of the bookshelves, with her back to the door. Netra stealthily made her way to her seat. Without turning around, Brelisha said, "As though I wouldn't notice that half my students were late."

"Sorry, Brelisha," Netra said, resisting the impulse to make a face at her back. She'd learned through experience that Brelisha had a way of knowing when she did that. "I was busy—"

"Save it," she said curtly, cutting her off. "Whatever it is, I'm sure I've heard it."

"Well?" Cara whispered, when Brelisha continued standing with her back to them.

"Well, what?" Netra whispered back.

"Are you going to tell her?"

Netra groaned. She should have known Cara wouldn't let it go easily. "I'm going to tell Siena. Later." In truth, she had decided to keep it to herself until after Treeside. She didn't want to do anything to jeopardize that trip.

Brelisha came over to the table carrying a slim black volume. Her lips were pursed and she held it with two fingers only, as if it was distasteful to her.

"We're going to read from this today."

"What is it?" Cara asked, craning her neck to see the cover. "It looks like…" She paused, a surprised look on her face. "But I thought you said we'd never read the Book of Sorrows." Cara had asked Brelisha once before if they could study the book and had been soundly rebuffed. The Book of Sorrows, Brelisha had informed her, was false. It directly contradicted an important tenet of the Book of Xochitl, which contained the wisdom of the Mother herself.

"I did." Brelisha frowned at the book.

"Then why…?"

Brelisha gave each girl a hard look. "If Jolene is more than just a fool woman poking her nose where it doesn't belong, if anything she thinks she saw is true, then black times are coming. We have to learn everything we can."

Cara's eyes went wide and she instinctively clutched Netra's hand under the table. Netra was shocked too. It wasn't like Brelisha to fly off in a panic. She had only the harshest criticism for people who worked themselves into a fit without being sure the facts were complete.

Brelisha opened the book and began to read.

They were filing out to the chapel for the ritual—every woman encumbered by the bulky gowns and costumes required for the ritual—when the rider galloped onto the Haven's grounds. He reined the horse towards them, and he didn't slow down but came straight for them as if meaning to ride them down. There were cries from some of the women as they scattered. But at the last moment the rider hauled back on the reins and the horse skidded to a stop in a cloud of dust.

He slid off the horse and stood there looking at them, clearly trying to decide who the leader was. He was a stocky man, with the calloused hands and weathered features of one who has spent his life in the sun working hard. His eyes settled on Brelisha and he stumped over to her, taking off his shapeless hat as he went. "Beg pardon, Sister. I don't mean to interrupt, but I've a problem and none else can help me." His words were deferential, but his tone was not. His tone was harsh, almost angry. He was not happy about being here.

"You'd do a lot better not riding in here like the Gray Slayer himself, scaring a bunch of women." Brelisha hadn't moved a foot when he raced up; she stood now with her arms folded and her eyes blazing.

Then Siena stepped up. Putting one hand on Brelisha's arm she said softly, "What she means to say, sir, is how can we help you?"

"I've a bull shatren. My best one. He's foaming and he keeps pawing at the ground. His stomach's hurting him bad. Been like this for two days and he's starting to go down. We're going to lose him, I know it. I've tried every remedy I know and the bloodletter's had his hand but none of it's any good. So I came to you, thinking maybe you would have some luck with him. Can't hurt anyway." Now Netra knew why he was so angry. The people of Tornith didn't often ask for help from the Tenders.

Brelisha tried to pull her arm away from Siena's grip. "Our healing has nothing to do with luck. It's by the grace of Xochitl and I've a mind to…"

But he never heard what Brelisha had a mind to because Siena cut her off. "That is enough!" She didn't raise her voice, but her tone was forceful and Brelisha subsided. "Now," she said, looking at the man again, "what did you say your name was?"

A new respect slowly dawned in the man's eyes and he turned slightly away from Brelisha. "My name's Brennan." He inclined his head slightly. "And who might I be speaking with?"

"I am Siena, Haven Mother of Rane Haven. And we'll be happy to help you, sir, just as soon as we've finished our ritual dance."

Netra could have sworn the man's eyes popped out slightly when Siena said this. His huge hands wadded his hat up into a bunch. "Let me get this right," he said, biting off each word. "You'll help me after your dance?"

"It's not just a dance. It's the Dance of All Circles," Karyn piped up. Her tone said anyone should know that.

"How long will this dance take?" Brennan asked, taking in their costumes. Netra suddenly felt extremely silly in hers.

"Only a few hours."

"My bull will be dead in a few hours."

"As the Mother wills."

Brennan stood unmoving. Then, with something like a snarl he stomped to his horse and climbed on. "Mery said I was a fool to come. She said you wouldn't help. I should have listened to her."

"Nevertheless," Siena said mildly. "We will come. As soon as we are able. I suggest that until then you pray to Xochitl."

"Sure," he snorted. "And to the moon and the stones in my fields at the same time. For all the good any of them does."

Brelisha opened her mouth to spit something angry out but Siena dug her fingernails into her forearm. "We will come," she said quietly. But the man was already wheeling his horse and he either didn't hear her or didn't care. In moments he was gone.

Netra stared after him and then turned to Siena, disbelieving. "You mean we aren't going to do anything?" she blurted out.

"Weren't you listening?" Brelisha said icily. "Of course we're going to do something."

"But isn't saving a life, any life, more important than some ritual?"

"This is not some ritual," Brelisha said curtly. "It is the Dance of All Circles. And it is vitally important. You'd know that if you paid attention to your lessons."

Netra started to reply, but Siena silenced her with a gesture. "After the ceremony," she promised. "Nothing more until then."

Netra looked after the disappearing rider one last time and then followed her sisters into the chapel, shaking her head.

When the last slow, formal movements had been completed—contrary to its name, the Dance of All Circles did not involve any actual dancing, rather a lengthy series of slow, ritualized steps—and the last lines had been said, Netra headed for the door of the chapel, tugging at the buttons on her gown. There might still be time. They might still be able to save the man's bull. But before she could get outside, Brelisha cut her off.

"You're not going. Owina and Karyn will handle it."

"But no one here's better with animals than I am," Netra protested, looking to Siena for help. Brelisha saw her look and gave Siena one of her own, laden with meaning.

Siena sighed. "No, Netra. Listen to Brelisha."

"But it's not fair," Netra pleaded.

"And fair is you getting your way?" Brelisha said. "Ruining one of our most important ceremonies through your childishness, is that fair?"

Netra suddenly felt the weight of all their eyes on her and she shrank under it. Beside her, Cara was looking down, twisting the hem of her robe in her hands. "Okay," she said softly.

And then she watched from the garden, gripping weeds in both hands, while Owina and Karyn slowly got ready. It took them forever to gather their medicine bags and trudge out of the Haven yard.

When they were gone she threw the weeds down, fighting tears of frustration. They were too late. She knew that already, knew it in her heart. They'd had a chance. Not just to save a life, but to show the people of Tornith that they were worth something. And they'd failed.

A few minutes later Cara came out to the garden carrying a mug of water. She handed it to Netra, who took it wordlessly. "I thought you might be thirsty." After Netra had taken a drink, she said timidly, "Do you feel better now?"

"No, I don't feel better," Netra snapped. "And neither does that man's shatren."

"But surely you can understand what Siena was saying. It was a very important ritual—"

"Stop. I don't want to hear it. I hope the prison cracks like it says in the Book of Sorrows," Netra said bitterly. "Maybe then the women around here would crawl out of their shells and see the sky."

"Netra! You can't mean that!" Cara's eyes were wide and round.

Netra took a deep breath. "I'm sorry. You're right. I don't really want that. And I don't want to take it out on you. I know you're just trying to help me feel better. It's just…just so frustrating being here, watching everyone slowly die."

"I don't think you mean that either, Netra. Not really. It's not that bad. This is our home. This is our family. We have a good life here. Why can't you just be happy with what we have?"

"I don't know," Netra said honestly. "I just have this feeling that there's supposed to be something more. There's supposed to be some purpose to our lives. Without a purpose, what are we but a bunch of women waiting for the years to come and claim us? I want to serve Xochitl and her creation. I want to live the vows we take every morning, not just mouth them." She felt tears starting to creep into her voice and they angered her. "Forget it. You wouldn't understand."

"Maybe I understand more than you think," Cara replied. She lowered her head and seemed about to walk away, then lifted her eyes in sudden defiance. "Maybe I just don't have the courage you do. Maybe I know there's not much I can do and so I just try to do what little I can. Maybe all I can do is try and make people feel a little bit better by trying to help them in some little way." She closed her mouth and blinked, looking almost surprised at her own words. Then she spun and hurried away.

"I'm sorry!" Netra called after her, but she didn't turn back. Netra sat down on the ground and put her head in her hands. That was stupid. And cruel, she told herself. She was only trying to help and I had to go and attack her. Why would I do that? Why would I strike out at the only one who has always been on my side? She groaned. Was there anything else she could do to mess things up? How much worse could things get?

CHAPTER 28

"I think I see it!" Netra exclaimed, pointing. They were stopped, while Gerath examined an old corn on her toe that was hurting her. Gerath looked up irritably, brushing sweaty hair out of her face. The late spring afternoon was hot, though it was far from where it would be in another couple moons. Gerath squinted at the horizon, then shook her head.

"Right there." Netra pointed again, trying to keep the frustration out of her voice. They could have been there hours ago, if Gerath didn't have to stop every hundred paces. "See? You can just see the smoke. That must be Treeside."

Gerath pulled her shoe back on and stood up, shading her eyes to get a better look. "Blessed Mother, I believe it is. And none too soon. I can't wait to get off these feet of mine. Why Brelisha sent me on this cursed task I'll never know."

Because you're fat and lazy and you never go more than fifty steps from the Haven anymore, is what Netra wanted to say, but she wasn't that dumb. She didn't need that much trouble. Instead she said, "Want me to carry your pack again for a while?"

Gerath peered at her. Her pale complexion had reddened in the sun and Netra knew she would be complaining tonight about sunburn. She seemed about to accept Netra's offer, then frowned and shook her head. "It won't do to have them see me show up looking like I can't even carry my own weight. These people need to respect the Tenders. I'll carry my own pack."

"Okay," Netra said. She started off down the trail.

"Come back here, girl."

Netra stopped and turned around. Gerath was still standing on the same spot, her frown deeper than ever. She snapped her fingers and pointed at the ground at her feet. Netra took a deep breath, then walked back to her, fighting to keep her expression neutral. It was late afternoon already. If they didn't hurry it would be dark before they got there.

"How many times have I told you to walk behind me? I am the elder Tender on this journey. You will stay behind me."

"Yes, Gerath," Netra said meekly. It was becoming harder to keep her anger from showing.

"And...?" Gerath tapped her foot.

"I'm sorry, Gerath." Netra was losing her battle, so she kept her face lowered.

"Good." Gerath picked up her pack. She seemed to spend an interminable amount of time adjusting the straps and buckles. Then she carefully realigned the case containing her *sonkrill*. Netra tried to remember what her *sonkrill* looked like. It had been years since she'd seen Gerath take it out of her room. She found it hard to imagine the heavyset woman ever Questing. She probably never went further than the garden.

Drawing herself up straight, Gerath squared her shoulders and patted her hair into place. Netra almost laughed out loud. Did she think she was getting an audience with the king? They were still more than an hour away from the town—two, probably, the way Gerath walked. Was she going to hold herself like that the whole way?

Limping slightly, Gerath started off again. They hadn't gone far before Netra stepped on the back of Gerath's heel while watching a hawk wheel overhead. The older woman spun on her angrily.

"Watch where you're putting those big feet of yours, girl!"

"Sorry," Netra mumbled. "I was looking at a hawk." The comment about her feet stung. So they were a little big. So what? She was taller than every other Tender at Rane Haven except Bronwyn. What good would little feet do her?

"You'd like to have broken my ankle." Still grumbling about girls too young to buckle their own shoes, Gerath started off. Netra let her get a few steps ahead before following.

I am too tall, she thought miserably. Too tall, too awkward, too plain. What she wouldn't give to look more like Cara. Next to her, Netra felt like a horse, all big feet and coarse hair. Cara was as slender and finely made as a china vase. Her hair was blond and soft. Netra pulled on her own hair. It was reddish-brown and her braid was as big around as her wrist.

Netra thought back to last year, when a peddler had come by the Haven. She was in a nearby ravine, crawling on her belly through a haldane thicket, trying to track a lizard through the dust, when she heard the peddler call out, announcing his presence. When she came running up, there was the peddler, standing at the back of his horse-drawn cart, all the Tenders gathered around oohing and aahing over his wares. He sold new pots and mended old ones, but he also sold bright bits of jewelry, hand-carved combs and bolts of cloth. He even had a small hand mirror, set in carved ironwood.

But Netra didn't see any of it. She didn't care much for such things anyway. What caught her eye was his son. The young man was about her age. He had long, black hair and forearms that rippled with muscle as he lifted packages out of the back of the cart. He lifted his head as she approached, looked her way, and smiled.

Suddenly Netra, who had never cared at all how she looked, felt very self-conscious of the leaves in her hair, the dust on her clothes. Desperately she ran her fingers through her hair, trying to force it into some semblance of order while she smiled waveringly back at him.

Then Cara came up beside her and she knew with awful certainty that he wasn't looking at her at all.

He gave Cara a tiny hairpin, carved to look like a dove, while Netra ran and hid in the Haven. Cara saw how much it hurt Netra, and that night she tried to give the hairpin to her.

Even now, a year later, Netra winced at the memory.

"Watch it! You're kicking dirt all over me!"

Mumbling apologies, Netra pulled up just before she stepped on Gerath's heel again.

"Foolish girl. Always daydreaming. You need to plant your feet in the here and now and stop wasting your time mooning. I swear, I don't know why Siena... "

Gerath droned on and on, carefully listing all of Netra's faults and what should be done about them. Finally, Netra just stuck her tongue out at her back, and immediately felt better. So what if she was big and ugly? She was here, getting to go on her first real journey, while Cara was still stuck with Brelisha, memorizing those boring old histories. It was a beautiful day and she was outdoors. There was a lot to be happy about. Realizing that Gerath had finally paused for breath, Netra said dutifully, "Yes, Gerath."

That appeared to satisfy Gerath and she shut up, concentrating on maneuvering her sore feet along the rocky trail. Netra watched her trip over a rock jutting out of the ground, then snag her robe on a limb. She shook her head. Wasn't this woman supposed to be a Tender of Xochitl? For that matter, few of the Tenders at Rane Haven did any better outdoors that Gerath did. They were all supposed to be Tenders of the Arc of Animals. How could they all be so awkward and out-of-place outdoors?

It was because they all spent too much time indoors, Netra decided. If she were Haven Mother, she'd make it mandatory for everyone to be outside for a certain number of hours every day. Get off their fat behinds and get out, even just to work in the garden, instead of making the younger Tenders do it all. She couldn't help smiling at the thought of the complaints that would cause. Brelisha would be apoplectic. She'd get red and thump her wrinkled fist on the table.

"But I'd make them do it anyway."

"What's that?" Gerath said. "What would you make who do?"

Netra clapped her hand over her mouth.

"Speak up, girl. What would you make who do?"

The old stubbornness that had gotten her in trouble so many times before suddenly flared up inside Netra and before she could stop herself she blurted out, "My name is Netra. I'm not a 'girl', I'm a full Tender."

Gerath stopped like a log that has just run up against a boulder in mid-stream. Slowly she turned, her fists on her broad hips. "What did you say?"

Netra meant to apologize, she really did, but when she opened her mouth what came out was "I don't like being called 'girl'. I am a Tender, same as you." *And more of one than you'll ever be.*

Gerath eyed her up and down as if she were a stranger she'd never seen before. "You have a difficult time with respect, girl. You always have; I've always said it. Why Siena babies you I don't know. You've needed a good, stout switch for too long now." When Netra tried to speak she raised one chubby finger and silenced her. "No. Not another word. I am the senior Tender on this mission. I say what goes and what doesn't.

"And you don't." She pointed at a flattened boulder beside the trail. "You will wait here until my work in Treeside is done and I return. Is that clear?"

"But, Sister—"

"No buts. I am done troubling with you. You will sit there and think of how to mend yourself. If you do not argue, if you do not move from this spot, when we get back to the Haven maybe Brelisha will not go so hard on you. Though I doubt it."

She turned and stalked away, every inch of her bearing righteous and indignant. Netra considered throwing a rock at her, then threw herself down on the boulder. She fumed and muttered for the next few minutes while Gerath disappeared from sight over the next rise.

Then she jumped to her feet, pulled up the hem of her robe and tucked it into her belt so it wouldn't twist around her legs so easily. Leaving the trail, she took off at a fast trot, taking a course that would lead her around to the side of Gerath and to the village before she got there. She didn't care what the old hag said. She'd come this far and she was going to see Treeside.

The hamlet of Treeside sat on the slopes of the Firkath Mountains, right at the line where high desert scrub oak, manzanita and jojoba gave way to the pines and firs that dominated the upper reaches of the mountains. It was situated in a narrow ravine. A nameless stream ran down the ravine, through the town, sinking into the ground and disappearing long before it struck the desert floor.

Treeside's security lay in its remoteness. It was far from any of the rough roads that ran between the cities of Atria, as the lands making up the remnants of the old Empire were collectively known. It possessed no mineral wealth and no discernible arable land other than a few tiny plots along the bottom of the ravine. Its inhabitants eked out a living with their sheep and goats, augmented by what little they could grow or scratch out of the surrounding landscape. They had little to do with the outside world and they liked it that way.

It was nearing sunset when Netra reached the town. She was, to say the least, disappointed when she crested the edge of the ravine and looked down on Treeside. The towns of Tornith and Tark—the only other towns she'd ever been to—were not exactly fairy tale cities, but they were impressive compared to Treeside.

There were less than a dozen buildings in Treeside, mean structures of roughly-stacked stone with lodge pole roofs. They sat huddled together around a wide spot in the stream like old men too tired to wander off to die. Nearby was a stone corral for penning the sheep and goats.

But the way Treeside looked was the least of her disappointment. The town was so ordinary. This was where Jolene's vision sent them? It didn't look like anything had ever happened here. It didn't look like anything ever would happen here.

Netra crept closer, using great care to stay hidden. It wouldn't do to have Gerath arrive and find the people of Treeside shouting and pointing to where she was crouched on the hillside. She peered off down the hill. Gerath was just visible, plodding up the trail. In front of her was a small boy, running towards the village with news of their visitor.

Soon the residents of Treeside were gathering and Netra had a chance to see them better. There were about thirty of them and they were dressed in cured leather rather than cloth. Netra's interest perked up. These were not people spending their days indoors as the Tenders at Rane did. Clearly they were living closer to the Mother than most, taking only what the land could give and no more. Some of the men carried weapons but they were not iron. Chipped stone spearheads and arrowheads. Netra almost growled in frustration. How she would have loved to talk to these people. There was so much she could learn from them.

She ducked lower as Gerath approached but there was no need to worry. Everyone in Treeside was staring at the newcomer and Gerath herself was busy trying to look regal and imposing. Netra had to stifle a laugh at the sight of her. She'd taken off her traveling cloak to reveal her brown Tender robe and was holding the hem up with one hand, trying to keep her back straight and her face emotionless, all while maneuvering across the rough, uneven ground.

Netra actually did laugh when Gerath tripped and nearly fell, barely catching herself in time. Then she started moving closer. She had to hear this. Netra made her way to a tangled pile of boulders on the hillside overlooking the village. She was able to find a spot in them where she could watch what was happening without being seen herself.

Gerath stopped before the assembled villagers and drew herself up haughtily. She had taken her *sonkrill* out of its pouch and it hung around her neck, a nondescript piece of gray-white bone. Hers was not one of the real ones.

"I am the Tender Gerath, from Rane Haven, and I have come to Test your daughters for their ability to hear LifeSong." Netra raised an eyebrow. She had wondered what Gerath would say and it appeared she was acting as if this were an ordinary Testing. "Any found worthy can come with me, to be raised in the ways of the Mother," Gerath said regally.

There was a long moment of silence while the Treesiders stared at her. Then they all burst out laughing.

Gerath looked like she'd been hit between the eyes with a club. Her mouth worked while a slow flush crept up her neck.

"Perhaps you do not understand," she managed finally.

A man stepped forward. He had grizzled gray hair and his animal hide clothing was dyed with streaks of red and black. In his ears were many earrings of what looked to be carved bone.

"We understand, Tender." His speech was difficult to understand, but it was the same language. Brelisha had taught Netra that during the time of the Empire, all peoples of the Empire were forced to switch to a common tongue and by the time the Empire fell, the switch had been long enough that it had become the first language for most people.

"You will take none of our women away," he continued, and now there was a hardness in his eyes. "Foolish woman of Xochitl. We remember the past, what you did to us during the Empire. You will not shadow us again."

"You are confused. We never…"

"Go." Now he pointed his spear at her and the threat was palpable.

Suddenly, Netra heard something approaching through the trees on the far side of the village. She looked up just as something huge shouldered its way through the trees, snapping limbs and trunks, and stepped into the village.

CHAPTER 29

It was twice the height of a man and it stood on two legs, a creature of reddish granite, like stone brought to life. Long arms ended in blunt hands like small boulders. Its legs were the thickness of tree trunks. It roared once and then ran into the village. For all its size, it moved fast, running bent over on all fours using its hands to help propel it. It was among the villagers before they could react, while they stood gaping in stunned disbelief. There it paused, the huge head swiveling as if searching for something. A deep gash ran diagonally across its face, taking out one eye and slicing across its mouth. From the depths of the gash came a flickering red glow.

Abruptly the villagers' paralysis broke and they scattered. It ignored them.

Gerath stood frozen a short way away, her mouth open. The massive head turned towards her. Netra wanted to scream at Gerath to run, but there was no air in her lungs.

"Tender of Xochitl," it growled, its voice the crunch of stone on stone. "Your god did this to me. I can't find her, but I found you." It took a step towards her.

With a small cry, Gerath fell back and held up one hand.

The monster bent and slammed its fists into the ground. The ground shook, so hard that Gerath fell down.

She scrambled to her feet and ran.

For another moment the monster paused, sniffing the air. "You are weak, helpless." A parody of a smile crossed its shattered face.

"Time to die."

It ran after her and when it was only two strides from her it leapt into the air and landed full on her.

Gerath only screamed once.

For one long, frightening minute the monster stomped on her remains and howled in mindless rage while Netra looked on, stunned and horrified. When its fury was spent it straightened and looked straight at the pile of boulders where Netra was hiding.

Netra shrank back into the boulders, into a gap between where two of them leaned against each other, her heart pounding. She could no longer see the monster. Surely it couldn't see her.

The monster sniffed the air. "I smell your Song," it grumbled. "You can't hide."

Netra cowered amongst the rocks, shaking. Raw power radiated from the monster, the force of it palpable, as if a forest fire was closing on her. Every instinct screamed at her to run but when she looked around she realized there was no way out except the way she'd come in.

She was going to die.

"You are weak too," it said, in its gravel voice. "You have forgotten the power your kind used to hold." It slammed its fists on the ground, hard enough that the boulder pile shook and several stones came loose and rolled down the hillside. Netra clamped her hand over her mouth to keep from crying out.

"Now you die too." She could hear its ponderous footsteps as it shambled toward her. It did not hurry, knowing its prey could not escape.

"Please, Mother," Netra prayed in a whisper. "Please help me."

As she prayed, she put her hand into her robe and fumbled for the *sonkrill* that hung around her neck. When her fingers made contact with it, a sudden jolt ran through her, the normal world fell away and she unexpectedly found herself *beyond*.

The mists of *beyond*, normally placid, were being whipped furiously, as if a fierce wind was blowing from the monster. Through the mists, Netra could *see* the monster as it approached. There was no glow of an *akirma* to mark its presence, only a cold darkness limned in the faintest of red glows.

The stone monster was only a few strides away. She was out of time. Panic rose in her, making it hard to think. She pressed back deeper into the gap.

All at once she had a feeling she was no longer alone. She turned her head. She could just *see* a glow in the mists off to the side. It seemed to be a four-legged creature. Then she knew what it was.

It was her spirit guide, the rock lion she had encountered during her Songquest.

With the realization of its presence, Netra felt a strange calm come over her. The panic receded and she could once again think clearly.

She looked back at the stone monster and remembered something Brelisha had taught her, about the powers of the old Tenders. By focusing Selfsong in their hands, they were able to take hold of flows of LifeSong, which were otherwise ethereal and couldn't be touched.

But Netra knew that even if she could manage it, there was no way she was strong enough—nor did she have the training—to channel enough power to even slow the monster down.

It was hopeless. Unless…

A crazy idea occurred to her. Doubtful that it would work, but what choice did she have?

The stone monster reached the boulders. It bent to sniff at the gap where she was hiding. The gap was too small for it to get its body in, so it reached in with one huge hand. Netra squirmed backwards as far as she could go. Its fingers groped blindly mere inches from her face. Its arm withdrew.

Netra stared at her hands, willing her Selfsong to gather there.

Nothing happened.

The monster put its shoulder against one of the boulders and began to push. The boulder shifted. Dust drifted down around Netra.

Panic rose up inside her once again. Netra's vision wavered and she almost slipped out of *beyond*.

Focus! she told herself.

With a crunch of stone, the monster pushed the boulder aside, far enough that it could now force its way in.

Netra blocked out the sound, blocked out the terror, focusing on her hands desperately.

They began to glow faintly.

Quickly Netra took hold of the flow of Song that was attached to her *akirma*. With a jerk, she ripped it away from her.

The effect was immediate. It was as if she jumped into a depthless black pool of freezing water. Light and air were gone. She gasped, utterly bereft, adrift in emptiness.

The monster stopped. It turned its head side to side, sniffing for its prey. "Where are you?" it growled. "Where did you go?"

Netra lay there, knowing she was dying. Cold was seeping into her. The light of life within her was going out. She could feel the severed flow nearby and more than anything she wanted to reach for it.

The monster roared and slammed its fists into the boulders. Chips of stone flew in all directions.

There came a loud, coughing growl from the forest nearby. Even in the midst of her suffering, Netra knew that sound. It was a rock lion.

The monster turned toward the sound.

The rock lion growled again.

The monster struck the boulders one more time, then walked away into the forest.

Netra waited as long as she could, until her Selfsong began to flicker and she knew she was about to die, then she groped for the flow of Song, missed it, caught it, and pressed it to her. Light and air and life returned in a rush.

On her hands and knees she gasped, trying to get a hold of herself. She was trembling violently and blood pounded in her ears.

Staggering upright, she looked one more time at the broken form of Gerath lying down below, then she stumbled down the hill, toward home.

CHAPTER 30

Unable to sleep, Siena rose when the night was still black. She drew back the curtain that enclosed the alcove she slept in and stepped out. The stone floor was cold under her feet. Pulling her nightdress close around her, she went to her desk and lit a candle. The Book of Xochitl lay on the table open. For a moment she paused over it, her eyes running over the words that had brought her solace so many times.

But they were only ink on paper now, guttering candles ready to puff out before the storm. Suddenly angry, she slammed the book. The action took something out of her and she leaned against the desk, trying to keep her panting from turning to sobs.

"What comes for us, Xochitl?" she whispered. "Where are you when we need you?"

As always, there was no answer. Taking the candle, Siena left her quarters and went out into the common room. It was a huge room, with a high, domed ceiling. A large sycamore tree grew up in the center of the room, flowers and other plants crowding around its base. Leaded glass skylights were set into the domed ceiling, providing light for Tenders and plants alike. No one knew how to make that glass anymore—no one within reach of Rane Haven anyway—and two had broken over the years, their panes replaced with crude plaster.

Rane Haven had been built by Roxin Delanteran during the height of Tender power, in the last century of the Empire. A powerful and influential Tender, Roxin had been exiled from the imperial court, sent out here to the middle of nowhere. But she had not lost everything and she had used her still-considerable wealth to see that she and those women who were exiled with her did not live in squalor. Years of inadequate maintenance had stolen much of its grandeur, but it was still an impressive building and Siena liked to walk around the rooms in the early morning darkness, gazing at statuettes set into alcoves in the walls, or admiring an old mosaic set into a ceiling. The candlelight was friendlier than the harsh daylight, softening broken edges, hiding cracks and glossing dulled colors.

As Siena stood before the sycamore tree she noticed something she had not seen before, what looked like a black stain low on the trunk. She held up the candle and went closer. The stain seemed to be oozing some sort of dark fluid with almost a purplish hue to it. Siena reached out to touch it but a sudden sense of wrongness assailed her and she pulled her hand back and rubbed it on her nightdress. She peered closer at the dark wetness. It stank of decay and it almost seemed—

A sudden pounding at the front door made her jump.

Alarmed, Siena hurried down the hallway. "Who is it?" she called, not unbarring the door.

"Let me in! It's me, Netra!"

Hurriedly, Siena unbarred the door and opened it. Netra fell into her arms, sobbing. Her robe was torn, her hair in wild disarray. There was a long scratch down the side of her face. Siena looked over her shoulder into the faint light of early morning. Netra was alone.

"Netra." Siena gave her a little shake to get her attention. "Netra, where is Gerath?"

"She's...dead," Netra choked. "It...killed her."

Dread filled Siena's heart. So the nightmare was beginning in earnest. She helped the young woman back along the hallway to the common room, wondering how she would ever find words to comfort her when she had none to comfort herself. She sat down with her on the hearth and then just held her, not speaking, waiting until Netra was ready to speak on her own. In truth, she did not know if she was ready to hear what Netra had to say. Gerath was dead, and she, Siena, had sent her to her death. *What have I done?* Curious faces began to poke into the room, but Siena warned them back with a shake of her head. Netra had been through enough already. She didn't need everyone standing around staring at her. The faces left grudgingly, until only Brelisha remained, her arms folded over her chest. But she came no closer.

At last Netra's shaking subsided and she pulled away from Siena. Her eyes tried to find Siena's and failed. Siena took Netra's hands and held them, forcing herself to appear calmer than she felt. There was no place now for her own fears. Netra needed her. Everything else must wait.

"It was…some kind of monster." Her voice was raw. "It…jumped on Gerath…she…didn't have a chance." She shuddered and squeezed Siena's hands so tightly it hurt.

"It's okay, Netra. You're safe now." Even to Siena the words sounded hollow.

Netra's eyes were shadows. Fatigue and horror etched her face. The scratch was livid in the dim light. "No, I'm not. None of us are. Nowhere's safe from…from that thing."

Siena felt the weight on her heart grow heavier and she had to fight to keep her voice even. "Tell me what happened from the beginning."

"We…we were almost there, when Gerath got mad at me and told me to stay behind. But I went ahead anyway. It wasn't fair of her." Some of Netra's natural defiance seemed to assert itself and she sat up straighter, but she still didn't meet Siena's eyes.

"It's not important now," Siena murmured.

"I hid. I was watching when she got to the village." Now she did look at Siena. "They laughed at her when she told them she was there for Testing. They just…laughed." For a moment she forgot her horror, reliving this.

Then she winced, as if something struck her. "Then it came. It…it was looking for her. Looking for us! It didn't even go after anyone else, it just wanted to kill us because we're Tenders." She pulled her hands away from Siena and wrapped her arms around herself. "Why would it do that? Why does it hate us so much?" She turned her haunted gaze back on Siena. "Why did Xochitl send us there? Why did she want Gerath to die?"

It wasn't Xochitl who sent you there, Netra. It was me, was what Siena wanted to say. "What was it, Netra? What did it look like?"

"Like…it was made of red granite. There was a deep gash across its face. It was huge."

"Are you sure it wasn't a bear or some other wild animal?" Siena asked this without hope. She already knew it wasn't. Her own sense of foreboding was like bile in her throat. She clutched at straws, knowing they would break under her.

"I would know a bear or any other animal," Netra said angrily. "You know me better than that. And you didn't…you didn't *see* what I did. It had no *akirma*. No flow of Song was connected to it."

"You *saw* it? You were *beyond*? But you can't go *beyond* yet. I just asked Brelisha about it…"

Netra looked away. "I've been doing it for a while now. I was going to tell you."

Siena looked at her skeptically. Going *beyond* took a great deal of concentration. She couldn't imagine how Netra could have done it while some monster was attacking her.

As if knowing what she was thinking, Netra drew out her *sonkrill* and clasped it tightly. "I didn't do it on my own. My *sonkrill* helped me."

"Your *sonkrill* helped you go *beyond*?" That was even harder to believe.

"I touched it and I was there. And then it helped me hide from the creature. Without its help I'd be dead like..." She trailed off with a sob.

Siena gaped at her. "It helped you hide from the monster? How can that be?" Something suspiciously like hope wanted to flare up inside her.

"I know how it sounds, but it did. I really believe it," Netra said, somewhat defiantly. "I'm not making it up."

"No," Siena said weakly, "I mean, I believe you. It's just...a lot to take in at once." Did she believe? It seemed impossible. Netra had been through a terrible ordeal; she might have imagined almost anything under the strain. But she *wanted* to believe. If Netra's *sonkrill* helped her then it might mean that Xochitl was finally listening to them once again. Now, when they needed hope most of all. "You need to rest now," she said, standing and taking Netra's hand. "We can talk about it more later."

Netra allowed herself to be helped to her feet. "What are we going to do?" she whispered. "It hates Tenders. What if it comes here? What if it followed me?" She shot a frightened look at the windows, as if expecting them to burst inward at that moment.

"Don't worry about that now, Netra." She led Netra to her room. Netra burrowed under her blankets and turned away as soon as she lay down on her bed. Siena looked down on her for a moment, wishing there was something more she could do, some solace she could offer. But the truth was that she was just as frightened as this girl and she had no idea what they could do, what they should do. She motioned to Cara, who was sitting wide-eyed on her bed, and together they left the room. Siena shut the door softly behind them.

"What happened, Haven Mother?" Cara's hair was still tangled with sleep and her face was pale. "Where's Gerath?"

"I'll tell you when I tell the rest. Go and gather them now, if there are any who are still sleeping."

Most were already coming out of their rooms, those that were in this wing anyway. Cara ran off to the other wing of the Haven to get the rest. In a few minutes they were all gathered in the common room. They were eight in all.

Siena waited for them to get themselves settled before she spoke. "Gerath was killed," she said. A stricken silence settled over the room and eyes went to the sagging chair that Gerath always sat in.

Jolene put a bandaged hand over her mouth and choked out, "I'm sorry. So sorry." Her eyes filled with tears. "It's my fault. I should never have—"

"Stop it," Siena said sternly. "It was my decision. I sent them there, not you." *Mother forgive me. I sent Gerath to die.*

"What happened?" Bronwyn asked quietly.

"They were…they were attacked." Her legs felt weak suddenly and she sat down.

"By what?"

"Some kind of monster apparently," Brelisha interrupted. "Really. A monster. That girl has too much imagination. I told you she should not be allowed to go. I told you the whole thing was a bad idea." The bony woman's chin quivered as if the very idea of a monster outraged her and she fixed Siena with an accusing glare.

"Brelisha. Please." This was already hard enough. Siena didn't need Brelisha making it harder. "This is not some flight of fancy. Whatever her other faults, Netra has a clear head. And she's not a girl anymore, she's a young woman."

"Then it must have been some kind of wild animal. A bear perhaps," Bronwyn said.

"Netra's probably seen more bears than all of us put together. I don't believe that and neither do you. If she says some kind of monster attacked them, then I believe a monster attacked them, hard as it may be to believe." She thought of the Book of Sorrows then. *Around him came legions of dark, twisted creatures…*

"But a monster?" Donae said. She was a thin, nervous woman. "All unnatural creatures were banished by the Mother during the Banishment, when Melekath and his spawn were sealed away. It says so in the Book." She looked to the other women for support. A couple nodded with her.

"And what if the prison has cracked?" Siena felt the quiver of fear inside her as she voiced every Tender's nightmare aloud for the first time.

The Tenders reacted as if she'd stuck them full of cactus needles. All traces of sleepiness were gone now. Immediately the room was filled with the babble of voices. Cara turned white. Brelisha just glared at her.

"Stop," Siena said. When the babble continued she rapped her knuckles hard on the table. "Be quiet!" she yelled. Gradually the others subsided.

"I'm only bringing this up as a possibility." She looked at the women around her, wondering how many of them had also noticed the dissonance in LifeSong. Jolene caught her eye and Siena was reminded of their conversation in the garden a few nights ago. *What if it's not Melekath? What if it's poison leaking through from the abyss? Which is worse?*

"Just because Netra thought she saw a monster is no reason to jump to the conclusion that Melekath is breaking free of his prison," Brelisha said. "There are many other, less drastic explanations."

"Name one."

Brelisha looked surprised. "Well I...I don't know right off hand. But I'm sure that careful questioning of Netra will give us some place to start. Some of us will need to go talk to the villagers as well, find out what they saw."

"Would you just stop denying it!" Siena shouted suddenly, all the worry and the fear of the past few days boiling over at once. "Stop lying to yourself! You've heard the dissonance too. You've read the Book of Sorrows. What else can it be?"

The others stared at her, shocked by her outburst. Even Brelisha looked a little surprised. But then she drew her haughtiness around her like a blanket. "I don't know what else it could be. But I won't run off like a scalded cat without more information. We need to know more. We should try a *remembering*." A *remembering* could be used to look into a person's memories, play them back and experience them again. It was difficult and these days required two Tenders to manage it. Unfortunately, it was also often painful for the one undergoing it, especially since she had to relive the experience as if it was happening for the first time. "Then we could see and judge for ourselves what she says she saw."

Siena sagged back in her chair. "That is a lot to ask of her after what she's been through."

"Then what else do you think we should do?"

213

"What if we join in a circle and look into the River? If the prison has weakened, we may be able to *see* it there." All events in the world of living creatures and plants, their causes and resulting effects, were reflected in the currents and ripples of the River. No one Tender had the strength or the stability to go that deep but, by joining together, they just might be able to boost one deep enough to do it.

"No one has gone that deep since the days of Empire," Brelisha said. "It's too dangerous. If our joint control isn't perfect, if we push too hard, we could lose hold of whoever we sent there. She would be torn apart. Even if we did manage it, which of us has the knowledge to read the currents there?"

"I still don't—" Siena began, but a voice from the doorway cut her off.

"It's okay, Siena. I'll do it."

"Netra!" Siena said, coming out of her chair. "You need to be in bed, sleeping."

"I can't sleep," Netra said, coming in to stand before them. There were hurts in the angles of her face that no young woman should carry. Her eyes rested on Brelisha. "Gerath only screamed once," she said.

Brelisha paled, her hand coming to her throat.

"We can do it tomorrow," Siena said. "You need time to—"

"No. Let's do it now. Let's get it over with."

The Tenders filed out to the chapel quietly, not speaking or looking at each other. The same chill gripped them all. Siena was last, having gone back to her rooms to get her *sonkrill*. Brelisha looked at her oddly as she entered the chapel with it hanging around her neck, but said nothing. Siena went to the front of the room and stood for a moment looking up at the statue of Xochitl. The Mother looked back at her, a serene expression on her face, her arms reaching out, palms up. As a young girl she had always felt as if the Mother was reaching out to embrace her every time she entered this place.

That was so long ago, she thought. Everything was so different then. Back then the statue had had both its arms. Now one of them was broken off at the elbow. Siena remembered clearly how that had happened. It was nearly thirty years ago, during a time of terrible drought. Just when the drought was at its worst, a plague of anthraxis descended on the area. Like grasshoppers, but equipped with a stinger and jaws strong enough to tear flesh, the anthraxis devoured everything edible and then turned on the people.

When the swarm moved on, a crowd of irrational, frightened farmers and townspeople showed up at Rane Haven. The toll of drought and pestilence had been too much for them and they'd come in a mob to burn out the only ones they could blame.

Ivorie was still the Haven Mother then, a beautiful woman in her prime, with a strong, calm voice. She met them at the door of the Haven. Siena remembered that day clearly, how strong the Mother was in Ivorie. With only the power of her voice, the Haven Mother calmed the mob and sent them home, but not before several attacked the chapel and tipped over the statue of Xochitl.

She turned around and saw the others kneeling in a circle, with Netra and Brelisha in the middle. She remembered kneeling here in this very room, beside Netra's mother, whispering as they waited for morning vows to start. Like Netra, Shakre always took the vows to heart too. And when she was around, it was easy to believe, so strong was her faith. Looking back, she saw that it was the loss of Shakre that was the beginning of the end of her faith.

Netra lay on her back, staring up at nothing. Siena knelt on the other side from Brelisha and took Netra's hand. "Are you sure?" she whispered. Netra didn't respond, but just closed her eyes. Siena thought how much she looked like her mother at this moment and her heart hurt.

"Then let us begin," Brelisha said. Siena heard a difference in her voice and she looked up. The woman was staring down at Netra, her perpetual frown lessened. Gently she laid a hand on Netra's forehead, and Siena felt something ease inside. Regardless of how she might act, Brelisha was not heartless or unfeeling. She was, after all, one of the Mother's chosen, and she had helped raise Netra nearly as much as Siena had. In her own way she cared for her as much as Siena did.

Siena lowered her head and took her *sonkrill* in both hands, wondering as she did so why she had it with her. It had been a long time since she really believed it helped focus her will or made her any stronger *beyond*. But she could not stop thinking about Netra's assertion that her *sonkrill* had come to her aid when she most needed it. She turned the lifeless bone in her hands, staring at the familiar smooth surface, and prayed that it might help her some in what was to come.

She was surprised to look up and see Brelisha take her *sonkrill* from a pocket in her robe. Brelisha caught Siena looking at her and gave her a defiant look before turning her eyes away. She'd heard what Netra said too. She longed to believe as much as Siena did. Brelisha's *sonkrill* was the lower jawbone of a badger, the tough, strong little animals who could sometimes be found down here in the desert. And unlike some of the other Tenders, Brelisha had not simply gone out and wandered around until she found some bones that she could bring back and claim had been shown to her by a spirit guide. She had Quested four times before she had been visited by a spirit guide and led to her *sonkrill*. If there was one thing a person could say about Brelisha, it was that she was persistent. Siena sometimes thought she would still be Questing to this day if she'd hadn't found her spirit guide.

Siena began a soft chant to calm her mind, and heard Brelisha join in. She let the words of the chant quiet and center her thoughts. Calmness descended over her as the fears and worries of the world were put away where they could not touch her. For her, going *beyond* was like opening a door. She visualized it in every detail until it was clear in her mind. Then she opened it and entered. Her body slipped away and the mists washed over her. She continued deeper into *beyond* and the mists parted, revealing the glowing outlines of Brelisha's *akirma* nearby.

Even had Brelisha stood in a crowd Siena would have had no trouble identifying her. She had seen Brelisha's *akirma* many times and recognized it easily. *Akirmas* were not just a uniform white glow. There were traces of other colors mixed in, along with patterns distinct to each individual. Most noticeable in Brelisha's *akirma* were the streaks of dull red, the anger that Brelisha carried with her always. She clung to her anger fiercely, and Siena suspected that the other woman needed her anger to face the daily battle that was her life, much as a soldier needed his sword.

The next part was harder. Siena concentrated. Dimly she was aware of her *sonkrill*, clutched tight in her hands. She would take any help she could get from it now.

Siena and Brelisha were still chanting. Now, as if on cue, each altered her chant, infusing it with Selfsong, brought forth from within. What sprang forth from them was a *song* of joining. It was one of the simpler *songs* of power, one of the few remaining to the Tenders.

In response to the *song*, a tiny thread of light emerged from Siena's heart, while another came from Brelisha. The two threads met and Siena felt the small charge as contact was made. They were joined now, the two of them able to pool their abilities and strengths, though only one could be the focal point of their efforts. Brelisha's Selfsong was stronger, but Siena had better control, making her the logical one to lead here. As she'd expected, Siena had to wrest control from Brelisha. Letting go just didn't come naturally to Brelisha.

Together they turned to Netra. The glow of Selfsong within her *akirma* was brighter than theirs—what was only a small blaze within the two older women was a furnace inside Netra.

At first the white glow of Netra's *akirma* was undisturbed, with only faint colors and hints of patterns moving across its surface. Then a shifting blotch of fiery orange and cobalt blue surfaced. That was what they were looking for. The orange was pain, the deep blue, sorrow.

Siena acted quickly, before the blotch submerged again. From the thread of light that stretched between the two older women a new thread sprouted. It reached out and settled on the blotch.

Siena paused. So far, so good. Now came the painful part, for them as well as for Netra. Already she could feel Netra's pain and she recoiled from it. She gathered herself, squeezed her *sonkrill* tighter, and then she pushed, going deeper into the memory. At the same time, she released some of her Selfsong into the connection.

This was where being joined with Brelisha was essential, for Siena did not have the strength to do this on her own, nor would Brelisha have had the fine control necessary to do this without harming Netra. Pushing too hard, or releasing too much Selfsong into another person's *akirma*, could seriously damage them, on any or all levels: physically, mentally or emotionally. What she needed to do was to revive the memory—like blowing on the embers of a dying fire—without adding so much Song that it flared up and burned out of control, becoming a forest fire that raged through Netra's *akirma* and perhaps even flashing back through the connection and harming the two older Tenders as well.

Even from the depths of *beyond*, Siena heard Netra cry out.

Then the memory came back to life and from inside Netra they relived the experience all over again.

They saw the monster come out of the forest. They heard what it said to Gerath. Gerath ran, and the monster chased her. But when the monster leaped on Gerath, Netra convulsed and a burst of energy exploded outward from her, flaring back down the thread of light connecting her to the two older women.

Siena and Brelisha were thrown backwards and the link was broken.

Siena opened her eyes to see Karyn bent over her, her brow lined with worry. "I'm okay," Siena said, struggling to sit up. "How is Netra?"

Netra lay on the floor, not moving. She appeared to be unconscious. Brelisha knelt over her, her face pale, tears in the corners of her eyes. Siena had to take several deep breaths, trying to push away the image of the creature stomping on Gerath until she was only pulp, then she crawled over to Netra. Brelisha moved aside and Siena gathered Netra's head into her lap. For a time, no one spoke while Siena rocked back and forth, soothing Netra as she had soothed her when she was a little girl.

Brelisha was the first to stand. Being second in the connection she had not experienced the memory quite as strongly as Siena, but she had gotten enough. She left the circle and touched the remaining hand of the Mother's statue as if to gather strength, then turned to her sisters. They stared up at her, except for Siena, who was still lost in Netra.

"That thing is a minion of Melekath. Of that I am sure." Some of her resolve returned as she spoke and her face hardened. Brelisha was stubborn and opinionated, but she was not blind. Once she was proven wrong, she would change her stance. Once she got moving, she was an implacable force. Now she agreed with Siena, and no one would argue with her. She lowered her head and charged on.

"Furthermore, I believe that thing was one of the Guardians."

A collective gasp went through the little group.

"You all know how much I have studied the history of our order, especially the time of the Banishment." Not only had Brelisha read and reread the books in the Haven's small library, in her younger days she had journeyed to several of the closer Havens to study the books they held. It was no accident that her quarters adjoined the library, or that she was responsible for teaching new Tenders. "What I saw in Netra's memories—" Here her eyes flickered to the young woman lying on the floor, and she winced slightly. "I believe matches the description of Tharn."

Fearful exclamations arose from the Tenders. They looked nervously around them, fearing what might already be coming for them. "What do we do?" Donae whimpered.

"We need to tell the FirstMother in Qarath. Maybe she has received some sign," Bronwyn said.

"Qarath is days and days away. Which one of us will go that far and will it be too late when we return? If we return?" Karyn tried to appear calm and emotionless, but her voice caught as she finished and she shot a glance over her shoulder.

"Maybe we should go to Nelton and tell the king," Owina said.

Nelton was the closest city, only two days away.

"The king is nothing," Karyn snorted. "His power barely extends beyond his own city walls and he thinks of nothing besides his dream potions."

"For now I need help getting Netra to bed. Then we can meet in the common room and discuss this," Siena said calmly, far more calmly than she felt. "It's not as dire as it seems, sisters. I think it's highly unlikely that Tharn is coming here any time soon. Remember, Netra escaped from him, and he did not pursue her here."

She caught Brelisha's eye and they exchanged looks, each knowing what the other was thinking. Both had seen how the Guardian went only for Gerath, ignoring the villagers. The truth was that things were direr than they seemed. The prison truly was cracked. The only real question left was when. When would Melekath be free? When would the Guardian come for them? The others—with the exception perhaps of Jolene, kneeling curled in on herself, her black hair hanging down, hiding her face—didn't know this yet and they didn't need to know. There was no need to send them into a panic.

As she helped Netra from the room, Siena wondered how she was going to keep herself from panicking.

CHAPTER 31

Netra slept straight through until early evening, when she gasped suddenly and clawed her way back to wakefulness.

"It's okay, Netra. It's okay, now."

Cara's hands were cool and soft. She stroked Netra's hair back from her face.

"No. It's not okay," Netra replied. Everything was far from okay.

"How do you feel?" Cara asked.

"Raw. Sore." The side of her face hurt where she'd gotten scratched during her flight. Her whole body felt like one big bruise. But the worst hurts were on the inside. She kept hearing Gerath's scream. Kept seeing that thing coming for her. In her sleep she had run from it over and over.

Cara drew her robe closer about her and shivered. "You were feverish for a while."

Netra nodded, and realized her neck hurt too. The clawed tip of her *sonkrill* was digging into her hand from gripping it too tightly and she forced herself to let go.

A tear slid down Cara's face. "I've been praying for you the whole day."

For once her tears didn't annoy Netra. Her friend's obvious concern made her own eyes well up in response. "Now look what you've done," she said, trying to smile, afraid to cry, afraid she wouldn't be able to stop.

"I was so worried. I must have had Karyn in here six times to look at you. The last time I couldn't find her. I think she's hiding from me."

Now Netra did smile, and it felt good. She squeezed Cara's hand. "How is everyone else?" Cara's eyes showed her puzzlement. "I mean, how are they handling it? Probably building barricades at all the doors, right?" She tried to laugh at her own joke and saw again the monster moving the boulder. Barricades wouldn't do any good when it found them.

"Oh, they're all right. We all are. Siena and Brelisha talked to us for a while and explained how unlikely it was the Guardian would come here."

Netra bolted upright in bed, causing every muscle and bone to cry out in protest. "That was a Guardian?!"

Cara's hands fluttered around her and her pretty face crumpled. "I'm sorry, Netra. I forgot you were asleep when Brelisha told us that was what it was. I didn't mean to scare you."

"A Guardian?" Netra still couldn't quite accept it. Guardians were Melekath's chief minions, his most fearsome demons. They were the worst nightmares of the Book come to life. She had never guessed that that was what that thing was.

"But they explained to us that there was no reason to think it would ever come here after us," Cara said. "After all, you got away from it and that was a long way from here."

"They told you what? But that thing said—" Abruptly Netra broke off. Cara's eyes were widening in alarm and she suddenly realized that the two older Tenders had kept some things to themselves, and why they had done so.

"It spoke to you?" Cara's hand hovered by her mouth. "What did it say?"

"Nothing," Netra said. They were right, of course. There was nothing to be gained by scaring everyone to death. Especially since there wasn't a single thing any of them could do to stop the thing anyway, or even escape from it if it came here.

Except me. I hid from it once. Would I be able to do it again?

The problem was that she wasn't sure she'd be able to repeat what she'd done. She wasn't even sure how she'd done it in the first place.

"I have to get up."

"But shouldn't you be staying in bed? At least until Karyn has a look at you?"

Netra made herself smile and touched her friend's arm. "How about we go find Karyn together and see what she thinks?" Cara still looked unsure so Netra said, "I'm okay, really. I'm made of strong stuff, remember?"

"You are," Cara replied.

She helped Netra up, but after Netra was standing she didn't let go of her arm. Netra walked a few steps and when Cara still didn't let go of her arm she pulled away gently and said, "Really, I'm okay."

The others were in the common room, sitting at the long dining table. They stopped talking and everyone stared at Netra. She felt like a winged pig, some oddity that no one had ever seen before. She wondered if she threw her arms up and yelled "Boo!" if they would all run out of the room.

"Here," Bronwyn said, getting up and pulling a chair out for her. "What can I get for you?" Three people reached for the stewpot at the same time and Donae started pouring her a mug of water.

"I'm okay," Netra insisted, feeling very uncomfortable under all the attention. Couldn't they see that what she needed now was to be left alone? "I'm really not even hungry."

"But you have to eat!" Donae insisted, her voice a little too shrill. "You have to keep up your strength!"

"Later," Netra insisted, gently removing Cara's hand, which had once again attached to her arm. "I promise." She eyed the door leading to Siena's quarters. "I think I'm going to go talk to Siena for a little while first."

"An excellent idea," Brelisha declared, setting her spoon down. She stood up. "I'll come with you."

"But I'd really rather talk to her alone," Netra protested.

"We have matters to discuss," Brelisha said firmly, giving her a look that spoke volumes. She knew more than everyone else, but not as much as she intended to. Netra knew there was no point in arguing further. Not when Brelisha was like this. She held the door open for Netra and then pulled it shut behind them.

"You have your *sonkrill* with you right now, don't you?" Brelisha asked, as soon as they were alone.

"Of course. I always do."

"Good. You have some explaining to do."

"You know, don't you?"

Brelisha stopped and turned to face her. "I know you can go *beyond*."

"I was going to tell you."

"When?"

"Soon. I don't know."

"How soon?"

"I don't know! You would have just given me a bunch of boring exercises to do. It's special to me. I don't want it ruined."

"Those 'boring exercises' are vital. Going *beyond* is not some kind of game. It's dangerous in there and without the proper guidance you could become lost or hurt yourself or worse."

"I know," Netra said, the steam going out of her suddenly. "I was going to tell you," she repeated.

"Netra," Brelisha said, her voice faltering for a moment in a way that surprised Netra. "You must believe me that everything I've done has been for your own good. If I've pushed you hard it's because I see how much potential you have. The Mother has blessed you with gifts that...that are very special. If you only knew how much..." She looked away, and Netra never would have guessed what came next. Brelisha's next words were nearly inaudible. They were broken, dredged up from some nether region of Brelisha's heart.

"How much I envy you. I have worked so hard for so many years for things that just come naturally to you."

Netra stared at her. "I never...I'm sorry..." She glimpsed briefly the full depths of how selfish and immature she was.

"I don't want your apology. I only want your promise that you won't throw away what the Mother has given you."

Netra nodded slowly. "I won't. I promise."

Brelisha stared hard at her, judging the depths of her sincerity. "Good," she said at last, taking Netra's arm and steering her down the hall again. "Now I want some answers."

Siena was waiting for them, sitting at her desk, an odd, tentative look on her face. She gave Netra a hug as soon as she came in and stared deeply into her eyes. Netra felt things welling up inside her again, too much, too fast, and she pulled away.

"Tell me everything," Brelisha said. "Everything."

So Netra did. She sat down on one of the room's two extra chairs and told them how when she touched her *sonkrill* she went *beyond*, how she *saw* the glowing figure of a rock lion.

"Wait," Brelisha said, sitting down in one of the other chairs. "You *saw* your spirit guide *beyond*?"

"I did."

"Are you sure?"

"Of course I'm sure." Was she though, really? She *could* have imagined it.

"You told Siena that your spirit guide helped you hide from the Guardian."

"Well...I'm not sure that it helped me. Not exactly. It was more like

223

it helped me be calm and that was when I had an idea."

Both women were staring at her raptly. "What sort of idea?" Brelisha asked. The intensity in her gaze was a little unnerving.

"It was something you taught us, about how the old Tenders could concentrate their Selfsong in their hands and then they could take hold of flows of Song."

"You took *hold* of a flow?" Brelisha looked like she was ready to choke.

"I did. The one attached to my *akirma*."

"Then what did you do?" Siena asked.

"I ripped it off."

They stared at her. They stared at each other. "But…how come you're still alive?" Siena finally asked. "People can't survive cut off from Song."

"I put it back."

"That's…incredible," Siena said. "It's been a thousand years at least since a Tender could do that."

Brelisha looked suspicious. "Hmm."

Siena turned on her. "You don't believe her? You think she's lying to us?"

"I don't think she's lying to us. But I do think that she nearly died and under that kind of extreme stress people imagine all sorts of things."

"Which doesn't explain how she hid from the Guardian."

Netra felt strange sitting there, listening to them talk about her like she wasn't there, but she kept her mouth shut. She wasn't sure she knew what happened either.

"No, it doesn't," Brelisha replied. "But there may be other, more prosaic, explanations for her survival."

"Such as?"

"Maybe its eyesight is poor. Maybe it was simply unable to find her. Or maybe Tharn wanted her to live, to return here."

"Why on earth would it want that?"

Brelisha shrugged. "We have no way of knowing that. Remember, this is a creature completely alien to us, with motives we can't possibly understand. It might have been following some order given by its master, an order designed to accomplish a deeper purpose that we know nothing about."

Siena sat there for a minute without replying. Then she said, "You choose your explanation, Brelisha. I will choose mine." She pulled her chair closer and took Netra's hands in hers. "I choose to believe you survived because it is the will of Xochitl. The Mother favors you and has chosen you for an important role in the war to come."

"Be careful, Siena," Brelisha warned. "You fill her head with such thoughts but you have no idea what the consequences may be."

"I don't care," Siena replied. "I see this as a message of hope. Xochitl will return to face Melekath and she wishes for the Tenders to help her. We finally have a chance to redeem ourselves in her eyes."

Netra hardly heard her. Her head was still spinning from her earlier words. Was it as Siena said? Had the Mother really chosen *her*? A strange thrill went through her, accompanied by a sense of dread. She had a faint intimation that being special might become a terrible burden, one big enough to crush her beneath it.

"I'm not dead. I desire hope as well," Brelisha said. "But we have been long in darkness and I fear it has not lifted yet."

"Why not just say it, Brelisha?"

"Say what?"

"That you are afraid to hope. That you can't bear the thought of hoping and then finding out you were wrong."

Netra gave Siena a startled look. This didn't sound like her at all. She was normally so conciliatory.

"Maybe you're right."

Now it was Brelisha who surprised her. When had she ever absorbed such pointed words and not retaliated? Brelisha seemed very small and frail suddenly, sitting in her chair with her head down.

"I hope you are," Brelisha added.

"I think it is time we go to Nelton," Siena said. "We need to reach out to the Haven there and share information. If the Tenders are to aid Xochitl in what is to come, we need to stand together."

Some of the fire returned to Brelisha then. "After what happened in Treeside you would risk another life for what might be nothing?"

"No, I wouldn't. That's why *I'm* going."

"And I'll come with you," Netra said instantly.

"Out of the question," Brelisha replied. "You need to rest up and you and I have much to discuss. You need to learn—"

Netra cut her off. "I'm going whether you agree or not."

Brelisha flared at her challenge. "You will not talk to me like that, young woman."

"How do you want me to talk to you? Like a child? Is that it? Because I'm not a child anymore. Is it that you're trying to protect me?

225

Because I've experienced more than any Tender has in a thousand years. Or is it that you want to control me because you're jealous of what I can do?"

As soon as Netra said the last words, she wished she could have them back. She saw how they pierced Brelisha and sorrow struck her.

"I'm sorry, Brelisha. I just..."

Brelisha waved her off and stood. "It is of no importance." She headed for the door. "Do what you want to do. It is what you have always done anyway."

Then Netra and Siena were left there alone together. Netra gave Siena a rueful look. "I'm an idiot."

"What you are is impulsive. But you're also right. You're not a child and these are not normal times." She leaned over and squeezed Netra's arm. "The truth is that I wanted to ask you to come with me anyway."

"I didn't mean to hurt her feelings."

"Brelisha will be all right. She's just upset right now. We're all upset. It's enough to make us all do things we regret."

Netra sighed. "It's just that I can't sit around here right now. If I do, I'm just going to keep reliving that awful scene over and over. I need to move. I need to *do* something."

"What you should do right now is get some rest. I want to leave first thing in the morning."

CHAPTER 32

When Melekath saw the first humans created by the Mother, he was
filled with jealousy. Bitterness grew in his heart until at last he went
away in secret and created the Gift, which he gave to those humans
who were seduced by his lies. But the Gift made them into
abominations. Left alone, they would have destroyed all that Xochitl
had created. She raised the lesser gods to war against Melekath and
besieged the unholy city of Durag'otal. After many great battles the
city still stood. Finally, Xochitl had no choice but to reach into the
earth and seal Durag'otal in stone, imprisoning Melekath and his
spawn. As the prison sank beneath the earth, Melekath cried out a
curse on Xochitl and all who followed Her, his voice shaking the
land like thunder. He swore to break free someday and destroy all
Life.

The Book of Xochitl

Netra and Siena left in the morning after breakfast, taking small
packs and enough food for several days. As they were getting ready to
leave, Netra several times noticed Siena touching something under her
traveling cloak, on her chest. Looking closely, Netra saw the leather
thong around Siena's neck when she turned her head and knew she
carried her *sonkrill*. Siena's Selfsong was calmer than it had been in a
while, some of the fear she had been radiating gone. Such was the
power of hope.

In contrast, Brelisha's Song was brittle and somehow raw. Netra's
sense was that she had slept poorly or not at all last night. She never
once looked at either Siena or Netra during breakfast and didn't react

at all when Siena told the rest of the women where they were going. It bothered Netra to see her like that and she realized then how much she had always relied on Brelisha's iron strength.

It was a beautiful morning. The ground felt good under Netra's feet, the sun welcome on her face. The desert was bursting with life. A jackrabbit paused under a palo verde tree, twitching its ears, and a hawk lifted off from its perch and caught the breeze. Out here, surrounded by the majesty of Xochitl's creation, it was hard to believe Melekath was making plans to destroy it all. In the light of day, it just didn't seem real.

"Brelisha gets mad because I'm always ducking my lessons. She thinks I don't care about anything, but it's not true. That's not why I get out of the Haven whenever I can."

Siena looked at her. "Then why do you?"

"I'm afraid," Netra admitted.

"Afraid of what?"

"Of ending up like the rest of you." Her words trailed off and Netra looked away, fearing she had said too much, that now she had hurt Siena's feelings as well. When would she learn to just keep her mouth shut? "I didn't mean it like that," she added softly.

Siena smiled at her. "I know that."

"It's just that I love this world so much," Netra said suddenly. "There's so much to see, to experience. When I'm out in nature I feel so close to the Mother. I never feel that way when I'm reading some old book. I've never understood how the rest of you can spend so much of your time indoors where it's broken and decaying when out here it's so vital, so alive."

Siena said nothing for a bit, looking around her at the morning as if she hadn't seen it in a while. "I remember feeling the same way once." There was sadness in her voice.

"What happened? How did you lose it?"

Siena shrugged. "Life. The passing of years. They go by faster and faster and then one day you look around and realize you're not the same person anymore."

Netra thought about this as they walked. "I don't want that to happen to me."

"I pray that it doesn't."

After that they walked in silence until Netra said, "Melekath is still in the prison, right? He's not free yet?"

"No. I think we would feel it if he was free."

"Then how come Tharn is free?"

"The Book does not specifically say what happened to the Guardians when the prison was created, so no one knows for sure. But over the years many Tender scholars have speculated that the Guardians were not trapped when the prison was sealed, that Melekath sent them out of the city beforehand."

"Then how come they were never seen before…?" Netra saw again Gerath's death and could not say the words.

"Again, it is all speculation, but some believe that although they were able to flee the city in time, they were caught in the Gur al Krin desert and have been trapped there ever since."

"But now that the prison is weakened they were able to leave?"

Siena nodded.

"Tharn said…" Netra's words trailed off and she swallowed hard. A tear slid unbidden down her cheek. "It said it hates us, Siena. Why?"

"It hates us because we are the chosen of Xochitl and it is a minion of Melekath. It hates us because our forebears stood with Xochitl at the Banishment." Siena sounded like she was reading straight out of the Book.

"I know all that," Netra said. "That's not what I mean. I mean, why does it hate *us*? The Banishment was so long ago. The Tenders who were there are all long dead."

"I suspect it doesn't seem so long ago to Tharn, who is immortal. A prisoner does not forget the prison he lives in—or the jailer who put him there."

"But it wasn't *us*."

"It doesn't matter. Tharn has had nothing to do but hate, nothing to think of but hate, for thousands of years while it waited in the desert."

Netra tried to imagine what it would be like to spend thousands of years trapped in the Krin, hating the ones who put her there. She'd never spent much time thinking about the Banishment. It had never really seemed all that real, just something she read about in a book. Another thought occurred to her. "What about the Children, those people who followed Melekath to Durag'otal?" Netra asked. "What do you think happened to them?"

"They must have died soon after the Banishment," Siena said. "There is no way they could have survived for very long."

"Couldn't Melekath have kept them alive somehow?"

"How? The Book states that no LifeSong can enter the prison. Nothing can live without LifeSong."

Netra remembered what it had felt like when she broke the flow of Song connected to her. Utter abandonment. Despair. Was that how those people felt when the prison rose around them, blotting out the sun? What went through their thoughts? How long did they live afterwards? She shuddered.

"Why did Xochitl imprison them too?" Netra asked. "Couldn't she have just let them go?"

"They were abominations. They betrayed the Mother and chose to follow Melekath into evil."

"But maybe they were just confused. Maybe Melekath lied to them."

"Most assuredly he did lie to them."

"Then why didn't Xochitl give them a chance to repent? She is supposed to be all loving and merciful. Why would she condemn all of them to die?"

Siena shrugged. "I don't know."

"It just doesn't seem fair."

"To us it doesn't. But we do not know her mind. We have to trust that she had her reasons. That's all we can do."

"Now you sound like Brelisha. 'Stop asking questions, Netra. Trust in the Mother.' I don't see what's so bad about asking questions."

"Maybe it's because asking questions leads to doubt. Doubt makes a person vulnerable to Melekath's lies. Maybe that's how he was able to lead all those people astray."

"I guess," Netra said. She didn't feel very convinced. This was another reason why she didn't like studying the Book. Too many parts of it didn't add up, but when she started questioning it, someone was always telling her to stop asking. Have faith, they said. As if having faith meant to stop using her mind and just accept whatever was told to her. What if the Book was wrong?

A squirrel scurried across the road ahead of her and stopped on top of a rock, looking at them with its bright eyes. Being out in nature was so much simpler. Out here it was easy to have faith. There was so much evidence of Xochitl's love everywhere. Out here it all made sense.

Lost in her thoughts, Netra hardly saw Tornith as they entered it. Like Rane Haven, Tornith sat in the foothills of the Firkath Mountains. It was a dusty, sleepy place, the homes built of baked mud bricks and stone. Most of the inhabitants made their living off the herds of shatren and sheep they grazed in the valley, or from the hardscrabble fields that dotted the rocky earth around the town. Although it was still fairly early when they got there, the day was already growing hot. Dogs barked at them from shady nooks under porches as they passed.

As they approached the center of town, Netra looked up and saw a familiar figure come out of a shop and climb onto his horse. It was the farmer who had come to them for help with the sick bull shatren. He scowled when he saw them. Ashamed, Netra turned her face away. He spat on the ground and spurred his horse past them. Siena kept her expression neutral, but Netra could hear the change in her Song, the way it wavered slightly.

The road left town and dropped down out of the foothills to skirt along the edge of the Tark Valley. The valley floor was flat, dotted with waxy-leafed greasewood so evenly spaced that they seemed almost to have been planted, and the walking was easy. Mixed in with the greasewood were mesquite trees and cholla cactus, bristling with long thorns. Small gray birds flitted between the greasewood bushes as they passed and a stripetail lizard darted across the road, pausing in the shade on the far side, its tail curling over its back. Far overhead, a pair of buzzards scribed lazy circles against the vastness of the sky.

By late afternoon they had climbed the rough escarpment that marked the eastern end of the Tark Valley and entered the band of broken, stony hills that separated the valley from the Plains of Dem. As the sun began to slide to the horizon Netra began to get more and more nervous. Every patch of reddish stone was Tharn, every unusual noise was the Guardian stalking them.

"I thought you said we'd be in Critnell by now," Netra said.

Siena stopped and wiped sweat from her face. She was breathing hard and stray hairs had worked their way loose from her bun. "I thought we would. It is further than I remember."

"I'll carry your pack if you want," Netra said.

"No. I'm fine. Just give me a moment to catch my breath. I'm sure we're almost there."

The road led up the bottom of a sandy wash and curled between two low volcanic peaks. The shadows grew longer but still the town did not appear.

"We have to go faster. I don't want to spend the night out here," Netra said. All too well she remembered running through the darkness, afraid that Tharn was chasing her. She had dreamed about it all night.

"We're almost there," Siena panted, holding her side. She pointed to a hill in the distance. "See that black hill? If I remember right, Critnell is at the base of that."

The sun dropped below the horizon as the hill slowly drew closer. More than once Netra realized she had gotten too far ahead of Siena and had to stop and wait for her. Finally, they emerged from a copse of the green-limbed palo verde trees and she could see the outermost homes up ahead.

"Do you think someone will take us in?"

"It is the only hospitable thing to do for travelers," Siena reassured her. "Especially since we carry our own food."

"But we're Tenders…"

"No. We're only two women in brown robes. Keep your *sonkrill* hidden. We'll have no problems." Siena spoke calmly but Netra knew she was nervous.

Critnell wasn't much, a dozen homes huddled up against the black volcanic rock of the hill. But right then it looked like an island in a stormy sea. Netra was holding onto Siena's arm, trying to hurry her forward, when the wrongness struck her and she stopped in her tracks.

"What is it?" Siena asked, and then she heard it too.

The Song coming from the town buzzed and seethed with pestilence, so strong that Netra's skin started to itch and she half expected to see hives all over her arms.

Siena's face went pale and she put her hand over her mouth. "Close yourself to it, Netra," she said.

Netra swallowed against a sudden urge to vomit. Then she began to seal herself off from the poisoned Song. It was normally not that difficult to do, somewhat akin to holding her breath when confronted with a powerfully bad smell like a skunk, but the feeling of sickness was so strong that it was hard to concentrate.

Then she managed to succeed, and the nausea subsided. Now the poisoned Song was like a wasp trapped behind glass, unable to get to her, but still there, buzzing angrily in the distance.

In the town, nothing moved. No fires burned, no dogs barked, no sheep bleated. Netra took Siena's hand and the two women went forward cautiously. With each step she took Netra felt the sense of wrongness increase. The *sonkrill* felt hot against her skin.

They stopped a stone's throw from the first house. It was built of the same black rock as the hill. There was movement inside, a pale smear at a window, and then a woman crawled out of the open door and collapsed on the ground. Even at this distance they could see the blue-black lesions on her arms and the side of her face.

"We have to try and help her," Siena said. She took a reluctant step forward.

"It's too late. There's nothing you can do," a voice said from behind them.

CHAPTER 33

The two women jumped and Netra gave a little cry.

A man about Siena's age stood behind them, holding up his hands. "Didn't mean to startle you ladies," he said. His clothes were simple homespun cloth and he had a large, floppy hat on his head. A large pouch was slung over one shoulder.

Siena had her hand over her heart and was trying to calm her breathing. Netra wasn't sure if she was breathing at all. "Who…are you?" Siena managed finally.

"Just old Dorn." He made an odd movement with his hand, like a bird taking flight. "A breath of wind. A chaser of dreams."

"Do you live here? What's happened to this town?"

"I live…" He spread his hands to indicate the horizon in all directions. "But not there. No. Or I'd be like them. Poor souls."

"What kind of disease could do that?" Siena looked back at the house and shuddered. The woman wasn't moving.

"You think it's a disease?"

"Are you saying it's not?" Siena said.

"You're Tenders, aren't you?"

The two women shared a look. Siena shook her head imperceptibly, but for some reason Netra felt she could trust this man. He was odd, but she sensed nothing hostile about him. "We are."

"Then take another look at the town. What do you *see*?" He was staring at Netra as he spoke, his head cocked to the side, peering out from under the brim of his hat, his eyes oddly bright. "

Netra frowned.

"Go on, lass," he said gently. "*See*."

Netra turned back to the town. Holding herself very still, she slowed her breathing and focused on it. In. Out. When she was ready, she caught hold of an exhalation and let it pull her out of herself. All at once she was *beyond*, the mists swirling around her. She concentrated and went deeper. The mists cleared and she could *see*.

She gasped.

Sickly yellow flows wrapped the town like some cancerous web. There were almost no normal flows of Song visible. On the edge of the yellow web was a dim glow. The dying woman's *akirma*. There was a flash of light as it disintegrated.

Netra pulled out of *beyond*. Siena was staring at her. "What is it, Netra? What did you *see*?"

Netra told her and Siena's eyes widened in alarm. "I've *seen* one of those sickly yellow flows before," Netra added. She looked at her arm. The mark it had made was faint, but still there. "The night Jolene had her vision. I was outside and I went *beyond*. It touched me on my left forearm, right here. It felt like it burned me."

"Why didn't you tell me this?" Siena asked.

"I was going to," Netra admitted. "But I was afraid you wouldn't let me go to Treeside and then…and then I forgot."

"You should have told me."

"I know, I know. I'm sorry."

Siena turned to Dorn. "What do you know about what happened here?"

"We can talk more, but best we go now. Sometimes other things follow those flows, or grow out of them. I don't know which. We don't want to be here either way."

He took them in a wide arc that led around the town. He moved like a much younger man, his steps light and sure. Netra, following him and checking his tracks out of old habit, noticed that he left almost no trace of his passage. She hurried to walk beside him.

"How did you know?" she asked him.

"How do you think I knew?"

"You can *see*?" The idea was astonishing to her.

"Perception is not limited to your order, lass."

"But the Book of Xochitl says that only women, and only those women favored by the Mother, can go *beyond*."

"Is that what it says?"

Netra hesitated. She felt foolish suddenly, like a girl who believes the moon is made of curdled milk. "It's what I was always taught."

"Be careful about what you're taught, lass. Sometimes those doing the teaching have other motives."

"But why would anyone do that?"

"Fear is one reason. Control is another."

"But the Book is the word of Xochitl, given directly to our order before she left."

"Is it now? Because there are some histories that say your Book was written long after she left."

"I...I don't really know."

Siena had caught up with them without Netra noticing. "The Book contains the wisdom of Xochitl. Nothing else," she said.

"Well, there you have it," Dorn said. "The voice of truth."

"I will thank you to keep your heretical opinions to yourself, sir," Siena said in an icy tone.

"It wouldn't do for the lass to get ideas of her own now, would it?" he replied and for the first time Netra heard a darker undertone in his voice. "She might start thinking and then where would we all be?"

"It's not like that," Siena replied.

Dorn came to a stop and he swung around to face Siena. "Then how is it like?"

"Look, we are grateful for your warning," she said. "But I think it is best if we go our separate ways now."

"But why?" Netra interjected. "I want to hear what he has to say."

"There's hope for you yet, lass."

"Stop that!" Siena exclaimed. "I won't have you twisting things around and confusing her."

"Are you confused, Netra?" he asked her in a gentle tone. She nodded. "Maybe it's because you've been fed a story that doesn't hold up in the real world."

"That's it! Netra, come with me. This man has nothing to say that we want to hear."

"Why don't you let the lass make up her own mind?"

"Because what you're saying is the same mix of lies and half-truths that Melekath used to lead the Children astray and I won't have you doing it to Netra." Siena's face had gone red.

"A thousand years since the Empire fell and still the Tenders haven't learned a thing," Dorn said in a cold voice.

"You know *nothing* about us," Siena rejoined.

"Can you both just please stop?" Netra asked. "It's too much. I don't want to hear it right now." She looked from one to the other, pleading.

Dorn was the first to bend. "My apologies, lass. Sometimes I don't know when to keep my own mouth shut."

"I'm sorry, Netra," Siena said, putting her arm around her. "I know you've been through a lot lately. I don't mean to make it worse."

"It's okay," Netra said. "Can we just make camp already? I'm tired."

"I'd like to stop," Siena said. "Do you think we're far enough from the town?" she asked Dorn.

"I can't say for sure," he replied. "But my gut tells me we're okay." He smiled, his good humor returning all at once. "Or it could be I'm just hungry." He patted his belly. He looked around. "There's a good spot in that clump of trees up ahead. How about we make camp there?"

As they walked toward the trees, Netra asked him. "What were you doing there, outside that town?"

"I've been there most of the day. I felt it start this morning and came as quickly as I could."

"Why?"

He gave her a sideways look. "To witness," he said. "No one should have to start the last journey alone. The living should always be near to watch the light leave."

Netra looked over her shoulder. Siena was a few steps back. She spoke in a low voice so Siena wouldn't hear. "How do you go *beyond*?"

He gave her a pat on the shoulder. "It's quite a bit different for me than it is for you, I imagine."

Netra frowned. "What do you mean by that?"

"There's other ways to the deeper knowledge," he said cryptically.

That immediately fascinated Netra. *Other ways?* "What ways?"

"Later," he said. "I've upset your friend enough for now. I say we eat and then, if you're still interested, I'll do better than tell you. I'll show you." He continued on.

Netra stared after him, wondering. There were complexities to his Selfsong that she had never heard before. His Song held a wildness, a raw edge, that she didn't quite understand. Something unusual had mixed with his Song and changed him.

They reached the spot and he had a small cook fire going in minutes. "Try not to let this bother you too much," he said when he had it going. He pulled a dead squirrel out of his pouch, drew his knife and began to quickly, expertly skin it.

"I don't...it's okay," Netra said, trying to ignore the sound of the skin pulling away from the flesh. The Tenders of Rane Haven were of the Arc of Animals and thus didn't eat meat. "It doesn't bother me."

"I'm glad to hear that," Dorn said, cutting the squirrel's head off and setting it aside. He skewered the squirrel and began to cook it over the fire. The smell of cooking flesh reached Netra and she started to feel ill. She had to swallow hard several times to keep from retching. To take her mind off the smell she started talking.

"You said you would tell us more about those strange yellow flows."

Dorn nodded. "They only appeared recently." He looked up from the fire. "You're going to find this hard to believe, but I think someone, or something, is poisoning the River itself."

"That's impossible," Siena said.

But there was something odd about her expression when she said it, and something in her Song as well that made Netra wonder. It was as if Dorn was giving voice to something she already feared and didn't want put into words.

"You saw the town," he said quietly. "That's not the only place it's happening. Tainted flows are popping up everywhere. How else would the poison get into all those flows, unless it was coming from the River itself?"

"I don't know how it got there or what it is, I just know it's impossible," Siena said stubbornly.

"Saying it's impossible doesn't make it so," he said mildly.

"What could poison the River?" Netra asked.

"That's one question, isn't it?" Dorn said. "The other question is why?"

"It's Melekath, taking his revenge like the Book says," Netra said.

"Well, he'd certainly have his reasons for revenge, wouldn't he?"

"What do you mean by that?" Siena was scowling at Dorn.

"I mean if you were imprisoned for a few thousand years, you might want some revenge too. It's only natural."

"Melekath corrupted and perverted people," Siena snapped. "He got what he deserved."

"Did he corrupt people or did he just offer them a different choice?"

"He corrupted them and turned them into abominations!" Siena's voice was rising.

"So your holy book says. But there's other sources say other things. They say the people of Durag'otal just wanted to live in peace and the other gods made war on them for no reason."

"That's ridiculous. What are these sources you speak of?"

"I think you know."

Siena came to her feet. She pointed at Dorn. "You're a Windcaller."

Netra stared at Dorn. A *Windcaller?* Brelisha had warned her and Cara about Windcallers. Windcallers claimed to be able to hear the wind, even call the wind to them. To the Tenders they were fakes at best and blasphemers at worst.

"That I am," Dorn agreed, taking off his floppy hat and setting it on the ground beside him. "You make it sound like a crime."

"It is a crime." Siena's face was flushed.

"Not anymore. Not since the Tenders lost power." He shifted his attention to Netra. "During the days of Empire my kind were hunted ruthlessly, almost to extinction."

"Because of your crimes," Siena interjected.

"And what crimes were those? Asking questions? Maybe the same questions that Melekath and his followers asked?"

"Do you see what he's doing?" Siena said to Netra.

"Faith is a wonderful thing," Dorn continued, "but not if it's used to close the mind."

"See the traps he weaves with words," Siena said.

"There is more to the world than you have been taught, lass," Dorn said gently. "You will never find out who you are and where you fit in this world if you blind yourself." He looked at Siena. "A healthy curiosity is not a bad thing."

"The wrong questions can lead a person into darkness," she snapped.

"Can you two just stop!" Netra blurted out suddenly. "Do you have to fight about this right now?"

"I'm sorry," Siena murmured.

"Accept my apologies as well. We fight an old battle and we have no right to put you in the middle." He pulled the squirrel off the fire and began eating it.

At the sight of Dorn eating the squirrel, Netra started feeling sick again and had to look away. She'd never seen anyone eat meat before.

When Dorn was done he stood. "If you're still interested in knowing about my ways..." He shrugged. "Up to you." He walked off into the desert.

Netra stood up to follow and Siena grabbed her arm. There was worry in her eyes. "Don't trust him, Netra. Don't let him fill you with his lies. That way lies separation from the Mother. He and his kind will never find the way to her embrace."

"How can it hurt to just talk to him? What's so bad about wanting to learn something new?"

"That's what your..." Siena broke off. When she didn't say anything more, Netra left.

"Once you start down that path you may never get off it," Siena called after her.

Netra hadn't gone far when she realized she didn't know where Dorn had gone. She stood in the darkness, quieting her thoughts, listening.

It wasn't long before she was able to pick his Song out of the background. It was definitely unusual. She followed it and in a small clearing she found Dorn. He had something in his hand.

"Can you really call the wind?" she asked.

"Sometimes. When they are willing."

"Who are you talking about?"

"*Aranti.*"

"What are those?"

"Be patient. You'll see." He held out the thing in his hand. It had a leather thong tied to it. It was too dark to see it clearly, but it looked to be bone, or maybe sun-bleached wood, about the size of her hand, irregularly shaped, with a number of tiny holes in it.

On one side of the clearing was a small pile of boulders. Dorn climbed on top of them. He began to swing the thing around his head. The thong was only a couple feet long and the circles the object inscribed were small. But as Netra watched, the circles began to get larger and larger. Soon it was cutting a huge circle in the air, a dozen feet across or more. She blinked. The object seemed to have grown larger as well. It was bigger than a man's head and an eerie whistling came from it. She started to back away and realized she was sitting on the ground, though she couldn't remember doing so.

The wind began to blow. Just a soft breeze at first, it quickly picked up. Chills ran up Netra's back. There were sounds in the wind. Voices. Perhaps even laughter. But utterly alien.

Still twirling the object, Dorn looked at her. Netra thought his eyes were glowing. He pointed at her with his free hand. With one finger he made a tapping motion, for all the world as if he was tapping on a window to get her attention.

Netra felt the taps like small concussions and her world reeled. Slowly she toppled over onto her back. Now she was looking up at the sky, and she could see creatures in the wind.

Formless, ethereal beings, they raced and cavorted in the sky. She smiled. They were laughing, calling to each other, making childlike noises, meaningless and joyful.

How long she watched them she couldn't tell. But at length she saw that there were fewer of them. They were dissipating, and then they were gone. She blinked. The sky was empty. Dorn appeared, looking down at her.

"They are somewhat mindless, at least in the way we understand. They don't care much for what happens in our world."

"Were those *aranti*?" she asked.

"Yes. They dwell in the wind, in the Sphere of Sky. Pieces of their Sphere lie within you and me, within all Life, though so far back we can't separate them anymore. There would be no Life without the Sky, just as there would be no Life without Stone and Sea as well. The Three coming together to form the One."

"What does that mean, the Three forming the One?"

"The Circle of Life borrows from the Spheres of Stone, Sea and Sky. Then we die, and what we have borrowed is returned."

"Are the *aranti* gods?" The question sounded foolish even to her.

Dorn laughed gently and helped her to her feet. "Forget about gods. The term is only a restrictive word for things beyond our understanding. Just know that they exist and they are not the only things beyond your narrow beliefs. There is far more to this world than either you or I realize."

"How do they help you go *beyond*?"

"I don't really go *beyond*, not in the sense that you do."

"Then how do you know the things you do?"

"Sometimes, when I let them, they blow through me and carry me away with them. Not my body, you understand, but my spirit."

"You mean like how the old Tenders were able to spirit-walk and travel great distances?"

"Something like that. When I go with them I can see the world through their eyes and they see far different things than you or I do."

"They know about the poison in Song?"

"They are frightened by it, by what it means. In their hatred, the Guardians open doors that should be left closed. There are things even the most powerful of the Shapers cannot control."

Netra's head was spinning. It was so much information, so fast. She had so many questions she didn't know which to ask first. "What are Shapers? What doors are you talking about?"

Dorn patted her hand. "There are things you are not yet ready to hear. You should go back to your friend now. She worries about you, and for all her narrow-minded views, she loves you. Love is not something to be tossed aside lightly, even when it delivers burdens."

Netra tensed. "You think I'm just a child."

"That's not it at all, lass."

"Then why won't you answer my questions?"

"Because there's still so much I don't know. Interpreting what I learn through the *aranti* is very difficult and I may be wrong about much of it. I don't want to frighten you unnecessarily."

"I think it's too late for that."

"Go now. Keep your mind open." He gave her a gentle shove back toward the camp.

Netra went a few steps and then she had a feeling and stopped to look back. "What is it?" she asked. "You want to warn me of something."

Dorn sighed. "Be careful, lass. You have so much potential and so much passion. You're capable of so much more than you realize."

He paused and Netra said, "That doesn't sound too threatening."

"Passion is a wonderful thing, so long as it does not get away from you. Unchecked, fear and despair can take over. You may wake up one day to find you have gone so far off your path you can no longer find it. You may find that you have become like the very thing you hate."

His words chilled Netra. "There's no way that would ever happen to me," she said, but her words lacked real conviction.

"I hope not. As I said, there is much I do not know."

Siena was already lying down wrapped in her blanket when Netra got back to the camp. Netra dug her blanket out of her pack and lay there on the ground by the dying fire, looking at the stars, feeling very small and insignificant. Only a few days ago the world had seemed a predictable, understandable place, where the worst thing that could happen was that she would be given extra chores as punishment for avoiding her lessons. Now there were monsters loose in the world, terrible prophecies coming true, poisonous flows that wiped out entire villages, and looming over it all, the menacing figure of Melekath.

She thought of the *aranti* Dorn had showed her and in spite of her fears she smiled. Who would have thought such creatures existed? She had been raised to believe that the sum of all necessary knowledge and wisdom was contained between the covers of the Book of Xochitl. And, until recently, she had believed it. Now she didn't know what to think.

Clearly there was far more to the world than she had been taught. It was both frightening and exciting to imagine what else might lie out there, things she had never dreamed of.

CHAPTER 34

"What do you know about the *aranti*?" Netra asked Siena the next morning. They'd been walking for an hour and Siena hadn't said a word. Netra was tired of pretending nothing had happened.

"The what?" Siena didn't look at Netra. She looked older today and her steps were slower.

"The *aranti*. Creatures that live in the wind."

"The Windcaller showed them to you."

"Yes."

Siena sighed. "I suppose it will do no good to try and convince you that what he showed you was a lie."

"A lie? I saw them."

"You saw something. Something a stranger told you were *aranti*. That's all you know for sure."

"You know what else I know for sure? You're hiding something from me. The way you two argued—I think you already know Dorn."

Siena shook her head. "I can promise you I have never met the man."

"Then what are you hiding from me?"

Siena walked to a flat rock beside the road and sat down. Netra joined her. For a couple of minutes Siena didn't say anything, just sat there with her head down. She seemed to be praying. Netra didn't know what to expect, but she wasn't prepared for what Siena said.

"It's time you learned about your mother."

Netra looked at her suspiciously. "What is there to learn? You said my mother died during childbirth."

"It's not true. None of what I told you was true. Your mother was one of us."

Netra gaped at her. "My mother was a Tender?"

"She was my best friend. She still is." The hand Siena laid on Netra's knee was shaking.

It took a long moment for what Siena said to sink in.

"She's...still alive?" Netra croaked.

The words hung in the air between them while each woman grappled with how to handle what came next.

"I think so." Siena stared off into the distance. Then her voice grew stronger. "No, I know so. In my heart I would know if she died. Almost I feel I can hear her Song when I am very still."

"Where is she?" Netra jumped up, as if she could run and find her mother right then.

"I don't know. I haven't seen her since she left."

"Why didn't you tell me about her before? Why did you lie to me all this time?"

"I couldn't. I made a promise. Let me start at the beginning, please. Hopefully it will all make sense then. Will you sit back down?"

Netra eyed her warily, then sat back down.

"Shakre and I were very close. Like you and Cara. We shared everything. She was the best of us, you know. She had such an openness, such an affinity with all life. She could hear subtleties in LifeSong that none of the rest of us could. I think she was open to LifeSong all the time, as if she were constantly *beyond*. She would have been Haven Mother instead of me. She would have deserved it."

"What happened?" Netra could feel the tears in her eyes and she brushed at them angrily.

"She was too much for us. She needed to be in a large Haven, perhaps the main temple during the Empire, or at the side of the Emperor himself. She had too many questions, too much energy. Life in a sleepy Haven out in the middle of nowhere was not enough for her. She was always digging, always trying to find more." She turned toward Netra but still could not meet her eyes.

"One day we heard in town that there was a man living in a cave in the foothills to the west. No one knew where he had come from or why he was there. It was as if he just appeared. People whispered that he was a Windcaller.

"From the first time she heard of him, your mother was fascinated by him. Oh, we'd been warned about Windcallers, but that didn't seem to do anything but make her more interested. One night she told me she was going to see him. Then. That night. She just had to meet him. She'd be back before dawn and none of the others would know she'd ever left."

Siena ran a shaking hand across her face. "Why didn't I tell the Haven Mother?" Her voice dropped to almost a whisper. "Why didn't I go with her? Maybe I could have kept her from...what happened."

Netra couldn't breathe. She stared at Siena, willing her to continue.

"After that she went nearly every night and she came back late, her eyes shining with what she had seen and done. It was as if a new fire was stoked inside her. It flared brighter and brighter every day until I was sure the others would see it. I was miserable. I wanted to tell, to save her before it was too late, but over and over she swore me to secrecy. I could never refuse her. I could never break a vow I made to her.

"Until now."

"They found out," Netra breathed.

"Even a Tender who was blind could not have missed it. She was changed, glowing from within. She began to argue with the other Tenders, saying we didn't know half of what the world was about, telling us we were blind and deaf to the true wonders around us. Finally, Ivorie, the Haven Mother, confronted her and she confessed.

"By then her pregnancy could no longer be hidden."

Netra drew a sharp breath. She felt unsteady.

"Not only had she consorted with a blasphemer, but she lay with him. The other Tenders were outraged. Prinel—you don't remember her, but she made Brelisha look cheerful—would have had her flogged on the spot and driven from us naked, if Ivorie hadn't stayed her hand.

"But there was no denying that she would have to go. Short of taking a person's life, your mother committed the most grievous crime imaginable. I know you don't agree, but Windcallers are evil men. They are followers of Melekath as we are followers of Xochitl. To bear one's child—it was unforgivable. And your mother was unrepentant.

"They locked her in her room while they decided what to do with her. They wouldn't even let me in to talk to her. It didn't take them long to make their decision: she would be exiled, her name stricken from our records. Her name would never be spoken on the premises again. It would be as if she had never existed."

"That's horrible," Netra managed.

Siena nodded. "At the last it seemed to finally occur to your mother what she had done. She threw herself before them and actually begged. Never did I think I would see such a thing. She begged, but not for herself.

"She begged for you."

Now Siena did meet her eyes and the tears there matched Netra's own. "She knew you were a girl. And she wanted you raised a Tender. She begged them to let her stay until the birth, that she would go away then and never trouble us again.

"When she handed you to me and walked away for the last time it was the most painful moment of my life. She never looked back. I've never heard from her since. And until this day I have always honored the last vow she extracted from me: never to tell you of her. She wanted you to think her dead rather than know her shame." Siena was crying hard now and Netra could not stop her own tears.

When she once again had herself under control, Siena asked her, "Do you hate me? For not telling you?"

"No," Netra said, standing up and brushing at her tears. "I don't think so." She wanted to run away. She was breathing hard.

"You see now why Brelisha has always been so hard on you. She is afraid you will follow your mother's path."

"I don't hate you," Netra said, turning away. "I don't hate Brelisha either. But I don't think I can ever forgive you."

Then something occurred to her and she turned back. "You think Dorn is that Windcaller, don't you? You think he's my father."

"I don't know. I never met him."

"I might have just met my father, but I didn't have a chance to ask him because you never told me the truth. How could you do that to me?"

Siena had no response.

Nelton wasn't much, as cities go. The defensive wall was mud, baked in the hot desert sun to the consistency of stone. It couldn't have been home to more than ten thousand souls, scratching by on the arid soil surrounding the city, augmenting their crops with herds of shatren and sheep that grazed on the sparse desert vegetation. A river ran right by the city, except that it wasn't much of a river, being strictly dry sand for most of the year. A sudden, harsh rain could bring the river to brief life, boiling brown and frothy over its banks. But two or three days later it was as dry as ever, only some scattered damp spots and leftover debris clinging to the boles of the cottonwood trees along its banks giving proof that there was ever water there at all.

Still, the water wasn't too far below the surface, especially by desert standards, and with wells and water screws turned by teams of mules, the residents of Nelton managed to bring up enough to support hardy crops and supply themselves with the necessary drinking water.

It wasn't much of a city, but to Netra it might have been Kaetria itself. She'd never been to a town larger than Tornith. She and Siena crested a low ridge and there was Nelton down below, its whitewashed mud brick walls gleaming in the late afternoon sun. To her it looked like a jewel, a perfect piece of quartz stumbled on in the dirt. In that moment her wonder washed away the hurt and confusion that had dogged her since Siena's confession.

"Oh," she said. "Look."

Siena stopped with her and looked down on the city she hadn't seen in twenty years. "Mostly like I remembered it," she said, wiping sweat from her face with a cloth.

"There are so many people. Look at them all." They seemed as numerous as ants, swarming back and forth meaninglessly. "How can so many of them live all together in one place? Don't they feel crowded?"

"Some of them do, I imagine," Siena replied. "Most of them have grown used to it and don't notice."

Netra started down the hill, not too far from breaking into a run.

"Just a moment!" Siena called after her. Netra waited impatiently while she caught up. "Put your traveling cloak on, so no one can see your robe."

"Do you really think we need to? We're going to roast with those things on."

Siena shrugged. "I just think it's best to be careful until we know more about what's going on."

Netra sighed and dug her cloak from her pack, thinking longingly about her trousers and shirt. That's what she'd really like to be wearing. Siena would be scandalized.

"What Arc do the sisters in Nelton belong to?" she asked, digging out her cloak and wrapping it around her. "They're not browns too, are they?"

"The sisters of Nelton Haven are of the Arc of Plants," Siena replied, carefully buttoning her cloak.

"Greens," Netra said. "From the looks of those fields I would think the farmers would be happy for any help they could get."

"Unfortunately, they face the same prejudices we do in Tornith."

"They're probably about as helpful as we are too," Netra replied, thinking of a dying bull shatren.

It was late afternoon when they finally got to the city. Up close the wall had long cracks in it and large chunks had fallen out at the base. The gate was a miserable thing of sagging timbers and dry rot and the only guard paid little attention to the people passing through. He wore a dirty uniform and sat on a rough stool in the shade of the gate, drinking now and then from a large clay jug at his feet. Quite a few people were passing through the gate, all of them heading into the city. Some drove sheep or goats and there were several pack mules heavily laden.

Netra stopped when they got near the gate and put her hand to her temple, a worried look on her face.

"What is it?" Siena asked.

"There's something wrong here."

"Something wrong?" Siena asked, suddenly alarmed. "You mean like Critnell?"

"No. It's not like that. I don't know what it is exactly. Something in the Song." She got a curious look on her face. "There's something else, too. Something in the background. It's powerful and it's old."

"Maybe you're just tired." Siena was anxious to get into the city. She wasn't ready to spend another night outdoors. She'd slept hardly at all last night. Part of it was that she couldn't get comfortable on the ground, but mostly it was because she'd felt so vulnerable out there. She kept feeling like at any moment some monster was going to charge out of the darkness and attack them.

"I don't think that's it."

"I really don't want to stand here and talk about it. We're blocking the way. We've come a long way, we're going in. Come on." She took Netra's arm and steered her toward the gate.

Siena nodded at the guard as they passed through the gate. He gave her a look of general apathy. Inside, the heat and stench were appalling, the air thick with sweat and urine. No breezes stirred the air. The street was packed with people. Siena guided Netra over to the side of the street, somewhat out of the press.

"It's worse in here," Netra said. "There's something definitely wrong with the Selfsongs of the people here. Can't you hear it?"

Siena tried, but there were too many people around, too much activity, and she couldn't concentrate. She shrugged. "It sounds okay to me."

"Really?"

"Really. Look, Netra, we're here for a reason, remember? We need to connect with as many of our order as we can so we can be ready when Xochitl returns. We can't do that if we turn and run every time something doesn't feel just right to you."

Netra gave her a skeptical look. "You can't hear Song right now, can you?"

"No, I can't," Siena admitted. "I'm tired, my feet hurt, and I want to go to the Haven. It's getting late and I don't want to be wandering these streets in the dark. Do I need to remind you that we don't have any money to pay for a room?"

Netra looked undecided. Siena felt herself getting impatient. It felt to her like far too many people were looking at them and those looks weren't very friendly. The longer they stood here, the greater the chance something would happen. They needed to get to the safety of the Haven.

"Maybe I should just wait outside the city," Netra said.

"No. Absolutely not. We stick together. We're not discussing this anymore. Let's go." Siena started down a side street. She was relieved when Netra followed.

They were skirting a large pile of rotting garbage, replete with rats that seemed to have no fear of people, when Netra said, "Was it this dirty the last time you were here?"

"I don't know. Maybe. It's been almost twenty years." Siena had to admit that the place was pretty foul. How come there was no breeze at all? Outside the walls it had seemed pretty windy. A breeze would go a long way toward lifting at least some of the stench.

"Are you sure you remember where the Haven is?"

"I talked to Bronwyn before we left. Remember, she was here just a few years ago. Between what she told me and what I remember, we should have no problems."

They turned a corner and nearly tripped over a man lying sprawled in the street. He had no visible wounds, but there were large sores on his body and he wasn't moving. Netra paused as if to check on him.

"No, Netra. There's nothing we can do for him." She plucked at Netra's arm, trying to pull her away from him.

"How do you know? We haven't looked at him."

"It's not our problem. We're here for another reason." Netra scowled but let herself be pulled on past.

"How could they just leave him there like that?" Netra asked. "Why doesn't anyone do anything?"

"It's a city."

"What does that mean?"

"Cities have beggars and homeless people. It's just how they are."

"His clothes weren't dirty. I don't think he was a beggar."

"Then maybe he was attacked. Whatever it is, it's a job for the city watch, not us. We don't want to be nearby when they show up."

"He definitely wasn't attacked. I think whatever's wrong with him is what's wrong with this whole place. There's some kind of sickness here. He's not the only one, either. Look at that woman."

She pointed at a young woman who was leaning against a wall. She seemed to be gasping for breath. There was a large sore on the back of one hand.

"All the more reason why we want to hurry," Siena replied. "The longer we stay out here in the open, the greater the risk to us."

As they continued on she had to admit that there were quite a few people who looked unwell. Some were coughing. A fair number had sores. Others just looked kind of listless. "Maybe there's some kind of plague here."

"If there is, it's no ordinary plague," Netra replied. She rubbed her arms. "I'm telling you, there's something wrong here and I don't think it's a normal illness."

"How do you know that?" Siena said irritably. Netra was starting to frighten her. She was even starting to question whether they should have entered the city at all. Why couldn't Netra just be quiet and follow?

"I don't know. It's just a feeling I have. I can practically feel it on my skin." She rubbed her arms again. "I feel like I'm getting a rash."

"We're not leaving just because of a feeling. We've come too far."

The street opened up onto a small square. "Look," Siena said, feeling relieved. "There's the red sign, just like Bronwyn said. All we have to do is go down that street for a few minutes and we'll be there. You'll feel better once we're in the Haven, you'll see."

"I don't think I will."

Siena spun on her. "Okay, Netra, I get it. You're angry with me for not telling you about your mother. I apologized and I know it doesn't mean anything to you but there's nothing else I can do right now besides that. You wanted to come along. No one made you."

"I know. It's just that—"

"Stop. I don't want to hear it. You're just getting yourself all worked up. The people here are poor, okay? That's what's wrong with the place.

It's the *only* thing wrong with this place."

Netra looked unconvinced. She was still rubbing her arms.

"So we can continue on now?"

"Do we have to stay the night here? Can't we just meet with them quickly and leave?"

"Really, Netra? The sun's almost down. It will be dark soon. Wouldn't you rather sleep indoors, in a Haven with your sisters?"

"No. I'd rather get out of here right now."

"That's not going to happen. Besides, they're probably locking the front gate right about now."

Netra's eyes widened. "They're locking the gate? We're trapped here?"

"Not trapped. It's what they do in cities. It's to keep people safe."

"I don't feel safe."

Siena tried to force herself to be calm. She took Netra's hand. "You've been through a lot lately. It's normal to be frightened. But we're safe here. As safe as anywhere. You need to just calm down. We're going to go to the Haven. You'll feel better once we're indoors. Who knows, you might even make a new friend there."

Netra nodded slowly. "I still say there's something wrong here, but I won't say anything more. Maybe I *am* just overreacting."

"That's better. Everything is going to be okay. You'll see."

Siena almost gasped with relief a few minutes later when they finally reached the Haven. It sat at the end of a narrow dirt street, its windows hooded with heavy shutters. Like so many of its neighbors, the Haven was a drab little building of baked mud bricks. It had been whitewashed once, far in the past, but now that whitewash had mostly worn away and there were lizards hiding in the cracks in its walls.

Siena rapped on the door, which was made of badly-warped, rough-cut wood planks. Her knees hurt and a deep weariness ran up the back of her legs and along her spine. It felt like she had been on her feet for forever. She rubbed at her eyes and they were gritty and sore.

The door opened. The woman standing there was skinny. Her green robe was old and covered in stains, at least one of which seemed to be blood.

"I...we're Tenders from Rane Haven," Siena said. "We've come to talk with you."

The woman just stared at her as if she was speaking a foreign language, then Siena realized she recognized her.

"Wendin?"

The Tender looked at her oddly. "Do I know you?"

"It's Siena. I met you years ago, when I came to Nelton. Don't you remember?"

The woman squinted at her and then a crooked smile played across her lips. "I do, I do," she said. "Sorry, you surprised me. We don't get visitors very often. Come in. You're just in time."

Siena wondered what they were just in time for, but decided not to ask right then. They followed Wendin down a dim, low-ceilinged hallway. The hallway led to a room lit only by a window high up in one wall. There was one other woman in the room, sitting at a rough table, staring at a knife lying on the table before her. She was younger than Wendin by a couple of decades, probably in her mid-thirties, though it was hard to tell for sure.

"Sit down, sit down," Wendin said. "I'd offer you something but the truth is we're about to go out so all that will have to wait. Why have you come? Are you here to listen to the Voice?"

"No, I…" What voice was she talking about? "We bring rather bad news, I'm afraid."

Wendin grew serious. "What bad news?"

Siena took a deep breath. Was there any good way to say this? "We think the prison is cracked. We think Melekath may be escaping."

"Oh, we already know about that," Wendin said lightly. "You had me worried when you said you had bad news."

"You don't consider this bad news?"

"Of course not! Why would we be upset that Father is returning?" Seeing the stunned look on Siena's face, she added, "Sorry. I'm being silly. You've not heard the Voice yet. That's why you're confused. You don't know the blessings we are all about to receive."

Siena looked at Netra. Netra looked just as confused as she felt. "What in the world are you talking about? How can Melekath's escape be considered good news? Why are you calling him Father?"

"I could explain it to you, but we really haven't the time and it would be much better if you just listened to the Voice, who explains it much better than I possibly can. We're just about to go to the nightly gathering. You can come with us."

Suddenly Siena wished she had listened to Netra and left the city. Clearly Melekath had already corrupted this place and the Tenders here as well. She stood up. "Maybe we should just go. We don't want to intrude. We can talk with you after the gathering."

"Nonsense. You're not intruding at all. The Voice wants us to spread the word to as many as possible. You must come with us."

"We're tired and we've come a long way so—"

The other woman spoke for the first time. "You're coming with us." She was eying them suspiciously and Siena realized with alarm that the knife was now in her hand. It was a large knife.

"There's really no need to threaten them, Tara," Wendin said. "They just don't know yet."

Tara just continued to stare at them.

"Shall we go then?" Wendin said. "We don't want to be late and miss anything."

Siena and Netra exchanged looks. Siena wished she could apologize right then, tell Netra she should have listened to her. She would have to tell her later.

If there was a later.

CHAPTER 35

The sun had gone down while they were inside. The street was filled with new shadows that curled out from doorways and flowed down from the eaves. A cat yowled from a rooftop. A stray breeze blew a scrap of cloth along the ground. There was smoke in the air.

"You'll see," Wendin said, closing the door behind them. "Wait until you hear the Voice. Then you'll see."

Still holding the knife, Tara waved them down the street and then fell in behind them. Wendin seemed to have forgotten about the knife. She chattered on as they walked, telling them about the wonders of the world to come when Melekath returned and how lucky they were to be among the first to follow him.

Netra wanted nothing more than to run. If Siena hadn't been with her, she probably would have. Tara didn't look all that healthy. Netra was sure she could outrun her.

"I'm sorry, Netra," Siena whispered to her. "I should have listened to you."

"I don't like your whispering," Tara said, putting her hand on Siena's shoulder and bringing the knife close to her back. "It makes me think you will be among the faithless."

"I'm sure that's not it," Wendin said with a skittering laugh that died as soon as it was born. "They're just nervous. Remember how we were nervous our first time?"

"The faithless receive no mercy," Tara said into Siena's ear.

"There is no need to threaten us," Siena said. Her face was pale. "We agreed to go, and go we will."

They turned onto a street that was crowded, everyone heading toward the center of the city. The street led to a large plaza in the center of the city. People filled every inch of the plaza and more were crammed onto rooftops. Mothers carrying babies, elderly people leaning on canes, children, young men—it looked as if every person in Nelton had come to the gathering.

Fires guttered on braziers around the plaza, lighting up a wooden platform that had been constructed on the far side, up against the palace wall. The palace gate opened and a man dressed in rich robes emerged, followed by several other men who were also well-dressed. They climbed up onto the platform.

"Kneel," Tara said, going to her knees and pulling Netra down with her. Everyone else was going to their knees as well.

"Is he the Voice?" Siena whispered to Wendin once they were settled.

"No," Wendin whispered back. "He's the king. But he speaks for the Voice."

"It is once again my pleasure to speak to you of wonderful news," the king said. Though he did not shout, somehow his voice carried easily to them. "Father is returning!"

A cheer went up from the crowd.

"The prison will collapse any day now!"

More cheers. Some people were openly crying.

The king waited for silence to return before speaking again. "He wants me to tell you that he misses you, as he missed all who have come and gone since he was locked away. He wants you to know that he does not blame you for what others did so long ago, when they warred on him and his Children."

Now a great many people were weeping. Netra exchanged looks with Siena. This was not what she had expected at all. What was going on here?

"When Father is once again free," the king continued, "he will come here and he will offer you the Gift, the same Gift he gave his Children so long ago."

A sigh went over the crowd. Netra wished she were far away. The Book of Xochitl said Melekath's Gift perverted those people who took it, turned them into abominations. Why did these people want it? What was wrong with them?

"That is enough from me," the king said. "I know it is not me that you came to see. With no further delay, I present to you the Voice!"

An awed hush fell over the crowd. From the palace gate emerged a very tall, slender figure, cloaked and hooded in white. The figure climbed the platform and looked out over them. It towered over the king and was probably eight feet tall.

The figure pushed the cloak back, revealing a face of wondrous beauty and long, golden hair.

Netra felt Siena squeeze her hand. Her confusion increased. The Voice was so beautiful. Why had she been afraid of it? It seemed as well that she could no longer hear the wrongness in the Song that she'd heard before. How could she have been so wrong?

The Voice tilted its head back—its beauty was androgynous, neither male nor female—and began to sing.

There were no words. It was utterly amazing. Netra had never heard a sound so beautiful, so rich. It was so calm, so perfect. She felt her fears slip away and a deep sense of peace and calm descend over her. She had been a fool to be afraid. Father was coming. He would take care of everything.

From the Voice's mouth came a cloud of tiny golden flakes, like bits of sunlight. The flakes flew up into the sky and out over the crowd, and then they began to settle. Still kneeling, people reached up, crying with delight as the flakes settled on them. Netra and Siena reached up as well.

Netra longed for the touch of those flakes of gold. She wanted the peace that the Voice was offering. So far they had only settled on those people closest to the Voice. Those further away, like she was, would have to wait.

But something was nagging at her. It felt like there was a weight hanging around her neck. She wanted to be rid of it and reached to pull it off.

Her hand closed on her *sonkrill* and suddenly she was pulled *beyond*.

Netra gasped at what she *saw*.

The flakes were not golden, but black, like ashes. The beautiful figure of the Voice was gone and in its place stood a creature of pestilence and disease. It was gaunt, withered, the bones standing out sharply under the skin. It was bald. The eyes were empty holes, the mouth gaping and toothless. Weeping sores covered much of its body.

The black flakes were settling on people nearby and when they landed on people's *akirmas* they stuck there, black stains that joined stains that were already there. This was what was affecting the Song here. These people were diseased at a fundamental level.

Netra left *beyond* and turned to Siena. "We have to go!"

But Siena did not reply. She had her arms over her head, a huge, beatific smile on her face.

Netra shook her. "We can't let those things touch us! They're not what you think they are!"

Siena tried to shake her off. The flakes were very close now. They had only seconds. Even if they were to run now, it probably wouldn't help.

Desperately, Netra grabbed the edge of Siena's traveling cloak and jerked it over her head, pulling her onto her side and covering her as best she could. Then she pulled her cloak over herself and threw herself on top of Siena, pinning her to the ground.

Siena struggled underneath her and cried out, but Netra held on as best she could. It didn't have to be long. Soon the flakes would all settle to the ground and then she could let her go. She only prayed that she'd guessed right and the cloaks would protect them.

The first flakes fell. Even through the cloak she could feel them. Netra held her breath, hoping.

"What are you doing?" she heard Tara yell. Hands grabbed her and pulled her off.

Netra rolled over and saw with relief that there were no more flakes above her.

Then she saw the glint of the knife in Tara's hand and felt a new fear.

⚔ ⚔ ⚔

"You refused his blessing!" Tara said shrilly, holding up the knife. Her face was contorted with rage. She had moved in front of Netra, her back to the platform where the Voice stood.

"No, we didn't." Netra jumped up and tried to back away, but she only got a couple steps. People were packed too closely around them and a number of them were starting to look at her accusingly.

Suddenly, Netra sensed something malevolent and she glanced away from Tara, over her shoulder. The Voice was staring at her, its gaze palpable even from this distance.

"I knew we couldn't trust you," Tara hissed, grabbing onto Netra's cloak. "Now I'm going to cut you."

Then the Voice raised one arm. Its hand opened and something black and toothy and snake-like appeared in its palm.

The toothy thing lifted into the air and shot at Netra.

Netra jerked back, trying to free herself, but Tara tightened her grip, her teeth baring in a snarl.

"You'll pay for—"

At the last instant, Netra shoved her.

The toothy thing struck Tara in the back and her eyes went very wide. Her mouth worked soundlessly. Almost instantly the veins in her face turned black and swollen.

Then she toppled forward, trying with her last strength to swing the knife at Netra.

Netra stood there frozen, staring down at Tara's corpse, trying to grapple with what she had just done.

Siena reacted first. She grabbed Netra's arm, pulling her down into a crouch. "Get down!" she yelled.

The man directly behind Netra shrieked as another of the black, toothy things struck him in the chest, just missing Netra.

Running bent over, the two women fled the plaza. More screams as other people were struck but the Voice could no longer see them and as the panic spread others began to flee the plaza as well, the chaos that ensued helping them escape.

CHAPTER 36

Fortunately, the city gate stood open. There were no guards to be seen anywhere as the two women fled the city. They ran as long as they could, until Siena bent over, gasping for breath.

Netra bent over, breathing hard. "What have I done?" she moaned. "What have I done?"

Siena's hand rested on her back. "I saw it. You had no choice."

"Of course I had a choice!" Netra said brokenly, pushing Siena's hand away and standing up. "I chose my life over hers."

"It wasn't like that."

"Yes it was! I killed her. I killed Tara." She held her hands up, staring at them in horror. "I pushed her in front of that black thing and she died."

"You're not being fair to yourself."

Netra turned away and began walking. Siena hurried after her.

"I won't let you do this to yourself. I saw it all. Tara was going to stab you. Even if the Voice hadn't attacked you, she would have. And she denounced you. The crowd would have torn us apart. You did what anyone would have done."

Netra looked at her. "I'm not anyone. I'm a Tender. I broke our most sacred vow."

"I know it's hard, Netra, but—"

"No. You don't know. You've never killed anyone. Is this all I am? A Guardian appears and I hide while my sister is killed. Then that thing in there appears and I kill another sister to save myself. What's next? Why don't I just go into the Krin and open Melekath's prison right now?"

"I'm your sister and I would have died if you'd done nothing.

Doesn't that mean anything?"

Netra had no reply. She kept walking. The road behind them was empty. No one emerged from the city to chase them. It was as if no one cared that she had killed a woman. It was as if nothing had happened. But Netra knew she would never be the same. What she had done could never be forgiven.

They walked for some time in silence. Then Siena said, "I still can't believe what happened in that plaza. It was like I became someone else. I forgot everything I believe, just threw it away. If it wasn't for you…" She trailed off and was silent for a while. "I wanted what that thing was offering. The Mother help me, I wanted it more than anything."

"I did too," Netra admitted.

"Those poor people. If it wasn't for you, Netra, I'd be like them now." Siena shuddered. "How did you know? How did you resist?"

"It was my *sonkrill*. It felt so heavy. When I took hold of it to take it off, I slipped *beyond* and then I saw through the illusion."

Siena stopped her and turned Netra to face her. She took both her hands. "But this is wonderful, don't you see?" she breathed. "Clearly Xochitl is watching over you, protecting you. Twice your *sonkrill* has saved you."

Netra pulled her hands away and resumed walking. She could feel Tara clinging to her as the life left her.

Siena followed. "What did you *see*?"

"The Voice is gaunt and withered, little more than a skeleton. There are open sores on its face."

"What about the golden flakes?"

"They are black. Where they touch, they stain the *akirma*."

"Good Mother," Siena said. "That's horrible."

"That's not all, either. Those people…they're changing. They're becoming something else."

"What?"

Netra shrugged, the gesture lost in the darkness.

Netra was quiet the next day as they walked. She seemed to be in shock. She kept her eyes down, not seeing any of the land they moved through, not responding to Siena's periodic attempts to draw her into conversation. Siena became worried about her. She had been through a great deal lately. She shouldn't have let Netra accompany her to Nelton. There was only so much one person could take.

In the afternoon they came up on the dead town of Critnell. Rather than walk through it, they left the road and began to circle around the town. As they did so, Netra kept looking at the town. Siena saw the pain that was written on her face and her heart ached in response.

"Do you want to stop and offer a prayer for them?" Siena asked, slowing down and catching hold of Netra's arm.

Netra kept her head down. "Why? It won't make any difference to them." She pulled away and continued on.

Oh, Netra. "But it might to you and me."

Netra stopped, though she did not turn around. "Go ahead if you want to." Her voice was dull and distant.

She stood there, facing away from Siena, away from the town, as Siena voiced a prayer to Xochitl to receive the spirits of those who had died.

Then they continued on. Desperate to do something, Siena started talking, hoping somehow to pull Netra out of herself.

"You look so much like her, your mother. You have her eyes."

Netra gave no indication that she had heard.

"I think that's what I see most clearly when I close my eyes and picture your mother: her eyes. They were so intent. She didn't seem to miss anything. She saw things that I never even noticed. She'd say to me, 'Did you notice the way Yrva kept touching her cheek when she was arguing with Lendl? I think she's afraid of her.' She was always noticing details like that, observing people, seeing what was really happening in any situation." Siena shifted her pack to a more comfortable position and was quiet for a minute, waiting to see if Netra would respond. When she didn't, Siena continued.

"Her eyes were so expressive. There was never anything hidden in them like there is with so many people. When you looked into her eyes you knew exactly what she was feeling. She never had any use for pretense and got so disgusted with people who did.

"Like you, she was strong willed." Siena gave a little laugh. "That's an understatement. No one could tell your mother anything. She had to find out for herself. If you said the stove was hot she had to touch it first before she would agree with you. She never just accepted what someone else told her about something without thinking it through on her own, arguing with it, holding it up to her own inner light and seeing if it made sense. Oh, she used to make Greta, our teacher, so mad. Greta would be teaching us something from the Book and Shakre would stop her and question her on some point she just made. 'Why do you say it's like that?' she'd say. 'That doesn't make any sense. Why wouldn't it be like this?' Greta would get so frustrated. She was a good teacher, she knew the Book inside and out, but she didn't have much imagination and she couldn't understand your mother's need to question, especially when she was handing down wisdom that had been accepted for thousands of years. I honestly think she thought your mother asked her that stuff just to get to her, but she didn't. Shakre just wanted to know the how, and the why behind everything. She didn't have much use for book learning or sitting quietly and letting someone else spoon feed her. She wanted to experience it herself, to touch the fire and know for herself it was hot, instead of just taking someone else's word for it."

They walked in silence for a few minutes. They got back on the road and the walking was easier.

"She was always wandering through the hills like you too, dragging me with her whenever I'd go, even Brelisha sometimes, though they didn't get along all that well. She had your affinity with animals, even wild ones. Squirrels, coyotes, birds, whatever, they'd let her get right up close to them, sometimes take food from her hand. They seemed to sense that she meant them no harm. She had a way of finding sick or wounded creatures and she'd bring them back to the Haven and nurse them back to health, usually in our room.

"One time she found where a coyote had killed and eaten a rabbit and she backtracked the rabbit to its hole." Siena shook her head. It was still hard for her to believe. "I don't know how she did it. She would take me out and show me tracks in the dirt and say, 'Look, can you see where the mouse stopped here to eat a seed?' But I never could. I couldn't see anything but dirt, but to her it was as plain as writing on a page.

"Anyway, she backtracked this rabbit to its hole and sure enough there was a whole litter of baby rabbits in there, only a couple days old and still blind. Now, everyone knows you can't raise a wild rabbit by hand. They won't eat. They die of fright or something. Lendl tried to tell her it was no use when she showed up with them in her robe. It was a waste of time. Everyone said so. Everyone but Ivorie that is. She just watched and waited.

"Not a single one of those rabbits died. They all grew up healthy and strong. They wouldn't let anyone else touch them but they followed Shakre all over the place." There was wonder in Siena's voice and for a moment she was a girl again, in awe of the friend she could never quite imagine living up to.

"Then there was the time she brought the javelina back to the

263

Haven. The thing was full grown, a boar I think, and you know how heavy they are. Almost as big as a pig. She'd built a travois out of sticks and tied it up with strips torn from her robe, then dragged the thing all the way back to the Haven. You should have seen the fuss when she brought the thing into the yard. Even Ivorie wasn't about to let her bring that thing inside. You know how mean those things can be, and they smell when you get up close. But your mother didn't care. She nursed the thing back to health. None of the rest of us could even go near it. Not that we wanted to. But for her it was as docile as a lamb."

And so Siena went on as the afternoon waned and evening came on and they finally stopped for the night. She told Netra every story she could remember. She spoke of childhood secrets she and Shakre had shared as girls, things they'd whispered about deep into the night when they were supposed to be asleep. She spoke of her feelings for her closest friend, still undiminished after all these years. As she talked she realized gradually that the things she was saying were for herself as much as for Netra. Ever since Shakre had left the Haven in disgrace Siena had been forbidden to speak of her, to even say her name aloud. For so many years these memories and feelings had lain inside her and suddenly all of them wanted to come out at once. There were times she cried as she talked, so badly did she miss her childhood friend, and times when she laughed out loud when she recounted one of Shakre's antics. It felt good, it felt cleansing and when, at last, she stopped, she felt she had finally put something to rest. As if she had finally, after all these years, paid her friend the tribute she deserved and could now let her go.

She stared into the flames of the small campfire they had built while she was talking and she said, "I loved your mother, Netra. I loved her more than I've ever loved anyone else. She was my best friend, my closest companion. So many times I've wished I'd gone with her, and maybe I would have if she had not handed you over to me. I've missed her every day and I'll never stop missing her."

Still Netra said nothing, but Siena saw that her shoulders were shaking. She wrapped Netra in a hug and held her as she cried.

CHAPTER 37

Jolene was standing out front when they reached the Haven the next afternoon. Her hair blew in an unruly mass around her head and she looked thinner than ever, the lines in her face stark and raw. She looked from Siena to Netra and then back to Siena, but she did not speak.

"Gather everyone, please," Siena told Jolene. Jolene left them and Siena squeezed Netra's arm. "Thank the Mother we're home."

"Yes," Netra said, but the Haven no longer looked the same. The solid, comfortable place, the place that had sheltered and comforted her for her entire life, had changed. It looked old and fragile. It looked like it would fall down in the first hard wind. She followed Siena inside.

The Tenders of Rane Haven gathered in the common room and Siena told them everything that had happened. When she was done there was silence at the table. The nine women sat there, lost in their thoughts, trying to absorb what was happening to the world they thought they knew.

"The Voice. Some texts refer to the Guardian Gulagh as the Voice," Brelisha said. She took a sip from her cup of tea. Her hands were shaking slightly. "Tharn is also known as the Fist. We must assume that Kasai, the last of his Guardians, known as the Eye, is out there somewhere as well."

"I'm scared," Donae said. She twirled her hair nervously between her fingers.

"We all are," Siena replied.

"Well, if there was any lingering doubt that the prison is weakening, it is gone now," Brelisha declared. She rubbed her swollen knuckles and grimaced. "It is only a matter of time."

"It can't be that bad. Surely Xochitl will not abandon the life she created to Melekath," Donae said, looking from one face to another, seeking comfort somewhere, anywhere. "Surely she will save us."

"Of course she will," Karyn said. "Even if she has not forgiven her Tenders, she will not stand by and let Melekath destroy all Life."

That hung in the air for a minute.

Donae pulled at her hair and shifted in her chair, her eyes darting around the table. "It seems…" She hesitated, then blurted out the rest. "You said Melekath is offering forgiveness to those people in Nelton, because they were not the ones who made war on him. Then why won't Xochitl forgive us? We weren't the ones who used her powers to kill. The ones who did that are all long dead."

Brelisha turned a stern eye on her and Donae shrank in her chair. "Melekath offers only lies. You can be sure of that." Donae nodded meekly, a child reprimanded for an outburst.

"Xochitl defeated Melekath once before," Bronwyn said, gazing at each of them in turn as if to drive her point home. "She will do so again."

"With the help of seven other gods," Karyn, ever the scholar, reminded them.

The next morning Netra was standing outside one of the back doors of the Haven, looking at the desert and wondering why it looked so different, when Brelisha came up to her.

"You weren't there for the vows this morning," she said.

Netra gave her a sidelong look. Brelisha's hair was pulled back in its usual severe bun. The morning sun cast her hawk-like features in sharp relief, outlining every wrinkle and age spot. "I don't think I belong there," Netra said. She felt immensely tired. She had barely slept. There was too much rushing around in her mind and it wouldn't leave her be.

"Because of Tara."

"Yes, Brelisha. Because of Tara. I killed her. Tenders aren't supposed to kill. I don't know that I am one of you anymore."

"It's not as simple as that," Brelisha snapped.

Netra sighed and turned to face her. "Isn't it?"

"You were under extraordinary pressure. You reacted. Maybe you made a mistake."

"*Maybe* I made a mistake?"

"Tara had given herself to Melekath. As did those who followed him to Durag'otal. For that betrayal, Xochitl condemned them to die in the prison."

"That's it, then? You turn to Melekath so you're guilty. Guilty and condemned to die"—she snapped her fingers—"just like that."

"Though I would not put it that way, yes. Just like that." Brelisha stood like a woman sure of her ground, sure she was right.

"To use your own words, 'It's not as simple as that.'"

"Explain."

"You weren't there. You didn't hear the Voice. You didn't feel its call. Tara, the rest of those people, they had no real choice."

Brelisha faltered, her brows drawing together in a frown. "Well...perhaps..."

"And maybe there's even more to it than that. How long since Xochitl turned her back on us? How long since she turned her back on the whole world?" She advanced a step and Brelisha fell back a step, suddenly uncertain. "How long do we have to keep paying for the sins of our ancestors? Is there no end to it?"

"We...cannot know the mind of the Mother."

"Empty words." Netra felt anger rising within her. "People can only live on those for so long. Then here comes a messenger from Melekath and you know what the first thing is he says? Do you?"

"No."

"Melekath doesn't blame you for what your ancestors did. He *forgives* you."

Brelisha held her hands up in surrender, but Netra was implacable. She leaned in closer.

"Why would anyone *not* listen to an offer like that?" She tapped herself on the chest. "I was there. When he said those words something jumped inside me. Yes, there is a seductive power in the Voice, but maybe its real power comes from the fact that it says what we all want to hear most."

Brelisha struggled to get herself back together. She clenched her hands by her sides. "Netra, you may have...well, there is something to what you say. Perhaps it is not so simple as that. I just..." She bit her lip, a sign of weakness Netra had never seen before. "Can we leave this for now? I came to ask you to come to your lessons. Cara is already waiting in the library." Netra opened her mouth to refuse but Brelisha forestalled her and what she said next stunned Netra. "Please? I know I can't compel you, I know you don't have to, but it would mean something to me. Can you just...one more time?"

Her eyes glistened. Never had Netra seen her so vulnerable. She remembered then what Owina had said to her that night in the garment room, about ritual and the comfort it gave people in frightening times.

"Okay. I'll come."

She followed Brelisha to the library where Cara was sitting. Cara smiled up at her and Netra knew Cara was trying to reassure her. She wanted to reciprocate. She wanted to smile back, but she couldn't. She took the chair next to Cara and forced herself not to pull away when Cara squeezed her hand. The truth was that ever since she'd returned from Nelton, she was finding it increasingly difficult to be near her old friend. Cara's every gesture, every expression, seemed so needy, so clinging. She wanted to yell at her, to tell Cara that she was lost too, that she had nothing to offer her, nothing at all.

But she knew that even a hint of those thoughts and Cara would crumple and Netra already had too much guilt in her heart. She couldn't take anymore.

Brelisha had only just begun the lesson when Cara surprised Netra, surprised Brelisha too, by the look on her face.

"There's something that's been bothering me since last night, Brelisha," Cara said. "The Voice called Melekath Father."

Brelisha's eyebrows rose. She looked at Netra, then back at Cara.

"What does that mean?" Cara asked.

"It means nothing. Melekath lies." Brelisha's lips were drawn very thin. "Xochitl is the Mother."

"At least, that's what we've been told," Netra said. Beside her, Cara looked at her in astonishment.

"You *doubt* this?" Brelisha's voice was a croak.

Netra actually felt sorry for her, but she seemed to have tapped into something that had been festering in the back of her heart, something that once she started to release, she couldn't stop. "I don't know what I believe anymore."

"You should be very careful if you walk down that road." Brelisha gripped the edge of the table very tightly, as if she might topple over without it.

"Maybe he is our father," Netra said. "Maybe everything in the Book is a lie." Cara was pulling on her arm. Netra shook her off, staring hard at Brelisha.

Brelisha came to her feet, her face mottled. "You will not say such things in here."

"Why not? When did it become a crime to ask questions?"

"This is beyond that. This is heresy. Xochitl created Life."

"So we were told. But what if it's not true?"

"I don't want to talk about this." Brelisha picked up the book lying on the table and held it before her like a shield.

"The world won't go away just because you refuse to see it."

"I understand that you've been through something very difficult, but—"

"No. You don't understand. Why? Because you never leave this building. You live in here with your moldy old books and you stare at the past while 'now' happens all around you."

Abruptly the air seemed to leave Brelisha. She sat down, her eyes empty. "Why are you doing this, Netra?"

"I'm only asking questions. What if the Book is full of lies?"

"Tell me why," Brelisha said tiredly.

"You want to know why? Because I don't know what to believe anymore!" Now it was Netra's turn to raise her voice. "I used to think I knew what to believe, but then I went out there. Now I don't know what's real." She fought sudden tears.

Brelisha put her head in her hands. "I don't know what to tell you. Maybe it is all lies," she said, gesturing at the walls filled with books. "But what else do we have? We have to believe something."

"And that's it, isn't it? We have to believe something, so we end up believing anything."

"Please go, Netra. Please…just go."

Netra felt Cara's pleading gaze on her but she turned her face away. Slowly she walked to the door. Even then she wanted to turn back and apologize. She didn't really want to hurt Brelisha and she knew she had. Deeply. But her world had been turned upside down. Thoughts and feelings charged around wildly inside her, with a life of their own. She couldn't hold them in any longer. She didn't know what was happening to her.

Netra spent the rest of the day wandering the hills around the Haven, trying to find in nature some measure of peace. But there was none to be found. The land seemed empty of wild creatures; even the birds were curiously absent, as if everything had sensed her mood and fled before her. She tried prayer but that felt even emptier than the landscape. There were no answers to be found there. Xochitl was silent. She was always silent. Had she abandoned them completely? Did she no longer care for her children at all?

There were too many questions and no answers.

Netra sat on a stone for a while, took off her *sonkrill* and simply stared at it. Twice now it had saved her from a Guardian. That had to be some kind of sign from Xochitl, didn't it? Some proof that she was watching over her offspring?

But it was only an old claw, dull in the bright light and lined with miniscule cracks she had never noticed before. The help it gave was all in her mind. She attached meaning to it, so it had meaning. Nothing more than that.

She did not put it back around her neck, but stuck it in her pocket.

When darkness fell, Netra trudged back to the Haven. The others would be at the evening meal. She did not really want to see them. She didn't want to see Brelisha's hurt or anger. She didn't want to see Cara's need. She didn't want to see their sympathy for her. But at the same time she could not bear being alone right now. She needed something, anything, to pull her from the thoughts that tormented her.

The meal was over and they were all sitting there, trapped in some fragile, unseen net together, when Netra spoke for the first time.

"What are we going to do now?"

"What do you mean, Netra?" Siena asked gently.

Her tone irked Netra. She was not a troubled child who must be placated. Her tone was sharp when she spoke again. "I mean, what are we going to do? About Melekath. About his Guardians. About everything."

"But what can we possibly do?" Donae cried, as if Netra had asked her personally.

"Indeed," Brelisha said, turning on Netra with a darkness in her eyes. "What would you have us do?"

"I don't know. I've been asking myself that all day. But we have to do something. The Guardians are free. One of them is less than two days from us. Maybe we should go to Qarath."

"To get to Qarath we'd have to pass by Nelton," Owina said. Outwardly, the older woman looked as calm and refined as ever, but there was sweat on her brow.

"And what would we find there anyway?" Bronwyn asked, sounding as if she was speaking to a thoughtless child. She was only a few years older than Netra and Cara, but she had always acted mature beyond her years. "Maybe Kasai is there. We might be walking right into a Guardian's hands."

"We can't just sit here and do nothing," Netra maintained

stubbornly. "We have to do something."

"Look around you, Netra," Siena said. "We are not soldiers. We are not heroes. We are only a handful of women. There is nothing we can do."

"What about all your talk about joining together with our sisters to be ready when Xochitl needs us?"

"We tried," Siena said. "You saw what happened."

"So now we're just going to sit here? Wait for the end with our hands folded?"

"We will pray," Siena said softly.

"That's it?" Netra asked. "Pray? What good will that do?"

"More good than haring off around the countryside," Brelisha replied sharply.

"If we are sincere, and our hearts are pure, the Mother will hear our prayers," Owina said.

"Well, that leaves me out," Netra said. "Now that I'm a murderer."

A dead silence greeted her words. Netra stared around the table but only Brelisha would meet her eyes. The rest turned their faces away.

The moment stretched out, seeming to freeze in Netra's mind. She saw them as if they were a painting. Donae, small, thin, afraid of her own shadow. Karyn, middle-aged like Donae, taking refuge as always in her intellect. Bronwyn, tall, capable, rarely rattled. Owina, prim and proper as a nobleman's wife, but with strength hidden under the softness. Jolene, hesitant, quiet, living in a world none of the rest of them could see. Cara, her best friend, wanting nothing more than to make and keep the peace. Siena, like a mother to her. Brelisha, cold and distant, a scathing word always ready on her thin lips. They were her family and she loved them, but right then she knew she would never fit in with them again.

Netra knew that whatever they said, however they reasoned, they did nothing because they were frightened. She found herself wondering, if her mother were with them at that moment, what would she do?

She would act. This Netra knew. She would fight, even if it did no good.

At that moment, Netra made the decision that had been lurking in the back of her mind since Nelton.

She was leaving.

The thought hurt her more than she'd expected. Her whole life had been spent here, with these women. But she no longer belonged here.

She had killed. In her heart she was no longer a Tender. It was a title she no longer deserved. Brelisha was saying something, arguing some point, but Netra wasn't listening. What was the point anymore?

"Okay, Brelisha," she said, getting to her feet. "You're right." Then she left the room and they stared after her.

⚔ ⚔ ⚔

"You told her about her mother? I thought you promised Shakre you wouldn't."

Brelisha had followed Siena to her quarters. Siena sat down wearily and regarded the stern-faced woman.

"I had to. You should have seen her after the Windcaller left. I had to warn her."

"Just like her mother," Brelisha said dismissively.

"I think she deserves to know, don't you?"

Brelisha thought about that. "Probably. But I think your timing was bad. Right now, with everything else going on."

Siena took off her *sonkrill* and laid it on the desk before her. She stroked it with one finger. "There isn't anything we can do, is there?"

Brelisha stiffened, and for a moment something very vulnerable peeked out from behind her eyes. Then it was gone. "Faith. That's what we can do. We can hold to our faith. If the Mother has use for us, she will let us know."

⚔ ⚔ ⚔

"Were you going to leave without telling me goodbye?"

It was dark. The evening meal had been over for an hour. Netra was sitting on the stone bench out back of the Haven, by the garden. Siena sat down next to her. There was a great sadness in her face.

Netra started to ask how she knew, but gave it up. Siena had always known more than she let on. "Probably," Netra said, unable to meet Siena's eyes.

Siena sighed.

"Don't try and talk me out of it. My mind is made up. I don't expect you to understand."

"I didn't come out here to talk you out of it, Netra. I know better than that." She sighed again. "And I think I understand better than you realize." She took hold of Netra's hand. "I think I always knew this day would come. Just as I always knew the day would come when your mother would leave. What is a sanctuary to us is a prison to women like you."

"I just…I can't be here right now," Netra said, her voice breaking. She would not cry, she told herself fiercely. "I killed Tara. I don't think I deserve to call myself a Tender, no matter what everyone says. And I…I want to find my mother. I have to talk to her." She had to pause to take hold of herself. "I have to know."

"It's all right. You don't have to explain yourself. You're a grown woman now. You have a right to make your own decisions." Siena rubbed her eyes and gave a shaky laugh. "I hope that sounded good, because it felt awful. I know I have to let you go, to let you live your own life—that's what a real mother does—but more than anything I just want to lock you in your room and keep you here. I'm going to miss you. More than you can possibly realize."

Then Netra did cry. She didn't fight it when Siena wrapped her in a hug and pulled her close. "Why?" she asked brokenly. "Why?"

"I don't know," Siena replied, not asking which question Netra referred to. "Only you, and the Mother, know that."

"I need some answers. I don't know what's real anymore."

"I don't think any of us knows. Oh, we act like we do. Maybe because it's what we're supposed to know as adults. Maybe it's just to convince ourselves to make it through another day. But none of us knows. We just muddle through as best we can. Mother knows, that's what I do. It might not be much, but it's all I've got."

Netra pulled back, looked at Siena through tear-stained eyes. "That wasn't very helpful, you know." She forced a half smile to take the sting from her words.

"Welcome to the world of adulthood. It's that time where you realize the adults don't know half as much as you thought they did. When you have to make real decisions and you've got no real idea what you're doing."

Netra laughed then, and cried a little more. "Do you think I'll find her? I don't know where to look."

"I don't know if it's any help, but your mother went north and west when she left. I got the feeling she was circling around the edge of the Firkaths and going north."

"I'll come back."

"Of course you will."

Netra pulled back. It was hard to see Siena's face. "You're not angry with me?"

"No. I'm not angry." She took both of Netra's hands. "Be careful. It can be a dangerous world out there."

"I will. You know that."

"You've survived two Guardians. I don't know what else the world can throw at you."

After that they sat there in silence for a long time without speaking.

"I know what you think of me," Cara said.

It was late and Netra was getting ready for bed, knowing she had to tell Cara she was leaving, and dreading it. Netra looked up at Cara's words. Her friend was sitting on her bed, her face turned down. She'd been brushing her hair and she was turning the brush over and over in her hands.

"I know you think I'm weak and afraid—"

"I don't think—" Netra began, but Cara cut her off, her face suddenly twisting with anger.

"Stop it! Stop lying to me!"

Netra stared at her old friend in surprise, waiting for the flood of tears to start as they always did. But to her surprise, Cara's eyes stayed dry.

"You think, 'It's Cara. Nice enough, but soft. Always afraid. Never standing up for herself. Nothing but a mouse.'"

"That's too harsh," Netra said quietly.

"Just let me finish!" Cara snapped, and Netra leaned back in surprise. "I *am* afraid. I don't mind admitting that. I'm not brave like you. I wish I was, I really do. You have no idea how hard I've tried, but I just can't do it. It's not in me. I'm not you, no matter how hard I try." She was pulling hair out of the brush with abrupt, angry motions. Then she looked up, locked eyes with Netra.

"I'm not you. I'm me. That's all I can be. I'm sorry I can't be more."

Netra went over and sat beside her. Cara flinched, and then leaned against her.

"I'm sorry," Cara said again.

"Don't be," Netra said. "I'm the one who should be sorry."

"It's just that I want people to get along. Can you understand that? I hate it when there is conflict. I just don't understand why people have to fight. What do we gain from it? What does it get us but misery?" She was gripping the brush very tightly.

"And that's one of your best traits, Cara. It's part of what makes you special. Trust me, the world needs more people who feel like you do." Surprisingly, Netra meant what she said. The truth was that she had always kind of looked down on Cara for being weak, but now she was starting to see that she had a different kind of strength in her.

"When were you going to tell me?" Cara asked. "*Were* you going to tell me? Or were you just going to leave?"

"I just...I couldn't find a good way to say it."

"I love you, Netra. You're my sister. You're my closest friend. All you have to do is tell me."

"I was afraid you wouldn't understand."

"I don't understand. But I'm your friend. It doesn't matter if I understand. It's your decision. That's what counts. I will miss you—more than you can imagine—but I accept that it is your choice."

Now it was Netra who began to cry. She put her arms around Cara and sobbed.

CHAPTER 38

Netra awakened very early the next morning, while it was still dark outside. She got out of bed as quietly as she could, then turned to see that Cara was awake, looking at her. Wordlessly she picked up her pack and the two of them walked to the front door. Outside, Cara threw her arms around her and gave her a long, hard hug.

"I love you," Cara murmured, and at that Netra felt herself losing hold, starting to fall again and she had to bite her lip until it hurt before she again felt steady. She hugged her back then and a moment later pulled away.

"Tell the others goodbye for me, will you?" She felt like a deer caught out in the open. "Try to explain to them that I…I just couldn't…"

Cara nodded, her hair silver in the fading moonlight. Netra turned and walked away. She did not look back but felt her friend's eyes on her until after she was out of sight of the Haven.

The End
The story continues in
LANDSEND PLATEAU
Available now at
EricTKnight.com

Glossary

abyss — according to the Book of Xochitl, the place the Eight reached into to create Melekath's prison. Gulagh drew poison from the abyss and released it into the River, which is what is causing the strange diseases and mutations plaguing the land.

akirma — the luminous glow that surrounds every living thing. Contained within it is Selfsong. When it is torn, Selfsong escapes. It also acts as a sort of transformative filter, changing raw LifeSong, which is actually unusable by living things, into Selfsong.

anthraxis – like grasshoppers, but equipped with a stinger and jaws strong enough to tear flesh.

aranti – creatures that dwell in the wind, in the Sphere of Sky.

Arnele – old Tender who taught Quyloc about Song.

Atria – (AY-tree-uh) name commonly used to refer to the landmass where the story takes place. It is a derivation of the name Kaetria, which was the name of the old Empire.

Banishment – when the Eight sank the city of Durag'otal underground.

Bereth – one of the old gods.

beyond – also known as "in the mists," the inner place where Tenders go to *see* Song.

Book of Xochitl – the Tenders' sacred book.

Brelisha – old Tender at Rane Haven who teaches the young Tenders.

Caller – shortened form of Windcaller, men reputed to be able to call things in the wind. They are considered blasphemers by the Tenders.

Cara – Netra's best friend.

chaos power—power of the abyss.

Children – the ones who followed Melekath to the city of Durag'otal and were Banished with him.

Critnell – diseased town that Netra and Siena come across on their way to Nelton.

Crodin – nomadic people who live along the edge of the Gur al Krin desert. After they die the Crodin believe that their spirits are drawn into the desert, to the gates of Har Adrim, the dread city where their god awaits: Gomen nai, the Faceless One.

Donae – (DOE-nay) Tender at Rane Haven.

Dorn – Windcaller Netra and Siena meet on the way to Nelton.

Durag'otal – (DER-awg oh-TAL) city founded by Melekath as a haven for his Children. It was sunk underground in the Banishment.

Eight – eight of the old gods, led by Xochitl, who besieged the city of Durag'otal and sank it underground.

feeder lines – the intermediate sized current of LifeSong, between the trunk lines, which come off the River directly, and the flows, which sustain individual creatures.

Firkath Mountains – mountains just to the north of Rane Haven.

FirstMother – title of the leader of the Tenders.

flows – the smallest currents of LifeSong. One of these is attached to each living thing and acts as a conduit to constantly replenish the energy that radiates outward from the *akirma* and dissipates. If the flow attached to a living thing is severed, it will only live for at most a few hours longer.

Gerath – Tender who goes with Netra to the town of Treeside. She is killed by Tharn.

Gift – something that was given by Melekath to his Children. The nature of it is not known, but it was said to turn them into abominations, with great powers and greater hungers.

Gomen nai – god of the Crodin. They believe he will someday emerge from his dark fortress at Har Adrim to devour their souls.

Gorim – one of the old gods.

Guardians – three powerful beings who serve Melekath and are sworn to protect his Children.

Gulagh – one of the three Guardians of the Children, also known as the Voice, in control of the city of Nelton. It has discovered a way to make a small opening into the abyss and when chaos power leaks out, use a living person to feed that power back up the flow of LifeSong sustaining that person and ultimately into the River itself. It is this poison in the River which is causing the strange diseases and mutations plaguing the land.

Gur al Krin – desert that formed over the spot where Durag'otal was sunk underground. Means "sands of the angry god" in the Crodin language.

Hame Terinoth – Tender who stood with the Eight during the siege of Durag'otal.

Har Adrim – the dark fortress where the Crodin believe Gomen nai (Melekath) dwells.

Heartglow - the denser glow of Selfsong in the center of a person's or animal's *akirma*. When it goes out, life ends.

Ivorie – Haven Mother at Rane Haven before Siena.

Kaetria – (KAY-tree-uh) capital city of the Old Empire.

Karthije – (CAR-thidge) city-state neighboring Qarath to the northwest.

Karyn – (CARE-in) Tender at Rane Haven

Kasai — one of the three Guardians of Melekath, also known as the Eye.

Lenda – simpleminded Tender at the Haven in Qarath.

LifeSong – energy that flows from the River and to all living things. It turns into Selfsong after it passes through the *akirma*, which acts as a sort of filter to turn the raw energy of LifeSong into something usable by the living thing.

Lowellin – (low-ELL-in) strange man who shows up in Qarath claiming to be the Protector spoken of in the Book of Xochitl.

macht – title from the old Empire meaning supreme military leader of all the phalanxes. Adopted by Rome for himself instead of king.

Melanine – the FirstMother in Qarath when Lowellin first shows up.

Melekath – the ancient god who was imprisoned along with his Children in the Banishment.

Musician – one of a highly secretive brotherhood who can manipulate LifeSong to create Music that transports the listener. Followers of the god Othen.

Nalene – FirstMother in Qarath after Melanine abdicates.

Nelton – town a few days from Rane Haven where Netra and Siena are nearly caught by Gulagh.

nemesis – what the Crodin call the Guardians, believing them to be dread lords who guard the entrance to Har Adrim.

Netra – a young Tender of Rane Haven.

Owina – one of the Tenders from Rane Haven.

Pente Akka – the shadow world that Lowellin shows Quyloc how to access.

Perganon – palace historian/librarian. He meets with Rome to read to him from the old histories. Also runs an informal network of informants.

Qarath – (kuh-RATH) city ruled by Rome and Quyloc.

Quyloc – (KWY-lock) Macht Rome's chief advisor.

Rane Haven – where Netra grew up.

Reminder – a many-pointed star enclosed in a circle. The holy symbol of the Tenders, illegal to own in Qarath.

seeing – the act of perception while *beyond*. It is an extrasensory perception, having nothing to do with the eyes yet what the mind perceives while *seeing* is interpreted by the brain as visual imagery.

Selfsong — when LifeSong passes through a person's *akirma* it becomes Selfsong, which is the energy of Life in a form that can be utilized by the body. It dissipates at death. It is continually replenished, yet retains a pattern that is unique to each individual.

Sertith – high grassland area to the north of Qarath. Nomadic horse warriors live there.

Shakre – Netra's mother, who broke Tender law and was banished from the Order.

shatren – animal similar to a cow, though smaller.

sklath – demons that the Crodin believe inhabit the Gur al Krin. They are believed to be responsible for raising the pillars of fire when the wind blows.

sonkrill – talismans that the Tenders receive/discover at the end of their Songquest.

Song – the energy that flows through living things.

Songquest – ritual that Tenders go through to acquire their *sonkrill*. They fast and wander the land until a spirit guide appears and leads them to their *sonkrill*.

sulbit – creature that Nalene finds in the River when Ilsith takes her there.

Tairus (TEAR-us) – General of the army.

Tharn – one of the three Guardians charged with protecting Melekath's Children, also known as the Fist. It kills Gerath at Treeside.

Thrikyl – city-state south of Qarath where Rome used the black axe to bring down the walls.

Tornith – town nearest to Rane Haven.

Trakar Kurnash – Crodin leader Rome is chasing when he is ambushed and forced to flee into the Gur al Krin.

Treeside – small village in the Firkath Mountains where Netra and Gerath encounter Tharn.

trunk lines – the huge flows of LifeSong that branch directly off the River. From the trunk lines the feeder lines branch off, and off the feeder lines come the individual flows that directly sustain every living thing.

Windcaller – men reputed to be able to call the wind and make it serve them. They are considered blasphemers by the Tenders.

Wreckers Gate – the name of the main gate at Ankha del'Ath, ancestral home of the Takare. According to legend there was a terrible battle there that led to the fall of the old Empire. The Tenders believe that that was where they committed their greatest sin against the Mother, and that after that is when they lost their power.

Wulf Rome – leader of Qarath.

Xochitl (so-SHEEL) – also known as the Mother of Life, the deity followed by the Tenders.

Yuon She – Tender from the past who used the dream powder with disastrous results. Author of the Book of Sorrows that predicted Melekath would free himself from the prison.

ABOUT THE AUTHOR

Born in 1965, I grew up on a working cattle ranch in the desert thirty miles from Wickenburg, Arizona, which at that time was exactly the middle of nowhere. Work, cactus and heat were plentiful, forms of recreation were not. The TV got two channels when it wanted to, and only in the evening after someone hand cranked the balky diesel generator to life. All of which meant that my primary form of escape was reading.

At 18 I escaped to Tucson where I attended the University of Arizona. A number of fruitless attempts at productive majors followed, none of which stuck. Discovering I liked writing, I tried journalism two separate times, but had to drop it when I realized that I had no intention of conducting interviews with actual people but preferred simply making them up.

After graduating with a degree in Creative Writing in 1989, I backpacked Europe with a friend and caught the travel bug. With no meaningful job prospects, I hitchhiked around the U.S. for a while then went back to school to learn to be a high school English teacher. I got a teaching job right out of school in the middle of the year. The job lasted exactly one semester, or until I received my summer pay and realized I actually had money to continue backpacking.

The next stop was Australia, where I hoped to spend six months, working wherever I could, then a few months in New Zealand and the South Pacific Islands. However, my plans changed irrevocably when I met a lovely Swiss woman, Claudia, in Alice Springs. Undoubtedly swept away by my lack of a job or real future, she agreed to allow me to follow her back to Switzerland where, a few months later, she gave up her job to continue traveling with me. Over the next couple years we backpacked the U.S., Eastern Europe and Australia/New Zealand, before marrying and settling in the mountains of Colorado, in a small town called Salida.

In Colorado we started our own electronics business (because, you know, my Creative Writing background totally prepared me for installing home theater systems), and had a couple of sons, Dylan and Daniel. In 2005 we shut the business down and moved back to Tucson where we currently live.